This book is dedicated to my girlfriend, cheerleader, soulmate, and president of the Larry LaDell Robertson fan club, my lovely, supportive, and understanding wife—Ramona. Again, I hope I've made you proud. And to my daughters, Jesseca and Jazzmin, thanks for your encouraging words and your hugs and kisses while I was at the keyboard. You kept me going!

I also dedicate this book to every man who is working hard to be and live his authentic, unique, and unrepeatable self. Be encouraged.

PROLOGUE

Well done, Dr. Beauregard Jeremiah Jackson.

October 15, 2014

"Bo promised us that he would be the first to die," Vine said, deliberately pausing to solicit the attention of the congregants. A quick scan of the sea of emotional faces validated that he had garnered their undivided attention. "It was the summer of 2008, and the economy was falling fiercely like chunks of an iceberg into the Arctic Ocean. Bo, Sam, Chivas, and I were bemoaning about our hemorrhaging 401[k] accounts and other investments earmarked for retirement. Ironically, it was the year Bo paid off his three-flat building in Woodlawn, retired from Streets and Sanitation with forty years of service, and announced the mortgage burning of his former residence in Beverly. Bo was smiling like a mouse who knew where to find the secret stash of cheese in an abandoned house. He said, 'You Negroes [his term of endearment for the group] have worked hard your entire lives. All the money and financial security you need should be had by now. I told y'all a long time ago to take your loot out of your mattresses and savings accounts and invest it in real estate, but no, you didn't listen to me. I was just a waste management specialist.' He never liked the pejorative title of *garbage man*. He said it made it seem like he was playing in garbage all day. We would respond, often in unison, 'You do.'" This time, there was laughter from the pews and choir loft behind him.

"'I'm going to die first, leave you all a bunch of money, and rest in glory,' he'd say," Vine continued the story. "'And don't think I'm doing this for you. I'm really doing it for me. It will be grand to listen to Ella, Mahalia, and Nina up there instead of you Negroes singing about being broke down here.'" This was a special day. He paced and tempered himself, being careful to use the right words. It wasn't just a eulogy to deliver; it was a point to prove. The church was admirably engaged. It was as if the congregation of mourners was anxious about what Vine was going to say next. Vine had a reputation for making church folks uneasy.

The Reverend Divine (Vine) Oliver was not only a full-fledged member but he also deduced and created the name Jolly Boys. He and Bo were the same age, seventy-two, with Arie (Chivas) Eubanks, the eldest at seventy-three, and Samaritan (Sam) Ladeaux, the baby of the bunch at seventy-one years young. They met at an investment seminar series sponsored by the Urban League. After a few interactions, the fellas introduced themselves to one another and began to develop a friendship. While the other gentlemen were skirt-chasing or showing off their deep and wide knowledge of the Bears, Bulls, and White Sox, these four discussed everything from organized religion to the faulty "pullout method" of birth control. Vine was playing around with the first letter of their last names and came up with *J-O-L-E*, thus the name Jolly Boys. *Jolly Men* just sounded dumb.

When it was time to drink, Vine sat at the table with the other fellas like a hungry field hand summoned to sustenance by a triangular dinner bell. When it was time to smoke, he lit everyone's legal and illegal cigarette before lighting his own, with his Tiffany sterling silver engraved lighter. When it was time to cuss, he bedazzled his friends with his undeniable ability to make the simplest and benign cusswords sound so low-down and foul. His limited repertoire of profane prose consisted of *shit*, *damn*, and *ass*. When it was time to gamble, his feet got hot with anxious anticipation. The mere mention of lottery, casino, or racetrack caused him to feverishly pat his thighs and hips, checking on the whereabouts of his car keys. An avid down-low gambler, he always had his disguise in tow. Vine would never venture to (what he referred to as) a "gambling opportunity" without his wig, hat, and press-on mustache. When teased by the fellas, he would always respond with "What if one of the saints sees me?" Bo would answer, "They'd know what we know. You ain't nowhere near saved, and if sanctification saw you coming, it would run in the opposite direction."

Vine was a handsome man, upright with perfect posture at six feet and two hundred pounds. He was of medium build and well-groomed with a faint mustache and beard. After the fellas ridiculed him for his "comb-over" approach to age-related hair loss, he shaved his perfectly oval-shaped head, which made him look even younger. He wasn't a pretty boy like Sam, but his presence was not a stranger to lingering stares, wide smiles, and a wink or two from both sisters and brothers in the pews. Vine was a private person. He never married, but he did date every now and then. If he did, he certainly didn't talk about it. Even though Jackie (Bo's wife) attempted and pledged to match him up with a neighbor, Vine cultivated a lonely heart but for his older sisters Anne and Pearl and, of course, the Jolly Boys. At one time, he was a prominent and respected spiritual leader in Chicago, serving as the seventh pastor of the Historic Grand Ole Baptist (GOB) Church of Chicago—that is, until his change. And it wasn't the drinking, gambling, or smoking that was his problem: it was his inability to collaborate, cooperate, and essentially work with church folks. Delivering the eulogy at his best friend's funeral was the first time he had been back in GOB's pulpit in years. Now standing again at the helm of the Grand Ole Baptist Church of Chicago, the flock he once led, he was hoping that it was God helping him showcase his spiritual value.

"When Jackie told me that I was to be the officiate today, I immediately railed against the idea," he continued. "So much has happened, so much has been said, so much has been misunderstood. Surely, I was not the one. But when she looked at me and said, 'You would not have one night of rest if you allowed someone else to perform this duty,' I had no choice but to step to the challenge. Today isn't about me. It's about Bo and our individual and collective love for this respected, highly regarded, beautiful, handsome gaze, the literal translation of his French name."

"Take your time, Pastor!" a woman yelled out.

"Let Him use you!" another woman yelled in similar sentiment. Vine missed the cheers and encouragement from the pews.

"I wish I could tell you that I was sad, but I can't," Vine continued his delivery. "I wish I could tell you that I have not been able to eat or sleep over Bo's transition, but I can't. I wish I could tell you that I can't stop crying, sobbing even, but I can't. I am glad Bo received his healing and made his transition back to perfection. Before you get all mad, let me explain. You see, the last six months were horrific for Bo. Back in April, he was diagnosed with stage 3 pancreatic cancer in his body. Right before the diagnosis, he would get these pains in his stomach and in his back that bent him over in agony. He said it felt like someone was drilling a foot-long screw through his upper stomach and out of his lower back. He finally went to the Mayo Clinic. I was sitting with him when the doctor confirmed the diagnosis. He tried every medication, every treatment known to man. Them Jolly Boys even made plans to take him out of the country in search of an experimental or nonconventional cure for this killer in his body. He likened cancer to a venomous serpent, slithering through his insides, striking and poisoning every organ and healthy cell in its path. But you know Bo. His spirits were up, and he didn't talk about his challenge. He was always jolly. But last month, all that changed. He knew he had been defeated. This tall, big, powerful James Earl Jones-lookalike moaned in agony in a fetal position for hours day after day after day. He was in pain, severe and serious pain. It was hard seeing him. I wanted to take him out of his pain. He even instructed us to take a gun to his head for an escape and instant relief as the three seconds of destructive pain would be better than what he was experiencing. I prayed that he received his healing. Last week, he put down that diseased body and moved onto his next experience. I know some of you won't like this, but principle is principle anyhow, whether you like it or not. Healing is freedom from pain. Death, when your spirit frees itself from your body assignment, is healing no matter who you are, what church you go to, or what you think about me. It's truth. I loved this man to the bone. And although he will be missed and can never be replaced, I'm happy that he's out of pain. These feelings that I'm feeling and that you're feeling, we can take care of them. We're going to be all right. I'm just glad that my friend, my agent, my promoter, my counselor, my banker, my disciplinarian, my business partner, my benefactor, and my brother will never ever have another day, hour, or minute in pain. So you see, I'm not a cold, or a callous person. It's why I'm not sad."

PART ONE

Getting Together

Life is partly what we make it, and partly what it is made by the friends we choose.

—Tennessee Williams

CHAPTER 1

Circa 1998

"What the hell is a pub crawl?" Samaritan (Sam) asked in earnest. "Sounds like some White-folks shit to me."

"*Pub* is a nineteenth-century English word for 'tavern or bar,'" Arie (Chivas) responded.

"Wow, you actually had to go to class, study, and take tests to be a gym teacher," Sam said. "Chivas, I'm impressed."

"First of all, we don't call it *gym* anymore," Chivas shot back. "It's called physical education. Secondly, were you equally impressed when your mother had to go to street-walking school to be a—"

Bo stopped him. "Come on now," Bo said. "Mothers, wives, and daughters are off-limits. Chivas, you know better than that, and, Vine, stop laughing. It ain't funny."

"You a lie," Vine said. "This shit is funny as hell. But explain what we're supposed to do on this pub-walk thing. Do I need my disguise?"

Sam shook his head.

"Crawl, Negro. Pub crawl," Bo replied. "So we'll meet at my house, drive to Forest Park, and park around Harlem and Madison. West of Harlem on Madison, there are about three blocks of bars on both sides of the street. We'll start with dinner at the Thigh and Leg and then travel down the street, stopping at as many bars as we want. We'll have at least one drink at each one and continue until we're at the Starbucks right by Harlem and Madison where we started. The goal is not to get drunk or to see how many pubs you can hit before you get drunk."

"Like I said, sounds like some White-folks shit," Sam repeated. "We live in the third largest city in the union. There are more clubs and pubs in Chicago that gladly accepted Black folks more than the law should allow. Downtown, on the south side, and up north, we got bars sprinkled like grass seeds onto fresh black dirt. Why in the world do we need to drive to a lily-white suburb to patronize a bunch of honky bars?"

"Aw, for God's sake, Sam," Chivas chimed in. "We haven't been colored, and they haven't been honkies in a long time, man. That's derogatory as hell."

"The White man didn't change our name," Sam said. "We changed our name. And I'm sorry to burst your bubble, but we haven't overcome that much. When 'Whitey' sees me, he sees a drug-addicted, uneducated, oversexed criminal that's yet to be imprisoned. Things have gotten better, but I ain't letting my guard down. We are far from truly being overcome. The White devil is alive and kicking, my Yankee friend."

"Sam, you got to let some of that shit go, man," Vine said. "You can't walk around with all that hate in you. The Bible says to follow peace with all men."

"Where was that verse when I was running from the police dogs?" Sam replied. "Where was it when I had to drink out of a separate fountain or ride the back of the bus? The Bible wasn't written yesterday. Wasn't nobody quoting that verse back then? I am not the White man's friend, and he sure as hell ain't mine."

Samaritan (Sam) Ladeaux was born on January 27, 1944, in Belle Chasse, Louisiana. He was the middle son of three who both proceeded him in death. Sam was the "pretty boy" of the group. He was tall and physically fit with skin the color of overmilked coffee. He was the most virile, well-kept man in his fifties that you've ever seen. His stereotypical creole features made him look Hispanic. His sunken hazel eyes, full pink lips, and other keen qualities secured him a lifelong position in the "high yellow" or "red bone" African American subculture. He has been married to Marsaleen for many long and tumultuous years. They lived in the same house but have not slept together in years. His twin daughters, Samaritan and Samita, lived in Atlanta. Samaritana or Lil Sam was a nurse, and Samita, the hell-raiser, was a grammar-school principal. Lil Sam was definitely her father's child, while Samita had been trying to get her mother to leave him for years.

As vices would go, Sam's primary vice (other than shoes and clothes) was his love and lust of the opposite sex. Perhaps it came from not having to try very hard or from his self-congratulatory bedroom skills. Whatever the genesis of his iniquity, Sam loved women. Thin, thick, fat, skinny, long hair, bald, dark, light, pretty, and even ugly, there was nothing in the world that meant more to him than being in the company of a woman. The fellas told him he was just a sugar daddy, but he paid them no mind. In his opinion, sponsoring a trip to the beauty shop, nail salon, grocery store, Best Buy, or the car dealership was a small price to pay for the incomparable taste and touch of God's greatest creation. Vine once told him that if we collected all the clothes and appliances Sam had been tricked into purchasing by the beguiling enticement of women, we could open the world's largest resale department store.

Opposite his love and passion for women was his complete and total disdain and abhorrence for members of the White race. Ask Sam what he'd call all the White people in the Chicago vicinity stiff on the floor of Lake Michigan, he would respond "a good start." According to him, the collective "they" could under no circumstances be trusted. His doctor was Black, his dentist was Asian, his lawyer was Panamanian, and his housekeeper was Hispanic. No White person played anything close to a significant role in his life.

"And it's not like I'm jumping on some sort of hate-against-the-White-folks bandwagon," he continued. "I've been this way all the time. My contempt didn't start with King, Martin, or Rodney. It was 1962, and I was eighteen years old. I had just graduated from high school and made the decision to work as a porter on the train like my daddy instead of going into the service or to college. See, we were not your stereotypical poor Negroes back then. My daddy worked for the railroad and made good money—good back then. And my mother was the only woman in Belle Chasse who did hair. Me and my brothers were well taken care of. Papa made sure we lived in a nice house, ate high on the hog, and dressed like we were well to do. He was eighteen when he started working as a custodian on the train. Day after day, night after night, he'd clean up after White folks. Trash, shit, and everything disposable and some things not—he cleaned it, shined it, and made the train sparkle. After a few years as a custodian, he was promoted to porter and then subsequently promoted to lead porter. He used his influence to get me on and assured me that if I was never late, never sick, and played the role of a happy, indentured servant, I would be a lead porter in no time. I had no intentions of being a custodian, porter, or no one's servant, not for long. I was going to be an engineer. I was going to be up high and in front, with my hands on the throttle and my eyes on the rail. My daddy laughed at me when I shared my divergent career plans with him. He said he had never seen a Black engineer, but if that's what I wanted, 'don't let nothing or no one stop you.'"

"Yes, Lord," Vine chimed in. "A few more years and you'll have fifty years there. You gonna retire on time then, I suppose?"

"You better believe it," Sam said.

"Gone with the rest of the story," Chivas said. "I got to hear why it's okay to use *honky* again."

"So on the weekend before I was to start my job, me and my daddy and older brother Billy took a quick trip to Jackson, Mississippi, to see my aunt Liz," he continued. He squinted and focused down and away from the eyes of the fellas as if he was reading from a tablet in his memory. "She had suddenly taken ill, and the prognosis wasn't good. She was my daddy's oldest sister and our favorite aunt, so we wanted to see her before she slipped away. My mama stayed home with my little brother, Oscar. She packed us a good meal of chicken legs and stuffed eggs, and at seven o'clock, we were on the road on our way. It was only a three-and-a-half-hour drive to Jackson from Belle Chasse, so we waited until Papa got off work. We listened to the radio, talked about one another, and went on our way without a care in the world. At nine, it was pitch black, and the mood in the car suddenly changed. Quietly and individually, we realized we had made a grave mistake leaving home so late. In 1962 in Mississippi, three Black men, regardless of a nearly White hue, had no business on the highway. We sat still in concentration as if our quietness would ward off evil and racist spirits. We had about an hour to go. It felt like an hour and a day. Papa focused ahead and to the left. Billy, sitting in the front, focused ahead and to the right. I looked into the darkness behind us. Now there was only thirty more minutes to go. We were coming down the hilly highway when we noticed a Mississippi State Trooper parked on the side of the road behind someone who was obviously in violation. Papa slowed down to pass. I ducked down instinctively for no other apparent reason than fear. Once clear and out of sight, Papa picked up speed. The sign up ahead read 'Jackson 15.' I breathed a sigh of relief and spoke.

"'Papa, I think we're going to be all right now,' I whispered. My whisper pierced the silence in the car like a hammer to a pane of glass.

"'Shut your mouth, boy,' Papa said through clenched teeth, glaring at me through the rearview mirror. 'Don't jinx our good fortune. What was I thinking, Lord? We should have never left home so late.'

"'You were thinking like a regular man,' Billy said. 'We are tax-paying citizens just like White folks. We should be able to travel up and down the highway without fear of being killed by some racist troopers.' After a minute, red, blue, and white lights began to flash. I looked back. The troopers we had passed a few minutes ago were now behind us. Papa pulled over slowly.

"'Sit still, everybody,' he said. 'Sam, get on the floor. Don't nobody move a muscle, and don't open your mouths.' The two troopers exited the car and walked up on both sides of us. Papa rolled down the window before being asked to do so. 'Is there something wrong, Officer, sir?'

"'Did I say something was wrong, boy?' the short, portly man said. 'You boys up to no good out here? It's awfully late for two half-breed Negras to be flying down the highway.'

"'Officer, I wasn't speeding,' Papa said. 'I am a careful driver.'

"'You calling me a liar boy?' he asked, placing his hand on the exposed handle of his gun, which was still in the hoister.

"'What I meant to say is that I don't believe I was speeding,' Papa said. 'But if you say I was, I'll gladly accept a ticket and be on my way. I'm going to see my dying sister in Jackson.'

"'This is some bullshit,' Billy said much louder than he should have. 'We were not speeding.'

"'What you say, boy?' the officer on the passenger side said, tapping on the window. Billy lowered his window. 'What you say, boy? Were you cussing at me?'

"'No, I mean no disrespect, Officer,' Billy said. 'I just said we weren't speeding.'

"'But my partner said you were,' he said. 'So what we gonna do now, James? We got us two high-yella Negras who disagree with us. Get out of the car.'

"'Billy, don't move,' Papa said as he reached down to find the door handle in the dark. He opened the door and stepped out with his hands in the air.

"'You need a special invitation, boy,' the other officer asked Billy. 'Get you Black ass out of this car.' When Billy stood with his hands in the air, the officer punched him in the stomach and delivered an uppercut blow to his face. Papa turned his head and yelled, 'Don't!' The other officer kneed Papa in the groin and then pushed him down onto the pavement. I resumed my position on the floor. I couldn't see anything, but I could hear everything. Every punch, kick, and moan. I heard what sounded like bones breaking, blood gurgling, and final breaths.

"'Now you niggas get back into your pretty stolen Cadillac car and head on back to the jungle where you came from," I heard the portly officer say. Papa was the first in the car, but I didn't hear Billy. I prayed, *Please don't let Billy be dead.* All of a sudden, I heard one gun shot. I heard another. I heard one more.

"'No!' Papa screamed. 'Billy, no, no, Billy. Please, God, please spare my son.' I couldn't hold it any longer. I knew my brother was dead. I wept, still lying on the floor of the back seat. Minutes later, the back door opened. Billy told me to get up front. I jumped over the seat. All three doors slammed in unison, and Daddy skidded back onto the open road."

"Was Billy shot?" Vine asked. "Who got shot?"

"As Billy was crawling back to the car and the troopers were walking back to their car, Billy pulled a gun he had strapped to his calf and shot both officers," Sam continued the story. "Papa could hardly see through the blood from his gashed-in eye. He pulled over, and I took the wheel. Billy threw the gun up front next to me on the seat.

"'If another White man approaches this car other than Jesus, don't say a word,' he commanded. 'Shoot to kill.'

"Papa and Billy road the rest of the trip in bloody agony and pain," Sam said. "When we got to Aunt Liz's house, family members and neighbors pitched in to help. Though they were both in bad shape, neither could go to the hospital. Papa and Billy would have been hanged for shooting one White state trooper, let alone two. Papa called Mama to tell her what happened and to strategize. The next day, the family put me on the train and sent me back to Belle Chasse. Papa and Billy followed a few days later."

"Did they find out that Billy shot the officer?" Chivas asked.

"Oh hell naw," Sam said. "They would have killed them both. I know that for sure. Papa and Billy took the plates off the car, wiped it down on the inside, and pushed it into the river. We never spoke of it again. My father wasn't the same after that. He could never get his jolly spirit back. It was a horrid reminder that no matter how fair his skin was or how hard he worked or all the money he had, he was a Black man in the South and therefore a part of an endangered species."

"You know what, scrap this pub-crawl idea," Bo said. "Some White woman will burp or break wind, and this Negro might have a flashback and blow her brains out."

"Yeah, let's think of something else," Vine said.

"Man, you got any Chivas Regal around here?" Chivas asked. "After that story, I need a drink."

"Please, you need a drink after Sunday school," Vine said. The fellas were laughing. The jolly was coming back. "Shit. I picked him up one Sunday for church. He got in the car and said he'd forgotten something. He went in the house and came back with nothing in his hands. I asked him what he'd forgotten. He said he forgot to gargle. Breath smelled like he had gone to Tennessee and fallen into a vat of Chivas Regal."

"For your information and edification," Chivas responded, "Chivas Regal is made by the Chivas Brothers, and they produce the blended scotch whiskey in Speyside Scotland, you country bastard. I have a shot a day to keep my heart pumping."

"Please, ain't nothing wrong with you heart," Vine said. "You teach jumping jacks ands and sit-ups. You don't actually do the shit yourself. And I'm from Duck Hill. That ain't the country."

"You a damn lie," Chivas said. "Duck Hill is as country as a dozen of double-yoked eggs." The fellas continued their unalarming banter and spent the rest of the evening drinking Chivas Regal, telling stories and lies, and enjoying the peace and comradery of a new brotherhood. It's also the night that Arie got his official nickname: Chivas.

CHAPTER 2

October 8, 1998

"You act like you've known these Negroes your entire life," Louise said, irritated at Chivas who was rushing her to get dressed. "You just met them a few months ago, and now that's all you talk about—them damn Jolly Boys. Y'all forming some kind of gang or something?"

"So when I was walking around here complaining about not having friends, you were okay, but now that I actually have some, you are irritated," Chivas said. Fully dressed, he was standing in the doorway of their bedroom, watching his partner get dressed. Of course, he was clutching a crystal highball glass containing ice, a little water, and a lot of Chivas Regal. "You travel the country and abroad with your little teacher friends. Why can't I be friends with a few distinguished men of my choosing?"

"You can have as many friends as you want," she replied. "I just don't understand why I have to be involved. And besides, I don't like Bo's wife, Helen, and I'm tired of meeting the whores Sam brings to these functions. We've been to a couple dinners and a party since you all have been hanging out, and he has brought a different woman every time. I'm starting to believe he doesn't have a wife."

"That's funny," Chivas said while laughing. "We've been saying the same thing. We don't think Marsaleen actually exists. Wouldn't it be funny if he actually showed up with his wife tonight? And why don't you like Helen?"

"Because she thinks she's better than everybody because she has her own business," Louise said. "And what she does, anyone can do. Black folks ain't gonna spend their hard-earned money having her come over and organize their closets, cabinets, basements, and attics.

She gets on my damn nerves. Speaking of closets, is Vine joining the party tonight?"

"Aw, here you go," Chivas said. "Just because Vine keeps his personal life to himself doesn't mean he's gay. I wish you would stop that."

"Any man in his fifties, never married, no children, and no woman is gay as hell," Louise said. "I'm going to ask him tonight. Have you all ever asked him?"

"No, we have not, and no, you aren't going to either," Chivas said. Louise slid on her shoes and held her necklace up, signaling Chivas for some help. He stepped into the bedroom, placed the glass on the dresser, and fastened the clasp of his lover's necklace. He then hugged her from behind while admiring their embrace in the mirror atop of the dresser. "You are such a sexy, smart, and beautiful woman. I definitely have the baddest chick in the bunch." She looked at the picture before her and smiled. "I love you, baby."

"I love you too, Arie, probably more than you love me," she said.

"Why would you say that?" he asked.

"Because I'm not Mrs. Arie Eubanks," she said. He sighed heavily and released her. "That's one of the reasons I don't like going to these gatherings and probably the underpinning of my dislike for Helen. I'm not a wife."

Arie (Chivas) Eubanks was the elder jolly boy. He was born October 16, 1942, in Brooklyn, New York. As looks would go, Arie was indisputably the shortest of the tribe at a modest five foot seven. He was almond brown and plump, especially his protruding stomach referred to by the fellas as his "front porch." He sported a classic low salt-n-pepper afro and beard of the same palette. But for his beard, people could easily mistake him for Andrew Young. He was truly a native New Yorker—accent, speedy cadence, short-tempered and all. His parents were both educators in the New York City school system, so it was assumed that he would go to college and subsequently become a teacher as well. In 1961, he began his studies at New York University.

While attending NYU, Chivas dated probably more than he should have not because he was promiscuous or some sort of sexual fiend but because he was selective. The woman who had a place on his arm had to be perfect: beautifully light brown, long, well-conditioned, and cared-for hair (preferably black); perfect regulation softball-sized breasts; small waist; sculptured hips, thighs, and ass; big hairless legs; and delicate, unabused feet absent of corns and knots. He considered himself an intellectual, so besides being stunning and fetching, his ideal woman had to be brilliant with a lexicon that showcased a logical mind and ability to engage others past casual conversation. He preferred to be toyed with. A sister playing hard-to-get was attractive to him. This was his reputation on campus. His nickname was Oda (one-date Arie), and he wore it like a badge of honor.

In the fall following his graduation, he began his teaching career at Frederick Douglas Elementary School in the Bronx. He taught home economics and physical education. There were not many men who were teachers, let alone elementary school teachers in the sixties. For two years, he and the principal were the only two men on staff. For the most part, the teachers were all married or had failed to meet his criteria for companionship. Two years into his teaching career, all that changed.

In the fall of 1967, the love of his life walked into his classroom. "Excuse me, Mr. Eubanks, can you please help me?" she said. "The teacher's desk in my classroom is just in the wrong place. I don't want to scratch up the beautifully varnished floors. Can I get you to help me move my desk?" Arie stood in silence and disbelief. As he listened with his ears and took her all in with his eyes, he was checking off all the criteria boxes in his mind. "Mr. Eubanks, your help, please."

"I'm sorry, I don't know who you are," he said.

"My apologies." She smiled and walked toward him with an extended hand. "I'm Catherine Nero Quinn. I'm one of the new English teachers."

"And you are also the most beautiful Catherine Nero Quinn I have ever seen," Arie said through the biggest and brightest smile he had had in a long time. "It would be my pleasure to help you."

Catherine smiled and exited his classroom and led the way to hers just across the corridor. Once in her classroom, he nodded. Her assessment was correct. "So where do you want it? In front of the short wall or the long wall?"

"I'm thinking the long wall," she replied. "What do you think?"

"Well, from how I view the world, long is always better than short." She rolled her eyes and lifted one end of the desk and helped carry it to the preferred position. "How is that? Does that feel right to you?"

"Yes, it's perfect," she said. "Thank you, Mr. Eubanks. You have a great rest of your day."

"Ms. Quinn," Arie said, "do you think Mr. Quinn would mind us having lunch together this afternoon? And we're dating now, so you can call me Arie."

"Arie," Catherine said, leaning on the repositioned desk, "first, there is no Mr. Quinn. My mother's maiden name was Nero, so I took it as a middle name. My father's last name, of course, was Quinn."

"How modern and cosmopolitan of you," Arie said.

"Also, we are not dating," Catherine continued. "I know this for two reasons: I don't date people I work with, and I don't like you."

"You don't like me?" Arie said, nearly coming unglued at the undeserved dismissal. "Of course, you like me. Everyone likes me. I'm that guy. You know, the guy on the job that everyone likes. What do you mean you don't like me?"

Catherine began to laugh. Arie was faking offense. Realizing that her intention was simply to discourage and not emasculate, she tried a softer touch. "Arie, I'm sorry," she said. "I shouldn't have said I didn't like you. I don't even know you. It's just my first year teaching. I'm in a new city, and I don't have time to manage a relationship, especially with someone I work with."

"Catherine, it's just lunch," Arie said. "What harm can come from Kentucky Fried Chicken and grape pop? It's the least you could do since you broke my heart. I mean, you just snatched my heart right out of my chest and threw it against the wall. And then you picked it up and drowned it in a bucket of water. And then…"

"Okay, okay." She smiled, holding up both hands in surrender. "I get it. I hurt your feelings. Okay, yes, I will have lunch with you, but not today. I'm having lunch with the other English teachers today. It's sort of a welcome-to-Brooklyn lunch. How about next week before school starts?"

"How about tonight after work?" Arie asked.

"Mr. Eubanks, Arie, who eats lunch in the evening after work?" Catherine asked.

"We do." He smiled. She couldn't control her blush.

"Okay," she relented. "Lunch this evening after work is fine. I mean, if nothing can come from lunch, what could possibly come from dinner?"

"Oh, you'd be surprised," Arie said with a conqueror's smile.

On Christmas Eve 1968, Arie and Catherine married after a sixteen-month courtship. On December 15, 1969, Catherine gave birth to their twin boys, Arie Jr. and Nero. On December 6, 1988, on her way home from College Park, Maryland, Catherine was in a terrible car accident. It was the end of the semester for the boys who were attending the University of Maryland near DC. Catherine decided to take the day off, drive down the night before, and head home after Nero's last final at one. At one thirty, they were on the road without incident. Two hours into the drive, a major snowstorm began. The untreated roads became more and more treacherous by the minute. Traffic was almost at a halt. Catherine decided to safely rest on the side of the road under an overpass. As they sat safely and warm, the driver of an eighteen-wheeler was speeding and lost control of his truck. It plowed into Catherine's Ford Expedition. Catherine and Arie Jr. died on the scene. Nero passed away a month later. He had been hospitalized and on life support since the accident. As painful as it was, Arie realized that Nero would never enjoy the quality of life he deserved. He made the decision to let him go.

The deep and piercing pain that Arie felt was, at times, unbearable. He lost the love of his life and his boys of whom he dearly cherished all in a matter of thirty days. He didn't think he'd ever recover from it. He was on leave for a year and attended intense therapy twice a week. It was hard for him to pull himself out of bed every day. The curse of depression was his number 1 contender. But with therapy and support from his friends and Catherine's family, he was able to see that his life was worth living. He pulled himself together and decided to live the best life he possibly could. He received an eight-hundred-thousand-dollar settlement from the trucking company responsible for the accident. It was like receiving eight hundred thousand pennies considering the enormous pain he endured. He decided to return to work, but coming home to a memory-filled but empty house was impeding the progress of his recovery. He accepted a new job in Chicago as a system director of health and physical education for a charter high school system. He traveled regularly to the eight high schools in Chicago and neighboring suburbs. That's when he met Louise Hitchcock. She was the principal of one of the schools and interacted with him regularly. After a couple of years of dating, Arie and Louise moved in together. Their relationship was passionate and strong but for their impasse regarding marriage. Louise wanted to be Mrs. Arie Eubanks. For Arie, Mrs. Arie Eubanks was dead.

"Oh, here we go," Chivas said. "My daily reminder of how awful of a bastard I am for not wanting to get married."

"I never said you were awful, nor have I called you a bastard," she said, inspecting her makeup in the mirror. "It's what I really want, and I'm trying to understand why you are so adamantly opposed to something I really want. Are you ashamed of me or something? Am I ugly, loud, or brash? Just because I'm not slow about getting someone told does not mean I'm a bad person." Louise was a big girl but certainly not ugly, loud, or brash. With the aid of the right undergarments, her curves were disciplined tight and still and accentuated her beautifully oval caramel-hued face and matching features. Chivas was more than satisfied with his lover's appearance.

"Of course not," he said, somewhat annoyed. "How could you say something so ridiculous? I'm not a liar. When I say you're beautiful, I mean it. I'm just not ready to be a husband again. That might not be fair to you, but it's the truth that we've discussed plenty of times. When Cat died, a part of me went with her. I'm not a whole man anymore. I've tried counseling, and it saved my life. But it only took me so far. I'm a borderline alcoholic because I only feel 75 percent and only with the aid of Chivas Regal. You deserve a 100-percent husband."

"Baby, like I've told you before," Louise said, "I know you are in pain. Sure, the pain has gotten better over time. But you are still grieving for Catherine, and I understand that. But I can't believe Catherine would want you refusing to fully commit with me because of your love for her. It's hurtful to me. It makes me feel like I am competing with another woman, and I could hold my own with another woman switching her ass in front of you. It's not fair to expect me to do that with one who is no longer here." Chivas didn't like that comment. He gulped down the few remaining drops of his favorite drink and left the room.

Chivas and Louise rode to Bo's house through the usual Saturday-night Chicago traffic and silent conversation with each other. No, they were not speaking, but their thoughts were engaged in a heated shouting match. He couldn't understand why she was so insistent on getting married knowing the pain he endured in losing his wife and sons. She couldn't understand how he expected her to compete with a dead woman. Pulling into Bo's driveway, he broke the silence.

"Can we table this long enough to have some fun, please?" he said, looking straight out the window.

"Of course," Louise said. "I will not behave in a manner that calls attention to the fact that my boyfriend does not think I'm good enough to marry."

"I never said that," he said, striking the sterling wheel with his right fist. "You know what, do whatever you want. Give me the silent treatment, be rude to our hosts, hell, sit in the car all night if you want to, but don't put words into my mouth. Don't speak for me even in your head." Chivas opened the car door and heard voices behind him. Once he was able to focus, he saw Sam and his date walking toward him. Louise exited the car and joined the huddle.

"I see we're right on time," Sam said. His date was holding onto him for dear life. "Chivas, Louise, this is Carmella. Carmella, Louise and Arie, or Chivas, as we call him, the eldest Jolly Boy."

"It's a pleasure to meet you both," Carmella said.

"I hear an accent in your voice," Louise said. "Where are you from?"

"I'm from El Salvador," she said. "I was born there but moved to the United States when I was a teenager."

"So you haven't been here long?" Louise mistakenly said aloud. "I mean, you were not in El Salvador very long." The moment of awkwardness was happily welcomed by the arrival of Vine's sister, Pearl, and an unknown gentleman. "Oh, there is Pearl. That must be her date."

"Hello, everyone," Pearl said. "Why are you all standing out here in the cold?"

"We pretty much pulled up together," Sam said. "I was just introducing Chivas and Louise to my girl, Carmella."

"Hello, Pearl," Carmella said. "It's a pleasure to meet you. Is this your husband?"

"Oh, where are my manners?" Pearl said. "Chivas, Louise, Sam, Carmella, this is Deacon Charles Cotton. He is a friend of Vine's and a part of his inner circle. I thought he'd be pleasantly surprised to see him, so I invited him to join us."

"Good evening, everyone," Charles said. "His face is going to crack when he sees me." Charles was bit flamboyant for their liking. Another moment of awkwardness and silence fell upon the huddle. Suddenly, the front door opened, and Helen came out.

"What are you all doing out here in the cold?" she said. "We can yell 'Surprise!' once he gets into the house. We don't have to jump out of the bushes. Lord, help Black people. I wonder if my White friends would congregate outside minutes before a surprise birthday party." The six guests walked up the steps and into the foyer of Bo and Helen's home. A woman in a maid's uniform was standing off to the sides. "Everyone, give your coats to Francis and join Bo and I in the kitchen." Everyone removed their coats and handed them to this short, portly, and extremely dark woman and followed Helen into the kitchen. Once all were assembled, Helen focused in on Charles and Carmella. "I'm sorry, I don't know who you two are."

"I'm sorry, Helen. This is my girl, Carmella," Sam said.

"And this is a friend of Vine's, Deacon Charles Cotton," Pearl said.

"Well, hello, Carmella and Charlie," Helen said. "This is my husband, Beauregard or Bo, and I'm Helen. Welcome to our home. Charlie, I hope you don't mind me calling you that? My brother's name was Charles, and we called him Charlie. Of course, you don't mind."

"Actually, Helen, I really don't like the name Charlie," Charles said. "I'd prefer Charles, if you don't mind."

"Well, you're in my house uninvited and unannounced," Helen said. "I think you can let me off the hook for one night, can't you?"

Louise looked at Chivas and rolled her eyes.

"See, there you go," Bo interjected. "The man hasn't had a drink, and already you're making him uncomfortable. Charles, pay my wife no attention. We will call you Charles. Now I'm going to get some ice and get the drinks started."

"Oh, Francis, can you fill the ice bucket with ice for Mr. Jackson?" Helen said to her maid.

"You mean the ice that's in the freezer ten feet from where Mr. Jackson is standing with the ice bucket in his hands?" Francis said, pointing to the objects of her question as she spoke. Everyone other than Helen found Francis's quip amusing.

"Yes, that's exactly what I mean," Helen said.

"Francis, I'm sure you have something else to do," Bo said. "I'll get this."

"No, you will not get this," Helen snapped. "Francis, you are the maid, the maid who usually sits around all day doing much of nothing. Please don't get an attitude with me when you are actually asked to work."

"Ms. Helen, yes, I'm the maid, but I'm not a slave," Francis said. "Mr. Jackson is standing right there. I don't understand why he can't get the ice."

"My dear, you are a slave," Helen said.

"Oh, Helen, did you really just call this woman a slave?" Louise asked. She couldn't help herself from defending Ms. Francis.

"Yes, slaves are paid to do all the things their bosses don't want to do," Helen said. "The only difference is that I don't own her and she's free."

"That's enough, Helen," Bo snapped. "Francis, I can get the ice. You may leave for the evening. We'll revisit this tomorrow after our guests are gone. And besides, you've been working on getting the house ready for this party. You look tired."

"Thank you, Mr. Jackson," Francis said. "I am a bit tired. Good evening all." Everyone said goodbye to Francis except Helen. Helen and Francis stared at each other before Francis made her exit from the kitchen.

"Why would you do that?" Helen asked Bo. "It's enough that you don't support me and embarrass me in front of the help but…"

"But nothing, Helen," Bo said, slamming the freezer door shut after retrieving the ice. "We have guests, and Vine will be here any minute. Let's try to squash this nonsense and have a good evening."

"I'll drink to that," Chivas said.

"You'll drink to anything as long as Chivas Regal is involved," Helen snapped.

"See, if you had said those same words with a different inflection, it would have been funny," Chivas said. "But your tone was mean and insulting. Funny how inflection and tone can result in being misunderstood. I bet that happens to you a lot doesn't it, Helen?" Out of the corner of his eye, Chivas could see Louise smiling before dropping her head. She was trying very hard not to make matters worse by engaging in a full-blown, belly-wiggling laugh. When she looked up, Chivas winked at her. She continued to smile and winked back. That was a good sign. She and her partner were back in good graces.

"Francis was out-and-out disrespectful and insubordinate," Helen continued her rant and ignored Chiv's signification. "When she shows up tomorrow, that woman is fired."

"She is not," Bo said. "That woman is like a member of this family. That woman ain't going nowhere. While you were out jumping from job to job and business idea to business idea, that woman you just called a slave helped raise your daughters. When you were so depressed that you couldn't get out of bed because once again, your big-ass mouth got you fired, that woman fed, clothed, and got your kids to school. And when you started this professional organizing business, that woman was your first paying client. I know this because I gave her the money to pay you. And so you stand in this kitchen and call that woman who has been cooking for two days a slave, and when she refuses to let you disrespect her, you threaten her with her job? Not happening. Not here."

"I knew you didn't like me," Helen said to Bo. She was standing directly in front of him. "But I didn't know you hated me. All, please give my regards to Vine. I'm going to leave now. I really have no place here, not tonight."

"Aw, Helen, wait," Louise said.

"Let her go," Bo said. "It's best for everyone tonight."

"Well, it was a pleasure meeting you," Carmela said. All eyes turned to her as if she had just enunciated the dumbest thing they'd ever heard.

"Sometimes the meek carries the burden of grace."

"Well, come on, Grace. We've work to do," Louise said. "No hostess and no maid, the food won't serve itself. Gentlemen, go wait in the foyer for Vine while we check on the status of the vittles. Yell when you see him coming. And if one of you calls me a slave, a Negro will get cut this evening, I promise." Without pushback or commentary, Bo, Sam, Chivas, and Deacon Cotton headed to the living room, which was right off the foyer. They sat and engaged in casual and safe conversation—that is, until Chivas spoke.

"So, Bo, man, what are you gonna do about Helen?" he asked. "No judgment, but, bruh, you can't be happy with that attitude nor that mouth."

"I'm not," Bo said. "I haven't been happy with a woman since Elise Green in the sixth grade." The fellas had a hearty laugh in solidarity. "And speaking of sixth grade, what time is Carmela's curfew? I know it's Saturday night, but she must have homework or cheerleading duties tonight." Chivas, the only person ignoring Helen's rule of "no food or drink" in the living room, nearly dropped his Mikasa highball glass from laughing so hard.

"Ha ha." Sam laughed mockingly. "Very funny. She's forty, for your information and education."

"She's a lie," Bo said. "I still smell Similac on her breath. You better check her papers before you end up on 22nd and California, the jail."

"Check her papers?" Sam said. "I thought I was the racist in the group. It's small of you to think that just because she has an accent and is from El Salvador that she is illegal."

"You haven't checked, have you?" Chivas asked.

"No 'cause I'm scared," Sam said. "That stuff is so good. I can't bear thinking about my stuff on a boat back to El Salvador. I'd have to go with her."

"What is your Black ass gonna do in El Salvador?" Bo asked. "Sell bananas and corn from a shopping cart? And Marsaleen ain't giving up that easy. Does *la bonita seniorita* know you are married?"

"Yes, but she knows it's a bad marriage," Sam said.

"Young, illegal, and dumb," Chivas said. "She fell for the old bad-marriage rap." All were suddenly a bit uncomfortable with a stranger in the room. It was a good time to pivot the interrogation to the quiet deacon. "So, Cotton, how exactly to you know Vine?"

"I'm one of the deacons from Shining Star where Rev. Oliver pastors," Cotton said.

"Oh, Shining Star," Chivas replied. "That's the new church he's at, ain't it?

"Em, hmm," Cotton responded. "He's been with us for about a year now. Some people are having a hard time with his directness, but I find it refreshing. A church like Shining Star needs hard leadership."

"You mean strong leadership," Chivas corrected him.

"Oh, yes, em, hmm," Cotton said. Charles Cotton was your stereotypical, quintessential, middle-aged church queen. He was round all over and wore clothes that were the size he wanted to be and not the size he was. He perched his lips, batted his eyes, and kept his legs together while seated. He would definitely be a topic of discussion at the next Jolly-Boy meeting.

"I guess you are fortunate," Chivas continued. "Most people who are overly direct tend to be the hardest on people in their inner circle. Are you in his inner circle?"

"I want to say yes," Cotton said. "Our previous pastor was a very nice man but had his picks and chooses. And he was a pushover. When I saw how Rev. Oliver was running things, I got excited and threw myself at his feet. I stand at the ready to do whatever I can to help him be successful. I love discipline—I mean, the discipline he is trying to instill." Bo, Chivas, and Sam looked at one another in part amusement and part disbelief.

"Well, most grown folks don't need discipline," Bo said. "They need teaching and sound doctrine."

"Yes, but they need rules and structure too," Sam said. "Folks will run over you if you let them, especially so-called church folks."

"Well, no one is going to run over Pastor Oliver," Cotton said, standing and moving toward the window. "Not while I'm around. Oh, he's here. He's coming. He's coming."

"Probably screamed that in his wet dream last night," Chivas whispered to Sam. Sam elbowed him in the stomach to silence him. The fellas walked into the foyer. Chivas alerted the ladies in the kitchen. Everyone stood patiently around the door. Vine rang the doorbell, and Bo yelled for him to come in. When he entered, everyone yelled, "Surprise!"

"Aw, shit!" Vine yelled. "What the actual hell is happening? Surprise what?" He placed his hand on his chest as if he was having a cardiac episode. "Y'all trying to stop me from having another birthday?"

"Happy birthday, little brother," Pearl said, stepping forward and giving him a tight hug. "May you have many, many more."

"You all are too much," Vine said. Once the shock wore off, he was pleased and excited about celebrating his birthday with his new family of sorts. His eyes fell on Cotton. He displayed a look of confusion. "Deacon Cotton, what are you doing here?"

"I invited him," Pearl answered. "I didn't think you would mind. Other than these Jolly Boys, he's the only supportive person I would have invited from the church."

"Happy birthday, Pastor." Cotton stepped forward and hugged him. Vine kept his hands to the side, never embracing Cotton's portly body. Sam, Chivas, and Bo studied his response to Deacon Cotton, as if they were looking for a touch, word, or reaction to warrant any suspicion.

"Thank you" was all Vine could muster. The fellas couldn't tell whether Vine was happy or annoyed. "Thank you for coming, but I'm not Pastor tonight. It's my birthday. I'm Vine. Now where is the Chivas Regal?" Everyone enjoyed another hearty laugh and headed to the dining room. For the most part, Helen and Francis had all the food prepared. All the ladies had to do was heat it up and transfer the dishes to the fine serving platters and bowls. It was an exquisite menu: crown rib roast, roasted vegetables, twice-baked potatoes, collard greens, and red velvet cake (Vine's favorite) for dessert. The dinner was loud and festive like a true celebration. Everyone ate and drank and had a great time. Everyone was done with their meal but remained around the table to fellowship. Chivas refreshed everyone's drink and, of course, his own. With a tapping of glass, Vine sequestered everyone's attention.

"Before we start heading out, I wanted to thank Bo one more time for hosting this party and you for showing up," Vine said. "I'm officially in my midfifties now, and I don't feel no-ways tired. It's been a rough few years, but as the song says, I'm still here. Thank God and thank God for my new family. You came into my life just when I needed you. To the Jolly Boys." Vine raised his glass. All followed his gesture.

When Bo began clearing the table, Louise gently slapped his hand. He demurred and allowed the ladies to take on the task of clearing and getting the kitchen and dining room back in order. "Hell, Helen left pissed. She don't need to come home pissed," Louise said.

Bo signaled the gentlemen, and they all stood and followed him down the steps and through the basement to the outside patio. There in the midst of six high-end outdoor chairs sat his new stainless-steel firepit. He bought it several months ago but was waiting for a special occasion to use it. What occasion could be more special than his friend's fifty-fifth birthday? He placed a starter log at the bottom of the pit and lit it. He then placed regular firewood on top. After a little poking and prodding, the logs were inflamed and gave out a brilliant red, blue, and gold light. It, amidst the cool October darkness, added heat, and the ambiance needed to quietly end a very loud but festive evening. For a while, the men were silent, staring into the light, occasionally sipping on their libation of choice. Bo's deep baritone voice punctured the quiet like a nail to a tire.

"Man, I got woman problems," he said.

"Shit, we all do," Sam said. "Marsaleen hates me so much that she doesn't even care anymore—where I am, who I'm with, nor what time I'm coming home. She wouldn't care if I didn't come home."

"Louise thinks I should want to get married again," Chivas said. "And I want to, but just when I think I'm ready, all the memories of Catherine come flooding back in. It's like when we're in a good space, I'm overcome with a feeling of guilt. It feels like I'm cheating on my wife when I'm with Louise."

"What about you, Deacon?" Chivas asked. "You married or anything?"

"No, not yet," he said with a wide smile. "But I do have my eye on someone. The more I sip on this drink, the more I realize that they are not paying me much attention. It's a long shot, but what do I have to lose?"

"Vine, I guess you are lucky," Bo said. "As Bob Marley declared, 'No woman, no cry.'"

"That's where you're wrong," Vine said. "No, I don't do much crying, but I've got the biggest woman problem of all y'all. My wife is the church. The New Testament speaks of the coming of the bridegroom, who is God. The bride is the church. I am the bridegroom until he comes for the bride. I'm not defying my calling, but I'd trade places with any one of you if I could."

"You know, I've always wondered about this calling that ministers speak about," Sam said. "I mean, is it really like you're walking down the street and you hear your name being called? What did it say? 'Vine, go preach'?"

"I wouldn't call it a calling," Vine began his explanation. "To me, it's more like a stirring. The idea comes into your mind, and it stays and wrestles with you until you surrender." Vine looked at the glowing and inquisitive faces around the fire. He knew it was time to tell his story.

"Yalobusha County was the worst place in America for a Black man or woman, for that matter, especially in 1959," Vine said. "Rapes, beatings, lynchings. All the stuff you Northern folks had heard about was real—very real in the South. I was just sixteen when I fully realized that every day God gave me was truly a blessing. And contrary to the myth, light-skinned Black folks were treated just as badly as the dark-skinned ones.

"My daddy was a farmhand on a pig farm about two miles from our house. It was an awful job. But when you're Black and uneducated in Mississippi, having a job, even an awful one, was a blessing. It's probably one of the reasons I don't eat a lot of pork now. That smell was rancid. We could smell my daddy coming a mile before he got home. My mother stayed at home and took in laundry and ironing for White folks. Both Pearl and Anne cleaned houses to help out. The only thing I did was go to school and the church. I loved church. The music, the preaching, the praying, and the safety. Even the most ignorant racist White folks didn't bother us when we were in church. It just made me feel good even as a teenager. Other boys my age were chasing tail. I was chasing something completely different. Mama, Pearl, Anne, and I went on Wednesday nights for prayer meeting, Friday nights for choir rehearsal and tarrying service, and all day on Sunday. My daddy started drinking Friday afternoon with the pigs and didn't stop until he saw them again on Monday morning. We coped with the Lord. He coped with moonshine."

"What is tarrying service?" Chivas asked.

"That's when you sang and testified and waited or tarried for the Holy Ghost to come," Vine explained. "You sat on the mourner's bench until you got religion. Then you danced and shouted, and everyone celebrated your salvation. One Friday night, this old preacher came through town. He was from the Pentecostal church. Back then, it wasn't like it is now with denominations worshiping together. The Baptist and the sanctified folks steered clear of one another. We didn't know he was from the Pentecostal church until after he left, but we should have known something. That man preached for two hours, and good preaching too. When he was done, he was wringing wet. He had preached his socks down into his shoes. When he was done and things were calming down, he called me out of the choir. I thought he wanted me to sing, but he told me to go to the wall. That meant turn your face to the wall and pray like Hezekiah did in the Bible. I was terrified. Sure, I prayed every night before I went to bed and every morning when I woke up but never out loud in front of everybody."

"So what did you do?" Cotton asked. "I mean now, I love to hear you pray. It's hard to imagine that you were once nervous or afraid of praying out loud."

"Well, I was," Vine said. "That is for certain. I started soft, and the guest preacher would yell for me to speak louder. I got louder and louder, and the Spirit hit me like a ton of bricks. And they couldn't get me to shut up. I remember my mother coming behind me with a handkerchief. She stuffed it into my mouth and sat me down. I knew then that this was what I was supposed to do."

"Yes, but how did you know for sure?" Bo asked. "Like my pastor, he's all of twenty-something with little-to-no energy and couldn't preach wet into water. He walks around thinking he's a chosen vessel, and folks are leaving the church by the busloads. I listen to him and wonder, *Who called you*?" The fellas chuckled but on the edge of their seats for the rest of Vine's story.

"Well, after that, everyone, including my mother and sisters, told me I was going to be a preacher," he said. "But this was too important to go on someone else's words. I needed to know it for myself and for sure. I knew that if I found out for sure, if God Himself came down and told me, nothing would or could stop me. That was my prayer that night, and I went to sleep. In the middle of the night, I heard footsteps walking, slowing down the rickety wooden hallway to my room, which was at the back of the house. I sat up and looked toward the door. I was terrified. It was Yalobusha. I then saw a dim light through the door. As the footsteps got louder and louder, the light got brighter and brighter. When it was its brightest, the light was in my room, blinding my eyes. The voice said, 'Teach my people and preach my Word.' Then something grabbed my hands. Surges of electricity shot through my body. I couldn't move, and I couldn't speak. At one point, I thought I was screaming, but I didn't hear a sound. As I came down from wherever I had gone, I focused again on the doorway. The light moved out of my room and back down the rickety hallway. It got dimmer and dimmer. The sound of the footsteps got softer and softer. I looked at my palms, and they were glowing just like this fire we're staring at right now. And then I heard, 'If you marry the church and prepare her for the bridegroom, everything you touch will be blessed.' I thought I was dreaming, but I was wide awake."

"Vine, aren't you sensationalizing this just a little bit?" Chivas asked. "You have to be making this up."

"Don't get me wrong," Vine said, suddenly self-conscious about telling his calling story with a drink in his hand. He sat the glass on the cement beneath him. "I'm not above telling a good embellished story, but I will never make up the details of my encounter with God. This happened for real, my friend."

"Wow," Sam said. "I thought you were just another jive-ass preacher. You the real deal, man. I believe it."

"So were your ordained at sixteen?" Cotton asked.

"I left Mississippi in 1964 and moved to Memphis with Pearl," Vine said. "I went to preacher school and studied the Word. I was twenty-one when I was ordained and have been preaching and pastoring ever since. After Mama and Daddy died, we moved to Chicago."

"You know, there is a rumor floating about you," Bo said. Cotton was bracing himself for what Bo had to say. "The rumor is that you are very hard to get along with at church. How many churches have you pastored since you've been in Chicago?"

"Oh, let me see," Vine said, playing with his digits to answer the question. "Mount Olive, those people were crazy. They wanted me to work full-time and pastor full-time for 250 dollars a week. Greater Kingdom or dummy kingdom, I later discovered. Half the folks in there couldn't read or write. I don't do stupid well, so I left there. Alpha Temple, Omega, Greater Omega, Mount Calvary, Tabernacle, and Prince of Peace—eight."

"Eight churches in thirty-four years?" Bo asked. "Something wrong somewhere. And weren't you the founder of Tabernacle? How do you get fired from a church that you founded?"

"I founded Prince of Peace," Vine said. "And yes, they fired me. See, I believe the church is a dictatorship. I run it. No board or deacons will tell me what I can and cannot do. And I also believe in order. I can't stand church dummies bumping into one another out of order. Jesus said, 'On this rock, I build my church.' He was talking about Peter, not the deacon board. And I've been known to throw a *damn*, *shit*, *asshole*, or *bitch* out every now and then. Funny thing—church folks don't like that. Prince of Peace fired me because I asked a simple question."

"This will be good," Bo said. "What was the question, Vine?"

"It was two hundred degrees outside in the shade," Vine explained. "Folks were passing out and not from the Holy Ghost. I stopped preaching, walked over to the thermostat, and the air-conditioning was off. Someone thought they were saving the church money on electricity. I simply asked, 'What simpleminded ass turned off the damn air?' They had a little problem with that." Everyone including Cotton laughed at that one. "So you see, pastoring Black folks is like being in a bad marriage. You stay and deal with it until you just can't take it one more second. So long story short, I'm married to the church. I'm doing what I was told to do. I'm preparing the church for the bridegroom, and that is very hard work. It will make you cuss."

"Well, Pastor, me myself, I think you are doing a fabulous job," Cotton said. Chivas had to blink his eyes to make sure Cotton hadn't turned into a woman before his very eyes. He sure sounded like one with that comment.

"But you've never been married, never dated, no kids?" Chivas pushed back.

"I don't have time," Vine said. "My wife is the church, and that's a gracious plenty. Imagine dealing with your wife all day and then coming home and dealing with Louise, Helen, or Carmela. Wouldn't that be too much?"

"But what do you do when, you know," Chivas said.

Vine knew what he was hinting at, but he wanted to hear him say it. "*You know* what?" Vine asked with a mischievous grin.

"You know, when you want to…" Chivas said.

"When I want to what?" Vine asked.

"When your love comes down," Chivas said.

"My love comes down?" Vine asked. "What love? Come down from where?"

"What do you do when you get hard and you want some ass?" Bo asked.

Vine laughed. "I do what you all do," Vine said. "I go out and get my needs met," Vine said.

Cotton was coming unglued. "This conversation is making me incredibly uncomfortable," Cotton said. "I don't want to hear about my pastor's sexual escapades."

"I gets plenty," Vine said before sipping his now extremely watered-down drink. "And female plenty." He looked directly into Cotton's eyes. "Folks think that just because you are single with no kids, you must be gay. I'm not gay. I just don't tell my business."

"Well, if you gentlemen will excuse me, I'm going to call it a night," Cotton said. "Happy birthday, Rev. Oliver." He was almost in a hurry. When he disappeared back into the house, the fellas burst out into laughter.

"Poor baby," Vine said. "He thought he was going to be the first lady."

"Well, blow the dust off your résumé," Bo said. "Once the good deacons find about your little birthday party and what you do when your love comes down, you can kiss Shining Star goodbye. I hope Lilly of the Valley is hiring. Rose of Sharon has a pastor."

The fellas laughed and let the fire fizzle out on its own. It was a good time. No judgment, just authentic fellowship. The Jolly Boys were getting closer and closer.

CHAPTER 3

New Year's Eve 1999

"It amazes me that you all seem to always show up at the same time," Jackie said, greeting her guests at the door. One by one, the gentlemen and their companions for the evening kissed and hugged the gracious hostess, showering her with bottles of champagne, jars of caviar, flowers, and premade party trays. Francis helped receive the onslaught of gifts. "Oooh, I feel the love. I got some sweet sugar, some tight hugs, a pinch from Vine being mannish." The foyer turned silent. You could hear a mouse pee on a cotton ball. "Lighten up, everyone. I was only kidding. I'm the one who pinched Vine."

Jackie Addison Jackson was Bo's new wife. After Vine's surprise birthday party last year, Helen and Bo's relationship worsened by the day. Similar to that stirring Vine described in talking about his calling, Bo knew that his marriage had come to a grinding, screeching halt. Over the twenty years he was with Helen, they grew more and more apart instead of closer and closer together. The divorce was easy and amicable. In fact, Bo thought it was a bit too easy. Christmas 1999 was the first year in a long time that there were no presents under the tree bearing Helen's name.

Bo met Jackie years ago on the job. No, she was not a waste management specialist like him. She worked in Human Resources managing worker-compensation claims. He worked with her when he injured his back a few months ago. She helped him initiate his claim and navigate through the confusing and involved process. Jackie wasn't what you'd call stunning, but she had a genuine care and appreciation for people, which gave an alluring spark. She was dark brown with a full head of jet-black feathered hair. She had big eyes and lips and distinct dimples in her cheeks. She was bountiful and curvaceous all over. She'd give Oprah a run for her money. What Bo remembered and admired about her was her attitude and general disposition. She had a reputation at work for being genuinely friendly, caring, and upbeat. She had an energy about her that was sincere and comforting at the same time. Spending time with her even in discussing a disability claim made Bo want more. Her demeanor was the polar opposite of Helen's, which was one of the reasons she was so attractive to Bo. He wanted and needed authenticity over audacity.

After his divorce, he went into HR to change all his insurance records and payroll deductions. She had no business assisting employees with other HR matters outside of workers' compensation, but she went out of her way to help Bo. The truth was, she was attracted to him even more than he was attracted to her. She made a comment about him being back on the market and offered her support for him in any way that he needed it. She told Bo, "I can predict a success story years before it's told. You are a success story waiting to happen." She offered to fill his home with the smell of a home-cooked meal. He later jokingly told the fellas that the collard greens were so good he couldn't let her leave. They started dating, and three months later, she moved in. Five months after that, she was Mrs. Beauregard Jackson, the new and improved Mrs. Beauregard Jackson.

"And Sam, who is this beautiful young lady making you look even better than you normally look?" Jackie asked.

"Everyone, this is my girl Barbara," Sam said. "Barbara, these are the Jolly Boys—Bo, Vine, and Chivas. This is Vine's sister Pearl, and Chivas's girl Louise, and Bo's wife—"

"Hello, I'm Jackie," she interrupted. "Welcome to our home."

"Thank you, Jackie," Barbara said. "I just love your spirit. Are you always bubbly and upbeat?"

"I'm afraid so," she said. "Okay, everyone, make yourselves comfortable downstairs. We're about to drop the fish."

"Jackie, can I ask what's on the menu?" Louise asked, rubbing her stomach as if she was warning it of a hearty fill.

"Well, we're going country chic," Jackie replied. "When I was growing up in the South, we wanted a break from all the turkey and dressing from Thanksgiving and Christmas. So my grandfather would go fishing every day of the week between Christmas and New Year's, and we'd have a fish fry on New Year's Eve. We'd have dirty old bottom-feeding catfish from the river."

"I bet it was delicious, but I know it was filled with all kinds of junk and chemicals," Louise said.

"You're right on both accounts," Jackie said. "How do you think I got this naturally glowing skin? I'm sure it's mercury, radiation, and all kinds of chemicals in this old body. Tonight, however, we're having farm-raised catfish from the grocery store. And we're frying it in the turkey fryer outside. We're also having spaghetti, coleslaw, Texas toast, and cheesecake with fresh strawberries. We're real low-key tonight."

"Wait, no collard greens?" Vine asked. He was insulted. The look on his face was as if he'd just discovered that someone had stolen his wallet. "Now don't get me wrong. I love hanging out with y'all, but I was whistling while getting dressed thinking about those collards greens. Is this some sort of sick and twisted joke?"

"Baby, come on," Bo interjected. "Please let the man off the hook. He's one minute away from a breakdown."

"Yes, Vine," Jackie said. "There is a big stainless-steel pot of collard greens simmering on the stove, waiting for you."

"I knew I smelled ham hocks and salt pork," Vine said, both relieved and excited. "Jackie, when you gonna put down this zero and get with this hero?"

"I got your zero preacher, man," Bo responded to the signification but laughing all the way through as only Bo would do.

"Damn, Jackie, how much crack do you put in your greens?" Sam joked. "This fool looks like he's at a crack house or something."

Everyone eventually made their way to the warm and spacious lower level. All were impressed and knew Bo had married up. Two long utility tables were joined together and held a table scape that was unbelievable. From elevated serving bowls to gold-rimmed champagne flutes to speckles of edible gold dancing in a bath of spiked punch, Jackie was an over-the-top events planner in the making.

It didn't take long for everyone to get relaxed and comfortable. After all, it was Bo's house. At midnight, everyone hugged, kissed, and proposed a sequence of resolutions to bring in the new year. Jackie insisted that everyone participate in her three New Year's traditions: roll a large head of cabbage toward the East for good luck, eat at least seven black-eyed peas for good health, and eat a serving of collard greens with your fingers for a steady flow of money in the new year. Everyone gladly complied. Later, the ladies separated into a huddle of laughter and gossip, while the men found themselves in a room alone to talk real talk.

"Man, I got to tell you." Sam was the first to speak. "Jackie is the one to beat. She's beautiful, smart, and definitely the last of the sweet girls. You're a lucky man."

"Yes, I am," Bo said.

"Does Helen know you remarried?" Vine asked.

"Of course," Bo said. "The girls told her, and they also told her how much they liked her. Let's just say it didn't go over very well. Helen just can't believe that we got married so fast. She's telling everybody that we were messing around all along. Can you believe that?"

"Just validation that she needed to be replaced," Chivas said. "Louise loves her, and for Louise, that's a tall order. Hell, I don't know if Louise loves me."

"I know one thing: if she pinches my ass one more time, we're gonna have ourselves a situation," Vine said, making everyone laugh.

"Negro, ain't nobody put their hands on your itchy ass," Chivas said.

"I ain't lying," Vine said. "She pinched and then squeezed me. She made my eyes buck."

"Shut up, Vine," Sam said. "That woman ain't thinking about you or your ass."

"That's for sure," Bo said. "She's been to Egypt, but now she's in the promised land." Bo opened his arms wide as if Jackie was standing in front of him.

"Uh-oh," Chivas said. "Someone has been reading their Bible."

"Please, someone has been watching the *Ten Commandments*," Vine said.

"Okay, okay, listen, I got an idea I want to talk to y'all about," Sam said. "I want us to take a man's trip somewhere for my birthday later this month. Just a long weekend or something."

"Naw, that might not be a good idea," Bo said.

"I agree," Vine said. "Jackie can't be without me that long. She has her needs."

"Keep it up, Vine," Bo said, raising his fists. "Just keep it up."

"They say the way to break up a friendship is to travel with a friend," Bo continued. "We might come back hating one another."

"Aw, man, that's woman stuff," Sam said. "We've been friends for a couple of years, and I think we could have a good time tearing up the streets of Miami."

"Miami, aw, please," Vine said. "I'll go on a trip, but I ain't going to no plastic-Ken-and-Barbie Miami. I deal with phony people for a living. I don't need to go visit none. Your birthday is at the end of January. Let's go somewhere hot like Mexico."

"How about we go to my old stomping ground?" Chivas said. "Let's go to New York." The men continued to debate, but Vine was suddenly withdrawn as if he'd left the conversation all together. He started rubbing his arms as if he was chilled to the bone. "Vine, what's wrong man? You look like you've seen a ghost."

"I don't know," Vine said. "When you said New York, I got chills all through my body."

"Uh-oh, that's the universe talking," Bo said. "That rules out New York for me. This ought to bring Vine back to the conversation. How about Vegas? Vine, you hear me?"

"Yeah, I heard you," he said. "I hate getting this feeling. It usually means something bad is going to happen. I don't think we should go to New York."

"Man, you are a sentence or two behind," Bo said. "Las Vegas is on the table."

"Oh yes, oh yes, oh yes," Vine said. "Vegas is the answer for the world today."

"I think Andre Crouch said Jesus was the answer," Bo said.

"I bet you don't get chills from Vegas, do you?" Chivas said.

"Now I could do Vegas," Sam said. "We could leave on Thursday and come back Sunday night."

"I could do Vegas, but, Vine, if you come out of your room with that wig and hat on…" Chivas said.

"Yeah, I'm with Chivas on that one," Sam said. "You don't realize how ridiculous you look when you wear that getup."

"But what if I'm at the keno table or the blackjack table or the slots and someone comes up and recognizes me?" Vine asked in earnest. "How am I going to explain myself?"

"Well, you could just ask a question like, 'What are you doing here?'" Bo said. Vine was genuinely confused. "If it's so wrong being in a casino, the only way your religious connections would catch you is if they were wrong too. Ever think about that? And besides, we aren't like those folks down at that church. You don't have to be perfect to be my friend."

"Then it's settled," Sam said. "Vegas it is. Y'all get your airfare money together. I'll take care of the rooms. Everybody is getting their own room. That way, you can handle your business and not disturb anybody."

"What am I thinking?" Vine said out loud. "I can't afford airfare to Vegas right now. Pearl is opening that flower shop in a few months, and I promised her that I'd invest. And even if I splurged on airfare, I won't have money to gamble."

"I got you, Vine," Chivas said. "I'll pay for your airfare. We'll fly together. In fact, as a gift to Sam, I'll pay everyone's airfare. It's kind of silly to have all that money from Catherine's settlement and not spend it."

"We can't let you do that," Bo said.

"Sure, we can," Vine interjected. "And watch. You're going to have it all back before you know it. You watch and see."

"Thanks, Chivas man," Sam said. "But I'll pay for Clay's ticket."

"Who is Clay?" Vine, Bo, and Chivas asked in unison.

"One of my running buddies," Sam answered. "He's cool people. Y'all will like him."

"I don't know," Bo said. "This is a Jolly-Boy trip."

"Yeah, but he's my friend man," Sam said. "I can't really celebrate my birthday without my running buddy. We'll get along. It won't be a problem."

"You know," Bo said, "this brings up a very important issue. Are we going to ever let other men become Jolly Boys? I mean, will it always be only us four?" Everyone in the room was silent. Bo was right. It was a very important question, and unfortunately, no one had an immediate answer. Even Vine's quick wit and Chivas's intellect were on pause. After some intense pondering and head scratching, Sam spoke up.

"Well, I guess if we are a club, we have to let other people join," Sam said.

"Is that what we are? A club?" Bo asked.

"I'm having a hard time with this," Vine said. "I don't befriend easily, but it was easy with you three. I don't know if I can do that with other people. Not to go all punk, but I think we're more than just a club. We've been friends, close friends, for a couple of years now and have had no major conflicts. That probably means something. We're a brotherhood."

"Like a fraternity?" Sam asked. "People join fraternities."

"No, more like family," Chivas said. "I mean y'all know some things about me that no one knows. You don't get that from joining a club. I think it's bigger than that."

"Well, personally, I like the idea of having some brothers," Bo said. "I mean, think about the ladies. They have it all figured out. Every woman, unless she is just a pure hellion, has a friend or a couple of friends who are closer to her than some family members. They all have that one or those two or three sisters who they consider ride or die. Worse case, they have that one girlfriend who will tell you the truth without fear or judgment, and at the end of the day, they love one another for it."

"You're right about that," Vine said. "I tell people all the time: when God made woman, man was asleep. The sisters have it figured out, and it's kind of amazing. They will stomp someone into the ground for messing with their friend and when it's all over, cuss one another out for putting themselves in the situation to begin with."

"I think it's the sign of a good woman when she's a part of a circle of friends," Bo said. "Not a bunch of petty mess but a true group of friends. They go through life knowing that they have at least one person they can depend on, one person who has their back no matter what. And when one has a problem, they've both got a problem."

"I'm hip," Chivas said. "You find a woman who is always to herself, by herself, or always in conflict with another woman, that's a sign that something is wrong with her mentally and emotionally."

"Look at Jackie," Bo said. "She has tons of friend, but Diana, Carmen, and Ramona are like her sisters. I know she feels some kind of way that they are not here tonight, but I bet you a thousand dollars they'll be together tomorrow, hook or crook. But then you have women like Helen who think that every woman is a threat to her and immediately enter into competition without the benefit of knowing each other's name. Look how miserable she is."

"Well, at the club, if you find a woman who is sitting by herself, run," Sam added. "The sister to get next to is the woman with her girlfriends. They can size you up and either encourage her to give in to you or discourage her all in about five minutes."

"Where did you meet this new girl, Sam?" Chivas asked.

"She was at this tavern I go to near the house," Sam replied. "And she was sitting at the bar by herself. It was slim pickings that night, so I stepped to her, hit her with this rap, bought her a few drinks, and made her breakfast the next morning. And she's proving to be decent, but she's a bit too clingy for me. I can't make a move without her. And you know why? Because she ain't got no damn friends."

"I think we're drifting away from the point," Bo said. "Now I'm not suggesting we become a circle of cackling hens, but it sure would be nice to have the peace of mind knowing there was someone else on this planet, besides your family, you could trust and depend on."

"I'll drink to that," Chivas said, raising his glass.

"Well, as your brother, let's talk about all this drinking you do, Chivas," Vine said.

"Vine, leave him alone," Bo said. "Learn him don't change him. We all have some stuff we need to work on, seen and unseen." Vine's quick wit was squashed by a knock at the door. Before anyone could grant permission to enter, Jackie and Louise were inside.

"Hello, gentlemen," Jackie said. She held a small ice bucket in her hand, an unopened two-liter bottle of cola under her arm, and a fifth of Chivas in her other hand. Louise had a tray of chips and salsa. Both sat their goodies on the table in the center of the small room. "Since you all are having a little man summit in here, we thought we'd bring you some drinks and snacks."

"Thank you, baby," Bo said, "but I'm cutting these jokers off. If they keep drinking, they won't be able to drive themselves home."

"Oh, no one is going home until after breakfast later this morning," Jackie said. "No one is leaving his house, not on my watch. We want 2000 to be a memorable year, but not from mourning the death of one of our friends because some drunken fool thought he could multitask behind the wheel. Oh no, not today, Satan. And that's just the way it is up in here. Anybody got a problem with that?" The room was silent. "Good. That's settled. Now finish up your little he-man, woman-haters club meeting and come out here with us."

At 2:15 a.m., the Jolly Boys adjourned their meeting as directed and joined the ladies in the open rec. room. They played games, rolled cabbage heads through the doors for good luck, ate greens and black-eyed peas for prosperity, and drank champagne and fried more fish just because. At 4:00 a.m., Jackie was the only creature stirring. She made sure everyone was settled and comfortable in their chosen sleeping accommodation and joined her husband in the master bedroom to rest. Bo heard her get into bed and looked at the clock. He smiled at her care and concern for his friends. He pulled her in, and they drifted into REM land together.

CHAPTER 4

January 8, 2000

Where the other Jolly Boys enjoyed the calm and ease of a new year and decade, Vine began his year with organization, reorganization, and (as he calls it) "divine disruption." This was the year that he was going to transform Shining Star Baptist Church from a midsized country establishment to the popular and growing mega church it was destined to be under his leadership. He had a plan, and like a dog who possessed the only bone in the yard, nothing was going to dismiss or delay his plan. The new church transformation required more tithers, more members, and more discipline. Tonight when he meets with the deacons and trustees, he would reveal his plan and announce some needed changes. Some and probably most of the changes they wouldn't like, but he was about his calling of getting the church ready for the bridegroom. His notes were prepared, and he was ready for the 7:00 p.m. meeting.

Vine had a good forty-five minutes before the meeting, so he tackled the stack of mail he had moved from one corner to the next of his oversize desk. He hated going through the mail. To him, it always brought bad news. Whether bills or complaint letters from congregants, there were at least one hundred things Vine would rather do than open envelope after envelope of trouble. To his surprise, the first envelope he opened was from Chivas. It was the hotel confirmation and plane tickets for the Vegas trip next week. Chivas made good on his promise and secured four suites at The Mirage in Vegas. Vine was so excited. Vegas was one of his favorite places on the planet. Although he enjoyed the gambling, more than that, the vibe of the city in the middle of the desert gave him energy. Maybe it was the lights or the hustle and bustle. Whatever it was, Vine always returned from Vegas recharged, excited, and a little richer. Unfortunately, his excitement was short-lived when he thought about his financial challenge. He needed two or three thousand dollars to spend while he was there, and he didn't know where he was going to get it. His savings were low, considering his investment in Pearl's flower shop, and although Chivas could certainly help him, his pride was stopping him from the ask. At Bo and Jackie's New Year's party, Chivas, in his generosity, inquired about Pearl's business and wanted to be an investor. He ended up investing twenty thousand in Flowers By Pearl. That was enough for ten months of rent. Pearl and Vine were overjoyed. Vine couldn't ask for more. He placed the envelope in his briefcase and continued the chore of going through the mail. Somehow, he'd figure his way out of his challenge without losing his pride. He would let nothing keep him away from Vegas with the(m) Jolly Boys, so cancellation was not an option.

Vine continued going through the mail and lost track of time. It was 7:10 p.m., which meant he was officially ten minutes late and violator of his own rule of never being late for God's work. Sylvia, his inept part-time secretary, left without as much as a good night or reminder. He'd be sure to give it to her in spades when he saw her again. He scooped up his notes and other documents and headed to the conference room. When he walked in, everyone stood. This was another one of his rules. Just as White House staffers stood in respect and reverence of the president, church workers should stand in respect and reverence of the man of God. The room turned silent. He took his position at the head of the table. After a brief prayer, all the deacons and trustees took their seat.

"Good evening, everyone," he said. "Praise the Lord, everybody. Repeat after me. 'Jesus Christ is the head of this meeting. We now become open and receptive to His teachings and leadership.' I have been your minister for nearly two years now, and I want to apologize."

"No, you don't need to apologize to us, Pastor," Alice Green, one of the trustees, spoke. She was his number 1 fan. She supported everything he did. He had hoped that it was because she agreed with his decisions and vision, but later discovered it was because she was messy and loved drama. Alice Green would start a rumor about herself just to get and keep some mess going. "You are in charge, and if folks don't like what you do or what you say, they can find another church. Half of them ain't giving no money no way. We ain't gonna miss nothing but their faces."

"Sister Green, what are you talking about?" Vine asked.

"I'll tell you what she's talking about," Elder Brookins, the president of the trustee board, interjected. "I said I wasn't going to say nothing, but I can't hold my peace."

"Brookins, say what needs to be said," Vine said, still confused about the subject.

"People are leaving this church by the busloads," he said. "And it's not because of the music or the crowd or even the preaching. It's because of your temper and harsh words. You stand up in that pulpit every Sunday and just go off on people. You let the slightest little thing set you on fire. These folks are adult contributors to this church. You can't speak to adults, who pay your salary by the way, like they are disobedient children. It's turning people away. And when they turn away, they are taking their tithes and offerings with them. So we accept your apology, but you need to apologize to the congregation on Sunday. The word will spread, and maybe folks will come back."

"And I want to say something," Sister Fletcher spoke. She was in charge of the kitchen and banquet hall until Vine shut it down. "The clubs and auxiliaries are up in arms. When you closed the kitchen and required all the clubs to report 250 dollars a month, people lost their minds. How are they supposed to pay the 250 dollars if they can't sell dinners after church on Sundays? People have to eat, and most clubs raised upward of two thousand dollars every time they went in there. You can't have it both ways. You can't close the kitchen and expect everyone to pay the monthly assessment."

"And can we please go back to collecting the offering after the message?" the chair of the deacon board, Deacon Wilmington, spoke. "People like to give based on the sermon. That's the way it has always been. When you get up there and snap on people and then preach a good sermon, folks forget all about the sermon. All they want to do is get their checks back because you've pissed them off. Excuse me, y'all. I'm a little upset."

"I guess that's our overall issue," Brookins chimed in again. "Too much has changed. Before you came along and while Rev. James was alive, we were a nice little church, having good service and welcoming new people in every Sunday. Now people are unhappy with some of the changes you've made and are leaving. We take in four people on Sunday and lose six on Monday. You know Black people cannot handle a lot of change. So let me give you a suggestion—no, an order. Be nicer and watch how you talk to people. Open the kitchen up or get rid of the monthly club assessment. If you don't, at the summer congregation meeting, you might get voted out."

Vine's blood wasn't quite boiling, more of a simmer until Cotton spoke. "And God knows you have experienced that before," Deacon Cotton said. Vine and Cotton have not really spoken since Vine's birthday party last year. "Based on the many churches that have dismissed you in the past, the threat of being dismissed again probably doesn't scare you much." The indignation and tone of Cotton's voice took Vine right over the edge.

"Well, as someone recently dismissed, I'm sure you can attest to how it feels," Vine responded, staring directly into Cotton's eyes. "Lascivious behavior has no place in the church and especially not on the official board."

"Okay, this has gone far enough," Brookins said. "We are the official board of this church, and you are our employee. You can either meet our expectations and manage your tongue and temper, or you will be fired. It's about us and not about you."

"Well, I know very well from the poor attendance at Bible study and Sunday school, most of you don't study the Word," Vine stated. He was in full control of his emotions and was praying that he could maintain control although looking at the angry and disengaged faces around the table, he was not all that sure. "The Word is not a file for your lottery tickets and old obituaries."

"Pastor, we're just saying…" Wilmington spoke before Vine interrupted him.

"No, you're done telling me," he said. "It's time for you and your disloyal cohort to be told. Matthew 16:18 says, 'And I say also unto thee, thou art Peter, and upon this rock I build my church and the gates of hell shall not prevail against it.' When Jesus spoke those words, He wasn't talking about deacons and trustees. He was speaking about Peter. He was speaking about the one He chose, the anointed one, the leader, the rock. I am not your employee. I'm your leader. God sent me here to prepare you for the bridegroom. Your requirement is to follow the leader and not dictate what I'm to say or how I am to say it."

"But people are leaving," Sister Fletcher said.

"The right people are leaving, and the right people are coming," Vine said. "People who don't value truth, order, and growth cannot and will not be happy under me. So no, I'm not opening the kitchen. Come to Bible class and learn how to live a prosperous life. Prosperous churches don't have fish fries and chitterling struts. Prosperous churches tithe and give back a portion of what God has given to them. Greens, dressing, and all that isn't necessary to meet our financial obligations. More chickens have been killed and eaten to support the Black church than the law should allow. But not here. Not on my watch.

"And no, we are not moving the offering to the end of service. This is not a performance. You don't determine your tithe and offering by how well you enjoyed or agreed with the sermon. After the sermon, the only thing I want people thinking about is how to put what they heard into practice. And trustees shouldn't be counting money between services anyway. That should happen on Monday here in the office with security. People are coming in and out of this church all day on Sunday. We could get robbed. It's probably why so many mistakes are being made with the money. Every week, I get a notice from the bank informing me that the amount in the deposit was lower or higher than the actual amount of cash and checks in the bag. I didn't issue an official exam, but it was my assumption that grown men could count, write, and use a calculator.

"My insistence on decency and order will never wane. And I don't bite my tongue. Ministers and choir members shouldn't be in or near the pulpit in sandals and no socks. There's entirely too much walking during service. People in the congregation should not play the tambourine. And the beginning of service is for praise and worship. We're not in the country anymore. I don't need a bunch of tired spiritless deacons having devotion, singing Dr. Watts and those sad-ass slave songs. So yes, I went off on that minister in my pulpit wearing slides and no socks. Yes, I told the congregation about the proper way to play the tambourine from the pew. And yes, I sat the deacons down when they stood, against my direction, to have devotion. I don't bite my tongue. I'm trying to create a church without a spot or a wrinkle. We've got a long way to go.

"So put on your seat belts and pin your Walgreen wigs down because I'm going to make more changes and go off on more people until my directions are followed and my orders obeyed. If you want to stay the same old small dying church, vote me out this summer. Hell, vote me out tonight. But if you want to grow and thrive, follow the leader, the rock, the one whom the church was built on and, in the process, leave me the hell alone."

The room became awkwardly silent. The tension was heavy but floated above the table like a mirage or illusion. Vine gathered all he had brought to the meeting into a pile. He panned the room, piercing the very souls of the troublemakers one by one. He stood to leave. Sister Green was the only person who followed the protocol and stood in reverence and respect for her pastor. Vine left the room. Now back in his office, he sat in his oversize executive chair and closed his eyes. This posture and this emotional state were all too familiar. His brain was flooded with memories of reprimand, resistance, and discord. Once again, he was staring at another leadership failure. Thankfully, a loud knock pulled him up from his low place.

"Oh, you're still here?" Deacon Wilmington said. "This saves me a phone call." Vine moved closer to his desk and folded his arms. He knew this was it. The board had sent Wilmington to fire him. Wilmington held a wicker offering basket in his hands. He took a seat in front of Vine's desk and placed the basket on the floor beside him. This was yet another blatant act of defiance as Vine insisted that offering baskets were consecrated and should never be placed on the floor. He let it go. Wilmington sat staring at Vine as if he was deliberating whether or not to speak. The more the seconds ticked away, the more uncomfortable Vine became. He had had enough.

"Deacon Wilmington, your antagonistic silence is unwelcomed and unnecessary," Vine said. "Is there a reason you're here?"

"I want you out of this church," Wilmington said.

"Fine," Vine said. "I'll have my attorney contact the church lawyers about my severance and will prepare a statement for the congregation to read on Sunday."

"You didn't let me finish," Wilmington said. "I want you out, but the trustees and some of the deacons do not, at least not yet. *We* are not ready to be yet another church on the long list of churches listed on your résumé. So we are placing you on a two-week silence and suspension. Think of it as a decision-making leave."

"For me or for you?" Vine asked.

"For you and the church," Wilmington said. "I think you know now what it's going to take to make this work. You've got to decide if you want to do what it takes. We've got to decide if we actually give a damn. So two-weeks office work only. You are not allowed in the pulpit or the sanctuary. And here is the offering from both services on last Sunday. Since we don't know how to count and write to your satisfaction, you can do it yourself." Deacon Wilmington dropped the wicker basket full of bills, change, and envelopes in the center of Vine's desk and stood. Vine stood as well.

"It is highly inappropriate for me to handle the offering," Vine said. "Please put this in the safe until it can be counted and recorded properly."

"All you have to do is open the rest of the envelopes, record all the checks, count the cash, make a deposit slip, enter the amounts in the member profiles, drive to the bank, and make the deposit," Wilmington said. "Like you said, it can't be that hard." Wilmington released a sinister laugh and left Vine's office.

Two hours later, Vine had counted, recorded, and completely posted last Sunday's offering properly and as it should be. He would remember to inform Deacon Wilmington that if it only took two hours in quiet concentration to do it right, he had concern that three men couldn't do it faster with more controls and attention to detail. Vine had 8,048 dollars in checks and 3,765.40 dollars in cash. He was only 184.60 dollars shy of the usual 12,000 dollars weekly collection. He felt a since of accomplishment and satisfaction from the church's financial success, but that prideful feeling was soon pushed aside when he replayed the drama of the last few hours. He remained incensed at being excommunicated for two weeks and felt a need to vindicate himself or at least have the last word. He thought about writing an open letter to the congregation but soon remembered the famous quote from Ambrose Bierce: "Speak when you are angry, and you will make the best speech you will ever regret." His cool head began to prevail. Although it didn't feel good, time was on his side. Struggling to look on the bright side, he smiled when he realized that he didn't have to make up an excuse for his absence to Vegas. He was looking forward to that now more than ever before.

As he sat, he looked at the cash. His eyes widened as if God had handed him in miracle in a wicker basket. It would be greedy and extremely self-serving to do what he was thinking of doing. "I can't," he said out loud to his own thoughts. It would be wrong. It would be stealing. Depositing the checks but keeping the cash for Vegas was something he was almost ashamed of even contemplating. He tore up the deposit slip and created another without a cash figure. He retrieved the FedEx envelope from Chivas that held his flight and hotel information for Vegas. He scooped up the cashed and stuffed it into the envelope, returning it quickly to his briefcase as if someone was watching. "Lord, I'll replace it plus 10 percent. It's a loan. I always win in Vegas. It's okay."

Vine placed the checks and slip into the night depository bag and set it aside. He gathered all he needed or thought he would need during his time away. As he prepared to exit, he checked his emotions. He wasn't surprised when he realized that they were all over the place. In that moment of introspection, he knew his stint with Shining Star Baptist Church was coming to an end. In fact, the end was in his briefcase.

CHAPTER 5

January 9, 2000

For Marsaleen, Friday night was the best time during the week to shop for groceries. Most working adults living on the Southside of Chicago were at a tavern, bar, club, or perhaps at home preparing to visit a tavern, bar, or club. Regardless, there was certainly nothing sexy or exciting about spending Friday evening at the grocery store. It was also a therapeutic distraction from her worries and sadness. She loved her job, loved her children, and loved her husband. She hated her marriage.

Marsaleen Williams met Sam in the summer of 1973 at a little hole in the wall tavern called "Under the L" or UTL. It was smack in the middle of a row of storefronts on East 63rd street between Martin Luther King Drive and Eberhart under the elevated train or the *L*. It was a Black Cheers. Everyone knew everyone, at least the regulars, and both Sam and Marsaleen were regulars. The beer and wine were warm. The coffee was cold, but back then, it was all okay. You didn't go to UTL to necessarily get drunk or to enjoy a sobering beverage. You went to UTL alone hoping not to leave as you came.

Marsaleen had always been described as striking. She was a tall girl, statuettes with thighs, breasts, and a derriere to support her unfiled claim as a beautiful Black woman. Her skin was light, and her hair was long and authentically her own. But it was her smile, her perfect wide smile that could light up the darkest space. Sam, the indisputable pretty boy, was instantly drawn to her. In later years, he would jokingly brag that he married the finest woman in the UTL.

Marsaleen still laughed when she thought of Sam's first words to her. She was sitting at her favorite table by the window when he, from out of nowhere, eased next to her and placed his arm around the back of her chair. He said, "Are you good at long division? What do you get when you place me over you? Love, passion, and beautiful children." It was so dumb. It was so corny, but it was effective. After an hour or so of drinks and laughter, Marsaleen left UTL and spent the rest of the weekend with Sam. She was in love, and she knew it. A few months later in the spring of '74, she became Mrs. Marsaleen Williams Ladeaux and expectant mother. They were so happy and in love. Unfortunately, she stopped going to UTL. Her husband didn't.

His infidelity began right away. He wasn't cavalier about it, but he didn't go out of his way to hide it. She deemed it as her lot in life. She married a pretty boy. When you marry a pretty boy, you marry infidelity. But like many Black women of that day, Marsaleen let him play, knowing that one day, he'd "come back home" and they'd be happy again. But now, twenty-six years later, he has yet to mentally come back home. They live in the same house, but they sleep in separate rooms. She cooks, but they don't eat together. He pays all the bills, but she does not know what bills he pays. Outside looking in, they were housemates. There was love there, but the friendship had been gone for years. On any given day, Marsaleen can be found wondering how on earth she managed to have another child with Sam four years after their first.

Driving home from the supermarket, Marsaleen began thinking about her plans for yet another lonely Friday night. She'd fry a couple pieces of catfish, heat up what was left of the pole beans she had prepared earlier in the week, and plop down in her oversize La-Z-Boy in front of the television. And when she was done with that, she'd take a nice hot bath, satisfy herself, and have some wine, and Friday would be over. On Saturday, she'd get her hair done and hang out with her daughters, Samaritana and Samita, both named after their father. On Sunday, she'd cook a week worth of meals and do laundry. It would be Monday before she knew it.

When she pulled into the driveway and pressed the button to open the garage, she was so startled she jumped in her seat. It had been years since she had seen Sam's Cadillac in the garage on a Friday night. Scads of thoughts, mostly of suspicion, raced through her mind. She was overwhelmed. She had been waiting for him to metaphorically come back home. Was this the night that he did? Her brain was shutting down. She needed another brain to help her process. Hers was not functioning at full capacity. She dialed Lola's number.

"Hey, Leen," Lola sang into the phone. "You just now getting in from the grocery store? I was expecting this call an hour ago."

"Girl, you won't believe this," Marsaleen whispered as though Sam would hear her if she spoke too loudly.

"Oh, Lord, it finally happened," Lola interrupted. "You walked in and caught that bastard ass-in-air on top of some hoe. Don't touch her until I get there. I'm sick of this Negro. I'm about to put on my gym shoes, take off my earrings, and come over there. We are about to whoop dat ass."

"No, Sam's here," Marsaleen whispered. "He's actually here. I pulled into the garage, and his car is actually in the garage."

"They doing it in the garage?" Lola asked. "What kind of hoe is this?"

"Naw, girl," Marsaleen said. "It has been a decade or two since Sam has been home on a Friday night. I'm scared to go in. What if I walk in, and he's dead on the floor? Or what if he brought some woman home and died on top of her? Hell, what if she died on top of him? Oh, hell no, I ain't going in there."

"What you gonna do?" Lola asked. "Sit in the car all night? Hope you didn't buy ice cream. Sam ain't dead. If anything, he's getting ready to go out, or this is a brazen hoe that he's brought home. But he ain't dead. For some reason, I think you'd know if he were. Girl, go on in there and see what the story is. She might have picked him up. Sam is probably on his second rubber by now." Lola was indeed Marsaleen's best friend and confidant, but her words could sometimes sting. But for good intentions, her opinion and views would be discounted and disregarded.

"I'm not going in," Marsaleen again affirmed. "I don't know what's in there, but whatever it is, I ain't ready for it. I'm coming over there."

"And when you do, I'm going to send your ass right back home," Lola said. "That's your house, your home. Sam ain't' got enough power to make you stay away from your own home. Hell, if I were you, I'd have a little fun with it."

"What?" Marsaleen asked.

"There's this young fine Timberland-wearing boy two doors down from me," Lola said. "You should get him to go in with you. Pay him to fawn all over you. That will get his attention. What the young folks say: flip the script." Marsaleen couldn't help but laugh. Though crazy and sometimes harsh, Lola always landed on the right words to say to her friend who was often in marital distress.

"Okay, I'm going in," Marsaleen said. "But if you don't hear from me in an hour, you need to use your emergency key and get in here. There may definitely be a situation taking place."

"I got you, girl," Lola said. "I've taken out my earrings already. All I need to do is grease up my face and put on my gym shoes. So call me back and don't forget."

Marsaleen grabbed a few of the bags from the trunk. She opted to play it normal but braced herself for whatever went down. She walked in, sat the bags on the kitchen island, and listened. The house was quiet but for the muted sound of a television upstairs. She didn't call out but followed the sound up the stairs to the guest bedroom, also known as Sam's bedroom. He was in bed, fully dressed, and cloaked in a thin summer throw blanket in the fetal position, holding his stomach. He was as white as a brand-new pillowcase.

"Sam, what's the matter?" she asked. "Why are you home, and why do you look like you're dying?"

"Hey, Leen," he moaned. "I think I am dying. I'm as sick as a dog. Around two, I got the chills and started feeling achy."

Marsaleen walked over and touched his forehead. "You're clammy, but you don't have a fever," she said. She used both index fingers to feel his glands, and they were not swollen. "Open your mouth." He obliged. She reached into the nightstand to retrieve the flashlight. Sam had flashlights in every room just in case there was a power outage in the middle of the night. She examined his throat with the aid of the focused light. "Your throat seems to be clear. It's red, but I don't see signs of infection. How is your stomach?"

He looked into her eyes to see if she had the stamina for yet another lie. The truth was that last night, he had dinner with Barbara. Since he didn't spend Christmas or Thanksgiving with her, she surprised him with a traditional holiday meal of turkey and dressing, greens, yams, chitterlings, and potato salad. The food tasted different, like she had drizzled pickle juice over everything. Something was wrong, but not to hurt her feelings and to make sure he got what he really came over to get, he began to eat. Halfway through the meal after compliments and thankfulness for her going through so much trouble for him, Barbara revealed the truth. He was eating reheated leftovers from her Christmas dinner. He was outraged and remarked that Marsaleen would never serve reheated dressing or anything else from a meal prepared six weeks ago. He left in anger, and his stomach had been on fire ever since. This was a story Marsaleen didn't need to hear. No wife was going to accept an explanation or perform her professional nursing skills for a man who contracted food poisoning from his extramarital whore. His trump card was a lie, and it needed to be a good one.

"My stomach has been griping and bubbling since last night," Sam said. "And I can't stop going to the bathroom." Marsaleen, who was no stranger to the ways of her adulterous husband, smelled the foul stench of the forthcoming lie before it left his lips.

"You probably have a bad case of food poisoning," Marsaleen said. "What and where did you eat last night?"

"Uh, some of the other engineers and I had a post-New Year's potluck at the station yesterday," Sam said. "I'm sure I ate something there that made me sick."

"I've told you to stop eating everybody's cooking," Marsaleen said, giving him the "I know that whore poisoned your ass" look. "People don't have good hand-washing habits. I'm a nurse. I know what I'm talking about."

"Yes, I know, but I didn't want to hurt nobody's feelings," Sam said. "I couldn't even go to work today."

"Well, I'm going to make you a herbal-tea remedy that will get your system back in order quickly," Marsaleen said.

"Will it stop this gurgling and diarrhea?" Sam asked.

"Well, it will stop the cramping, but it won't stop the diarrhea," she said. "We've, I mean, you've got to flush the bad bacteria from some nasty woman's cooking out of your system before you get dehydrated. Then it's to the emergency room. But once you sip on my Jamaican grandmother's gut-well tea, you'll be fine in a few hours. You may still be able to go out tonight."

"I'm not going nowhere tonight," Sam said. "I feel sick and nasty."

"No comment," Marsaleen said. "I'm going to finish bringing in the groceries and make your tea. I'll be back in fifteen minutes."

Marsaleen made the tea and covered it too steep while she put away her grocery items. When she turned around to head upstairs, Sam was standing in the kitchen. His chest was bare and smooth. His thighs still had the muscular composition of a man in his twenties. His boxers were full in both the front and the back. She had almost forgotten just how fine her pretty-boy husband was.

"I thought I'd come get this miracle tea myself," he said. "I'll be okay by myself. Don't let me mess up your Friday-night plans."

"I don't have any plans," Marsaleen said. "I'm going to do what I always do on Friday nights: eat by myself, drink by myself, watch television by myself, and go to sleep by myself." Sam was without words. He knew that comment was directed at his absenteeism as both a husband and lover. "So no, you are not messing up any plans. Drink your tea, and I'll check on you later. Let me know if you need something, but please drink every drop of the tea. It's nasty, but it will do the trick." As Sam was walking away, Marsaleen's cell phone began to ring, snatching her ogling and admiration for the sight of Sam's meaty and enticing derriere.

"Hello," Marsaleen answered. She was embarrassed for her lustful stare. "Hey, Lola, everything is okay. Sam is home with some sort of stomach bug."

"Did you make him that Jamaican cure-all elixir?" Lola asked, "Or did you do what I would have done?"

"What's that?"

"Give him rat poison and baking soda," Lola howled on the phone. She made Marsaleen laugh, which was an all-too-frequent occurrence.

"No, I didn't envenom my husband," Marsaleen said. "He's upstairs drinking the magic potion now."

"Well, why don't you come over here tonight?" Lola said. "I know you are not going to want to be there when he starts his onslaught to the bathroom. That won't be sexy. Girl, I got some reefer I found on the train. We could have us a good ole time."

"You are crazy enough," Marsaleen said. "You don't need to fire up the herb. No, I'm going to stay at home tonight with my husband. Wow, it's been a long time since I've said that."

"I'm hip," Lola said. "Well, as long as you didn't find him dead or jumping up and down on some home-wrecker. I can stop worrying about you. And don't be over there acting fast either. I know your basement needs cleaning out, but they've got services that will do that. You know what I'm talking about too. Don't be looking up at the wall embarrassed. Don't seduce that man tonight."

"Sweetie, it's not being fast or seductive when it's your husband," Marsaleen said. "Now good night. I have some things to take care of. Me and the girls will see you tomorrow."

Like clockwork, Sam began disposing all remnants of poisons and toxins from his body. Marsaleen took a hot massaging shower and got into bed. For about six minutes, she entertained the idea of seducing her husband but instead inflicted the forecasted rejection upon herself. Although close, she was not at the point of desperation. At midnight, she heard a knock at her door. She cautiously ran to the door, unlocked it, and opened it.

"Sam, what's the matter?" she asked. He had just come out the shower. His body was wet and glistening from the soft beams of the hallway night-light, and he smelled fresh and appetizing. His towel was wrapped snuggly just below his developed stomach. "You need another mug of tea?"

"Since when do you lock the door?" he asked.

"Since I pretty much started living alone," she said with a cadence dripping with indignation. "What do you need?"

"I'd like to sleep in my bed with my wife," he said. "I miss you, Leeny." He was staring at her breasts. "Don't you miss me?"

"Whether or not I miss you doesn't matter," she said. "The other side of my bed is reserved for my husband when he decides to come home and not to the free clinic to see the nurse."

"What about sex?" He grinned. She was now in dangerous territory. That sexy devilish smile was what got her years ago at UTL. It was what probably got all the women he played around with as well. Now somewhat annoyed, Marsaleen folded her arms across the objects of his attention.

"I am a married woman," she said. "And I don't know about you, but I only have sex with my husband."

"Well, you haven't had sex with your husband in a while," he said, removing the towel and throwing it over his shoulder. All the energy in her body rose to her head. Her knees felt as if they couldn't support the weight of her body. One touch, one caress, one more amatory latent statement or suggestive gesture, and she would give in. She knew it. She stepped back from the door just to get her bearings and to mentally regroup.

"I'm waiting," she said. "You see, my husband is a beautiful, strong, passionate man. He's been this way his entire life. But his thinking is small and common. He has subscribed to the school of thought that suggests that it's in a man's nature to lay with as many women as possible before he actually commits to one woman—his wife. But one day, he'll realize that that school of thought is short-lived, and the only way he can be completely happy and satisfied is to come home. So when my husband comes home, there is nothing about me that I will withhold from him. Just like my mother did and my grandmother did and my cousins, sisters, and aunts did, I'm going to wait for my husband to come home. And just as my mother granny, aunties, cousins, and sisters, I'll be right here, ready to forget the past and hold hands and run into the future. Good night, Sam."

PART TWO

Friends and Their Issues

True friends aren't the ones who make your problems disappear. They are the ones who won't disappear when you're facing problems."

CHAPTER 6

Vegas, Day 1

Vine was neither anxious nor overly concerned about making it to the airport on time. With the bitter cold Chicago winds and the shards of falling snow, there was no way flight 2744 nonstop to Las Vegas was leaving on time, if at all. He was certain that the inclement weather was God's way of punishing him for pilfering the church's money. When he made it to O'Hare, he checked the departure board immediately. To his surprise, the flight was on time with boarding starting in about an hour. His subsequent thought changed to thinking God was telling him that his pilfering was okay, just this one time. Once he allowed himself to think about something other than himself, he began wondering where the other Jolly Boys were, especially Bo. He was never late. Ten minutes early was late for Bo. A familiar voice from behind answered his inquiry.

"Rev. Oliver, you sho is fine," the voice purred in his ear. "Wanna go out of town with me?"

"Okay, but what about your husband?" Vine said without turning around.

"He's going somewhere with his friends, and besides, I keep my sex life and my marriage separate," Jackie teased.

"Well, we may as well have some fun," Vine said. "We going to hell anyway." Vine turned to embrace Jackie and Bo.

"First lady, what are you doing here?" he asked Jackie. He recently started calling Jackie first lady, intimating what she would be called once they got married. "You can't stand to be without this old African for four days? You going with us?"

"Oh no, dear," she said. "I'm just playing chauffeur today. Hanging out with four old men with tight half-buttoned silk shirts showing off their medallions and their chest hair is not my idea of a good time." Both Vine and Bo laughed out loud. "I'm going to relax and catch up on my shows."

"Well, if Chivas and the birthday boy don't show up, we're all going to be catching up on our shows," Bo said, jokingly irritated. "One of the easiest things on planet Earth to be is on time. Why can't we get that right?"

"I'm with you on that one," Vine said. "CPT time (colored people time) is not fashionable nor cute." Bo, Jackie, and Vine began to scan the crowd for the missing Jolly Boys. Soon, both Chivas and Sam stepped out of a sea of travelers. Chivas pointed toward the group, and both hurried over. Jackie stepped aside to let the fellas hug and greet one another.

"Okay, if you all break out into some fraternity step or secret handshake, I know something," Jackie said. The men heard Jackie's cry for admiration and attention and hugged her in group formation. "Well, I'm gonna get out of the way and let you all loose on Vegas. I hope they're ready for you." Bo walked a few feet with his wife, gave her a passionate kiss, and slapped her behind as she was walking away. He returned to the group now sitting and engaged in casual conversation.

"Man, you know, you married way above your zip code," Vine said. "I can't wait until she put down the zero and get with this hero."

"Man, gone somewhere with all that extra mess," Bo said, sitting and resting his hands atop of his protruding stomach. "I got that on lock."

"Chivas, what's wrong with you?" Bo asked. "You wound up tighter than a cheap watch."

"Man, I ain't no punk, but I'm not too keen on flying," Chivas said. "Think about it. We are about to board a 735,000-pound machine with 200 other people, use engine power to propel 30,000 feet in the air, stay up there without ropes or rails for four hours, and then come down without injury or incident. That's a lot to ask God to do." Chivas reached into his bag and pulled out a sterling silver flask, lifted the top, and took a long gulp.

"I must be having a dream or nightmare because I know your ignorant ass didn't bring a flask for this flight," Bo said.

"I sure did," Chivas responded. "Now you have a choice. You can have me on this flight with my flask or me on Amtrak with a milkshake. Let me know what you prefer. I'm good either way."

"I can't believe you made it through security with that thing," Sam said. "If a fool can get through security with a flask, I know one can get through with a gun."

"I'm sure people bring on all kinds of stuff, but I bet they'd find a gun," Vine said. "Especially on a Black man. But mark my words. All this is going to change one day."

"Well, until it does, me and Mr. Regal will be flying together," Chivas said. "When I get to Vegas, I'm going to be more jolly than before, and there will be no tags on these toes."

"We're flying first class," Bo said. "Which means we'll hit the ground first. Our toes will be the first to be tagged."

"See, don't say stuff like that 'cause it ain't funny," Chivas said.

"Bo, you've done it again," Vine said. "You snatched the high right out of Chivas. He might need something stronger, like a Benadryl chaser."

"Naw, we need something stronger than that," Bo said, struggling to be audible through his near-hysterical laughter. "We need Mahalia Jackson."

"Yes, and not cute and made-up Mahalia," Vine said, trying like Bo to control his teasing. "We need Mahalia after she has been under those hot lights and that wig dripping with sweat and making those ugly Holy Ghost faces. 'Way over in Beulah, I see the captain beckoning to me,'" Vine began singing.

"Okay, okay," Chivas said. The fellas including Chivas were enjoying Vine's show. And a few of the passengers who understood Vine's reference enjoyed his performance as well.

"Chivas, you're an educator," Sam said. "I know it's just gym, but you teach people for a living. Where's your intellect and critical thinking? More people have died at the intersection of 79th, Stony

Island, and South Chicago than on American Airlines flights. Be cool."

The four-and-one-half-hour flight to Vegas was smooth and without incident. After about thirty minutes of small talk, Bo and Vine were sound asleep. Sam dosed on and off while reading the January issue of *GQ* magazine. Chivas, sitting next to him, assumed the duty of copilot, wide awake using the tray table as a steering apparatus for the plane. It was a wonder anyone could sleep with Chivas on board. Every dip, every bit of turbulence, and every turn was followed by Chivas's audible reaction. At first, Sam was annoyed and somewhat embarrassed, but after an hour or so, it turned amusing and entertaining.

Chivas made good on his promise and arranged for a stretch limo pickup from the airport. Sam's chest instantly puffed when he saw an older White gentleman holding a sign bearing his name. When the limo approached The Mirage hotel, it bypassed the main entrance and stopped in front of a private VIP entrance on the secluded side of the hotel. The men went straight to their rooms after receiving the keys from the driver. All had two-thousand-square-feet suites on the same floor but scattered except for Vine and Chivas who had adjoining suites. The fellas traveled the floor, inspecting one another's room and searching for evidence in support of their bragging of who had the most extravagant room. Fortunately, all the rooms were exactly the same. Sam's room would be the meetup room. Chivas had arranged delivery of a well-stocked bar and a cart of snacks for the fellas to share.

"Chivas man, I don't know how to begin to thank you for these rooms," Sam said. "And VIP limo service from the airport—this is blowing my mind. Thank you, man."

"Hey, it's a birthday gift," Chivas said. "I realized that holding onto that money is not going to bring Catherine back. She would want me to use it and enjoy my life. So no more thank-yous. We just need to relax and have a good time. So what are we doing tonight? My hand is itching. What does it mean when your hand itches?"

"Is it your right hand or your left?" Vine asked.

"My left," Chivas replied. "Why?"

"Because if your right hand itches, you're preparing for money to come," Vine answered. "But if it's your left, that means an important letter is on the way."

"What, you a preacher by day and a voodoo priest by night?" Bo said. "Where you get that country-backwoods stuff from?"

"From the country in the backwoods where I was raised," Vine said, almost prideful. "My mama used to say that all the time. And if you dream of fish, someone is pregnant. And if you dream of someone's death, they will live a long time."

"When you start dreaming of lottery numbers, let me know," Bo said.

"Aw, Bo, I already know you're going to be a rich man one day," Vine said. "I've already received divine intelligence on that."

"If y'all start swapping recipes, I know something," Chivas said. "So what are we doing tonight? It's eleven, and I'm in Vegas. It's time to do something."

"You all go right ahead," Bo said. "I'm going downstairs and get a hot dog, and then I'm going to bed. I want to hit the Bellagio Brunch in the morning."

"You come to Vegas, and all you want to do is eat," Vine said.

"No, I want to gamble and sleep as well," Bo said. "I'm starting with sleep. Y'all do what you want. I'm going to get my hot dog, take a shower, call to kiss my wife, and go to bed. Let's meet here at noon and head down to the Bellagio."

"That works," Sam said. "I'm tired as well. And tomorrow afternoon, I'm going to arrange for us to have some special fun."

"Vine, that just leaves you and me," Chivas said. "I know you want to hit the casino. Let's go downstairs for a minute."

"Cool," Vine said. "We'll see you Negroes at noon tomorrow."

After a quick shower and wardrobe change, Vine was ready to go. He was not in his usual casino disguise, but he was on a mission nonetheless. He placed his two good-luck silver dollars in his right shoe and salt and red pepper flakes in his left before dousing his palms with a pungent good-fortune oil he bought years ago on a voodoo tour in New Orleans. He knocked on Chivas's door, but his running buddy was still getting ready. Vine left for the casino floor with one thousand dollars of stolen church money in his pocket. Two hours had passed before Chivas caught up with Vine. Both had been entertaining their respective vices. Chivas was six sips away from intoxication. Vine was down nine hundred dollars. Chivas, with glass in hand, approached his friend who was at the twenty-five-dollar blackjack table. Even in his near inebriated state, he could see that Vine was in trouble.

"Hey, man, what's the good word?" Chivas asked, sitting himself in the empty chair next to Vine. A portly White gentleman who was also seated at the table rolled his eyes in Chivas and Vine's direction before leaving the table. "What's up with him? It's not my fault that he's giving his money away."

"Listen, this is serious business, so I don't have time to talk right now," Vine snapped. "If you're going to play, then play. Otherwise, I'll catch up with you later."

"What in the actual hell is the matter with you?" Chivas asked while retrieving three one-hundred-dollar bills from his billfold. "Why are you talking to me like that? And why are you looking at me like I'm ugly or something?" Chivas was trying to make light of the situation, but Vine wasn't having it. The dealer placed a short stack of twelve chips in front of Chivas. He slid two chips toward the dealer as his bet. Both stopped talking to play their hands. Vine lost his twenty-five-dollar bet with a 6, 8, and 9. Chivas won fifty dollars with an 8, 2, and 10, beating the dealer's pull of 4, 10, and 9.

"See, that is why I don't like to talk when I'm gambling," Vine said, even more frustrated and agitated than before. "In fact, most serious gamblers like quiet when they are playing. That's probably why that man left the table." Vine looked as though he was going to be sick.

"Man, relax," Chivas said. "This is supposed to be fun and entertaining. You making this out to be a life-or-death situation. You bring your mortgage money or something? Do you need to call the 1-800 number?"

"I'm treating this like a life-and-death situation because it is one," Vine raised his voice. "Life as I know it is at stake." Vine's expression suddenly changed. He instantly regretted making that last statement.

"Get your chips," Chivas said. "We need to have a talk." Chivas stood, collected his chips, and began walking toward the bar. Vine was reluctantly right behind him. After sitting, he ordered two Chivas Regal and ginger ale highballs. Once Vine was able to take a gulp and exhale, the conversation continued. "Now tell me what's going on with you. You wound up tighter than a wet knot in a rope. And don't tell me you're tired. Our vices give us energy. Talk, Negro."

"Man, I'm just stressed out," Vine said.

"No shit," Chivas said. "What about?"

"I did something that I'm now realizing was risky and stupid," Vine said.

"What?" Chivas pressed.

"I had a bad meeting with the church board earlier this week," Vine explained. "I was espousing my expectations, and they suspended me. I'm on a two-week silence and forbidden from preaching or entering the pulpit." Chivas, intuitive in nature, looked at his friend for the rest of the story. "So I took about four grand of Sunday's offering for spending money in Vegas. I promised myself that I'd pay it back plus 10 percent, but in the last two hours, I've lost close to a thousand of the money. If this continues, I'm going home broke, disgusted, and hell bound."

"Please tell me you're lying, Vine," Chivas said. "Please tell me you didn't take the hard-earned money of those people in that church and use it to finance your gambling for this trip. You didn't do that really, did you?"

"I did," Vine said and dropped his head. "But I didn't know what to do. I didn't have money for the trip, so somehow I thought the confrontation with the board was the universe giving me permission to—"

"Steal," Chivas said, cutting him off. "Do you really think God was giving you permission to steal the church's money? Why didn't you just ask me?"

"You bought the plane tickets and took care of the rooms and also invested in Pearl's flower shop," Vine said. "I couldn't ask you for more money. I wouldn't like the way that made me feel."

"It would feel a whole lot better than what you're feeling right now," Chivas said. "I'm not a religious man by any stretch of the imagination, and God knows I've got my own mess to deal with. But you are… Did you really think God would bless you when you stole from Him?"

"Yes," Vine said. "Yes, I thought there was no harm in taking this money and using it as long as I paid it back and an additional 10 percent."

"Look, we're going upstairs, and you are going to give me the rest of that money," Chivas said. "Tomorrow, I'm going to the bank. I'm going to write a four-thousand-dollar check to the church, get five-thousand dollars for you, and when I get home, I'm taking this cash and putting it in the offering plate. I ain't trying to go to hell either."

"No, I got myself in this situation, and I'm going to get myself out," Vine said.

"Yes, you got yourself into this mess, but you have no way of getting out," Chivas. "We're going to do this so tomorrow, maybe your good fortune will show up. You've allowed yourself to be cursed. You can't prevail from this. We're doing this. Finish your drink and let's go up."

CHAPTER 7

Vegas, day 2

On Friday morning at 10:00 a.m., the fellas received a phone call from the hotel concierge on Sam's behalf. It was January 27 and Sam's 56th birthday all day. Chivas, Bo, and Vine were to meet Sam at the world-renowned Buffet at Bellagio, where unforgettable flavor profiles were created that pleased every palate. They were instructed to meet there at 1:30 p.m. sharp. The rest of the itinerary for the day would be shared at that time. The final instruction was to dress athletically comfortable but fly. About five minutes after hanging up the phone, Vine could hear Chivas laughing hysterically in the adjacent room. He laughed as well and shook his head, resigning to reality of how crazy a day it was going to be with Samaritan Ladeaux in charge of the agenda.

At 1:30 and as instructed, the Jolly Boys gathered in the lobby of the Bellagio Hotel. Bo was the first one there, determined to savor every bite from each and every offering on the buffet. Vine was ready for a break from his morning gambling session. He had arrived a couple of hours early to see if the slot-machine experience was as rich and satisfying as the infamous and elegant smorgasbord. It was not. According to Vine, if the Wild Kingdom, Money Train, and Balloons of Fortune slot machines were food, they'd be dry, cold, and absolutely flavorless. Chivas, mister physical education teacher, opted to walk from the Mirage to the Bellagio. He was on time but the last to arrive nonetheless.

"Well, I certainly worked up an appetite," Chivas said, slowly but surely allowing his breathing to regulate back to normal. "When they say this shit is not as close as it looks, they mean it. I've been on escalators, elevators, overpasses, and even through a few tunnels. It felt like I was trying to escape Alcatraz."

"You should have stopped and taken a break," Bo said.

"Damn a break," Vine said. "His drunk ass should have stopped and taken a taxi." Chivas didn't find Vine's signifying comment amusing or funny, but he mustered up a disingenuous half-chuckle for the sake of peace.

"Well, we're all here," Bo said. "Let's get our eat on! I've been waiting on this for weeks. I'm about to show you ladies how to eat up in here. I'm going to eat them into the red today. They gonna remember me."

With the birthday boy at the helm, the gentleman made their way to the buffet. After being seated, they grabbed plates and made their first-trip selections. Bo was in heaven, emitting sounds of sheer bliss and satisfaction after every bite. In collective consciousness, the fellas couldn't decide what was more satisfying: eating the plentiful and delicious cuisine or watching Bo eat the plentiful and delicious cuisine.

"See, we need one of these in Chicago," Bo said. "It's high as hell, but Black people don't mind paying for good food and good service. Thigh and Leg is my spot back home, but they ain't got nothing on this. I'm adding this to my vision board. I'm going to open a high-end buffet-style restaurant for my people."

"What you gonna call it?" Sam asked. "Good Samaritan or Sam's Birthday Bistro sounds good."

"I'm thinking Beauregard's Buffet," Bo said. "Our motto will be 'Come and put something good in your mouth.'"

"See, that's just nasty," Vine said. After a second trip to the buffet, Sam shared the itinerary.

"So when we leave here, we're going to the outlet mall," Sam said. "They say that even the Las Vegas celebrities shop at the outlets in Vegas. We'll do some people watching and gambling at Caesars, go back and change, have a late dinner, and then we're off to the club."

"Club?" Chivas asked. "What kind of club? I haven't been to a club in years. I don't even know what the latest dance steps these days are."

"Not a dance club, country," Sam continued. "A gentlemen's club." All eyes fell on him in earnest ignorance. "Y'all slow as hell. A gentlemen's club with strippers."

"Naked strippers?" Vine asked.

"Wouldn't be much of a strip club if the dancers kept on their clothes," Chivas teased. "In that case, we might as well just go to the church." Bo almost choked to death from laughing. And he was in good company, except for Vine, of course. "More ass and titties shake on Sunday mornings at eleven than the law should allow."

"Anyway, I ain't going to no strip club," Vine decreed. "What if Jesus comes back tonight? Oh no, he won't catch me with some woman's big ass in my face and dollar bills in my hand."

"Wait, hold up," Bo said. "Vine, we've been wondering how you got down. You just told on yourself. You an ass man, ain't cha?"

"Naw, get it right," Chivas said. "He's a big-ass man." Even Vine had to laugh at that himself before swiftly getting back to matters at hand.

"Come on, y'all," Vine said. "I'm a minister. I'm no prude, but I am a minister. Yes, I have a nip now and then and love the casino, but a strip club just seems like I'm slapping God in the face. It's just a low, vile, and dirty place. I don't even understand why they call it a gentleman's club. Gentlemen don't go there."

"Look, it ain't like what you see on television," Sam said. "We'd be at a table. Some girls will come around and flirt a bit. Also, a couple of girls will be dancing on stage, but you can't get close to them. It's not like people are going to be walking around naked and dripping."

"Oh God, dripping, Sam?" Vine said.

"Vine, get a grip," Sam said. "It's an upscale establishment. And I ain't no preacher, but I do know a thing or two about sin. It's not a place but an act. Don't do nothing, and you won't be guilty of nothing. Besides, it's my birthday, and going to the strip club will be like a send-off or last hurrah."

The fellas looked at one another, and then all eyes fell on Sam. They were silent, dismissing each perilous thought that entered their head about Sam's existence. The silence had to be broken. Someone had to ask the question.

"What do you mean exactly by send-off and last hurrah?" Chivas asked. "I'm going to be monumentally pissed if you brought us to Vegas to tell us that you are dying or something."

"Dying?" Sam reacted. "I'm not dying. I'm talking about me and Marsaleen. I think it's time to bring it in now. I think it's time to put this womanizer crap down and go home. I want my wife back and only my wife."

"Wait, let me get this right," Chivas said. "You want to go to a strip club because after the strip club, you're done chasing tail. You are going to work on your marriage."

"That's it exactly," Sam said. "Man, when I was sick last week, Leen took care of me."

"Your wife is a nurse," Vine said. "That's what she's supposed to do. She took that hypocritical oath, didn't she?"

"Vine, that's for doctors, not nurses," Chivas said.

"Whatever. Same flavor," Vine said. "She lives in the same house with you, and she's your wife. What kind of human being would she be if she didn't take care of you?"

"Yeah, but we haven't heard the whole story," Bo said. "Not as much as you love women. Something you ain't telling us."

"Man, she rejected me," Sam said, slightly above the decibel of a whisper. "When I was feeling better, I took a shower and thought I'd reward her for taking care of me. I was going to make love to her, and we were going to sleep together in our bed. First, she had the door locked. When she answered the door, she turned me down, and it wasn't even a struggle for her to do so. I was standing there, plantation naked on brick right in front of her, and she turned me down like a Jehovah Witness at your door on Sunday morning. That was a sign. After tonight, I'm going back to being married. We might even renew our vows." The fellas waved Sam off and laughed as if they'd heard the most preposterous and fatuous words ever spoken.

"Negro, please," Vine said. "For five seconds, I thought you were serious. She didn't want you in her bed because ain't no telling what kind of foul and filthy gentleman-club diseases you got going on down there. You probably got a petri dish down there. Sam, you ain't the one-woman type. Why does everyone know that but you?"

"You know, I'm about sick of your hypocritical ass being so judgmental of everybody," Sam said. "Maybe if you kept your big ass mouth shut, you could hold a job for more than a month. And at least I have a wife to show my petri dish to. What you got?"

"Look, I'm just trying to be real," Vine said. "It is what it is. We all got our vices. The facts are the facts. You're a hoe, Bo's an over-eater, and Chivas is a drunk."

"See, I let it slide when you said that shit before, but you gonna stop calling me a drunk," Chivas said, pointing his four right fingers across the table in Vine's direction.

"I'm sorry," Vine said. "There goes my big-ass hypocritical mouth again. I meant to say *alcoholic*."

"I ain't no damn alcoholic," Chivas snapped. "I go to work every day sober and come home the same way. Alcoholics drink because they have to. I drink because I want to."

"Please," Vine said. "Your only complaint about this buffet was that they didn't serve liquor. And the first thing you gonna do when you walk out of here is find Chivas Regal."

"Like I said, I ain't no damn drunk," Chivas reported. "I wasn't drunk when I replaced all that money you stole."

"Money he stole?" Bo asked before stuffing his mouth with the other half of a crab cake. "What money you steal, Vine?"

"Chivas, this is really no one's business but ours," Vine said.

"Oh, so you blast us, but we gonna keep your hot pot of mess simmering on the back burner?" Chivas said. "Not today. So tell your friends about the four thousand dollars you stole from the church to fund your gambling habit."

"A typical phony-ass preacher," Sam said. "You are acting just how folks want you to act. Drive a big car and steal from the church."

"I didn't steal," Vine said. "It was a loan that I'm going to pay back with 10 percent interest."

"If I walk into a bank, ask for four thousand dollars, fill out an application, get approved, and get a check, that's a loan," Bo said. "If

I walk into a bank, walk into the vault, take four thousand dollars, and walk out, that's stealing."

"And would you believe that my drunk, alcoholic ass took that money back, gave him five thousand dollars, and plan on sending that unused stolen money back to the church, all to protect him?" Chivas said. "And if that was drunk, I can't imagine my philanthropy if I was sober."

"Vine, man, come on," Bo said. "How could you?"

"Why you so quiet now, Vine?" Chivas asked. "Don't feel so good staring your vices in the face, does it? When I walk out of here and get that drink, I'll have one for you too."

"Look," Vine snapped. "I made a mistake. You can't question my calling for making a mistake. I'm not hypocritical. I just have an opinion."

"Yeah, about everybody's issues but your own," Chivas said. "See, something told me not to do this. Something said folks show their natural asses when they travel. Just leave well enough alone. Everything with the fellas is good. You go to Vegas, it's going to fall apart, and look what's happening. And before you say it, yes, Vine, I want a drink. In fact, I want a bunch of them, but at least I can afford them."

"You know what," Vine said, pulling a rubber-banded roll of cash from his pocket and sitting it on the table. "I'm tired of you treating me like some welfare case. Take your damn money." He stood from the table. "I'm going back to my room. I don't need this foolery."

"Fine. I'm leaving too," Sam said. "Thanks for an unforgettable birthday. I should have known better."

"Sit down," Bo barked. Chivas, Sam, and Vine were more frightened than startled. No one moved. "Let me try this again. Sit your Black asses down." This time the cadence of his voice was demonically low and methodically paced. The entire section of the restaurant was staring in their direction. The gentlemen, now embarrassed, eased down into their seat.

"Everybody is looking at us," Vine said. "I'm a grown-ass man. I'm not to be—"

"Oh, you didn't let me finish," Bo said. "And shut the fuck up. You came all the way to Las Vegas to be typical. Four Black men ain't supposed to be able to be friends, brothers, confidants. We are supposed to be incapable of leaning on one another and helping one another. No one in the world, especially all these White folks looking at us right now, expects four Black men to be great individually, let alone greater together. So what y'all do? Play right into that expectation to the point you gonna walk out on one another. You are going to walk out on one another and the chance to build a friendship and bond that you need and like you've never had before. This was no accident. Us meeting was not some happenstance. This was supposed to happen, and I'll be damned if I let your typical, expected, and common antics ruin it. So stop acting like a klatch of catty women and pull up your manhood by the bootstraps. Tighten this shit up and fix this shit. We are boys. We're brothers. The world tears a Black man down every three seconds. The world don't need no help from us." The men had a solemn response to their chastisement. No one could find the words to combat the truth that Bo was speaking.

"Vine," Bo continued, "you ain't no priest, and this ain't the Catholic church. Don't nobody need you weighing in on their transgressions 'cause you got your own. We gonna help you use your mouth for good. Chivas, drinking ain't gonna bring Catherine back. Just like eating won't ease the pain, guilt, and grief from losing my grandson. But you tag us in when you need to. When that day comes where you start drinking because you have to and not because you want to, tag us in. You gonna be all right. And Sam, it doesn't matter if we believe what you say about Marsaleen and working on your marriage. As long as Marsaleen believes you, that's all that matters. We'll never help you get into trouble, but we'll always pull you out the fire."

"Everyone has a breaking point," Sam said. "It's just that I'm too old to…"

"Humbug and argue over stupid shit?" Bo said. "I'll agree with that. That's why we're not going to do this. We are going to have peace and brotherhood, not this signifying, insensitive nonsense that woman complain about all the time. And I ain't perfect. I got to work through some shit like eating everything I see. I got to work through some shit myself.

"I remember when Jarah, my oldest daughter, broke the news to me and her mother. It was the Sunday before she was to go back to high school after her spring break. She and this rail-headed Jamaican boy, Maxime, with their heads down in shame, informed me and Helen that she was pregnant. My seventeen-year-old junior-in-high-school daughter was pregnant. I could have fainted. This happens to other low-class ghetto people. Not us. Not the Jacksons. But there I was, modeling the statistic in living color. I was so angry. And then she said that she and Maxime, who had already dropped out of high school, discussed it and she was going to drop out too. Maxime had a good job at the Arlington Racecourse, and he could afford to take care of her and the baby. I was seeing red, white, and blue that day."

"She and Max discussed it and decided," Vine repeated. "Like she's grown. I would have knocked her out."

"Aw, man, I can't hit my girls," Bo said.

"Would you let him finish the story?" Sam said.

"Well, I didn't hit her, but she probably would have preferred a beating compared to how I snapped off," Bo said. "I let them both know that there was absolutely nothing to discuss. She was going to graduate and on time with everyone else. Yes, she would be showing at some point, but she should have thought about that before she had unprotected sex with Rasta man. She was so upset. In December, she gave birth to Beauregard Jeremiah Jackson II. That was my dude. We spent a lot of time together. I gave him the nicknames BoBo and Hercules. He was fast and strong. Seemed liked he gained a pound every night. He would crawl all over the house and onto anything that got in his way.

"One week, it was on a Wednesday, probably one of the reasons I hate Wednesdays, I elected to take a few days off. I had vacation time I was going to lose if I didn't use. So to help Jarrah and Helen out, I agreed to keep Hercules for one day. It was a normal day that ended in a nightmare. I laid down for an afternoon nap, and Hercules was right with me. I slept for about two hours before getting up. Hercules didn't budge, so I let him sleep. When Jarrah made it home, she made a beeline to her baby. She couldn't wake him. The hairs on my arm stand up every time I think about Jarrah's bloodcurdling scream. The baby would not wake up. We shook him, blew into him, turned him upside down, slapped his face, but nothing. Neither one of us knew CPR, but that didn't stop us from trying. While I was calling the paramedics, Jarrah was performing what she knew to be CPR. It was as if she would give up breathing herself if it meant her baby could breathe again. Eventually, her brain caught up to reality. She knew, we knew, he was gone. I fell to my knees. I can't begin to describe the pain. It was a deep and sharp pain that radiated from my heart through my entire body. And watching my baby grieve over her baby, it was almost too much for me. I thought I was going to die. When the paramedics arrived, I pried him from Jarrah and squeezed his heavy body into my chest. I thought that maybe if we connected, two males from different generations with the same name, maybe if we connected, just maybe he'd take one deep breath, and the nightmare would be over. But the nightmare continued."

"Bo, I don't know what to say, man," Sam said. "I've always wanted to ask what happened to your grandson, but I didn't know how. How did you get through that?"

"That's just it," Bo said. "I don't think I've gotten through it. Probably one of the reasons I eat so much and why I've gained so much weight over the last few years. I'm not through it. Not a day goes by that I don't think about my little dude."

"Did they ever find out the cause of death?" Vine asked. "Did he have a condition that was undetected or something?"

"They did an autopsy and concluded sudden infant death syndrome (SIDS)," Bo answered. "For some reason and usually from suffocation, some infants stop breathing while they are asleep. That's why newborns should always sleep on their backs. Newborns don't have the instinct to lift their heads and move if their mouth or nose is obstructed. But Hercules was eight months old. It wasn't suffocation for him. He just stopped breathing, and we'll never know why. I don't think I'll ever be able to forgive myself for his death. I often think, what if I did things differently that day? Instead of taking a nap with him, what if I just let him sleep by himself? Maybe we should have gone out for a stroll or ride in the car. Did he cry for help and I slept through it? Hell, maybe I should have lost my vacation time and gone to work."

"You gotta know by now that his death was not your fault," Chivas said. "That was a breakthrough for me in dealing with Catherine and the boy's death. I used to think that somehow, things would have been different if I went to pick them up or paid for the plane, train, or bus tickets. Maybe they would still be alive. Through therapy, I learned and accepted that there was nothing I could have done to stop an incompetent truck driver from killing my family. There is nothing you could have done to prevent SIDS with your grandson."

"I know that now, but for years, I blamed myself," Bo said, getting more and more emotional as the conversation continued. "And I went through that ordeal by myself. Jarrah, Helen, Maxime—everyone blamed me. They never came out and said it, but my relationships with all of them have changed. It's a heavy burden and situation that I've got to continue dealing with until I get my healing. So this nonsense y'all trying to beef about means nothing. What's important to know is you don't have to go through your crap alone. Now if you want to turn your back on that, get up and walk out. Walk away. But if you want the comfort and confidence of a brotherhood, you'll stay, check yourself, and hold your brothers up." The fellas sat in silence with their heads down, but no one walked away.

In true Vine Oliver-fashion, the witty and strategically irrelevant preacher brought the jolly back to the table. "Bo, you have two daughters right?" Bo, somewhat confused, nodded. "Your oldest daughter is named Jarrah. What's the name of the baby girl?"

"Maya, like Maya Angelou," Bod answered.

"Seriously, Jarrah and Maya, like Jeremiah?" Vine asked. "You and Helen should be horsewhipped. Why y'all do those babies like that?" Soon thereafter, the fellas were laughing and joking again with their recent discord far behind. There was no ceremony or declaration, but this was the day Bo became lead Jolly Boy, a title he would hold and cherish until his demise.

CHAPTER 8

Friday, January 27, 2000

With very little effort, the Jolly Boys moved past their first rough patch and recommitted themselves to making Sam's birthday a true celebration. Only as a sign of solidarity did Vine relent and agree to hitting up the strip club. Sam was so excited, and for some reason, so was Chivas. The fellas later learned that Chivas was not excited for the naked and seminaked ladies. He was looking forward to witnessing just how Vine was going to handle himself in a club of ill repute.

After a modest and late supper at the Venetian hotel, the fellas climbed into a limo and headed to the club. It was about a thirty-minute drive away from the city and strip. The club was called Pedestal, but one look would suggest that it was erroneously named, to say the least. After twenty minutes of nothing but desert darkness, a low and modestly lit building glowed in the distance. Up close, it was obvious that the Pedestal was an old banquet hall repurposed as a den of iniquity. The four men climbed out of the limo and took their place in the line. The next show began at 11:00 p.m., and they were an hour early. For that and other reasons, no one was in a hurry.

"So how much does it cost to get in?" Vine asked while taking out his wallet. "I'd prefer not to use a credit card. I don't want this mess showing up on my statement."

"Put your wallet away," Sam said. "This is an exclusive gentleman's club. You pay for admission when you make the reservation and order the car service. Look around. You don't see a lot of cars, do you? That's because they prefer you not drive but use their fleet."

"Well, that's smart," Bo commented. "Probably not a good idea to put a bunch of drunk and horny men on the open highway."

"Or have a bunch of drunk and horny men taking strippers home after the show," Chivas added. The group envisioned Chivas's commentary playing out in their minds and simply nodded. It was like they had finally understood the punch line of a bad joke. "I guess when you wake up the next morning with no evidence of the night before, it's worth the two hundred dollars."

"Wow, fifty dollars a person?" Vine asked.

"Naw, fool," Sam said. "Two-hundred dollars a person."

"See, that's just ridiculous," Bo said. "You could buy a whole vagina for two hundred dollars and have money left over for a buffet at the Bellagio. They better have a buffet up in here."

"Well, we know they ain't running low on vagina," Vine joked.

"Chill out," Sam whispered. "We're supposed to be wealthy businessmen from Chicago. Don't let nobody hear your cheap behinds complaining about money. Like I said, I took care of it. So try to be like me: suave and debonair."

The men walked into the lobby in a cloud of cautious curiosity and excitement. Two very tall and very wide Black gentlemen waved a metal detecting wand around their chests, backs, and pockets. Once clear, they were given a gold card and told to wait for their concierge to escort them into the Pedestal room. The gentleman huddled at the waiting area right in front of the theater doors. They engaged in nervous chitchat and took in all they could see. The benches were low and covered with purple velvet material. The casino-style patterned carpet was also purple with hints of gold and red letter *P*s. The amateur-painted lavender walls connected with thick and wide white molding underneath purple covered ceilings. Expansive French provincial chandeliers hung snuggly from the high ceilings. Underneath, all could feel the thumping base of the music from the main room.

"This is not at all what I expected," Bo said. "There are no women here. I expected to see ass and breasts coming out of the woodwork."

"Hello, gentlemen. I'm Addison," a sensual voice cooed from behind. Bo, Chivas, Sam, and Vine performed an about-face with military precision. No one uttered a word. They couldn't. The sight of Addison filled their eyes like hot cocoa being poured into a holiday mug. She was petite, perfect, and plump. She had a head full of auburn-brown hair that draped her bare brown shoulders. Her face and striking features were a canvas for a skillful makeup artist. Her body was draped in a long see-through duster, white to match her stiletto heels. Her smile was perfect and as inviting as her natural full lips.

"Lord Jesus," Vine allowed his prayer to be heard aloud. "You are the most beautiful woman I've ever seen." His eyes were fixated on her breasts, which he could see through her sheer covering.

"Oh, thank you, handsome," Addison said. "I'll be sure to come and see you before you leave. You can tell me how beautiful I am, and I'll let you touch the objects of your attention. Oh, how I love a breast man."

"You promise?" Vine asked with the cadence of a beggar.

"Yes, hun," Addison responded. "I promise."

"Now who is the birthday boy?" she asked. Both Vine and Sam raised their hands. Addison looked at Vine and chuckled. "Let's go with you since you have the golden ticket." She walked up to Sam and wrapped her arms around him and squeezed the cheeks of his buttocks. He did the same to her. She released a theatrical moan and stepped back. "Okay, fellas, the big show begins in the main room at eleven. I will be your concierge for the evening. If you need anything, let me know. Come on, birthday boy." She reached out and took Sam's hand and began walking to the big room.

"Walking behind her is worth two hundred dollars all by itself," Chivas said.

"I'm hip," said Bo. "Vine, you okay?"

"No, but I will be," he said. "Once my blood starts circulating again. Right now, it's pooling in one location." Chivas bent over laughing as if that was the funniest thing he had ever heard. This was truly going to be a night to remember and a key event in the Jolly-Boy evolution.

"You better hope the Lord don't come back tonight," Chivas said. "I don't think you could explain yourself out of this one."

"Naw, he ain't coming back tonight," Vine said. "Not at least until the show is over."

Addison escorted the fellas to the big room and sat them at a table directly in front of the round stage. In each corner of the room, there were smaller round stages with poles in the middle of each. Each stage showcased a beautiful and voluptuous dancer entertaining a circle of men. Sam looked at his watch and realized that there was only thirty minutes left until the main show began. He pulled a roll of dollar bills from his pocket and stood.

"Okay, you old men can sit here like deers in headlights, but I got a handful of money to give out and only thirty minutes to do it. See you in about a half hour."

"Wait, I'll roll with you," Chivas said.

"We'll stay here and guard the table," Bo said.

"Speak for yourself," Vine said. "I'm going to find Addison. That girl got me questioning my calling."

"Y'all go ahead," Bo said. "I'm going to stay here and guard our seats. Hopefully, someone will be coming around with some hors d'oeuvres to pass." Vine, Chivas, and Sam just shook their heads. They knew it was no point trying to wrestle with Bo's made-up mind and appetite, so they headed to the first stripper and her respective pole.

The flickering lights signaled the ending of the personal shows and the approaching start of the main event. Vine, Chivas, and Sam returned to their table, ready to describe their experience to the lead Jolly Boy in intimate detail. What they saw made Vine and Chivas break into hysterical laughter, while Sam fought to hold back his rage and embarrassment.

"Are you kidding me right now?" Sam asked Bo. "You are an inch from the stage of the most exclusive gentlemen's club in the entire state of Nevada, and you're sitting here with a paper napkin hanging from your collar eating buffalo wings?" Sam looked around. He was convinced that the entire room was looking at him.

"Those look delicious," Chivas said and reached for one of the wings.

Before he could get it to his lips, Sam spoke again. "Don't you dare," Sam said through clenched teeth. "Drop it." Chivas dropped the wing. He was shaking from laughter.

"Look, I'm a real man, and real men like to eat," Bo said. "Addison came over to check on me. She asked me what I needed and I told her, 'buffalo wings and Chivas Regal,' and within minutes, they appeared."

"Sam man, sit down and chill," Vine said. "Ain't nobody paying you no attention. Fix him a drink."

"Yes, fix me a drink, and when the show starts, those wings are going under the table," Sam said.

"You a lie, and a damn lie at that," Bo said. As if on cue, the lights dimmed, which brought the noise in the room down to a whisper. The MC announced the first dancer, and the stage began to rotate.

For the next two hours, beautiful women in various colors, shapes, and sizes erotically performed in front of a sea of excited men. The dances involved a variety of props from the traditional pole grip to whips, dog collars, and an enormous rubber replica of male genitalia. After the fifth dancer's performance, Sam was growing irritated. Dancers 6, 7, and 8 were all thin White girls and not up Sam's alley by a long shot. When dancer number 9 appeared, Sam acted as if he was repulsed.

"Damn, yet another flat-chested Barbie doll," Sam said. "See, they started strong with some bad babes. These pole-bean, dieting, nearly anorexic chicks do nothing for me. Booo, booo."

"Sam, shut the hell up," Vine said. "This ain't showtime at the Apollo."

Within minutes of Sam's outburst, Addison appeared at the table. "What's the matter with the birthday boy?" she asked. She positioned herself on his lap and wrapped her arms around his neck. "Now why are you booing my friend? Is that any way for a handsome, fine man who just turned forty to act?"

"Good question," Bo said. "Hand me the microphone."

"For what?" Chivas asked.

"Maybe we can find one and ask him," Bo said. "'Cause quiet as it's kept, you sitting on top of old smoky."

"Now calm yourself down," Addison said. "There's one more dancer, and I promise you will love her. Okay?" Sam nodded and vowed compliance with his head cradled in the cavern between Addison's perfect spherical breasts. After prying herself from his grip, Addison walked away.

"You heard that, didn't you?" Sam said, pushing his chest out in pride. "That woman thinks I'm forty. What you think about that?"

"That you are dumb as hell," Vine said. Chivas spit out his drink in Danny Thomas fashion. "That woman is around young, strong, and fine men all night every night. She know damn well you knocking the hell out of sixty."

As more playful banter ensued, the men paid little attention to what was happening on the stage. When they looked up, the stage crew was preparing for the next and final performance.

"I know one thing: if this is another pale, pasty, skinny White girl, we are up and out," Sam said.

"I bet you it's my Addison," Vine said. "Damn, now everybody is gonna know about my good thang."

"Negro, please," Chivas, Sam, and Bo said in unison.

The lights dimmed, and the stage stood still. Four muscle-bound shirtless men escorted the next dancer to the stage. When they walked past Sam, he nearly broke his neck to get a peak, but the glistening escorts blocked his view. All he saw was the back of her head, full of long tar-black hair. She took position on the other side of the stage, which meant that Sam would have to wait until the stage rotated her around in front of him. When the lights were full, she was drenched in brilliance and shine. The audience on the other side of the circle went wild. Men were throwing wads of cash onto the stage and beating their chests like amorous animals in the wild. With every inch of turn, the anticipated goddess approached. Sam's heart was beating dangerously wild. Based on thunderous applause and reaction from the audience, he knew this could not be another skinny White girl, but he wanted to see her up close and personal. Bo, Chivas, and Vine stood with their brother bracing themselves for something magical, magnificent, and incredible. When the stage finally brought the entertainer around and into view, the fellas were awestruck. None of them could move, speak, applaud, or blink. She was just that beautiful. The stage stopped rotating, positioning the dancer right in front of Sam. This was the day he'd remember for the rest of his life. It was the day he met Nevaeh. With the microphone in her hand and without much effort, she dropped to the floor of the stage and laid flat on her stomach. She was eye-to-eye level with Sam.

Nevaeh Jean Miller could easily be described as the baddest chick in the room regardless of whatever room she was in. No matter how beautifully decorated or furnished, how palatial or lavish, with Nevaeh inside, it was mere space and shelter from the elements. A little on the tall side but not statuette, she was the perfect height to compliment any man's arm. Her curvaceous size-twelve frame was thick and voluptuous from any and every angle. Her skin was expresso brown, evenly covering her body canvas from head to toe. With her perfect grapefruit-sized breasts, full stomach, bowing hips and thighs, sculptured derriere, and strong but sexy legs, she quickly and consistently sequestered the attention of every human being she encountered. Her facial features were strong and defined but not butch. Her sunken seductive eyes, high cheekbones, dimples, and natural full lips made her every woman's threat head to toe and everything in between. And her walk, though forced and theatrical, changed the energy in the atmosphere and called physic principles into question. No object, human, animal, or otherwise should be able to move their body the way Nevaeh did. But surprisingly for Sam, a confirmed ass and breast man, it was her smile that sealed the deal. Her brilliant dimple-framed smile intimated that she was one of the last of the soon-to-be-extinct sweet girls. With her show-horse strut, alluring beauty, confidence, sexual agility, and perfect smile, she brought with her a level of emotional danger that was not for the faint at heart.

"Hello, sexy Sam," she said into the microphone. "My girl Addison told me it was your fortieth birthday. My name is Nevaeh. Come here and let me give you your birthday licks." Before Sam's body could catch up with his eyes and brain, Nevaeh had his entire head in the grip of her palms. Starting from his hairy chin all the way up to his bald head, she licked his entire face in one slow moving stroke of her tongue. She then gently kissed him on his cheek and released her grip. "Happy birthday, sexy Sam." Nevaeh jumped to her feet and continued greeting the crowd as the stage began to turn again. On the second rotation, the stage began ascending. At its final position, Nevaeh was six feet higher and in the center of the circular stage.

"I get it now," Chivas said. "This is why they call it Pedestal. It's as if she is on a pedestal."

"Damn, Sam," Vine said. "Close your mouth and change the look on your face. You look like you are about to break out into tears. She's coming back down. Pull your shit together."

"Leave him alone," Bo said. "It's his last hurrah, remember? Let him have some fun."

"I have seen the promised land," Sam said. "I'm going to marry that girl."

"Well, goodbye, Marsaleen," Vine said.

"Who?" Sam responded loudly over the noise.

"Your wife, fool," Vine said. "You know. The one you're supposed to be working on your marriage with when you get back to Chicago. Her name is Marsaleen."

"I'm in love," Sam said again. "I've got to have her in my life, my world, my bed."

"And your pocket," Vine said.

"It would be worth every penny," Sam said.

Sam knew the show was nearing completion when the four escorts gathered to the left of the stage. Nevaeh ended her routine positioned flat on her back, legs open, and one thin garment away from being completely naked. The mounds of bills around her were scattered like green rose petals. Thunderous applause, catcalls, bills floating in air and landing on the stage, chest beating, and foot stomping in some respects mirrored a crime scene. The bare-chested escorts lifted her to her feet and whisked her off the circular stage.

"I wonder where they are taking her," Sam asked aloud.

"Probably to shower and change," Chiv said. "Although many wouldn't object, I'm sure she's not going to drive home butt-ass naked."

"No, I wonder if I could meet her," Sam said. "I've got to meet her. Y'all wouldn't understand. You didn't feel what I felt and know what she felt when our eyes met. There was something there. Something happened."

"It's called entertainment, Sam," Bo said. "That money on stage that they are sweeping up with push brooms was a giant tip. That girl, yes, that beautiful girl teased you and licked your face because that's what she's paid to do. Every time you come to Vegas, you'll be right here looking for her. That's what's supposed to happen. And tomorrow night and the night after that, she'll be licking some other man's face for his birthday. Ain't nothing happen between y'all. You had a good time. You had a great birthday. Now you're going home and square up with your wife."

"Look, we've got two more days in Vegas," Sam said. "I promise you and I promise myself that Nevaeh is going to fall asleep at least one of those nights on this chest and in these arms before I leave Vegas."

"Hey, fellas," Addison said. "Did you enjoy yourselves?"

"It was indeed an unbelievable experience," Vine said. "Where do we go to get the limo back to our hotel? It's two in the morning. It's bedtime for the bishop."

"Okay, slow down, Bishop," Addison said. The fact or idea that Vine was a minister or bishop didn't faze her. "Your check should be coming soon. Oh, here they come with the checks now."

"Check? What check?" Chiv asked. "It costed two bills to get in this joint. What could we possibly owe for?"

"You had a bottle of Chivas and a bucket of hot wings," Addison said with attitude. "Shit ain't free, and you need to tip me, your server. And did I mention me already?" A tall young man handed Addison what appeared to be a check. She read it and jerked her head in shock and disbelief. "Wow, this has never happened."

"Damn, how much is it?" Vine asked.

"Well, fellas, it's your lucky night," Addison said. "Your bill, including gratuities, has been taken care of, compliments of Nevaeh. She'd like y'all to join her in her dressing room for a birthday night-cap in sexy Sam's honor."

"Well, drop kick me, Jesus, through the goal post of life," Vine said.

"I told you," Sam said. He was so excited he could hardly still himself. "I know women. Something happened when we connected on that stage."

"Well, we'll see what Nevaeh has to say about that," Bo said.

"Addison, please tell Nevaeh that I graciously thank her for taking care of us, but I will be the only one joining her this evening for that nightcap," Sam said. "It's been a long day and night for my friends, so they are going to head back to the hotel."

"Wait, I'm not tired," Chiv said. "I'd love to have a nightcap with Nevaeh."

"No, you're going back to the Mirage," Sam said through clenched teeth. He pulled out a hundred-dollar bill and handed it to Addison. "Please make sure my friends get back safely."

"Wait, we don't get a say?" Chiv asked.

"Uh, no," Sam said. "My birthday, my rules. One man is all Nevaeh needs tonight, and that one man is Samaritan Ladeaux. I'll see y'all tomorrow night at dinner. Remember, we're eating at the Stratosphere at eight. Good night, my brothers. And please don't wait up." Sam walked away, following Addison to Nevaeh's dressing room. The fellas stood in disbelief.

"Well, he did say 'last hurrah,'" Vine commented. "Hell, I should have told Addison it was my birthday. I could have gotten licked and maybe not going home with you two hard legs."

"Shut up, Vine," Bo and Chiv cut in unison.

CHAPTER 9

January 28, 2000

At noon on Saturday, the Jolly Boys had lunch and discussed their plans for the day. With Chiv's help, Vine no longer had the stress and worry of winning enough money to settle his debt with the Lord. He was able to relax and enjoy the remainder of the trip with his new best friends. They were certain that they would not see Sam until dinner, so the three of them tossed around ideas to occupy their day. After a little debate, they decided to abstain from gambling for the day and take an excursion to Hoover Dam. They rented a car and made the 37.3-mile drive to the popular scenic wonder in about twenty-five minutes. After the tour and some souvenir shopping, they were back in the car to Vegas at five. This gave them plenty of time to nap and dress for dinner scheduled for eight with Sam.

The famous Top of the World restaurant on the 106th floor of the Stratosphere Hotel was a marvel in and of itself. The space was huge with floor to ceiling windows all around. And to everyone's surprise, the venue rotated, so views of Vegas were spectacular and vibrant. The clear sky was the perfect backdrop for some amazing vistas.

When eight-thirty rolled around, the fellas ordered dinner and enjoyed their evening without Sam. He was a no-show, and everyone knew why. At the end of dinner, the waiter informed the gentlemen that a Mr. Ladeaux sent his apologies and had paid for their meal. And he will meet at the airport on Monday afternoon.

"This is like some stuff you see in a movie or read in a romance novel," Vine said.

"Well, at least we know he's alive and okay," Chiv said.

"Oh, I never thought he wasn't okay," Bo said. "Put a self-proclaimed, light-skinned, clothes-horse pretty boy with a stripper—ain't nobody sad or in danger."

"I'm hip," Chiv said. "I just hope that girl knows that fool ain't forty. She keep jumping up and down on him, his fifty-six-year-old heart might attack him."

"I'd hate for my first conversation with Marsaleen to be me telling her that her husband died doing the hoochie-coochie with a Las Vegas stripper," Bo said.

"What a way to go," Vine said. "I'm a little jealous."

"Them light-skinned cats always get the girl," Bo said.

"Yeah, if I was light-bright and damn near White, Addison would be jumping up and down on me right now," Vine said. Chiv and Bo looked at each other.

"Shut up, Vine," they said in unison. They had gotten good at shutting Vine up in concert.

"Well, we got one more day in Vegas," Chiv said. "What should we do tomorrow?"

"Well, I don't know about y'all, but tomorrow at high noon, I'm executing my plan to win enough money to pay you [Chiv] back and give a 10-percent tithe to the church."

"Vine man, stop worrying about that," Chiv said. "We done with that. The church got their money back, and you don't have to pay me back, not right now."

"Naw, I've got to shake this off me," Vine said. "I don't like to owe nobody nothing. And who knows? One day, I might need you for some real life-or-death stuff. I want a clean slate. I've made up my mind. I'm dropping a grand at Caesar's, Harrah's, and the Mirage. Before my head hits the pillow tomorrow night, you'll have your money back, I'll have a big offering for next Sunday, with money left over to buy myself a new suit. When I fall into Shining Star Missionary Baptist Church next Sunday, I'm gonna be grinning and sharper than Al Gore at Bill Clinton's funeral."

"What you gonna play?" Chiv asked. "Slots ain't gonna set you out like that."

"Whatever the Spirit tells me," Vine said.

"You going to hell with a gasoline can in your hand," Bo said. "You're gonna blow hell up. The Lord ain't gonna tell you which games and machines to play."

"Of course, He will," Vine said. "The Bible says, 'In all thy way, acknowledge the Lord, and he will direct your path.' I don't put no limits on God. He can do anything, even this."

"I ain't gonna be nowhere around you," Chiv said. "He gonna strike your ass like Benjamin Franklin with a key and a kite."

As planned, Vine, with Bo and Chiv in his peripheral, was sitting in front of the Triple Diamond Wheel of Favor machine at Caesar's. The max bet was five dollars a pull. After he failed to get ahead and two hundred dollars later, he was in search of a new machine. He entered the high-limit section and immediately felt unwelcomed. Max bets on these machines were as high as one hundred dollars a pull. He didn't run. He focused. He walked around, touching every machine that wasn't occupied. He was truly looking for divine intervention, but if he couldn't have that, a sigh, hunch, or feeling would have to do. His wandering caught the attention of one of the plain-clothes security officers.

"Sir," the short female officer approached. "Are you okay? You appear lost. You know, you're in the high-limit section."

"Yes, I know, and you're right. I'm lost," Vine responded. "I'm not used to being in this section. Just trying to decide on a machine to play. What's hot over here these days?"

"Now you know, sir, I don't have that information," she said. "Contrary to popular speculation, we don't control the machines and their payouts. I wish we did. I'd fly away in a big ole money balloon." Vine laughed, but the guard did not. Her eyes widened as if she was trying to get Vine's attention. "A balloon filled with money, making drops all over the world." This time, the cadence of her voice was slow and choppy. She enunciated each syllable of her words. Vine dismissed her affect and strong behavior. "I love balloons. Wouldn't it be magical to have balloons to burst and release piles and piles of cash?" She pressed her earpiece further into her ear and dropped her head to focus on the message she was receiving. "Okay, sir. I must leave you now. We have some people upstairs misbehaving. Enjoy your balloons." The young lady hurried away before Vine could respond. As she walked away, he pondered her strange behavior but attributed it to the antics and strangeness of all things Las Vegas.

Vine walked around, continuing his search and listening for mystical inspiration. As he completed his circle, he heard a familiar tune blaring from one of the machines. It was an old song by the 5th Dimension. He recognized the lyrics right away: "Up, up and away in my beautiful balloon." He followed the song to a machine labeled Money Balloon. And then it hit him. The security guard, through her strange behavior, was telling him to play this machine. He studied the words and realized the max bet was one hundred dollars a pull. Without hesitation, he fed nine one-hundred-dollar bills into the machine. He took a deep breath, closed his eyes, and hit the spin button. A yellow, blue, and green 7 landed on the play line. This earned him seventy-five dollars. Technically, he was down twenty-five dollars. He hit the spin button again. He lost. He was now down 225 dollars. Again closing his eyes, he hit the spin button. One gold balloon, followed by another, landed on the play line. The last reel kept spinning and spinning. Finally, a third golden balloon, which earned him three hundred dollars and fifteen free spins. The machine was now in bonus mode. He couldn't watch. He hit the spin button to activate the bonus rounds and dropped his head.

The machine cranked out sounds of whimsical frenzy. He wasn't watching, but he surmised that he was winning from the sound of the machine. When the machine went silent, he finally looked up. The screen depicted balloons falling from the sky with the message flashing to pop the balloons. Vine went into action, frantically and virtually sending balloons down onto the grass on the screen with his fingers all over the screen. As he popped them with every digit on both hands, dollar amounts appeared ranging from 50 to 2,500 dollars. When he was done, he examined the screen. He had thirteen thousand dollars in credit with four free spins remaining. He hit the spin button again, but this time, he watched. When the golden balloons appeared on the play line again, he felt light-headed. His mouth was open, but no words came out. He had ten more free spins to go. He hit the button, and once again, three more balloons, which meant he now had twenty free games in play. He was finally able to break his silence and in a big way. His yelling and screaming caught everyone's attention. Before he realized it, there was a small crowd of well-wishers behind him.

"What the actual hell is happening?" he heard a familiar voice. "Vine, what are you doing?" It was Chiv and Bo.

"I'm winning ninja," Vine joked. "I told you. I told you."

"How much did you put in?" Bo asked. "And why are you in the high-limit area?"

"If you want to win high, you've got to play high," Vine said.

"Bruh, you have 28,000 credits," Chiv said. "Do you know what that means? You just won 28,000 dollars."

"Oh, I'm not done," Vine said. "I'm going to keep the twenty thousand dollars, but I'm playing the eight."

"The hell you are," Bo said and hit the cash-out button. When the ticket printed, Bo snatched it and began walking away. When Vine and Chiv caught up with him, they pulled him to a sudden stop.

"What are you doing?" Vine asked. "That machine is on fire. I hit three bonus runs. I can't stop now."

"You have been a nervous wreck since you've been in Vegas," Bo said. "You got more than you came for. You might hate me now, but one day, you'll thank me. Let's go to the cashier."

"You're right," Vine said. "The last time I won real big back home, I played it all back, and it was thousands of dollars. I do hate you, but I hate being broke more." The fellas headed to the cashier. Vine saw the guard as he walked through the casino. He winked. She winked back. Vine had to get a check for his payout thanks to the rules of the IRS. He received three thousand dollars in cash and the rest in a check. The fellas spent the rest of their day shopping in the Canal Shoppes at Caesar's and enjoying their remaining time in Sin City. He splurged on himself and his new friends and promised Bo one more trip to the Bellagio Buffet before heading to the airport tomorrow. Yet another memorable Jolly-Boy experience.

CHAPTER 10

Monday, January 30, 2000

Monday morning in Vegas brought a different vibe. It felt as though someone had turned down the volume and lifted the shades. The hustle, congestion, and magic in the air was calmer and more manageable than the weekend vibe. For the citizens of Vegas, it was time to separate the visitors from the natives, take a deep breath, and reset.

Vine, who was still walking three inches above ground from his miraculous winnings, treated Chiv and Bo to one more trip to his favorite buffet. It was a joy seeing the lead Jolly Boy enjoy his favorite source of Vegas sustenance. As this was his third trip in three days, he attacked his choice dishes with laser precision. The mood at the table was light and heavy at the same time. The topic, of course, was Sam. Each of the three had an opinion and perspective about the elder Jolly Boy's antics and behaviors on this their first brotherhood trip.

"I don't know if I'm jealous or disappointed," Chiv said. "I mean, ole boy pulled the baddest chick in Vegas just by being present. He didn't hit her with no strong rap or impress her with a wad of dough. He just pulled her in by virtue of being there. Ole girl licked the ninja's face on stage, and what she do that for? It blew his mind. Ain't no telling what she's been licking for the last few days."

"Let's not get vulgar," Vine said. "We are eating, you know. So why disappointed? I follow your jealousy commentary, but why disappointed?"

"I know this is all new," Chiv explained. "The four of us are new, but I think Sam played below our standard. We are men of veneration and honor. We don't do what everyone else does. Bedding a stripper and ducking out on your friends while on your birthday trip seems common and typical. We're not common nor typical."

"And you got a whole wife at home," Vine said. "Not to mention a harem of chicks on the side. I know that society accepts the indiscretions of a married man, but should we? I feel like I am the accomplice to some sort of crime. We should have found out where he was and went and got him. Instead, we ignored him."

"And when you knocked on her door and told her you were there to get Sam and Sam came to the door in his drawers with a big smile on his face and said wild horses couldn't get him to leave Nevaeh's house and that you should mind your own damn business, then what was you gonna do?" Bo posed. "I don't like it, but our friend is a grown man and a player at that. We can't save him, but we can't judge him either. Hell, Vine, if Addison had licked your face—"

"I would have rebuked that spirit of promiscuity and fled from her presence," Vine interrupted.

"Shut the hell up, Vine," Bo said through a laugh.

"I'm hip," Chiv added. "If you weren't a preacher and I wasn't sanctified, I would use the f-word."

"Sanctified?" Vine repeated with his eyes bucked. "Spell it!"

After brunch, the fellas headed for the airport where they'd meet Sam for their 3:00 p.m. flight back to reality. As all predicted, the airport was super busy. Once at the gate, they were glad of their decision to arrive a couple of hours before takeoff. Just as they sat down at the gate and took a deep breath, Sam appeared. He looked worn and sheepish, as if he was embarrassed. He stood in front of the semicircle of friends with his head partially lowered. *Finally*, they thought, *some remorse for being common.*

"Good afternoon, gentlemen," he said cautiously. "Everybody okay?"

"Yeah, we okay," Chiv said. "What's up with you?"

"And right now, I don't want to hear the details of your sexual conquering of that girl," Vine said. "Sit down and get yourself together. You look guilty as hell."

"Um, I'm not going to sit," Sam said. "Nevaeh is waiting for me outside. I'm not leaving today. I'm staying a couple more days. I just wanted to come say goodbye and thank you in person."

"Wait, what?" Bo asked, genuinely confused. "You are not going home today? Do you think that's a good idea, Sam?"

"I can't leave yet," Sam said. "I think I'm in love. I haven't been this happy in a long time. I know you all see her as just a stripper, but she is sweet, loving, and caring. I gotta figure this out before I go home."

"It's good sex bruh, but she ain't your wife," Chiv said. "I get the one-night stand, even the two- and three-night stands, but what about your wife? This ain't cool."

"I haven't completely lost my mind," Sam said. "I'm definitely going home on Wednesday," Sam said. "I'm just not ready to go back to being unhappy. I just want to be happy until Wednesday."

"Are you at least being careful?" Vine asked.

"Aw, she ain't got no man, and she ain't married," Sam said.

"What?" Vine shook his head. "I ain't talking about you getting your ass kicked, which is a possibility, quite frankly, I had not considered. Are you being careful in the bedroom? You look confused. Are you wearing rubbers?"

"Aw, man, she can't get pregnant," Sam said. Bo, Chiv, and Vine looked at one another as if they had heard the most absurd reasoning ever possible. "She had herself fixed. She had her tubes tied and burned."

"You are really starting to scare me," Vine said. Sam was genuinely confused. "Fool, did you watch her tie and burn them yourself? And have you ever heard the acronyms STD, HIV, or DAH? That stands for 'dumb as hell.' You could have all kinds of life-threatening diseases screwing a stripper without a rubber."

"Aw, man, chill out with that drama," Sam rebutted. "She is squeaky clean. She has perfect feminine hygiene. I know when a woman is nasty down there. She ain't nasty, and I ain't got nothing."

Bo dropped his head in embarrassment and disappointment. Vine was catapulted into sheer disbelief.

Chiv rubbed his face in frustration before speaking. "What time do you get in on Wednesday?" Chiv asked.

"My plane gets in at four," Sam answered.

"Good," Chiv said. "I'm picking you up from the airport, and we're going to the clinic. You are going to get an HIV and STD test. Don't open your mouth and say another word. My intellect cannot take another ounce of dumb shit out of your mouth.

"Whatever, man," Sam said. "I've had stuff before. I know my body, and I know hers. I'm squeaky. You'll see. All right, y'all be easy. Let's huddle this weekend." The fellas hugged it out. Before Sam left, Vine placed his hands on Sam's shoulders and prayed. When finished, Sam walked away. The mood turned somber and serene. Although the airport was loud and busy, for the fellas, the silence of care, worry, and concern was deafening.

On Wednesday, Sam pried himself from Nevaeh's grip and headed home. When he exited the airport doors at Midway Airport, Chiv blew his horn and flashed his headlights. He could tell that Sam was surprised and probably disappointed that he actually showed up. He forced a smile and an acknowledging wave before pushing his coatless body through the chilly Chicago air to Chiv's car. Chiv opened the trunk from inside. Sam placed his two bags in the trunk and closed it gently. He took a deep breath and got in. To his surprise and delight, Chiv was his normal, grounded, and jovial self.

"What's up, me brother?" Chiv asked rhetorically. "You look surprised to see me."

"I'm glad to see you," Sam said. "I am surprised but more glad than surprised. How you been? How hard was it going into work on Monday?"

"I wouldn't know," Chiv replied. "I was off yesterday and Monday. I'm getting too old for quick reentry. I needed a minute to get my head right after Vegas. You working tomorrow?"

"Oh yeah," Sam said. "Amtrak ain't so happy with my last-minute emergency that required two additional vacation days." Sam noticed that Chiv was driving North, the opposite of where his home was, which was South. He felt a lump in his throat and a ping in his gut. "Where exactly are we going?

"I found a doctor in a discrete location up North," Chiv said. "They specialize in what you need right now."

"And what is that, I dare to ask?" Sam said.

"Assurance, blessed and medical," Chiv said. "You've had unprotected sex with a prostitute. You need to get checked out."

Sam chuckled and looked out the window. "She's not a prostitute," Sam said. "Since when do *dancer* and *hoe* mean the same thing?"

"Oh, that happened right around the time that good feminine hygiene became synonymous with disease-free," Chiv replied. "You getting checked out. And the way you like to sow your seeds, this will prevent you from infecting someone else, and watch this: it may even save your life."

"Whatever, man," Sam said. "Like I said, I know my body, and I know hers. But if it will make you feel better, let's go. I hope this place is reasonable. I don't want to use my insurance. I don't want the Amtrak doctors seeing STD test on my medical records."

"It's very reasonable," Chiv reacted. "It's free."

"So I know y'all been dogging me out behind my back," Sam said. "I know Vine's self-righteous behind had a mouthful of hate on me."

"No hate, bruh," Chiv said. "Love and concern. Think about it: you went ghost for days and nights with a strange dancer, as you call her. We didn't know where you were or nothing. She could have cut your body up into little pieces and shipped you all over the world. We couldn't tell the police her name, address, nothing if we had to. Then we find out you were raw-dogging? Man, you playing with fire."

"Look, I know it's hard to believe and even harder to understand, but I'm in love, Chiv," Sam said soberly. "All y'all see is a stripper, but she's a good woman making her own dough. She's got a nice well-furnished crib in the suburbs, drives a nice car, and ain't on no drama. She wasn't hitting me up for money or nothing. She honestly enjoyed having a man in the house. She cooked. We went shopping and made love day and night. She's even thinking about going to school and getting out of the dancing business. I told her I'd help here."

"What's a stripper going to do with a bachelor's degree?" Chiv asked.

"You mean *a master's*," Sam proudly corrected Chiv. "She already has a bachelor's degree."

Chiv gave him a "yeah, right" look. "Help her?" Chiv asked. "Help her how?"

"Pay for school," Sam said. "I took her shopping."

"Sam, about how much did you spend on Nevaeh—just a guess," Chiv asked. Sam started laughing. "I know I'm being nosy, but how much?"

"It don't matter," Sam said. "And I offered. She didn't ask. My baby can't be going to the Laundromat and sleeping on no soft mattress."

"Please tell me you didn't," Chiv said, diverting his eyes away from the road to make visual contact with Sam. "She got you to buy her a washing machine and a new bed? She must have done things to you that have never been done."

"For sure," Sam said. "The girl got skills. She's named Heaven for a good reason. Well, her name is heaven spelled backward."

"Wait until I tell Vine heaven got strippers," Chiv said. They both cracked up.

After Sam and Chiv arrived at the clinic and checked in, they sat and waited to be seen. It was indeed discretely located, tucked away on the first floor of an old three-unit brownstone right on the Chicago-Evanston border. The walls were glossy white and filled with HIV and STD awareness and prevention posters and flyers. There were already two men and one woman seated in the waiting area, so they knew the wait wouldn't be quick. Sam and Chiv sat in silence, thumbing through old issues of *GQ* and *Sports Illustrated*.

"Man, this waiting is stirring up my nerves," Sam said.

"I see the reality of the situation has finally hit," Chiv said. "I thought you would come to yourself eventually. Ain't no ass worth dying for."

"I'm hip," Sam said. "What happens behind that door could change my entire life. Thanks for making me do this. Now I'm scared but glad I'm here."

"Hey, we them Jolly Boys," Chiv said. "This is what we do for one another."

"Mr. SL," a portly White nurse called out from behind the desk. Realizing that only initials were being used to protect privacy, Sam stood and approached the nurse.

"These people were here first," Sam said. "I can wait my turn."

"I'm running this, SL," she cut. "If I say it's your turn, it's your turn. Now follow me please." Sam disappeared behind the door without looking back. After about twenty minutes, Chiv's nerves had him jumpy. Every movement in the waiting area startled him. He took a few deep breaths to steady himself and continued flipping through the magazine. Just as he calmed himself, the men who were waiting and subsequently called in were coming out. One had his arm around the other one, trying to console his tears away. Chiv imagined himself in the same position with Sam. It was at this point when Chiv didn't want a drink but needed one. Chiv threw the magazine on the table, rested his head on the cold wall behind him, and closed his eyes. It was helpful in turning off the stimuli of his senses, but it did nothing to shut down his thoughts, mostly of gloom and doom.

After an hour-and-a-half wait, Chiv stood and walked toward the window. He folded his arms and studied the traffic from the single-story view. "Something must be going terribly wrong back there," he said to himself. "This is taking way too long. When I was here before for myself, it took twenty minutes: a mouth swab, blood draw, a needle in the ass, and a pamphlet. This can't be good."

"Chiv," a booming voice called his name from a daydream. Bo's voice made Chiv jump in surprise and fear. "What's the matter? Why you looking like that? Where is Sam?" He turned to face Bo and Vine.

"Y'all scared the hell out of me," Chiv said. "And don't say names out loud. This is supposed to be a private and anonymous visit."

"Sam still in there?" Vine asked. Chiv rolled his eyes and nodded the answer. "How long he been back there?"

"Ninety-one minutes to be exact," Chiv said, looking at his watch.

"Let's just consider that a sign of them being thorough," Bo said. "That's all it means."

"Absolutely," Vine said. "The devil meant this for bad, but God meant it for good."

"What's up, gentlemen?" Sam said, startling his brothers.

"Okay, can we get the hell out of here before somebody gives me a damn heart attack?" Chiv said.

"So what did the doctor say?" Vine asked.

"Can we talk about this outside?" Sam said.

"Hell no," Chiv said. "I'm not leaving here until you tell me something. I already saw this dude leaving here in tears. And I ain't had nothing to drink. I'm about to pop off. Start talking."

Sam pulled the guys further into the corner so he wouldn't be overheard. "The rapid HIV test was negative," Sam said. "They did take blood and will complete a thorough test. I'll get those results in a couple of weeks. The doctor told me to relax. Usually, the rapid showed positive, and the test showed negative. It normally didn't happen the opposite way."

"Thank you, God," Chiv said. "What else?"

"I have no symptoms of an STD, but it's only been a few days since my risky sexual experience," Sam said. "And after I described the details, he suggested a shot as a preventive measure. He said he'd be surprised if I didn't have something. So I got two shots, one for syphilis. They made me watch a video. That's what took so long. Man, there is some wild shit out here. Did you know a woman can get pregnant from anal sex?"

"Enough," Vine said. "You are well in Jesus's name. Don't pull no dumb shit like this again, or we gonna kick your pretty Black ass. Jumped up here and got me all excited and nervous. Now get me out of here. It feels like something crawling up my leg." The fellas started walking toward the door.

"Wait, you can get someone pregnant having anal sex?" Bo asked. "I don't believe that. That doctor don't know what he's talking about."

"Vine, it's a good thing that you're past your childbearing years," Chiv said, followed by an eruption of laughter.

"Good thing your dog is past her childbearing years," Vine shot back. "You'd have a litter of puppies who looked just like you."

"Somebody got to carry on the Eubanks name," Bo said. The fellas were glad to be laughing again. Grace and mercy prevailed.

CHAPTER 11

Circa 2001

When Bo, Chiv, Vine, and Sam looked up, they realized that eighteen months had passed in warp speed. Sam's health scare as a result of his reckless sexual abandon seemed as if it were just last month but certainly not last year. Time was moving, the world was changing, and the Jolly Boys were committed to not being left behind. Chiv made sure that everyone knew how to use a personal computer, had access to the World Wide Web, had an AOL account, had the latest iPod, and had a cell phone complete with a camera that easily slid into their front pocket.

Against Bo, Chiv, and Vine's approval, Sam continued to see Nevaeh as often as he could. He even took a small pay cut to run freight trains from Chicago to Vegas. It could be said that the railroad funded his indiscretions, which satisfied his desire to foster his relationship with Nevaeh. What he lost in wages, he gained in saving on airfare to and from Sin City. Sam had convinced himself that he was in love now more than before.

Chiv was still navigating through his commitment issues with Louise, working and coaching high school basketball and self-medicating with Chivas Regal and ginger ale as often as he could. His team or his "ninja warriors," as he called them, ended the season one win short of making it to the playoffs. Chiv was determined to win divisional esteem this year. Although school had not started, the ninja warriors were practicing in the steamy Chicago heat as if their bodies were designed to do so. Seeing their potential, the school board paid for their registration and airfare to a week-long basketball camp scheduled for the second week of the school year in New Rochelle,

New York, right outside of New York City and his old stomping ground. Chiv loved hanging with young people. It made him feel like he was making a contribution to the Black male population and most importantly, less old. It also left just the right amount of time to spend with Louise. According to Chiv, he and Louise would have been over years ago but for basketball, coaching, and the NWs.

After returning from Vegas, Vine endured one more week of being silenced by the church board and returned to his rightful place as the helm of Shining Star Baptist Church. Although he'd toned himself down a little, he was consistent in confronting people and rubbing them the wrong way. Unbeknownst to the church and the Jolly Boys, he was looking for a new congregation to lead.

It was now Friday, August 21, and Vine, Chiv, Sam, and Jackie were all at the hospital. Bo's complaint of stomach and back pain landed him in the hospital on the schedule for gallbladder surgery later that morning. He was comfortable but was looking forward to ridding himself of this ailment and the associated pain in his gut. Bo wasn't worried nor blithely unconcerned. He was just ready to move on and glad the fellas and his lovely wife were with him. In their minds and hearts, being somewhere else today would have seemed like a violation of the unwritten Jolly-Boy code. Jackie was in the reclining chair in the corner of his suite at Northwestern, sound asleep. The fellas sat around Bo and tried to keep their bantering to a minimal to not wake her. Tired of everyone sitting and staring at him, Bo, as usual, took control of the situation.

"So, Chiv, how are the nigga warriors looking this year?" Bo asked, barely able to finish his question without laughing. Vine and Sam hollered Jackie nearly out of her slumber.

"Ninja, nin-ja," Chiv enunciated. "That ain't even funny. As a people, we shouldn't use that word."

"Aw, man, come on," Bo said. "I don't care how much we think we've overcome. That word will be in our lexicon forever."

"I'm cool with it as long as one of these crackers don't say it," Sam said, reminding everyone of his bigoted disposition.

"Cracker, Sam?" Chiv questioned. "That's just as bad and wrong as the n-word."

"Vine, you mighty quiet on this subject," Bo said. "It's unusual for you to be quiet on any subject. What you thinking over there?"

"How wrong I must be," Vine said. "The other Sunday, I called the head usher a nigga from the pulpit."

"Stop lying, Vine," Chiv said. "You did not do that."

"I was speaking and was being so nice," Vine said. "You all would have been proud. I was giving compliments and just talking so nice to the people, giving them just what they wanted. But it was like every five minutes, I saw his big backside up walking the aisles. When I'm at the podium, everyone is supposed to be sitting and listening, but he could not sit down. It was starting to get on my nerves. Finally, I snapped. 'Nigga, would you please sit down?' I commanded. Half of the church laughed. The other half dropped their heads."

"What happened?" Bo asked, laughing so hard the bed shook.

"He sat his big ass down, that's what happened," Vine answered. "And didn't move again. My phone has been ringing about that one all weekend."

"See, that's wrong on multiple levels," Chiv said. "You owe that man and the congregation an apology."

"I already apologized to him," Vine said. "And Sunday, I'll apologize to the congregation. They'll love that. It doesn't happen too often."

"Can we make a Jolly Boy rule please?" Chiv asked. "It's the same rule I have with my team. The n-word and all the derivatives is prohibited by or in the presence of a Jolly Boy."

"I don't know," Sam said. "I mean, is there any real harm in saying the n-word among ourselves? I don't think I can be a true friend to Vine if I don't call him a nigga every now and then."

"No, not necessary and not allowed," Chiv said. "And the fine is one hundred dollars. As I tell the ninja warriors, we've got to be the change we want to see in our homes, classrooms, practice fields, and the world. That word is officially prohibited." All nodded in agreement and solidarity. It was anything to calm Chiv down and shut him up. All, including Chiv, knew that rule was as good as broken before it left Chiv's lips.

"Okay, Mr. Jackson," a beautiful Latina nurse said with an authentic accent. "I have some meds for you. And you have way too many people in here."

"Nurse, these are my husband's brothers," Jackie said. "Surely, you're not going to kick family out?"

"Of course not," she said, relaxing her initial stern tone. "And besides, once I give him this magic potion, it's going to get really quiet in here really quick." The nurse gave Bo a shot in his arm and then another through the IV. "This is the first dose. It will help you relax and normalize your blood pressure. People usually get a little excited when they are wheeled into the operating room. We'll give you the heavy-duty stuff once you're in the ER."

"How long will it take?" Chiv asked.

"About a couple of hours, start to finish, so not long," the nurse said. "Okay, Mr. Jackson, I'll see you on the other side." All conversation stopped. Everyone turned their heads in the nurse's direction. She had about five seconds to autocorrect, or she was going to get a cussing out the likes she'd had never seen. "On the other side of the operation, in recovery. That's what I meant."

"Oh, okay," Jackie said. "Something really bad was about to happen." Jackie squeezed Bo's hand. "How you feeling, baby?"

"Feeling nice, real nice," Bo said. "Makes me wonder why I stopped smoking reefer."

Sam laughed. "They don't call it that no more, man," Sam said. "They call it weed now."

"Sam, make sure you pick me up some of that weed," Bo said. "Bring it with you when you come back." The transport team came into the room to escort Bo to surgery. Jackie bent down and kissed him on the lips. "I love you, Jackie. Listen, fellas, if something happens to me...if I don't see y'all on the other side, take care of my wife. She should want for nothing."

"Oh, she won't want for a thing," Sam said. "I will personally ensure all her needs are met."

"Sam, I ain't worried," Bo said. "You with Jackie is like pushing a car up a hill with a rope." Everyone in the room including the two transport workers were howling. "Let's go y'all. I'm saving my good material for the operating room staff." The team did as expected and wheeled Bo out of the room and down the hall to the operating room.

"Jackie, you want us to wait with you?" Vine said. "I love hospital cafeteria food. I'll go get us something."

"No, no," Jackie said. "I'm good. Y'all go on with your day. Come by after he gets home. While y'all there, I can run some errands and do some shopping. Go on. I'm fine."

"Okay, but call us if you need anything," Chiv said. "We'll be sure to come through tomorrow if he's up for visitors." Vine, Chiv, and Sam hugged and kissed Jackie and made their exit. When they got to the parking lot, they were startled by loud noise and commotion. Sam stopped a gentleman and asked what was happening. The man told him that a car had caught on fire. The driver barely got out alive.

"Damn," Vine said and hugged himself as if he'd felt a chill.

"What's the matter, Vine?" Chiv asked.

"I just got that feeling again," Vine said. "That cold fear feeling just shot through my body. Whenever I feel this way, something terrible is about to happen. I feel it in my spirit."

"You don't think it's Bo, do you?" Chiv asked.

"I don't know," Vine said. He was unusually serious and focused as if he was receiving some sort of message directly from the universe to his brain. Although the fellas often joked with Vine, they believed in his calling and his spiritual abilities. All listened attentively. "I feel death and fire and smoke like an explosion in the sky. This car fire pales in comparison to what I see and feel. This is bad. I don't want no one traveling for a while. Everyone, keep your feet on the ground."

"I'm supposed to take the team to New Rochelle in a few weeks for the basketball camp," Chiv said.

"But y'all are going by bus, aren't you?" Vine asked.

"We're actually taking the train," Chiv said. "Airfare was too expensive."

"You can take the train, bus, or walk if you want," Vine said. "Just please don't fly. God, please protect us and keep us from all hurt, harm, and danger. Amen."

Bo's surgery was a success. With the exception of an unexpected hernia repair, the lead Jolly Boy shared only positive modifiers when describing his experience. He was released Saturday afternoon and spent Saturday evening relaxing in his favorite chair surrounded by Jackie, Vine, Sam, and Chiv.

Sam, Chiv, and Jackie informed Bo about Vine's recent prophecy and how convicted he was about what he saw. Just to look at Vine confirmed that the divine intelligence he had received was authentic and genuine. Vine's sermon the next day was all about his prophecy and the catastrophic death, suffering, and anguish that would be experienced by thousands. Although he had convinced himself that his revelation was not related to anything in the US but in lands far and away, he advised the congregation to be cautious and wise in their travels whether foot or air, near or far. On Tuesday morning, two weeks later, it all made sense.

"Hello," Vine answered the call that woke him.

"Hey, man, sorry to wake you," Chiv said.

"It's seven in the morning," Vine said. "Normally, I'd be awake and about my day by now, but I haven't been sleeping well."

"That's one of the reasons I called," Chiv said. "We're at the train station getting ready to leave for the basketball camp. I was trying to make sure you were okay before I left."

"I appreciate that," Vine said. "But you sound a little apprehensive yourself."

"Naw, man, I'm cool," Chiv lied. "I don't doubt that what you've predicted is true. I just think it's gonna happen overseas somewhere. I'm not worried about it. I'm more worried about you."

"I had another night of tossing and turning," Vine said. "It was like I would wake up every hour on the hour. I finally started sleeping well around four. That's the last time I remember until now."

"That ain't good for you," Chiv said. "Take some type of sleep aid tonight. You can get something over the counter."

"Okay, I just might do that," Vine said. "What time y'all leaving?"

"We were supposed to leave at 7:45, but this raggedy-ass train needed a new engine. So we're delayed until the new one gets here. They're saying eight-thirty. And then it's a full day and night of bouncing on those tracks with twenty teenage boys and one chaperone who is dumb as a Christmas tree ornament. It's like I have twenty-one teenagers."

"Is it a parent or one of the teachers?" Vine asked.

"One of the teachers," Chiv said. "He's a language arts teacher fresh out of college. And thinks he knows everything about everything. He has a big-shot friend who works in New York and doesn't get to Chicago often. It's probably his boyfriend. He seems a little sweet, if you know what I mean. My daddy used to call them gal-boys." Vine laughed, which made Chiv feel better about the mental state of his friend. "I'm trying not to drink in front of my boys, but if he keeps asking me these 'when, where, and what' questions, I'm going to need a shot of CR [Chivas Regal]." Vine chuckled again. Chiv was pleased that his witty disposition was successfully masking his fear and giving his friend some comic relief.

"Well, at least you don't have the responsibility for all those ninjas on your own," Vine said. "There's not much to do on the train, but once y'all get to New York, put him to work."

"That's the plan," Chiv said. "Well, I'll check on you later. I better get back to the team before someone comes up missing. I ain't trying to deliver no bad news to nobody's mama today."

"I wish you weren't moving around so much," Vine said.

"And I wish you would stop saying that," Chiv said. "Everything is fine. What do you always say? 'Nothing will happen today that me and God can't handle.'"

"Well, I won't argue with principle," Vine said. "All right, call me later and be careful. Good luck with the twenty-one ninjas."

"Thanks, and don't forget to get something to help you sleep," Chiv said and ended the call. After hanging up the phone, Vine laid flat on his back in bed. The white ceiling, desperately in need of a coat of paint, slowly turned black as his eyes closed on their own. At eight-thirty, Chiv called him back, once again deterring him from a much-needed slumber.

"Hello, Chiv," Vine said. "How can you be an advocate of over-the-counter sleep aids when you keep calling me and waking me up?"

"Turn on the television," Chiv said. His voice was low and disturbing. "At 7:45, 8:45 New York time, a hijacked American Airlines plane crashed into one of the towers of the World Trade Building in New York," Chiv said. "Then eighteen minutes later, another hit the south tower. We are under attack, Vine. I think, no, I know this is what you saw."

"Are you on the train?" Vine sat up in bed.

"No, they made us get off," Chiv said. "All trains are canceled. Mr. Parker, the teacher that was our chaperone, ran out of the station. His friend works in the World Trade Center. Vine, this is bad, really bad."

"And unfortunately, it's going to get worse," Vine said.

Vine was correct. At 9:45, a third plane crashed in the west side of the Pentagon in DC. Less than fifteen minutes after that back in New York, the south tower of the World Trade Center collapsed. Television screens were filled with up close and intimate pictures of thick clouds of dust and smoke from the collapsing structure. At ten-thirty, the north tower collapsed. This iconic structure that was the crown jewel of the New York skyline was reduced to a mound of concrete, steel, glass, and human remains. The bad news kept pouring in minute by minute in living color.

Just when Vine started to understand what it meant for the country to be under attack, more devastating and breaking news filled his big screen. A fourth California-bound plane was hijacked about four minutes after leaving the airport in New Jersey. It crashed in western Pennsylvania. There was no way anyone could have survived a plane that struck the ground at an estimated five hundred miles per hour. All forty-four people, including the crew, were killed. The destination of that plane was said to have been the White House or one of the several nuclear power plants along the eastern seaboard.

The so-called mastermind behind the September 11 attacks was terrorist Osama bin Laden. It's estimated that three thousand people—including firefighters, first responders, pedestrians, and passengers—were killed in the 9/11 attacks, including the friend of the chaperone teacher who worked for a venture capitalist firm on the eightieth floor of the north tower. He was on the phone with his mom when the wing of the plane sliced through the building.

No matter where you were in the world, hearts, minds, and souls were heavy. The cloud of catastrophic fear and sadness showed up in homes, workplaces, and even houses of worship. On Sunday the 16th, everyone including Louise and Jackie was at church. They needed something that only God could give: grace, mercy, and hope. Vine had the awesome responsibility of lifting a people up with his sermon.

"This morning, I'm not going to follow the lead of my minister friends and preach the wrong thing," Vine began. "I don't believe our souls need to hear how God is reminding us of the coming of the judgment or the rapture. People don't need to hear how God is so angry with how we are living, that he used Osama bin Laden to kill and harm nearly three thousand people and their families. This is not a test. God doesn't have to test nobody. I keep telling you that. He created you. He knows your thoughts before you think them. Why would he give you a test when he already knows if you will pass or fail?

"The tragedy of 9/11, as it's being called, has nothing to do with God or His will. A terrible man, low in his thoughts and regard for human life, devised a plan and recruited other low-minded and low-thinking individuals to carry out fatal and horrific harm to America under the banner of revenge and power. I'm not a fan of President Bush, but I was very proud of him and his ability to hear God speak. In his national address to the people of the United States, he spoke truth. God is our refuge and strength, an ever-present help in trouble. Therefore, we will not fear. Though the earth give way and the mountains fall into the heart of the sea, though the masterfully design and architecture give way and the towers fall, God will help us. We will not fall. Nations are in uproar, kingdoms fall, but God is our fortress. He is with us. I wish he had continued reciting the 46th division of Psalms because he left out some good stuff. It says, 'He makes wars to cease. He breaks the bow and shatters the spear. He burns the shields with fire. He is what our souls need today.' This is what you need to hear. 'Be still and know that I am God.'

"I want you to know this was not an act of God, nor was it in His will. He is benevolent. He is magnificent. He is good. All things that we hear, see, smell, taste, and touch that are good are pressed out of God. This was not an act of good. Therefore, it was not an act of God. We will heal from this. We will come back from this. Be still. I see another tower piercing through the clouds, filling the void in the skyline. I see widows and widowers finding love again. I see fatherless and motherless children growing up and becoming fathers and mothers to their own children. I see people in New York and all over the country hugging their neighbors, showing kindness to strangers, and treating their friends, family, and coworkers with love, concern, and respect—like it was their last chance to do so. I see people picking up litter in the streets and on the sidewalks because they care about their communities. I see an increase in volunteerism, charitable contributions, and activism. God didn't do this, but He and only He is able to bring us out of this kinder, gentler, and healthier than before."

Vine went on to conclude his sermon with the Aretha Franklin rendition of "What a Friend We Have in Jesus." His goal had been accomplished. Souls were lifted, and some hope was restored. Seven people joined the church that Sunday. Three were candidates for baptism. After service, all gathered at Bo and Jackie's house for an old-fashioned "after service" soul food feast prepared by Ms. Francis and Jackie.

"Have you ever just stood and watched her cook?" Sam asked those seated at the table. "What does she do to food that makes it taste so good?"

"Must be cocaine," Louise said. "I have baked, boiled, broiled, fried, and barbecued my sweet potatoes. I've never gotten them to taste like this."

"The secret is orange juice," Jackie said. "Instead of baking in water, she uses orange juice and four or five cloves. That's that unique flavor you're trying to figure out."

"The greens make my toes curl," Vine said.

"Man, come on," Bo said. "We're eating. This is the first real meal I've had in long time. Please don't ruin it talking about your crusty feet." The group laughed in unison.

"It feels good to laugh again, don't it?" Vine said. "It's good to end it with friends and family."

"Well, your sermon was on point today," Jackie said. "I am already tired of all the so-called theological theories about what happened and what's to come. You gave folks hope, Vine. You gave me hope. You are truly working your calling." Vine, somewhat embarrassed, smiled and dropped his head. "I'm serious. God is going to use you in a brand-new way. You just wait and see."

"And what's tripped out about it," Chiv said, "you've been feeling this event coming for years. Sometimes I think what we'd be doing right now if we had flown instead of taking the train or what if we got to New York and was in the middle of it all. Brings chills to my body."

"Vine said one of the teachers had a friend who worked in the north tower," Bo said. "Have they heard from him? Was he at work that day?"

"Well, he was on the phone talking to his mother when it happened," Chiv said. "His mother said the call just disconnected. She hasn't heard from him since. He was at work that morning. I'm sure he didn't make it. They are hopeful, but chances are that anyone who was at work Tuesday morning at the World Trade Center didn't make it out in time. They are hoping for a miracle."

"I'm just thankful that we're all okay," Vine said. "It's gonna take some time, but as I said today, we will return from this because the earth belongs to God. We cannot, will not, shall not fail."

CHAPTER 12

Circa 2005

"Arie, please explain this to me one more time," Louise said to Chiv. She refused to call him Chivas like them Jolly Boys did. "Vine is getting married? Am I the only one who knows that Vine is gay?"

"Oh my God," Chiv said, "you've got it all wrong. Vine is interested in the pastor position at Grand Ole Baptist. He heard that they would prefer a pastor who was married or seriously dating. Since he is neither, we have to find a woman for him who could and would perpetrate the fraud at least through the interview process and election. And he's not gay. Don't ever say that again."

"Fine, calm down," Louise said. "So how is this story gonna end? What happens after that? I mean, he can only go so long seriously dating. What's gonna happen when the jig is up?"

"We haven't gotten that far yet," Chiv said. "I can't imagine that it would be an issue. I mean, they may hire him because he's married, but I can't imagine that they'd fire him if he broke up with this girlfriend."

"With us Baptist, you'd be surprised what actually makes sense," Louise said. "We're a peculiar people."

"Come on, peculiar," Chiv said. "It's Jackie's turn, and I want to be on time to see this show from beginning to the end."

When Vine discussed his latest plight with the fellas, there was no light at the end of the tunnel, no rainbow over the horizon, or any chance in hell of finding a solution to this problem. But after the jokes ran out and the Chivas Regal began to flow, the fellas had figured out a way to help their friend. Sam, Bo, Chivas, Louise, Jackie, Anne, Pearl, and even Ms. Francis had a wager on the table. Each was confident that they'd be able to find a suitable escort for Vine. Each person had one shot at producing a girlfriend for Vine and introducing her in a forum where all could meet her. If Vine asked her out, the purveyor would walk away with 1,500 dollars. There was only one problem: satisfying Vine.

The acceptable candidate had to be on the taller side but not tall enough for tall-girl clothes or taller than him when she was wearing heels. She couldn't be darker than Oprah or lighter than Lena. She couldn't be a big girl, but she couldn't be thin. She had to be intelligent, soft-spoken, and have a head full of relaxed and professionally styled hair. When men saw them together, they should say, "What a catch." When women saw them, they should say the same thing. Bo, Chiv, Sam, Pearl, and Anne's candidates had all bombed. This afternoon, it was Jackie's turn at bat.

Jackie broke the pattern of a traditional dinner party and opted for an afternoon cookout. According to her plan, a three-hour barbecue beginning around three should place her candidate on Vine's arm later that night. Everyone gathered in Bo's backyard. Aside from must-have greens for Vine, the menu was light and easy: burgers, hot dogs, and fish kabobs. It was three thirty on a steamy August afternoon, and the proverbial stage was set. The only thing missing was the candidate.

"Okay, it's after three," Vine said to Jackie. "It ain't looking good."

"Just calm yourself down," Jackie said. She was frustrated that her candidate was late as well but couldn't allow it to show. "You have never been on time for a thing in your entire life. She'll be here. And besides, it's a lady's prerogative to be fashionably late."

"Well, while we wait, give us some information," Chiv said. "What does she look like? You said she worked for the city. What does she do?"

"She's a nurse in the public health department," Jackie said. "I sometimes go to her with workers'-compensation claims. She helps me with all the medical mumbo jumbo. Williams is a sweetheart. I can't imagine you not falling in love with her. You just better hope she has an appetite for the farce."

"Well, I can hardly wait," Vine said. Jackie heard the doorbell and ran into the house. "That must be her. Damn, I wish Jackie had told me her name. I really don't want to call her Nurse Williams."

Sam rolled his eyes and took the initiative to manage the grilling. Everyone was so focused on the mystery guest that no one thought about the food on the grill. He walked over and began playing grill master with his back to the door. Vine could hear Jackie and her guest laughing as they approached the backyard. Sam's ears picked up on the familiarity of the laugh. Suddenly, he thought, what if it was one of his many extramarital partners? How would he explain that to Vine? The more he focused on the stranger's distinct laugh, the more concerned he became. He closed the grill, spun around, and joined the gang, who had laser focus on the sliding doors.

When Vine saw her, a smile of relief and excitement filled his face. She was beautiful, stunning even, adorned in a simple but well-made, straight-cut pink sun dress and pink-and-white designer slides. Her jet-black hair was laid to the heavens and feathered just the way Vine liked it. As he walked toward her with an outstretched hand, their eyes met. Vine felt a ping in his chest, not his stomach. That was a sign that something was wrong. His spirit man was telling him that this vision of loveliness was too good to be true. For once, he was praying that his spirit man was wrong.

"Hello, I'm Divine, but everyone calls me Vine," he said. "Please tell me your name so I can tell you how happy I am to meet you."

"Her name is Marsaleen Ladeaux," Sam said with anger. He was nearly apoplectic, flared nostrils and all.

"Say what now?" Vine said before Marsaleen snatched her hand away from his.

"You heard me," Sam said. "The delicate hand you were drooling all over belongs to my wife."

Marsaleen was shocked, confused, and embarrassed all at the same time. How could this be happening? "Samaritan, what are you doing here?" she asked.

"I'm having a set-up barbecue for my friend with my friends," Sam said. "The one-hundred-thousand-dollar question is, what are you doing here? Did you come here knowing you were going to be hooked up with another man?"

"Wait, wait, just wait one minute," Jackie intervened. "You can't be Sam's wife. Your name is Williams. Everyone at work calls you Williams or Nurse Williams. No one calls you Marsaleen Ladeaux."

"I need to sit down," Vine said. "I knew my spirit man never lies. This is some freaky shit."

"So you out here playing strong, even letting your friends hook you up," Sam said. "You got an overnight bag in your car? You should have brought it in with you."

"Williams, Marsaleen, whatever your name is, why didn't you tell me you were married?" Jackie said. "I told you Vine was a minister. You should have told me you were married, girl. Why did you agree to come and meet him?"

"That's what I want to know," Sam said. Anger was welling up in his body to the point that he appeared swollen from head to toe.

"Easy, Sam," Bo said. "You're a Jolly Boy. Be cool."

"Yeah, be cool, Jolly Boy," Marsaleen said. "You've got a whole network of friends here that I know absolutely nothing about. Dare I ask what you say when they ask, 'Why didn't you bring your wife?' How many whores have you pranced and paraded in front of your friends? Yes, I wanted to meet Vine. Yes, I wanted a reason to get dressed up and get my hair and nails done. Yes, I wanted to be looked at and admired. My husband certainly doesn't give a damn about me anymore. Vine, I am sorry, but this will not work. Although that look in your eyes when you saw me did me a whole bunch of good, I wouldn't feel right having an affair with my husband's friend. Goodbye, everyone. I hope you enjoy your barbecue. He's actually good on the grill."

"I'll walk her out," Jackie said. She turned and raised a fist to Sam. He was indeed going to get a tongue lashing from her when she returned. Sam turned and looked at Vine, who was slowly railing back from a state of shock.

"Before you open your mouth to say one word to me, think," Vine said, shaking his index finger to emphasize his sentiment. "I mean it, Sam. You better think long and hard before you say something stupid to me."

"Take the damn meat off the grill before it burns," Sam said. "I'm going to talk to my wife." Sam walked quickly into and through the house to catch up with Marsaleen, who was standing in the driveway apologizing once again to Jackie. "Jackie, can I have a word with Marsaleen in private?"

Jackie looked to Marsaleen for some sort of gesticulation that it was safe to leave her alone with her husband. Marsaleen nodded, and Jackie walked back into the house. Sam and Marsaleen stood silent for a minute before Marsaleen spoke.

"So you have a whole family of friends, and I knew nothing about them," Marsaleen said. "Not only am I not part of it, I know nothing about it."

"Don't try to throw me off my square with the sideline bullshit," Sam said. "So you sleeping around now?" Sam asked, avoiding adding any commentary to her statement. "Someone you know at work offers to hook you up with someone they know, and you buy a new outfit, get your hair and nails done, and step to the invitation? Is this what we're doing now?"

"What I should be doing is slapping the shit out of you for signifying that I'm some sort of adulterous hoe," Marsaleen said. "All these years, all these years, you've been messing around on me, and the one time I even entertain the possibility of going on a date, you reduce me to a hoe? You got more nerve than a brass-ass monkey. You want to know what I do while you're out there screwing any and everything that will let you? I cook, drink, and smoke weed with my friend and go to work. I haven't been kissed, touched, or even treated to a nice dinner in years. I'm tired of being ignored and mistreated. So yes, I wanted to meet Vine. In fact, I've been excited all week about meeting Vine, sight unseen. What's good for the goose, well, you know the rest."

"So Jackie has been filling your head with information, I see," Sam said.

"Jackie hasn't been filling my head with a damn thing," Marsaleen replied. "I'm not stupid. I know your sexual appetite and prowess.

We were having sex three and four times a week. Do you think I'm dumb enough to think that when we stopped, you stopped? You've been out here shaking your big thang in the faces of every woman who still loves the light-skinned, shiny-head pretty boy. I'm not stupid." Sam dropped his head and looked away. "Exactly. So don't start acting like the jealous, mistreated husband. You can't be that without being a husband to begin with. And, baby, you ain't that."

"Oh, so I'm not your husband anymore?" Sam asked. "What you gonna do? You gonna change the locks? You gonna gather up my stuff in a pile in the driveway and burn it up like Bernadine in *Waiting to Exhale*?"

"I wish I had the gumption," Marsaleen said. "I wish I had the fight in me, Samaritan, but I don't. No, I'm not going to do any of those things. But trust me, my days of sitting at home or lying in bed with my toys are over. It's time for you to wonder where I am or if I'm coming home for a change. Your locks and clothes are safe. They'll be there whenever if ever you come home. Now if you'll excuse me, I suddenly remember somewhere I need to be." Marsaleen got into her car and drove away.

Sam ran his hand over his face. He was perplexed and worried. Sam walked through the house and back to the patio. When he appeared through the sliding doors, all conversation stopped. "I don't want to talk about it," he said.

"Well, that's just too bad, Samaritan," Jackie said. "That is a beautiful, sweet woman who, for whatever reason, is still in love with you. You ought to be ashamed of yourself. I hope whatever it is out in Vegas works out for you, but if you bring another woman to this house and her name isn't Marsaleen Williams Ladeaux, I will shoot your thang off and send it back to you in a FedEx envelope. Louise, Pearl, Vine, Chiv, honey, I'm going inside. I've lost my appetite." Louise and Pearl followed Jackie into the house.

Once the coast was clear, Chiv spoke. "Your best friend's wife set up your wife with your other best friend," Chiv said. "Vine was right. This is some freaky shit."

"Amen," Ms. Francis said. "Tyler Perry could do something with this. It's a hell of a story."

CHAPTER 13

February 10, 2006

In retrospect, 2005 was a year of both tragedy and comedy. Marsaleen, feeling unnecessarily guilty for hindering Vine's pursuit of a pastorship at a new church, offered up her best friend, Lola, as his pseudo-fiancée and companion. They actually started dating for real on the down low but fizzled out after a few short weeks. Vine thought Lola was a little too fast for him. Lola appraised Vine as slow in every regard. Vine applied anyway but didn't get the job. The church board was adamant. They wanted a chief executive minister who was married in order to dispel any rumors of promiscuity or homosexuality. Vine thought that was discriminatory and ridiculous. His intention was to sue them, but for now, Shining Star continued to be his home and employer.

Chiv and Louise, as well as Jackie and Bo, were fine and going strong. At one point during the year, Louise entertained the idea of motherhood but was soon dissuaded. She channeled her baby-making ideas into work, and luckily, the idea vanished into the air.

The worst tragedy came from Hurricane Katrina, which was said to be one of the deadliest hurricanes ever to hit the United States. An estimated 1,800 people died in the hurricane and the flooding that followed. Fatal engineering flaws in the levees around New Orleans precipitated most of the loss of lives. And to add insult to tragedy, assistance and relief was slow to arrive. People were trapped on rooftops and in high rises for days before seeing the first FEMA representative. Thousands of people, many separated from their family members, were displaced throughout the United States as far as Salt Lake City, Utah. Like 9/11, it would be years before New Orleans would recover. Today, however, was Bo's birthday. In true Jolly-Boy fashion, all were on hand to celebrate his sixty-three years of life. It was the end of yet another delicious meal at the Jackson household. Vine, Bo, Chivas, Sam, Louise, Anne, Pearl, and Ms. Francis enjoyed cake and coffee prepared and served by Jackie. It was a quiet but fun time.

"So, Bo," Jackie said, "aren't you gonna share your good news with everyone?"

"No, because it sounds like bragging," Bo replied. "No one wants to hear another person brag and boast."

"Aw, come on now," Vine said. "Ain't nothing wrong with bragging if you actually have something to brag about. Call it a praise report. In fact, when you're done, I've got a praise report myself."

"Me too," Chiv said.

"Uh-oh, girl," Jackie teased Louise, "you about to earn your MRS degree."

"Girl, please," Louise said. "Other than Walgreens having Chivas Regal on sale, Arie ain't got no praise report." Everyone thought that was funny except Chiv.

"Sam, you want time on the praise report agenda?" Jackie asked. Since the incident involving Marsaleen and Vine, Sam has kept his distance from Jackie. Feeling that distance, Jackie goes out of her way to make him uncomfortable.

"I've got nothing to contribute," Sam said.

"Well, I've got something," Pearl said. "After all these years, the flower shop is doing so well I'm opening another one over East, on 80th and Stony Island. I'm going to run the shop out here, and Anne is going to run the shop on Stony. We're hoping to open the first week in May before the wedding and prom seasons start."

"Oh, Pearl, that's wonderful news," Louise said. "Congratulations. Me and Jackie will plan your grand opening."

"Yes, we will," Jackie said. "See how easy that was, Beauregard? Now go on and tell them."

"Well, it looks like my three-flat in Oak Park will be paid off this summer," Bo said somewhat sheepishly.

"Wait, what about the old house?" Sam asked. "I didn't know you had a building in Oak Park."

"I let Helen take the old house," Bo said. "I bought the building years and years ago. I kept it after the divorce because it was mine before we got married. I have six more payments, and then it's mine."

"Naw, man," Chiv said. "Call them now. I bet your payoff is lower than the sum of those six payments. Call them and get the payoff amount as of today. You might be surprised to know that you don't owe as much as you think."

"Okay, I'll do that," Bo said. "So what's your good news, Arie?" Bo was mocking Louise, who never calls him Chiv or Chivas.

"No. Vine, you go next," Chiv said.

"Okay, well, I've been dating someone, and it's getting serious," Vine said.

"Wait, before we go any further," Pearl said, "is she married to anyone in this room? We've seen this movie already you know."

"Oh, I can assure you that the first time you meet her will be the first time you meet her," Vine said. "And she's an attorney. That's how we met. I was upset with Grand Ole Baptist for not hiring me that I contacted an attorney to see if I had a case. She was the attorney. I didn't have a case, but I brought my best mac game. And now I'm yoked up with a professional woman."

"Vine, you cheating on me?" Jackie teased.

"Yes, every chance I get," Vine played along. "It's taking you much too long to put down that zero and come get this hero."

"Don't get cussed out in here," Bo advised jokingly.

"What's her name?" Chiv asked. Chiv's enthusiasm was slow and reserved. It was as if he was irritated that Vine kept his new relationship a secret from him.

"Her name is Hadassah," Vine said.

"Odessa?" Sam asked.

"No, you heard what I said," Vine snapped. "Her name is Hadassah. I was going to bring her tonight, but I didn't want to take away from Bo's big night."

"Well, we can't wait to meet her," Jackie said.

"Yeah," Chiv said. "We'll see if she can pass the Jolly-Boy inspection."

"Okay, Chivas," Bo said. "It's your turn. Who has got the best deal on Chivas Regal this week? Walgreens or Rothchild's?"

After an overexaggerated eye roll and heavy sigh, Chiv turned his attention to Louise. "Lu, you came into my life at a very low point in my life," Chiv said. "I have experienced loss at a magnitude that I've never experienced before. The three people who represented my reason for living were gone in a matter of days. It was hard to handle. It was a hard thing to come back from, but I did, and on my way, I met you. I never thought I could experience love again, let alone be someone's husband again. But I think I can, Louise. I want you to be my wife." Chiv reached into his pocket and pulled out an aqua-colored Tiffany box before lowering himself onto one knee. "I know you've waited for a long time, and because of that, I will understand if you say no. But, Louise, will you marry me? You see…"

"Yes," she answered, interrupting his extended proposal speech.

"Well, damn, make a decision, why don't you?" Vine joked at her quick response.

"Yes, yes, and yes," Louise said and delivered a passionate kiss to his full lips. "But on one condition. I can only wear this ring if it's from a man who does not have a drinking problem. Arie, I love you, baby, but you are an alcoholic. You've ignored it, but you can't ignore it any longer. I won't let you. I cannot marry an alcoholic, functioning or otherwise. I want to so badly be Mrs. Arie Eubanks, but you've got to be sober."

"Makes sense, and that's fair," Vine said. "We'll help you, man. You can do this."

"I'm way ahead of you," Chiv said. "Today marks seven-days sober. I'm attending AA meetings and even have a sponsor. I don't need alcohol, but I do need you. Wear my ring please." Louise's face was so wet from crying tears rolled off her chin like a dripping faucet. In fact, there was not a dry eye in the house. When he stood, Bo was the first to embrace and congratulate him.

"Chivas, I mean Arie," Bo said, "I am so proud of you."

"Well, Ms. Francis," Sam said, "I guess it's just me and you in the bad-luck corner tonight."

"Oh, I ain't in no bad-luck corner with you," Francis said. "I've been skipping happy since Helen Jackson left this family. If there is a bad-luck corner, you're in it by yourself." Ms. Francis's words brought hearty laughter to the party.

"Come on, Sam," Bo said. "Don't break the chain. Certainly you have something good to report. How are things in Las Vegas?"

"Not good," Sam said. "I've worked three lines out there in the last three months and have not seen her."

"See, Sam?" Jackie said, "I knew you had some good news in there somewhere. But we're not going to stick around to hear the sorted tales about some home-wrecking whore. Come on, ladies. Let's go into the kitchen. We have a flower-shop grand opening and a wedding to plan." Jackie led Louise, Pearl, Anne, and Ms. Francis into the kitchen.

When the ladies were out of sight, Sam continued. "Something is wrong," Sam said. "Nevaeh has kinda gone ghost on me. We talk on the phone every day, but whenever I'm there, I never get to see her. She's always working or out of town. I think she's breaking up with me."

"Oh my God," Vine said. "You may be pretty, but you dumb as hell. How did you think this was going to end, Sam? A stripper or dancer, as you call her, whose name spells heaven backward, hooks up with a married man who lives on the other side of the continent, who sees her every other month. Did you think you two were going to end up hand in hand walking into the sunset? Men throw their money and ding-a-lings in the woman's face every night. She has played you like she's playing them."

"I'm Sam Ladeaux," he said. "Ain't no woman ever played me. I'm the player. I make the plays."

"The only thing you made were payments: telephone bill, car note, John M. Smith, Neiman-Marcus, and the Piggly Wiggly. Cut bait. Settle your losses and get back into bed with your wife."

"It's not over," Sam said. "Something is wrong. This woman knows me, and I know her. We're in love. She gonna be Mrs. Samaritan Ladeaux one day."

"I thought that position had been filled," Arie said.

"I'm hip," Bo reacted. "And you will remain in the bad-luck corner all by yourself until you do the right thing. You can't prosper doing the wrong thing."

"And I'm not just a destruction doom-and-gloom prophet," Vine said. "I can see good things too. We are all gonna be prosperous. Bo, not only are you gonna pay off that three-flat, you're going to pay for this and another one in the next three years. In fact, all our houses will be paid for. No one in this house will die broke. We're all gonna be millionaires."

"Well, I receive that," Bo said. "I know I'm gonna be rich before I die. And I'm going first, so then y'all will be rich too."

"So I got to wait until you die to be rich?" Arie asked.

"Hopefully not, but just in case," Bo said. "When I'm in heaven, I want to enjoy my peace and serenity. I don't want to listen to you broke ninjas complaining about money. And that's a promise. Sam, make a surprise trip to Vegas and end this nonsense with that girl. This has gone on long enough. You better get to your wife before someone else does." Remembering his first encounter with Marsaleen, a huge mischievous smile filled Vine's face.

"Divine Oliver, if you utter one word that's even close to the thoughts in your head right now, I'm kicking your big ass," Sam said. Vine howled in laughter and was soon joined by Bo and Arie. Sam left. When he got into the car, he couldn't help but laugh himself.

CHAPTER 14

SHE'S ALRIGHT

"Divine, why are you so irritable?" Hadassah asked. "I should be the one on edge about meeting your friends, not you. Please go wait for me in the living room. I'm not going to jump out the window and run away."

"That's good," Vine said, "because you might land wrong and get your dress and shoes dirty. I can't present you to the Jolly Boys, and you're looking unkept."

"Oh my God," Hadassah said. "You are being extra new-and-improved ridiculous right now. Living room, please, and work on your relationship with Levi. Take him for a quick walk."

"If I walk his ass, only one of us will come back," Vine said about Hadassah's English bulldog. "And of all things, a bulldog—Shouldn't you have one of those little toy dogs that you can just throw in your purse? No, not my girlfriend. She has to have a black bulldog with a spike collar."

"Go play with your stepson," Hadassah asked. "I need to find the right pumps, and then I'll be ready to go." She kissed Vine gently on the cheek and pushed him out of her spacious bedroom. As soon as his feet touched the kitchen floor, Levi began barking as if an intruder was approaching. Vine reached down to pet the puppy, but Levi turned and walked away. "You bitch-made ball licker," Vine said. When Hadassah came down, Vine and Levi were in their respective corners of the couch, gazing at the television as if they had just had an argument.

"This is too funny," she said. "You two are competing for alpha-male status in my house. I need to be filming this. Levi, go to your place. Mommy and Daddy have to go meet Daddy's friends."

Levi barked as if he understood but did not approve. He took his time, but he retreated to his kennel as directed. Hadassah closed and locked the kennel door, and then she and Vine were off to the restaurant. Bo had taken Chiv's advice and called the mortgage company for the payoff amount for his Oak Park building. Chiv was right. Bo only needed the equivalent of one-and-a-half-months mortgage payment, and he'd be done. He and Jackie treated the Jolly Boys and their guest to a celebratory mortgage-burning dinner at his favorite restaurant in Chicago, Lawry's Prime Rib on Ontario, right off Michigan Avenue.

The new couple spent the ten-minute ride from Hadassah's mansion in the downtown sky to the restaurant preparing for questions she would no doubt get from the gang—Pearl and Jackie, in particular. Hadassah found it unnecessary but amusing, so she went along with the program. By the time they reached the restaurant, Hadassah was more prepared for this meeting than a courtroom battle with a worthy opposing attorney. As they approach the private dining room reserved for the auspicious occasion, they quickly discovered the couple of honor had not arrived. Vine thought this was good and bad: good because it gave him more time to avoid the inquisition, but bad because Chiv, Louise, Sam, Miss Francis, Pearl, and Anne were already there.

When his friends laid eyes on Hadassah, the shock was evident and somewhat humorous. Vine knew they'd be shocked, but with the way they looked, you would think they'd never seen a strikingly beautiful White woman before. Not to appear racist, everyone quickly forced themselves to cover their mouths and pretend, at least until they got more information, that there was absolutely nothing wrong with Vine dating a woman who was "non-Black."

"Everyone, let me introduce you to my girlfriend, Hadassah. Sweetheart, this is Samaritan. We call him Sam. Chivas, I mean Arie, and his fiancé, Louise. Ms. Francis, who's the housekeeper and chef extraordinaire for the Jacksons, and my sisters Anne and Pearl."

"Hello, everyone," Hadassah said. "I can't tell you how excited I am to finally meet you." Hadassah Lehrman Locke was strikingly more beautiful than any woman the fellas could imagine with Vine. She was five feet, seven and a half-inches tall with heels, curvaceous, and sported a perfect auburn bob cut. Her clothes were well designed and made to perfectly fit her frame. She was gregarious and a master extrovert. When Vine turned her lose, she would be able to work the room like a Kennedy. With her alabaster skin and conspicuous Jewish lineage, she could be a stand-in for Debra Messing from the sitcom *Will and Grace*. She wasn't necessarily soft-spoken or dossal, and undenounced to Vine, she didn't come to play.

Arie, Louise, Anne, and Pearl were quick to get up close and personal. They embraced her and began trying not to appear uncomfortable, making her feel welcome and comfortable. Sam, not known for his coalescing with White folks, intentionally held back. Aware of his disdain for White people, Hadassah stepped right up to the lion, literally.

"Sam, it is a pleasure to meet you," Hadassah said, extending her hand.

"Hello, Odessa," he said.

"No, Hadassah," she quickly corrected Sam.

"My apologies," Sam said. "I'm used to easy names like Anne, Pearl, and Louise. You'll find that Black people are less audacious than your people."

"I'll remember that the next time I'm asked to represent Chiniqua or Quinita or Nobatambe," Hadassah said.

"Are you making fun of my people?" Sam said defensively.

"Now why would I do that?" Hadassah said. "Unless you're planning on making fun of mine?"

Sam smiled and nodded as if he was impressed with her forthrightness. He ignored her question and continued to engage.

"Your name is Jewish, isn't it?" Sam asked.

"Well, I think it's more biblical than Jewish," she said. "Depending on who you talk to, it's another name for Esther and

Myrtle—like the myrtle tree. I'm so glad my parents went with *Hadassah*. Esther and Myrtle sound a little…"

"Too Black for you?" Sam interrupted.

"No," Hadassah said. "A little too old."

"Of course," Sam said. "So is Locke your maiden name?"

"No," Hadassah responded, somewhat mirroring Sam's obvious disdain for her. "My maiden name is Lehrman. I married a Locke."

"Like Joseph Locke?" Sam asked. "The real-estate mogul who owns all kinds of office buildings and strip malls in the city? You are married to him?"

"I used to be married to him," Hadassah said. "We are divorced."

"So you're a rich Jew, huh?" Sam said.

"Sam, enough," Louise said. "Now you're just being rude and making the woman feel uncomfortable."

"Oh, I'm fine," she said to Louise. "I am not rich, Sam, in answer to your question. As Claire Huxtable said to Cliff, 'When you're rich, your money works for you.' I work extremely hard for my money. I'm not rich."

"Cute," Sam said. "And yes, I am impressed with the *Cosby Show* reference."

"Oh, my instincts tell me that it will take more than a television-show reference to impress you," Hadassah said. "You have a problem with me because I'm not Black, and you assume I have a problem with you because you are. But trust me, if I end up not liking you, it won't be because of your skin color. It will be because of who you are as a person and how you treat me."

"Straight talk," Sam said. "I just don't know how Vine could walk past a city full of beautiful Black women to get to a White woman. It's like stepping over a dollar bill to pick up a dime."

"Okay, Sam," Vine said. "I'm shutting this down. You starting to piss me off. Now I'm dating this woman whether you approve or not."

"But why couldn't she be a sister?" Sam asked.

"Well, I went with a White attorney after all the Black strippers were spoken for," Vine said. Sam took a deep breath, preparing to light into Vine, but Bo and Jackie finally arrived.

"Hey, everybody," Bo said. "Sorry we're late." Bo's eyes panned the room. When his eyes focused on Hadassah, he masked his shock well and greeted her. "You must be Vine's girlfriend, Hadassah. Welcome to the party. This is my wife, Jackie."

"Hello, Hadassah," Jackie said. "So glad you could join us, and sorry we're late. I hope everyone has made you feel welcomed."

"Everyone has been wonderful," Hadassah said. "Sam and I have some work to do, but other than that, all is well."

"Well, good luck with that," Chiv joked. "Y'all make me want to start drinking again."

As the evening progressed, the mood became lighter and lighter. Hadassah blended in well and appeared to have a lot of fun. It was also very obvious that she was not only smitten with Vine, he was very attentive and tactile toward her. And to everyone's surprise, she and Sam enjoyed each other's company immensely. By the end of the evening, the two were laughing, debating, and coalescing on a myriad of issues from FEMA's poor and slow response after Katrina to the need for the complete and total elimination of unions in Chicago. They even broached the subject of a female or Black president. She had won him over in a big way. After dinner and just before the mortgage-burning ceremony, the fellas gathered around the bar to conduct exclusive Jolly-Boy business.

"Well, well, well, preacher man," Sam began, "ain't you full of surprises. You went out and found you a White, Jewish, rich redhead girl with tig ole bitties. But the feat of them all is how you kept this one a secret. For someone who runs their mouth as much as you do, playing this hand close to your chest must have tired you out. You must be exhausted right now."

"Yes, I am exhausted, but I'm glad I kept it to myself," Vine said. "If I gave advance notice, you would have acted even a bigger fool than you did tonight. You were just about to show your natural Black-ass at one point, but you saw the look on my face."

"Aw, man, I was just trying to figure out if she was all right," Sam said.

"Of course, she's all right," Vine said. "Would I be with someone if they weren't all right?"

"I love that," Arie said. "Make sure she's all right. It's like there is a secret but understood code that White folks are racist and can't be trusted until we ask enough questions or provoke them to anger to see their real selves to make sure they don't have a problem with Black folks. It's amusing."

"It's necessary and a part of your heritage," Bo said. "I was smiling and going along because she's your girl, but I was listening to every word she said and watching every move she made. See, Arie, you didn't grow up below the Mason-Dixon line. You didn't see some of the stuff we saw. Now all the White folks weren't racist, but most were. Every now and again, you'd find one who was all right. And we didn't trust what we trusted because White folks are like the weather—they can change on you in a minute."

"But how will things change if we don't start judging people by the content of their character and not the color of their skin?" Arie asked. "I believe a great man suggested that we do so."

"When Martin said that, he was talking to us, but he wasn't talking about us," Sam said. "You best believe that while he was up on the mountaintop and looking over to the promised land at the glory of the coming of the Lord, he had ten or twenty of us at the foot of the mountain to make sure White folks didn't come up, unless, of course, they was all right."

"All I'm saying is that Hadassah is a good woman, one Vine may have missed if he was narrow in his thinking," Arie said.

"Speaking of narrow in their thinking," Sam said, "how is the riga marrow?"

"The what?" Vine asked. "What is the riga marrow?" Vine knew this question was going to come up.

"Come on, fool. Now you know what I'm talking about," Sam said. "Is she one of those chicks who's all buttoned up and demure by day and a stone freak at night?"

"Oh my God," Arie said. "I don't want to talk about this."

"You know what, Arie or Chiv or whatever the hell your name is," Sam said, "you stopped drinking and turned into a prude. I'm just asking the question that everyone wants to know. The question Jeffrey Osbourne asked: Can she woo, woo, woo?"

"Hell, I wouldn't know, know, know," Vine said. "We ain't done nothing yet."

"Negro, I know you lying," Sam said. "Y'all been out here for over a month now, and you ain't got no drawer at her crib yet?"

"Nope, not even close," Vine said. "I think she's afraid or something. She keeps saying the day will come, but she's just not ready to go there yet."

"What is she afraid of?" Arie asked.

"She probably think I'm so big I might hurt her," Vine said. "You know, the man-dingo snake theory." Bo, Arie, and Sam broke from Vine in three different directions, spitting out their drinks and holding their stomachs while laughing. "I guess if you're used to Vienna sausage in a can, a Jew Town polish might be a bit intimidating."

"Meeting adjourned," Bo said, wiping happy tears from his eyes. "Come on, Mande, and pray so I can burn up these papers."

Everyone stood around Bo and Jackie as the deed burned over the floor-standing ice bucket. The mood in the private dining room shifted from jovial and jolly to somber and serious. For the first time in the quiet, everyone took in how significant an accomplishment this was. It was a dream that could no longer tarry. It was a promised-land, mountaintop experience that none of them would ever forget.

"It's interesting," Bo said. "A Black man feels accomplished and successful when he buys his first Cadillac and when he pays off his home. I got two Caddies in the garage. Hell, I've got two garages. I may not have arrived yet, but I can see the sign."

As Sam drove home after the party, he reflected on how happy Vine was with Hadassah, the strong marriage Bo had with Jackie, and the love Chivas must have for Louise to give up Chivas Regal. He was jealous. He wanted to have something real. His marriage was officially on life support, and the love of his life was avoiding him. He needed a plan to get his life right again. He didn't know what the plan would entail, but it would start with getting things straight and clear with Nevaeh. He had convinced himself that regardless of what his friends thought, Nevaeh was the basket in which he'd put all his eggs. If he lost his friends but kept her, he'd have a shot at happiness.

He needed some help navigating through this one. He needed the help of his special neighbor. He dialed her number while driving.

"Hey, what you doing?" he asked. "I need some help figuring some stuff out. You got time for me tonight?"

"Sam, I will help you figure out whatever needs figuring out as long as you take care of me," she cooed. "You got the stuff to make me feel better."

"Are you speaking of wine?" Sam said, playing with her a bit. "I can stop and get you a bottle of red for your counsel tonight."

"When you get here, you'll have everything you need to settle your debt with me," she responded. "I'm going to slip into the tub. Use your key and let yourself in."

"Lola, aren't you a naughty girl," Sam said, "opening your legs for your best friend's husband."

"Oh, I don't think you'd have it any other way," Lola said. "I can always find another best friend, but what you're serving, now that's a different story. Now I've got to get freshened up. See you soon."

"I need to check to see if—" Sam said before Lola interrupted him.

"It's safe," Lola said. "She left here for home about an hour ago. Now hurry, please. I'll help you with your problem if you help me with mine."

"I'm not even going to ask," Sam said.

"You already know the answer," said Lola.

PART THREE

Everything Must Change

Change is inevitable, growth is optional.

—John Maxwell

CHAPTER 15

The first Sunday in April 2007

As Vine and Hadassah cruised down Lake Shore Drive, they experienced feelings of gratitude, favor, and a hint of disbelief. After Reverend Stroy Anderson was fired as pastor of Grand Ole Baptist in January, the chair of the board reached out to Vine to see if he was still interested. It would appear that GOB would rather have an unmarried pastor than one who was addicted to crack cocaine. That infamous Sunday when Reverend Anderson, who was as high as his body would let him be, started stripping out of his clothes while preaching was an indelible image sketched in the minds of the congregation. Luckily, security and his wife got to him before he reached for his boxer briefs. No one had seen Anderson since.

After a thorough and exhausting interview process, Vine's candidacy was presented to the congregation for an official vote. He successfully received more than the two-thirds vote he needed to win the seat. Today was installation Sunday. Against Vine's preference, the board sent a stretch limo to fetch Vine and Hadassah and bring them to church. They rode in silence, occasionally exchanging smiles and glances and then returning their attention to the beauty of the city along the shore.

"Divine, I cannot begin to tell you how proud I am of you," Hadassah said. "GOB is one of the oldest and respected churches in Chicago. That they chose you is a true honor."

"I still can't believe it," Vine said. "This is a pastor's dream job. The board is small, the staff is big, the sanctuary is new, the congregation is growing, and there is one year's worth of bills in the bank. I am in awe."

"You sound more surprised than in awe," Hadassah said.

"I think I am," Vine replied.

"Well, I'm not," she continued. "You are a good man and dynamic leader. You have some patience and anger issues, but you're working on those. It's what our synagogues and churches need today—strong leadership."

"Well, I may have been too stern in the past," Vine said. "How could they have chosen me? God did this, but somebody right here on earth had something to do with this. I just know it."

"I'm sure Shining Star is still scratching their heads, wondering how you pulled this off," Hadassah said.

"Seems like just yesterday I had that terrible meeting with the board," Vine said, recounting the meeting that ended his stint with Shining Star Missionary Baptist Church. "I should have known something was up when they wanted to meet on a Monday morning." Vine went on to retell the story of that day.

"It was another Sunday morning where again I had lost my temper in the pulpit. The choir was singing an old familiar hymn of the church, "I Know It Was the Blood. " In the middle of the chorus, I stood and stopped the song. I remember snapping on Eric Rockrose, the minister of music. There is no such word in the English language as *knowed*. It's 'I know it was the blood.' not 'I knowed it was the blood.' The song isn't past tense. It's present tense. 'We know,' 'you know,' 'I know it was the blood.' I don't see how you hold choir rehearsal each week and the choir says something stupid like that. He made some flip comment before jumping off the organ. He said something like 'Maybe if we had a pastor who supported us instead of tearing us down.' I then said something like 'If you sissies used choir rehearsal to actually learn the songs and not a meet-and-greet before going to the sissy bar, you wouldn't need support. Sit down, all of you. Just loud and wrong.'" Hadassah shifted her focus from the window into Vine's eyes. She was in a state of shock and really understood the depth of his perfectionist ways.

On Monday at 11:55 a.m., Vine walked into the boardroom of the church concerned but not afraid. This was a road frequently traveled for the anointed but sharp-tongued pastor and prophet. Just like the many meetings in the past, he knew how things would go: the board chair would express concerns, Vine would defend himself, they'd argue, and then Vine would relent. He'd promise to apologize, and the church would just roll on. To show growth and remorse and to get this over with, Vine planned to surprise the good deacon with an apology, agreement to a one-week silence, and beat the Monday traffic downtown to Hadassah's crib. As he walked to his seat, he was surprised to see the executive committee of the board around the table. His spirit man was telling him that this disciplinary meeting was going to be different and possibly his last. As he sat, he decided to change his strategy and do more listening than speaking. Deacon Mosley led the group in prayer and then called the meeting to order. That was another sign of danger lurking. Mosley deliberately broke one of Vine's rules. As the spiritual leader of the church, he should always be the first to pray. Something really bad was about to happen.

"Rev. Oliver," Mosley began, "need I say we've had our differences in the past, but there are some things that are surfacing and proving very disturbing to members of the board. Take yesterday, for example. Your harsh words to Eric and members of the choir were excessive, humiliating, unnecessary, and downright nasty. To call someone's sexual orientation into questions during one of your rants is so common. No body of believers would expect that behavior, tone, or language from their spiritual leader. The choir is one of the hardest, if not the hardest-working groups in the church. They should be celebrated and appreciated, not belittled and berated."

"You are correct," Vine said softly and calmly. Mosley was shocked and suspicious. "They are hardworking, but they are also well compensated. We spend close to four thousand dollars every Sunday for music. The minister of music, pianist, keyboard guy, guitar player, drummer, saxophonist, both choir directors, and bongo player get a check. And whoever sings lead on a song gets a check. I've never worked with a church who pays someone for leading a song. With that expense of nearly sixteen thousand dollars a month, we should expect songs to be rendered in proper and well-enunciated English. That said, my words were harsh. I will make it a priority to attend rehearsal Thursday night and apologize for snapping at them. Okay, shall we adjourn now?"

"Not just yet, Pastor," one of the officers said. "We have some other concerns."

"You have been spotted playing a slot machine at the casino out by the airport," said Lana Hughes, a newly appointed board member.

"That's not true," Vine said. "I don't go to that one. I go to the casinos in Aurora and Indiana."

"I was sent a picture," Hughes said, scrolling through her phone to find the picture. Sure enough, when she turned the screen around, there was Vine, sitting at the slot machine.

"And what's wrong with that?" Vine asked.

"It doesn't look good for a pastor to be gambling when gambling is a sin," Mosley completed her thought.

"Oh, please," Vine said. "I don't have a picture, but it's also a sin for a married board officer to be sleeping with the minister of music. Hughes, why exactly are you upset? Is it because I yelled at your boyfriend, or is it because you're embarrassed, finding out that your boyfriend is a sissy?" Hughes looked like she would die in place.

"But Hughes is not the pastor," Mosley said. "You are. People are watching you. It makes the church look bad."

"Fine. I will not go to any casinos in our area," Vine said. "Now are we ready to adjourn? I'm starting to get a bit uptight."

"And then to top it all off, you have the nerve to bring that White woman in here and present her as your partner," his once advocate and the board's secretary, Pamela, chimed in. "You would have done better by lining up all the Black women in the church and slapping them in the face one by one with open hand."

"First of all, that White woman's name is Hadassah, and she is an accomplished attorney and my girlfriend," Vine said. "And she has become a huge financial supporter of this ministry. In just a few short months, she has given more than you Negroes have given since you've been here. But I'm getting ahead of myself. I need to know why, who I sleep with is any of your business."

"Well, that answers my next question," Hughes said. "You are having premarital sex with that tramp. It's an abomination."

"See, that's why people who are not students of the Bible should not pretend to be," Vine said. "It is natural for a man to lay with woman, but I'm not so sure that's what you and Millicent Jeffries are doing two or three nights a week. Now that's not natural." Hughes glared at Vine as if she was staring down Satan himself. "And in the same beds that you lay with your husbands. And no doubt, the same beds where your children were conceived. I'm not a homophobe. Love is love, and God is love. But I don't think God would approve of your methods."

"Don't forget who you're talking to, Negro," Hughes said. "Your lies will not serve you well in keeping your job."

"And see, that's the problem," Vine said. "Just because I'm not walking around here with my nose in the air like your typical high prophet, you all forget that I am. It's a gift whether I've earned it or not."

"Well, as you're demonstrating right now, you are out of control," Mosley said. "And this church will not have a leader who is out of control—not on my watch. So I think—"

"Control," Vine interrupted. "That's an interesting word coming from you." Vine closed his eyes and was silent for a few seconds. He opened this eyes and established laser focus on Mosley, who was immediately concerned. He knew he wouldn't like what Vine had to say.

"What happened to your driver's license?" Vine asked. Mosley appeared as if his entire world was shaken.

"You shut your mouth right now, Vine!" Mosley yelled. "This is none of your concern."

"Oh, I'm being called on the carpet because I'm spending my money at the casino, but the chairman of the board of the one of the largest churches in Chicago loses his license for driving under the influence and I need to shut my mouth?" Vine said. "I think we all know that's not going to happen. And if the folks on that job find out that you faked that fall down the steps, which landed you on disability, oh, I'm sure they wouldn't like that either."

"This meeting is over," Mosley said. "I will not be spoken to any kind of way."

"Finally," Vine said. "I've been trying to end this shit show for an hour now. So unless you are firing me or someone else wants their prophetic read aloud, I suggest you leave me the chuck alone." Vine walked out of the meeting leaving the executive team shocked and dumbfounded. He sat in his office, steaming with anger and alone. A few minutes later, the phone rang. It was GOB wanting to resume discussions about his candidacy for the pastorship also known as chief executive minister. Vine pulled an offering envelope from his top drawer and wrote the words "I resign effective today" and signed his name. Without a thought of packing his personal belongings, he walked back to the boardroom. The executive committee was still assembled. He handed the envelope to Mosley and turned toward the door. Before his exit, he had one last suggestion. "I suggest that you send the severance agreement before the end of the day. Otherwise, I will feel it my responsibility to share the personal transgressions of our senior leadership team with the congregation. And let the minutes reflect, madame secretary. That's not a threat but a promise." He walked out and had not entered the doors of Shining Star Baptist since.

"Divine, can I ask you a question without you getting angry, my *bashert* [Jewish for "soul mate"]?" Hadassah asked. "Have you learned anything from all this? Not asking if you've learned your lesson as if you've been lucky enough to dodge punishment. I guess I'm asking, what are you going to do with this fresh start and extra chance?"

"The question doesn't upset me, *mispocha*," Vine replied. He had picked up a few Jewish words since dating Hadassah, including *mispocha,* which means "family." His use of them, especially at just the right time, made her smile. "I'm going to figure out how to have high standards and expectations without losing my patience and temper. I have not been called to prepare the church for the coming of the bridegroom. I have been chosen. Many are called, but only a few are chosen. No, Hadassah, I'm going to do this differently. You'll see."

"I'm so glad to hear that," she said. "Now I'm just hoping GOB can handle you having a White, Jewish redhead for a girlfriend."

"You forget *beautiful* and *delicious*," Vine said and made her blush.

"Divine, you are the devil," she said, slapping his hand. "Did Sam teach you that? As Louise once said to Arie when he was acting mannish, 'I never should have given you some.'"

Vine loved it when Hadassah genuinely tried to speak in the vernacular of his people. As she turned and looked out the window, he turned and looked at her. His spirit intelligence had already revealed that their relationship was not long-term, but he was falling in love with her. He knew better than to second guess the spirit, but in the moment, he couldn't imagine breaking her heart.

When their limo pulled up in front of the church, two women in expensive and stylish black pantsuits walked toward the car. "Rule number 1—women cannot wear pants in church," Vine whispered to Hadassah.

As the door opened and Vine began to exit, Hadassah grabbed his arm, bringing his ear close to her mouth. "Sweetheart, does the Lord really care if women wear pants when they come to worship?" she asked.

Vine smiled and gently attempted to escape her grip, but she wouldn't let him. "Hadassah, I'm old and country—" he said before she interrupted him.

"You didn't answer my question, darling," she said.

"During the week and out in the street, I really don't care, but in the church, women should not—" Vine said before being interrupted again.

"The answer to my question is no, isn't it?" she asked. "It's your preference, not a holy directive. Before you get out of this car and unleash on these women who have probably been wringing their hands with anxiety over taking care of you today, remember what we just talked about. Remember what you've learned and how you got here. Will you promise me that?"

"Yes, Hadassah," Vine said, portraying the role of a henpecked husband. When they finally exited the limo, one of the ladies stood next to Vine and the other next to Hadassah. After brief introductions, Vine learned that the ladies had been assigned as their professional assistants for the day. Kimberly, who was dark brown and plump all over, whisked Hadassah out of sight. The other woman, Donna, walked Vine to an entrance on the side of the building. While they walked, she shared the itinerary for the day. Regular service where he would sit in the pews would begin promptly at 11:00 a.m. His friend, Rev. Dr. Joseph Blair from the First Church of Peace, would deliver the installation sermon. After the offering, the installation service would begin. Once inside, she took him to a special vestment room that also served as his dressing room for the day as he was not allowed to use the pastoral office until after he was installed.

"What is all that?" Vine asked, looking at the garments that were laid out for him.

"These are your vestments for the day," Donna said. "You should wear the white robe or the alb during the morning service. Right before the installation pledge, the bishop will place the stole on the alb, and after the pledge, the board chair and your friend, Rev. Blair, will place the gold cape or the chasuble as it's called on you. You will be given the skull cap or zucchetto and then the hat or biretta by Rev. Blair to place on your head before your walk."

"My walk?" Vine asked.

"Yes," Donna answered. "Once you've taken the pledge and dressed, you are to consecrate the middle aisle as the new pastor by walking it. Do you want the shepherd's staff or crosier to carry?"

"No, this is all a little too Catholic for me," Vine said.

"Funny you should say that," Donna said. "From what I was told, the founder, Dr. Taylor, visited Rome in 1957 and attended his first Catholic mass. He was so turned on by the pageantry and vestments he brought it back to our church, redid his installation, and introduced all the garments. It's become a tradition, so yes, you are correct. It's all very Catholic. It's your decision on the crosier, but people may be offended if you break tradition."

"Well, let's use it," Vine said. He wished Hadassah could hear him demurring to tradition. She would be so pleased. "I'm sure you've heard that I'm a bit of a perfectionist and big on order, and I have to say, I am very impressed. You are truly a blessing to this ministry."

"Oh, thank you, Pastor—I mean, Pastor-elect," she said, almost giddy from his words. "I was told to keep you calm. I never knew it would be this easy. God is going to bless you like crazy. This church has a covering and anointing that is truly a blessing."

The installation service combined with the regular morning service made for a long Sunday. But for Vine, time flew by. He was extraordinarily pleased, happy, and proud. The congregation, board, ministers, and members made him feel not only welcomed but wanted and needed. This was his opportunity to begin again, doing what he was chosen to do.

A major high point of the day was when his friends trusted him to be their pastor. Bo, Jackie, Arie, Louise, Sam, Pearl, Anne, and even Ms. Francis joined GOB that Sunday to Vine's surprise. Although Hadassah could feel the pressure to support her man and his extended *mispocha*, she opted to continue on her spiritual journey as a practicing Jew. After services and the installation luncheon, the group gathered at Hadassah's for a late celebratory dinner and some much-needed wine.

"Hadassah, I'm jealous," Jackie said. "You have more room way up here on the 27th floor than I have down there in Beverly. This place is huge. It just keeps going and going."

"This is one of the oldest buildings on the Gold Coast," Hadassah explained. "This unit and the one above it on 28 have been in my family for four generations. When my great grandfather and great grandmother moved in, it was a rental. My grandmother bought it and the unit upstairs when the building went condo. She had the crazy idea to combine them into one unit, but that never panned out. My parents had them until they both died. Then it became mine. My sister and her husband live in the unit upstairs."

"You and your ex lived here?" Vine asked.

"Oh no," she answered quickly. "When I was married, I rented it out, but it's home now."

"Well, it's just beautiful," Louise said. "And Jackie was right. It just keeps going on and on."

"And with four bedrooms, you all have more than enough room when you start expanding your family," Bo joked.

"Yeah, Vine," Sam said through his near hysterical laughter, "what are you wishing for? A girl for you, and a boy for her?"

"Well, we already have a son," Hadassah said, pointing to her English bulldog, Levi. "I'm hoping for a girl."

"I'd rather walk through hell with a gasoline can in my hand," Vine said. "And besides, what would people say about a man in his late forties having a child?"

"I don't know," Hadassah said, "but when we find one, we'll be sure to ask." Vine playfully pushed Hadassah's arm while laughing himself.

"I don't know, Hadassah," Arie said. "I think you ought to do some more family research. You sounding more and more Black as the days go by. I think you got some Black in you."

"Maybe not right now, but later on tonight, she will," Vine said, giving Bo, Sam, and Arie high fives.

"See, that's just plain ole nasty," Jackie said while rolling her eyes at Bo. "Y'all are turning Vine into a dirty old man."

"And as the late Redd Foxx said, 'I'm going to be one until I'm a dead old man,'" Vine said. Laughter pushed away even the slightest hint of failure, worry, or doubt.

"Hadassah, what are you going to do with him?" Jackie teased.

"Try not to wake up your sister and brother-in-law with your moans and screams of sexual abandon and passion," Arie said. Hadassah was stunned.

"Well, honey, you are kinda loud," Vine said, not empathizing at all with her embarrassment.

"Divine!" Pearl screamed. His ease in engaging in sexual signification did not bode well with her overall prudish disposition. "I mean, really, Divine. Not even twelve hours ago, they had you adorned in gold vestments, hat, and cane. You looked like Pope John Paul II himself. Now you talking like you've never seen the inside of a church."

"Aw, sis," Vine said, "I'm just having fun. Don't be so tight. You wound out tighter than a girdle on a first lady."

"You know, Pearl, I been looking at you, and I know you been looking at me," Sam said. "Maybe I can help you loosen up a bit. You know what I mean?"

"Sam, I'd rather straddle a cactus with a fresh blossom of desert needles before getting anywhere near you," Pearl said. The sound of laughter slammed up to the ceiling and back down, filling everyone's ears.

"Y'all leave him alone," Hadassah said. "It's my fault."

"Please, how is it your fault?" Louise suspended her laugh to ask.

"I never should have given him some," Hadassah said.

"Let the good time roll, everybody," Bo said and lifted his glass. Everyone repeated his affirmation and lifted their glass in agreement.

CHAPTER 16

June 10, 2007—Broadway, New York

Earlier in the year, the fellas realized that it had been almost seven years since their Jolly-Boys trip to Vegas. One could say they were a motley crew with Bo eating everything, Arie drinking everything, Vine betting on everything, and Sam screwing everything. That trip was stressful to the point that the fellas had not attempted a trip since. So much has happened, good and not so good. Through the drama, however, the fellas have nurtured and cared for their friendship and bond. After a little debate, they decided it was time for another trip.

Discussing and deciding the destination of their trip would be a hellish task, to say the least. According to Vine, it would be easier to convince the pope to cancel Easter in Saint Peter's Square than the Jolly Boys agreeing on an acceptable destination for their next adventure, but they gave it a try. After days turned into weeks and weeks turned into months, something had to give to break the impasse. They elected to draw a name out of a hat. The person's name pulled would get the privilege to choose the destination absent of argument, debate, or fear of noncompliance. Arie won the privilege and opted for a trip to New York City for sightseeing but specifically to attend the critically acclaimed Broadway musical, *The Color Purple.* The scholarly gentleman of the bunch thought the brotherhood could use a little culture, so it was museums, tours, and the play. On the night of the show, the fellas dined at the popular B. Smith's just blocks from the theater. It was the culminating event of their trip as they were leaving the next day, Sunday, for home. Arie had endured a few days of eye rolling and loud sighing, so he was not looking forward to hearing everyone's complaints about their intellectually stimulating trip to the Big Apple, especially considering the news he had to share.

"This place is smaller than I thought it would be," Sam said, looking around the long and narrow restaurant. "I mean, B. Smith is the Black Martha Stewart. I thought it would be huge and at least two stories."

"It's New York," Arie said. "Everything is small and narrow especially in the TD—theater district. You'll get large and wide in California. But the food, the actual purpose of the establishment, is delicious. Her greens are almost better than Ms. Francis'."

"Hush your mouth, blasphemer," Vine said in the voice of a televangelist. "Lose here, Satan. Lose here."

"You are sick. Just plain sick," Chiv said.

After a few minutes of waiting in the foyer, the hostess escorted the men to their table, smack dab in the center of the restaurant. Immediately, a tall, dark, and lanky waiter began walking in their direction. Arie held up his hand, deterring the young waiter from approaching. Bo was the only one who noticed but dismissed the gesture. He knew it would eventually come out in the wash.

"You know, I rolled my eyes when we pulled your name, Arie," Sam said, "because I knew you'd have us doing something intellectual or educational, but this has been a great trip."

"Say what?" Arie leaned into the circle. "Was that a compliment?"

"Yes, it was," Sam said. "Don't get used to them."

"Well, I guess I have one too," Vine said. "I'm not a big museum person, but something about that Guggenheim. I actually gave a damn and read every description I came across. And the architecture was unbelievable. I'm going to build a church from the ground up one day. It's gonna look just like the Guggenheim. Now Ground Zero, that was a different story. I thought I would be able to handle it, but walking on the grounds felt like I was disturbing a crime scene or walking on headstones in the cemetery."

"Makes you think, don't it?" Bo said. "Makes you appreciate life."

"It sure does," Vine said. "So, Arie, good job, man."

"Thanks, and about the Arie business, you can go back to calling me Chivas," he said. All mouths fell open, and all eyes focused on Chiv's lips, waiting to hear confirmation of what they've suspected all along. "So I know you'll be disappointed, hell, I'm disappointed my damn self. I've started drinking again."

"Aw, naw, man, come on," Sam said. "I thought you had this beat. What the hell happened?"

"I don't know," Chiv said. "I started giving up. And I thought I was tricking myself with a glass of wine here and a beer there but eventually ended up right where I started: ice, ginger ale, and Chivas Regal. Ever since I proposed to Louise, I've been thinking about Catherine and the boys more and more. It hit me harder than hard one night, and I fell off the wagon. I'm seeing my old therapist when we get back. I know the signs of depression, and that's where I'm headed."

"Does Louise know?" Vine said.

"Oh no," Chiv said. "She'd take that ring off and throw it right in my face. No, I'm hoping to get this back under control without her having a clue. So don't tell Jackie, Pearl, Anne, or Ms. Francis. I don't need that pressure."

"We got you, man," Bo said. "Maybe take some time and get it out of your system for real. You'll lick it on the next try."

"Have you been talking to your sponsor and going to the AA meetings?" Vine asked.

"Well, not really," Chiv said. "Admitting I'm an alcoholic every time I want to speak ain't my idea of support or therapy. I just need a break—some relief."

"You know, I don't condone you drinking and should really kick your ass for starting up again, but I don't think I've ever seen you torn-down drunk," Sam said. The fellas all tilted their heads and squinted their eyes, searching their memories for an example.

"That's because I don't act an ass when I'm a little inebriated," Chiv said. "I get mellow and quiet. Most people don't even know I'm drunk when I'm drunk. I think that's why I've been able to talk myself out of so many traffic tickets."

"Aw, hell," Bo said. "This is sounding worse and worse the more you talk. My granddaddy used to say, 'Fool, don't be no fool. You can't get behind the wheel of a car, and you ain't got your shit together. You'll kill yourself and someone else who ain't even done nothing to you.'"

"I had an uncle who used to claim that he actually drove better when he was drunk," Sam said.

"Uh, Negro, you ain't helping me here," Bo said. "Promise me, promise us that before you get behind the wheel drunk, mellow or otherwise, you call one of us to come and get you."

"Fine," Chiv said. "I have the same agreement with my sponsor."

"Good," Vine said. "Have you and Louise picked a date yet? You better pick one before she changes her mind."

"Naw, not really," Chiv said. "It will be in 2008, next year, is all we know. She don't want to live in my house, and you couldn't pay me to live in her neighborhood. We're trying to save our money for a down payment for our new house."

"Have you spent all the money from the settlement?" Bo asked. "Hell, by my calculations, you should be able to pay cash for a nice crib right now in Beverly. We're in Beverly now, but we're at the bottom of the hill. I want that crib right next door to where the president of Chicago State University lives. It's been vacant for a minute. No one can afford it."

"Oh, Louise doesn't know about that money," Chiv said. "That's all mine, and I ain't sharing. That's my pain-and-suffering money. Now I'll give some toward the cause, but that's not for sharing, if you know what I mean." Everyone nodded in agreement with Chiv's reasoning. Finally, they were truly on one accord. "Just like every woman has money hidden in her secret panty drawer, every man has money hidden out in the garage somewhere. My stash happens to be in a safety deposit box at Chase Manhattan."

"Man, 2008 is gonna be a hell of a year," Bo said, rubbing his hands together. "I'm retiring, Chivas is getting married, and it's an election year."

"Who cares about an election?" Sam said. "I don't even vote no more. White folks, Democrats, nor Republicans get support from me. The White man is going to continue doing what he always does: he comes around at election time, shakes some hands, kisses some babies, and then it's off to Washington to forget all about us." The waiter was successful approaching on his second try. Chiv ordered Chivas and ginger ale for everyone at the table and an appetizer: fried green tomatoes and low-country caviar—mashed black-eyed peas and wedge toast.

"Naw, I think the times are changing and changing in our favor," Vine said. "Have y'all checked out the Black dude that's running, Broderick Bombanyan or something like that?"

"You mean Barack Obama," Bo said.

"Yeah, him," Vine said. "He's running, and folks are saying he's a serious candidate. Jesse tried, but we all knew and he knew, too, that he wasn't gonna win. It was for principle. This dude is serious. We could have a Black president one day. Wouldn't that be something? White folks would be mad as hell."

"That will never happen," Sam said. "The racist White folks of this country will never elect a woman, Black man, Mexican, gay, or Jew to be commander in chief. It's just not gonna happen. And we ain't ready for that, no way."

"I'm doing a lot of cussing today," Bo said. "Don't even start that shit. I am so tired of Black folks saying we're not ready for this; we ain't ready for that. We are ready for anything we want to be ready for. If every Black person went to the polls and voted for Obama, we could have a Black president. It's up to us, not him."

"And he is clean as a whistle," Vine said. "They can't find nothing on him. No baby mamas, no divorce, no sex tapes, no drugs, no chicks on the side, no dudes on the side—nothing but a pack of cigarettes. And he's Harvard-educated, an attorney, and so is his wife. They have two daughters who are smart and well-behaved. If we have any chance, it's with him. Jesse and Al aren't the great Black hope anymore. It's Obama."

"When I say we ain't ready, I'm talking about America, not Black people," Sam said. "If he takes the oath in January, he'd be dead by Valentine's Day. These White folks will kill him."

"So we shouldn't change the course of history and elect our first Black president because someone will kill him?" Chiv posed. "That's an excuse, and it's ridiculous. I'm going to influence history. I'm voting for him."

"And I didn't realize how dumb Donald Trump was," Bo said. "This idiot says that the man is not a US citizen. He questions the legitimacy of his birth certificate. I guess if you're Black and born in Hawaii, we should question your citizenship."

"See what I mean?" Sam said. "Folks are already acting an ass. Obama might be good for history, but not for our safety."

The waiter came back and took their meal orders. Modest and safe dialogue was in play. Leave it up to Vine to shake things up especially after a drink or two.

"So, Sam," Vine said after swallowing another bite of his meal, "dare I ask about Nevaeh. Y'all still seeing each other?"

"Aw, man, it's complicated," Sam said. "I don't think I even want to talk about it."

"You don't think you want to talk about it?" Chiv repeated. "What the hell does that mean? For more than five years, you been talking about it. Why you closing us out now?"

"Like I said, it's complicated," Sam said.

"When was the last time y'all saw each other for the riga marrow?" Vine asked.

"Well, I saw her last week, but there was no riga marrow," Sam said. "We haven't slept together in about a year."

Chiv nearly choked from both shock and having a mouth full of collard greens. "Say what now?" Chiv said. "Sam Ladeaux ain't had sex in about a year? You must be tarrying for the Holy Ghost. Vine, open the doors of the church."

"Oh no, my brother," Sam said. "I'm not built likc that. I gotta have some, as Vine says, riga marrow at least once a week, or I start turning into a different person."

"Let me get this straight: you cheating on your wife and your girlfriend," Vine said. "Lawd, touch, heal, and deliver. Who is this side piece? I bet it's Lola."

"Now why would you say that?" Sam said, suppressing his initial thought of 'How did you know?' "That's Marsaleen's best friend."

"'Cause I went out with Lola a few times, and she is easy as Crisco in a hot skillet," Vine said. "Let's just say, I've cooked in the pot before." Sam knew he'd have to temper his anger, or he'd give himself away. The thought of Vine and Sam "being with" the same woman managed to spoil Sam's appetite.

"Never mind all that," Sam said. "I think Nevaeh is hiding something from me."

"This will be good," Vine said. "Why you say that, Sam?"

"I was talking to someone about the situation, and she suggested that I not announce my next visit," Sam said. "I should just show up. It was sort of a test. If she was happy to see me, we'd be good. If she was pissed, something was wrong. And she was pissed. She came to the door in her robe, hair all over her head, and carrying a few extra pounds, I might add. I like 'em thick, but ole girl went from a 14 to 18 overnight. And was babysitting some kid, her nephew or something." The fellas squinted and looked at one another in disbelief. "She said that this, our relationship, wasn't working out and that maybe we should just put us on ice for a while. She was taking some time off to help raise her nephew. She was tired and broke and not in the mood to entertain or bed another woman's husband. I think she's trying to break up with me."

"You are a very handsome man, attractive even, but you dumb as hell," Vine said. "The woman tells you she's putting your relationship on ice, and you think she's trying to break up with you?"

"Yeah, I do," Sam said.

"Don't think it, Sam. Know it," Vine said. "She has broken up with you. She just forgot to tell you."

"Naw, she's just been busy with her nephew," Sam said. Bo shook his head, Vine dropped his head, and Chiv scratched his head. "What?"

"I'm a trained educator," Chiv said. "Let me see if I can help you. Hopefully, that old saying of 'when the student is ready, the teacher shows up' rings true here. You haven't had sex with Nevaeh for about a year. You went about six months without seeing her. She's not working, has gained weight, and taking care of a kid. What's the sum of this equation, Sam?"

"She has a lot on her plate?" Sam asked in earnest.

"And you got nothing on yours," Vine said. "The girl had a baby, fool, and it's probably yours."

"Aw, naw," Sam said. "She can't have kids."

"Did you see her medical records?" Bo asked. "Oh, I forgot. She had her tubes tied and burned."

"She told me," Sam said. "Who would lie about something like that? There are millions of women who want kids and can't have them. Women are touchy about stuff like that. She's taking care of her nephew."

"God, I feel like I'm talking to Rose Nylund on the *Golden Girls*," Vine said. "She's cranky and gained weight. Does that sound like a day in the life of a stripper?"

"I'm not going to keep correcting y'all," Sam said. "She's a dancer."

"She's a whore," Vine said.

"Okay, let me see if I can help Sam land this plane," Bo said. "The last time y'all did the riga marrow, did you use a condom?"

"Well, yes and no," Sam said.

"Oh, I can't take this no more," Vine said before slamming his fork onto the plate.

"Well, I ain't no one-hit wonder," Sam said. "We used a condom the first couple times but didn't for the rest of the trip. We kept getting caught up, and when a woman like Nevaeh is lying next to you, describing all the things she wants you to do to her, there isn't time to reach in the nightstand drawer." Sam's eyes widened. It was like he was focusing on some object off in the distance. His mouth opened in the very shock of his own thoughts.

"Bo, I think you did it," Vine said. "We are wheels down. Looks like the dummy plane is making its landing."

"Oh my God," Sam said. "That wasn't her nephew. That was my son. Oh my damn, y'all. No, nope, that couldn't be. She wouldn't hide something like that from me. She knows that I would leave

Marsaleen in a second. Why wouldn't she tell me?" Sam suddenly turned from dumbfounded to emotional.

"Okay, calm down," Chiv said. "Sip on your drink. Let your brain catch up. We don't know this for sure, and we don't know if it is yours. I think you need to make another surprise trip to Vegas, but only after the report comes in."

"What report?" Sam asked.

"The report of the private investigator I'm gonna hire for you," Chiv said. "My daddy used to say never ask a woman a question you don't already know the answer to. The next time you talk to dancer Nevaeh, you're going to know the answers to the questions before you ask. In the meantime, play it easy and chilly. Send her a little extra than you sending now. Be nice and kind, and then we'll see."

"What you gonna do, Sam?" Vine asked. "What if that is your baby? What you gonna do?"

"I'm gonna marry her and take care of her," Sam said. "I will divorce my wife and marry Nevaeh and take care of my son." Vine caught the attention of four Black ladies seated two tables down. He looked at his watch and then walked over to the table.

"Good evening, ladies," Vine said. "Have you ladies seen *The Color Purple* yet?"

The butch-looking woman spoke for the group. "No, we haven't," she said. "We took in a show last night and the night before that. Theater tickets are too expensive to see three Broadway shows in three days. Why do you ask?"

"I have four tickets to *The Color Purple,* which is starting in fifteen minutes," Vine said. "My friend over there has just realized that he's in more trouble than he thought. We're gonna grab a bottle and some cups and head over to Central Park and help him figure it out. Would you like our tickets?"

Without a moment's hesitation, the fellas surrendered their tickets to the ladies, who were nearly ecstatic. After a plethora of thank-yous and cautiously tight hugs, the ladies whisked out of the restaurant to get to the theater before showtime. The fellas stopped at a liquor store; got a brand-new bottle of Chivas Regal, cups, and ice;

and headed to Central Park by taxi. They didn't get ginger ale. This was going to be a straight, no-chaser night to remember.

After the Central Park meeting, the fella went back to their hotel rooms, spending the last night of their trip alone and under the ponderous influence of Mr. Regal. The travel and scheduling gods must have been working in their favor when they booked the trip. Their flight was scheduled to leave New York at four in the afternoon. They met for breakfast early and went back to their rooms to nap before checking out at 1:00 p.m. Separately, they were concerned about their individual plights, but the plight of their friend was top of mind. Chiv felt good that he had an approach for Sam. He wished he or someone else had an approach for him.

On Monday during an extended break in his day, Chiv contacted his buddy Jerry, who was a private detective. They talked, and Jerry was excited to get started on the Nevaeh Jean Miller case. It came with a price tag of a thousand dollars a day plus expenses, but it was a small price to pay to ensure order and a peace of mind for his brother Sam. He would be sure to lie about the price when discussing it with Sam. There was no need for Jolly-Boy pride to get in the way of bringing resolution to a seemingly unresolvable situation.

When Chiv made it home that night, Louise was not there. A brief moment of concern was quickly felt when he recalled her Monday-night card party with some of the teachers. A small group of teachers agreed to meet on Monday nights during the summer break for cards and conversation. They chose Monday night because there was really nothing else for an educator to do on Monday nights during the summer break but play cards. Chiv deduced that he had about 3.5 hours to himself. In that time, he could have a couple of drinks, gargle, and be asleep before Louise got home, hiding his addiction yet another day.

Chiv had the object of his addiction hidden in several spots throughout the house. They were small pint-size bottles, good for easy access and greater "hidability." Feeling safe and free, he went to his favorite place, the garage behind the snowblower, for the nearly full bottle. He brought it into the house and sat it on the counter. Normally, he'd drink out of a coffee mug to give the illusion of sobriety, but tonight, having quality alone time, he retrieved his favorite Waterford Crystal highball glass and filled it with ice. He covered the ice with the brown liquor and shook it in his hand. The clinking sound of ice swimming in deliciousness and slamming against the expensive crystal made him smile. He took a long quenching sip and then sat it on the counter. In that moment, he felt as if he had just committed a crime. Something wasn't right. No one should feel guilt when doing something they enjoyed and to their highest good. He called his sponsor, Eric.

"Hey, Eric, it's Arie," Chiv whispered. "I'm at home alone. I poured a drink, took a long gulp, and sat it down. I'm standing here now resisting the urge to take another sip."

"Why are you going to do that, Arie?" Eric asked.

"Because I'm an alcoholic and alcoholics drink alcohol," Chiv said.

"But you are an alcoholic who understands that you have an addiction and no addiction is good for you," Eric said. "Where are you?"

"I'm at home," Chiv said. "But I don't want you to come here. I just need you to talk me out of taking another sip."

"So you have taken a sip already?" Eric asked.

"Yes," Chiv replied.

"How did it taste?" Eric asked.

"Good," Chiv said.

"What would happen if you poured the rest down the sink?" Eric asked. "Would you feel better or worse than you feel right now?"

"I would feel worse but eventually better because I did the right thing," Chiv said.

"So I want you to go to the sink and pour out that drink," Eric said. "Listen to the sound of it going down the drain. Imagine that it's taking your addiction with it." Chiv took a deep breath and did as Eric had instructed. "How do you feel?"

"Disappointed because I really wanted to finish that drink," Chiv said.

"How do you think you'll feel when Louise comes home?" Eric asked.

"Okay, at ease, glad that I didn't get caught," Chiv said. "I'd feel good that I didn't have to hide or lie or make up stories."

"Wouldn't it be great to feel that way more often than not?" Eric asked.

"Of course, it would," Chiv said.

"So let's see if we can do that tomorrow too, and before you know it, you'll be living every day like today. But it starts with today," Eric said. "Can I get you to commit to tomorrow?"

"Yes, thanks, Eric," Chiv said. "I can do this."

"Good," Eric said. "Call me later, okay? And come to the meeting tomorrow."

"Okay," Chiv said. With a big smile of accomplishment on his face, Chiv poured out the rest of the bottle and threw it in the kitchen garbage. He undressed, took a shower, and made his way to his favorite chair in the television room. Before he knew it, Louise was walking through the garage door.

"Hey, baby," Chiv said as Louise walked toward him. "How was spades? How many times did you renege?"

"Hey, you," she said, ignoring his jab, bending over to kiss him. As she approached, he silently prayed that he had gargled well enough to mask the smell of alcohol on his breath. "How was your day today?"

"Good," he said. "Made a few phone calls and took care of some business. Got a call from the president. He wants me to act as summer principal for the network. I told him yes. It's an extra ten grand a month. We can use that for the wedding."

"Oh, wow, we can," Louise said through the sound of running water at the sink. "But you lose your summer."

"It's only half days, four days a week," he said. "It's worth 30k, don't you think? With that kind of money, we can have a great wedding and even a better honeymoon."

"From what I can tell, there probably won't be a wedding," she said.

"What?" he said and jerked his body around to look at her in the kitchen. "You want to go to city hall?"

"No, I want to know why you lied to me." she said. By the time he was able to focus, Louise was standing in front of him with an empty Chivas Regal bottle in her hand. "And before you lie, I smelled liquor on your breath. I didn't say anything, thinking it may have been the smell of liquor on my breath, but I didn't drink nothing tonight. It was you. You are drinking again."

"Okay, come sit down and let me explain," he said. His disposition was calm and cool. Surely all would be fine after he explained his temptation and breakthrough. Louise came and sat at a distance from him with the empty bottle in her hand. "So earlier, I found this bottle I had stashed away, and I was going to have a nice stiff drink just like old times. I got the glass and ice, poured to the rim, took one sip, and then stopped. I called Eric. He made me stop, and I poured the rest down the sink and threw the bottle in the garbage. That's why that bottle is in the garbage."

Louise got up and went to the garbage can. She opened it and retrieved the empty bottle. She resumed her seat across from him, now with two empty bottles in her hands. "Okay, that's the lie or alibi for this empty bottle in the garbage," she said, sitting it on the cocktail table. "What's the lie or alibi for this nearly empty pint bottle you had hidden behind the seasonings?"

"What?" Chiv said. He wanted to hear her ask the question again. It would give him time to come up with an alibi for the bottle he hid earlier this week. "What are you talking about?"

"I teach children. I'm not one," Louise said. "I just looked in the cabinet to see if my favorite tea was in stock, and on the seasoning shelf, I saw the top of the bottle. This is it. Why is there a nearly empty pint of Chivas Regal in the home of someone who is not drinking? You've been lying to me, Arie."

"Baby, that bottle has been there for months," he said.

"Do better, baby," Louise said. "That bottle has not been there for months, and you and I know it. Can you tell me the truth? You've been drinking."

"Okay, okay," he said, holding up his palms as if her words were attacking him like balls of snow in a snowball fight. "I did fall off the wagon, but I'm back on now. I only had a sip, and I poured out the rest."

"A sip, a fifth, a pint!" Louise yelled. "You are drinking again. I told you I would not be married to an alcoholic. Do you love alcohol that much? You've got to decide. It's me or Chivas Regal. I can't believe you. You are a sorry excuse of a man." The hairs on the back of his head rose. Louise was coming very close to crossing the line. "For years, I was competing against a dead woman and her children. Now I'm competing with this?" Chiv counted a second below-the-belt blow from Louise. She had one more to go. "It's all a bunch of weak-ass excuses. You've been hanging around Vine too much. You starting to act like a punk. Just like him." Before he knew it, his right hand was in the air, ready to strike his fiancée. Her scream halted his actions. "You were gonna hit me? You were going to slap me? Really, Arie?" Louise ran out of the television room into the adjoining kitchen. Chiv was right on her heels.

"Baby, baby, I'm sorry," he said. "I don't know what…" He paused. He was about to lie again. Instead, he opted for the truth. "Wait, wait, I'm not sorry. I'm not sorry because I didn't do anything. How dare you disrespect me by disparaging my wife and children like that? Don't you ever say another negative thing about my wife and kids again. Yes, I've been drinking. I've been drinking because I can't shake the pain of losing the three people in the world that I loved more than life itself. But I'm dealing with it. It's hard. Drinking makes the pain go away. So you can be mad at me for failing and you can be mad at me for lying, but don't you ever let another contemptuous word against my dead wife and children leave your mouth because if you do, you give me license to knock the ever-loving shit out of you." Chiv snatched one of the bottles out of her hand and threw it against the wall. He left the kitchen and reappeared with his wallet, phone, and car keys in hand and was headed for the garage door.

"Arie Eubanks, don't you dare walk out on me!" she screamed. "You threaten me and then draw your hand back to hit me and then you gonna walk out? Don't you dare. I don't think I can marry you."

"I don't think you can either," he said and slammed the door.

He was seething, banging his fist on the steering wheel at times during his ride to Vine's house. By the time he appeared on Vine's doorstep, his face was soaking wet with tears.

Vine opened the door. His eyes widened with shock. "Chivas, what the hell is wrong with you?" Vine said. "What happened?"

"Why did he do it?" he said with tears dripping from his face. "How could God take them from me? Didn't he know I wouldn't be able to take this? Didn't he know I would never be able to get over this? What have I done so wrong in my life to make God hate me so? Vine, help me understand?"

Vine wiped his own eyes and pulled his friend inside. He held him and rocked him and just let him be. When Chiv's legs started giving out, they both spiraled to the cold marble foyer floor. Vine's strong and protective arms never disconnected from Chiv. On the floor, Chiv laid his head on Vine's chest and cried. At one point, he screamed out, which sped up the flow of Vine's tears.

"That's it, man," Vine said, rocking his friend to comfort. "Cry out. Cry out."

"Lord, help me," Chiv cried aloud. "Help me, Lord, please." Vine could feel the years and years of hurt and anguish shake through Chiv's body. He needed the comfort only God could give.

"'I cried unto God with my voice, even unto God with my voice, and he gave ear unto me,'" Vine said, reciting verses from the 77th Psalms. "'In the day of my trouble, I sought the Lord. My sore ran in the night and ceased not. My soul refused to be comforted. I remembered God and was troubled. I complained, and my spirit was overwhelmed. Thou holds mine eyes waking. I am so troubled that I cannot speak. Will the Lord cast off forever? Will he be favorable no more? Is his mercy gone forever? Does his promise fail for evermore? Hath God forgotten to be gracious? Hath he in anger shut up his tender mercies? And I said, this is my infirmity but thou art the God that does wonders. Thou has declared thy strength among the people. The clouds poured out water. The skies sent out a sound. Thine arrows also went abroad. Thou leads thy people like a flock by the hand of Moses and Aaron. That they might set their hope in God and not forget the works of God but keep his commandments."

When Chiv calmed down, Vine stood him up. He grabbed his face with both hands and looked straight into his eyes. "You are a unique, unrepeatable expression of God. God is not depressed, anxious, despondent, heartbroken, or dismayed. He's not an abuser, alcoholic, or addicted to anything. This means that you cannot be these things. You are not these things, Arie. You are not these things." He walked him to the guest room and put him into bed. Vine sat with him.

The next morning when Vine woke, he was in his room in his bed with Chiv right next him. Someone on the outside looking in might appraise this as strange, unnatural, even sexually suspicious. In reality and truth, it was pure friendship and care from brother to brother. Vine made it to the kitchen to make a pot of coffee and a quick breakfast. While cooking, he called Bo.

"Hey, man, what you doing later?" Vine asked.

"Nothing really. What's the matter?" Bo asked.

"Man, Chiv showed up at my house last night a mess," Vine said. "From what I'm piecing together, Louise found out that he's been drinking and confronted him. Also sounds like she said some other foul shit in the process, which he didn't appreciate. They had a fight, and he left. He stayed here last night."

"Damn, he walked out of his own house?" Bo said. "He must have really been pissed. How is he this morning?"

"He hasn't gotten up yet," Vine said. "I'm cooking a quick breakfast, then I'll get him up. He's got to go to work, too, unless he's taking the day off. I'm just calling because I might need you to tag in. I mean, he was so bad last night he was boo-hoo crying. I think this alcoholism is just about over. I think he's sick and tired of being sick and tired."

"Naw, the drinking ain't going nowhere until he's done with Catherine's death," Bo said. "He was so excited to be done with the situation he left prematurely, and now he's right back there. We've got to get him to go back to therapy and this time, stay there until he gets better."

"I was thinking inpatient rehab," Vine whispered. "but he'd never agree to that."

"No, he won't, and that's not the root cause of the problem," Bo said. "He's got to get to the point where he misses Catherine and his boys, but he doesn't blame himself or God for that accident. Rehab ain't gonna help that. He's gonna have a nervous breakdown."

"The hell, he will," Vine said. "Not on my watch. We can't fix this, but God can."

"Well, I'll be over there after work," Bo said. "We gonna give the Lord some help."

"Well, you stopping home first, ain't you?" Vine asked.

"No, I'm not bringing Jackie," Bo said. "Chiv ain't gonna want to see no women tonight."

"No, I mean you stopping at your house to take a shower," Vine said. "I'm still airing out my crib from the last time you came over here right after work."

"If I didn't think God would send me to hell for calling a preacher an asshole, that's what I'd call you," Bo said.

"Touch not my anointed," Vine said.

"Negro, you ain't even appointed," Bo said, adding some levity to a heavy situation. "I'll be there around seven."

"Cool. See you then," Vine said. "Call Sam."

"Aw, shit, what is this?" Bo said. "Buy one Negro with issues, get another one free?" Vine dropped the phone laughing at Bo's quip, which brought Chiv to his feet.

"Hey, I'm back," Vine said. "Look, gotta go. Chiv is up."

"Who was that, Bo or Sam?" Chiv asked, slow-walking to the coffeepot.

"Bo," Vine said. "He's calling Sam."

"So what time is the intervention?" Chiv asked.

"Around seven," Vine said. "You know we got you, man. One of us go through it, we all go through it."

"Well, I can tell you now, that woman makes another smart-ass comment about my family, and I'm going to jail," Chiv said. "How could she be so cold and low-down?"

"I think she may have been hurt and disappointed," Vine said.

"No, she won't be satisfied until I tell her that I'm over Catherine and the boys and ready to focus on only her," Chiv said. "I can't see that happening for a long time. Louise cannot be my wife if she's gonna be so damn common."

"Don't start speaking in absolutes until you've had time to talk to Louise," Vine said. "Who knows? When you talk to her later, she may have replayed her words and now sorry for what she said."

"Oh, I'm not talking to Louise later today, tomorrow, or the next day," Chiv said. "If I go back to that house, my house, I might get arrested. No, I'm staying right here. I'm going out to the mall and buy a week's worth of clothes, and I'm staying right here, if that's all right, of course."

"Stay as long as you like," Vine said. "But stay in your own bed. What if I thought you were Hadassah in the middle of the night? You could be pregnant right now."

"You are stupid as hell," Chiv said. "But we may as well get used to it. If Sam finds out we slept together, we might have to stuff tube socks in his mouth to get his to shut up."

As arranged and scheduled, by 7:00 p.m., the fellas were assembled at Vine's for an Arie intervention. But first, Sam.

"Wait, wait," Sam said. "You two in love now?" Vine slipped and mentioned that Chiv woke up in his bed, and that's all Sam needed. He's been on a comedic roll ever since. "I always wanted a gay friend. Now I have two."

"Shut up, Sam," Chiv said. "Ignorant ass. What kind of friend are you, laughing at my pain?"

"I'm sorry, I'm sorry," Sam said, holding his stomach as if it were aching from laughter. "I just wish I could have seen Vine's face when he looked over and saw your old crusty ass lying next to him. Hold me, baby. Drive me crazy. Touch me all night long."

"Bo, you got your gun?" Chiv asked. "Shoot this bastard."

"Okay, okay, I just have one more question and then I'm done," Sam said on his knees, laughing. Bo, Vine, and Chiv couldn't help but laugh themselves. "Vine, when Chiv was giving it to you really good, did you call him Arie or Chiv?"

"Mr. Eubanks, ass hat," Vine said, and the entire house erupted with laughter. It was the Jolly-Boys approach to just about all issues—laughter. In reality, they really didn't know what to do with pain but laugh. "We'll see if you're laughing Sunday when I make a big announcement."

"Vine, please," Bo said, holding up his palms. "Our plates are full already with these two. I don't think I can take you getting fired from another church, not right now."

"God is taking me in a new direction," Vine said. "You'll see. I just need your support."

"Of course," Sam said. "Man, I'm just messing with you. You know we got you. We got one another. But, Chiv, you need to go back to your house and check Louise for what she said. That was foul. And you know, I thought about this driving over here. Ask her what she's going to do to help you heal. Why does healing from this have to be all on you? If she loves you, she should want you to be mentally healthy. Why is she sitting on the sidelines watching you come apart? That ain't cool. She loses big points for that shit."

"Bingo," Bo said. "Sam, you hit the nail on the head. Chiv, you need to go back in therapy, and she should go with you. That's the ultimatum to be stated. Go with me to therapy or go away."

"But these are issues that I personally have to unpack," Chiv said. "How is family therapy going to help?"

"It's a visible gesture that you don't have to go through it by yourself," Bo said. "If a woman is really by your side, your best friend, your ride-or-die, she will use every resource, spend every dollar, give up her own happiness for her man. You will be able to tell a lot about Louise on how she handles this. Watch and see."

CHAPTER 17

Sunday, June 18, 2007

Even Chiv was surprised that he was in his seat, ready for Sunday morning service a whole half an hour before church was to start. It had been a long week full of worry, inquiry, and scenario planning. He was happy to be in the haven of rest if only for two short hours. Chiv ended up staying with Vine until Saturday when he finally went home to Louise. Although he followed Vine's directive and stayed in his own assigned bed, the two spent their evenings talking and coming to grips with the things that were top of mind in their individual and collective worlds. Chiv spoke to Louise every day and assured her he'd be home soon. He just needed some time alone with his thoughts and the comfort and nonconfrontational ethos of a strong and loving friendship. Louise apologized, admitting that she was foul and over the line with her comments about his deceased wife and kids. She asked for his forgiveness, which he gave without trepidation. She even agreed to join him in counseling. She passed the trust, love, and devotion test created by Bo himself with flying colors.

As Chiv sat, watched, and listened to all the preshow activities, his eyes fell on Eric Rockrose, his sponsor. Eric was ushered to the front row. Usually dignitaries and other key visitors sat up front. Why was Eric at his church, and why was he being treated as a dignitary? He'd soon find out. At 11:00 a.m. on the dot, Chiv heard the organ prelude and Vine's voice booming through the new arena-worthy sound system. "The Lord is in His holy temple. Let all the earth keep silent before him." As the choir chanted the opening prayer, Vine made his way down the center aisle and to the pulpit. His best friend was adorned in a brilliant white-and-purple robe that was hemmed perfectly to not dust the floor or show the cuff of his pants. He studied his friend's face. If he didn't know better, he would swear that Vine looked tentative and somewhat brittle. He remembered Vine's mention of a "Sunday to remember." Maybe that was the cause of his uneasiness, which was written all over his face. After the giving, praying, singing, and shouting, it was time for preaching. Vine stood at the podium microphone, fanned out his materials and hesitated, bowing his head in silent prayer. He lifted his head, opened his eyes, smiled, and began speaking.

"Good morning, all," he greeted the congregation, which was at capacity and was unusual for a third Sunday. "It's good to be here and to be with you. I have something exciting I want to talk about today, but before the lesson, I'd like to introduce you to brother Eric Rockrose. Come on up, Eric. Eric was the minister of music at Shining Star. I treated him very badly and said some things I shouldn't have said, but that was a long time ago. Time brings about a change, and change signals growth. And grow we must. I've asked Eric to join the Grand Ole Baptist family as our first director of diversity and inclusion. Jesus had a fundamental purpose in coming to earth, and that was to show us the way. To illustrate and model how to live as a spiritual being in a mortal world and be governed by spiritual principles. Jesus never pushed anyone away or rejected anyone. Only the thieves in the temple who depraved the house of prayer by selling their goods and wares. Jesus pulled in and accepted everyone from the servants to the sick and from the sinful to the saved. I think the church should do the same thing. We are going to be a church that embraces diversity and inclusion. The church, particularly the Baptist church, is quick to dismiss and disenfranchise difference. That's not Christ-like. We are going to let our Christian light shine that the entire city, state, even the world may see us following the example of Jesus. Eric's job will be to develop programs to attract and retain people from underrepresented demographics into the church. Whether you're White or Hispanic, upper class or lower class, young or old, gay or straight, GOB is a haven of rest for you. Amen? That sure was a weak Amen. I said Amen, church." The subsequent response was just as weak as the first, but Vine kept going.

"As an openly gay Black man, Eric knows all too well how your soul feels rejected by the so-called body of Christ. Not here. Not no more. We are followers of Christ, and as such, we embrace and appreciate difference. That's what Jesus would do. That's what we're going to do." As Chiv sat and listened, he was proud of his friend's courage in this regard, but from the mumblings of the congregants behind him and beside him, he knew Vine was in trouble.

"Girl, I don't know about this," a woman said to another in the pew in front of his. "We already have an unmarried pastor bedding a White Jew. Now we're going to have a bunch of sissies running around here smacking and voguing. Next thing you know, we'll have cross-dressers sashaying through here. I can't raise my boys in a gay church." Chiv was tempted to rebuke their gossip but decided against it. Change was hard for some people especially for church folks. He had to trust that his friend knew what he was doing and that these two busybodies would soon come around.

"Come on, GOB. Let's give brother Rockrose a welcoming round of applause," Vine said. "May God bless you, Eric, for answering the call." Every eye was on Eric, silently praying that he didn't display any feminine mannerisms. Chiv was secretly hoping Eric would smack his lips or bat his eyes or walk with a switch just to keep it interesting, but he didn't, defying the stereotype. Chiv was proud of his sponsor and even more proud of his best friend.

"Today and for the next six Sundays, I will be preaching a series of sermons entitled 'And Then Jesus Said,'" Vine announced. "Not Peter, Paul, or Mary, but Jesus. Now don't get me wrong. The Bible and all its contributors and characters are important, but what's most important is what Jesus said. The stuff that's in red writing in your Bible, that's what we're going to talk about during these six weeks. And Sister Mildred, you aren't going to be in that wheelchair long. The Lord told me to tell you that by the end of this series, you will be running around this church thanking and praising God because he said, 'Take up your bed and walk.' There is power in the words of the way-shower church. Power to do exceedingly and above anything we could ever ask. That's why this diversity and inclusion ministry is so important because he said, 'Come unto me all you that labor and are heavy laden, and I will give you rest.' That's why we can't walk around with hate and malice against our brothers and sisters for what they've done to us. He said, 'Forgive,' so we must forgive. Oh, it's gonna be a good series. I wouldn't miss it if I were you."

Vine went on to preach a dynamic sermon on inclusion that worked the congregation up to a crescendo of praise and worship. When the doors of the church opened, fourteen people including Eric joined. Vine was right. Diversity and inclusion is important to ministry. Chiv just hoped other people got it as well.

After the service, Chiv made his way to Eric to personally welcome him to GOB. As Chiv approached Eric, he lit up with excitement. "Oh my God," Eric said, opening his arms to embrace Chiv. "What are you doing here? Don't tell me this is your church?"

"It sure is," Chiv said. "I joined when my best friend became the pastor."

"That's what's up," Eric said. "You know, when he insulted me from the pulpit a few years ago, I thought I'd never see him again. Now I'm back in his employ leading a brand-new ministry. I know I have your support."

"Oh, I ain't gay," Chiv said.

"I know that," Eric said. "Us gays can spot a family member from across a football field. I meant with other inclusion efforts like young people and people with disabilities and from other ethnicities. Diversity and inclusion is more than LGBT."

"Oh, I guess," Chiv said. "This is radical for the old and the Baptist. Put your seat belt on. This road is going to be bumpy as hell—I mean *heck*."

"No, you were right the first time," Eric said. "Believe me. I know. So Reverend Oliver is your best friend?"

"That's correct," Chiv said. "What's the matter, Mr. diversity and inclusion? A minister can't have a friend who is an alcoholic?"

"No, no," Eric said. That was exactly what he was thinking, but he pivoted quickly. "I'm just thinking how small the world is. It seems the older I get, the degrees of separation get smaller and smaller. How are you doing otherwise?"

"It's been a bumpy week, but I'm not drinking," Chiv said. "And my fiancée has agreed to join me in counseling. I really have no complaints."

"All things work together for the good of them who love the Lord," Eric said. "Well, I gotta go. I have a date." Chiv reacted as if he was startled. "Are you reacting to me having a date on a Sunday or having a date period?"

"I don't know why I'm reacting to tell you the truth," Chiv said.

"Well, you'll run right out of here when I tell you that my date is with my partner and my daughter and four of her friends. We're going to Chuck E. Cheese."

"You have a daughter?" Chiv asked. "She must be adopted."

"No, when I was married, my wife and I had a child," Eric said. "Maybe I better cancel my date and go have a meal with you. There's a lot you need to learn about being gay."

"No, I'm good on that," Chiv said. "I'll take it in small doses, if you don't mind. I'm actually going to see what Vine, I mean Reverend Oliver, has planned for this afternoon. We may hang for a while."

"Well, it was good seeing you, and stay strong and come to the meetings, Arie," Eric said. "They are the secret sauce of sobriety."

"Have fun at Chuckie's or wherever," Chiv said. As Eric walked toward the door and Chiv walked toward Vine's office, he was thankful that his conversation with Eric was over. That was just too much to process in such a short time. A gay, alcoholic, father musician who was once married to a woman and now has a partner was a bit much for his mental computer to handle.

As he approached Vine's office, he was stopped by two men who were standing right outside of his door. *This is new*, he thought to himself. "Excuse me, gentlemen, I'm going in to see the pastor. I'm his best friend."

"Hold on, sir, what is your name?" one of the gentlemen asked.

"Well, before I had the sex-change operation, my name was Odessa," Chiv said. "Now they call me *O* for short. Tell him his friend O is here to see him." The other gentleman went into Vine's office. Ten seconds later, he could hear Vine's loud laugh through the door.

"Get in here, Odessa," Vine said, standing in the doorway. "Gentlemen, this is my good friend Chivas, I mean Arie. He is welcomed in my office unannounced any time."

"Yes, Pastor," the shorter man said. "Sorry, O."

"Have you received death threats or something?" Chiv asked, sitting in the chair in front of Vine's desk. "Why you need security detail?"

"I don't," he said. "I guess it comes with the job. So what did you think about today?"

"Man, I hope you know what you're doing," Chiv said. "You know how ignorant some folks can be. Two old bitties in front of me have already predicted that we will become a gay church. I was gonna get her straight, but I decided against it. And Eric. Did you know he was my sponsor?"

"Eric is an alcoholic?" Vine whispered.

"Oh, maybe I shouldn't have said that," Chiv said.

"Well, with him, I'll just add it to the list," Vine said. "He's gay, lives with a man, has a daughter, now he's an alcoholic."

"Yeah, you check a lot of boxes with that one," Chiv said.

"But he's a good man," Vine said. "And he's excited about the D & I ministry. Let the church roll on. How you doing? How are things at the Eubanks crib?"

"Fine. I was going to invite you out for after-church brunch," Chiv said.

"I can't," Vine said. "Hadassah and I are going to some concert at Ravinia."

"That's that outdoor theater up in Highland Park where the rich White folks live," Chiv said. "Who y'all going to see, Debbie Boone?"

"Some *farkakteh* folk singer named Joni Mitchell," Vine said.

"Did you just say the f-word?" Chiv asked. "What the hell does farkakteh mean, Sammy David Jr.?"

"Oh, it's Jewish for 'silly or ridiculous,'" Vine said.

"Sounds like the f-word to me," Chiv said.

"Why don't you want to go home to your fiancée?" Vine asked. "Sunday afternoon is a good time for some riga marrow."

"It's not that I don't want to go home," Chiv said. "I was just thinking we could have a meal together, but I'll check in with Sam or Bo. Maybe they…"

"Go home, Chiv," Vine said. "Just because all is forgiven between you two doesn't mean you can stop working on your relationship. Go home and talk to Louise some more."

"That's just it," Chiv said. "All is not forgiven. Yes, I said I forgave her, but I keep hearing those words she said about Catherine and the boys and seeing that look she had on her face. That cut right through me. And I know I'm going to have to deal with it, but I ain't ready. Last night when I came home, we hugged and kissed and did a few other things and went to sleep. This morning, she was still in bed when I left. We really haven't talked about it."

"That's why I'm telling you to go home so you can talk about it," Vine said. "If it's worth talking about. If she's worth it. After all, this is the woman you asked to marry you. You two are going to get married next year, remember? You better fix this, whatever this is, now before you can't or you don't want to. Go home, man."

Chiv left Vine's office and headed home per instructions. He stopped and picked up a couple of dinners from Jackie's Soul Food before going home. When he arrived, to his surprise and pleasure, Louise wasn't there. He was relieved to delay the evitable conversation if only for a few hours more. He ate his turkey wing and dressing combo with freshly brewed iced tea and relaxed. He wanted to drink. He needed to drink, but he didn't.

Sunday, June 16, 2007

Four weeks had passed since Vine introduced his new sermon series. Today was sermon number 5, entitled "Who Do You Say I Am?" It was also the first Sunday in a while that all four Jolly Boys were together at church. Afterward, they hung out in Vine's office to catch up.

"You big time now, ain't cha, big pimpin'?" Bo teased. "You got bodyguards and whatnot. It's a waste of money, if you ask me. Ain't nobody coming up in here to get your Black ass."

"See, why you gotta hate on me?" Vine said. "My members take good care of their leader, ass hat."

"Reverend Oliver, your language," Sam said. "I just wanna know if you and Hadassah have had relations on this holy desk."

"See, that's just nasty," Vine said. "But why am I surprised?"

"And you got some fine women joining the flock," Sam said. "I think I should be in the welcoming ministry."

"Speaking of hoeing," Vine said, "Chiv, have you heard from the investigator?"

"No," Sam answered. "That jive Negro ain't came up with nothing. He said Nevaeh don't even live in Vegas anymore."

"He's doing the best he can, Sam," Chiv said. "We didn't give him much information to work with. All we know at this point is that she's living in Indianapolis with her sister."

"And she is not returning my calls," Sam said. "At first, I was concerned and worried. Now I'm pissed. How you gonna have my baby and then go into hiding? I would roll up on her ass, but I can't get none of y'all to roll with me."

"I got a bad feeling about this, Sam," Bo said. "I think you should just leave that girl alone. It's obvious that she's moved on. You should do the same."

"Yeah, I hate to admit it, but I think you're right," Sam said.

"How you and Marsaleen doing?" Vine asked.

"Coexisting," he said. "I love my wife, but I don't like her. It's like we're strangers. But I got me a little young freak who keeps me satisfied, if you know what I mean."

"Ain't you tired of giving your money away?" Bo said.

"See, there y'all go," Sam said. "Who said I was giving this girl anything?"

"Of course, you are," Bo said. "Why do you think she's with you?"

"Because I'm fine and know how to please a woman," Sam said.

"Yeah, the more bills you pay and the more you sponsor weekly hair and nail treatments, the louder she screams and moans," Vine said. "You should have peeped that game already."

"So what if I'm generous?" Sam said. "I like my women all dolled up. What's a hundred a week for hair and nails? As long as I'm getting what I'm supposed to get, it's just money."

"I'm so tired of shaking my head at you my neck hurts," Vine said. "And you better not be hollering at any of the women in this church. I'd hate to have to put you out."

"I can't make no promises," Sam said. "They coming in here fine as ever, two by two. Now there's a blessing for your ass: beautiful Black women two at a time. I ain't got that much energy."

"You ain't got that much money," Bo said. "Let's get out of here. I'm hungry."

The fellas followed one another from the church to their favorite restaurant, Leg and Thigh in Oak Park. They climbed into their favorite booth by the window and settled in. They loved this booth. It was the booth they sat in for their first Jolly-Boy meal more than ten years ago. Although their waitress presented each with a menu, no one opened it. They had patronized the mom-and-pop eatery so much over the years they had committed the menu to memory. And for an added treat, Ms. Gina was there.

Gina Bartalozzi was part owner of Leg and Thigh. She and her husband, Oscar, opened the small Italian bistro thirty-two years ago in their backyard in Berwyn, Illinois, just a few miles west of Oak Park. After the Cook County Department of Health threatened to shut them down for operating a restaurant without a license, Oscar secured a small business loan, and they moved to larger quarters at Lake and Harlem, still in Oak Park. Word of Gina's homemade classics transcended through the western suburbs and parts of Chicago. Business was booming. They moved again to a larger spot in the art district of Oak Park, doubling in size and ability to host small events including weddings, repasses, and kids' parties. When Oscar retired from the Oak Park Police Department, he channeled all his energy into the restaurant, allowing his wife to focus on the food and him on the operations of the business. Oscar had a debilitating stroke about ten years ago and relinquished control to his oldest son, Oscar Junior. Oscar was a college graduate and loved running the business. Unfortunately, he loved cocaine more, and soon, Leg and Thigh found itself near peril. Gina knew she had to do it all on her own, so she downsized, focused on making less dishes but making them well and hired pretty and handsome young people to serve. She's now a small mom-and-pop again, and she loved it. When she visited, she always walked around and greeted her customers. She was short and petite with a big mouth and risqué sense of humor, the striking image of Sophia Petrillo on the television sitcom, the *Golden Girls.* She loved hanging out with the Jolly Boys and flirting with Bo.

"Well, well, well," Gina said, walking to their booth. "If it isn't boys in the hood." Normally and commonly, most Black people would be offended by that comment, but Gina didn't have a prejudiced bone in her body. Gina was all right. "And, Bo, you look more and more like James Earl Jones every day. Can I sit on your lap?"

"Gina, to be an old married woman, you are so nasty," Bo teased. "You ought to be ashamed of yourself. Aren't you shame?"

"No, I'm not," she said. "What I am is hot on fire. I got needs, Bo, and I'm not going to wait forever."

"Gina, as tempting as that is, I'm going to have only eyes for my wife," Bo said.

"And Black women don't share well," Vine said.

"Not true," she said and then leaned in to whisper. "Some of the best sex I've ever had was in a three-way with a Black couple. She was big and fat, and he was six eight and athletic."

Chiv gripped his forehead and closed his eyes before speaking. "Gina, are you trying to tell us that you were in a three-way with another woman and a basketball player?" Chiv asked.

"I'm not saying a thing," she said. "You will never get me to talk about Juanita's husband like that." Gina let out a laugh that made heads turn. She was a character, if there ever was one.

"You are telling an Italian lie," Sam said.

"Hey, they're the best lies to tell," Gina said.

"Is that why you named this place Leg and Thigh because you like dark meat?" Chiv asked.

"Shhhh," Gina responded. "If some of these racist White people find out that a big, strong, strapping Black man was my inspiration, they'd walk out today and picket tomorrow. Ain't nothing like a firm and muscular leg and thigh of a Black man. Stand up, Bo. Let me see what's going on."

"Go on now, Gina," Bo said. "Stop being nasty."

"I'm just in love with you guys, and I'm going to miss you," she said, leaning in again. "I'm closing down next summer, but don't tell anyone yet. It's time to retire and spend some quality time with my husband."

"Oh no," the fellas said in unison.

"Yes, it's time," Gina said. "I've been doing this for thirty-two years. It's time to sell and sit down, you know."

"Who are you selling to?" Bo asked.

"No one yet, but I'm going to be very selective in who I turn these keys over to," Gina said. "Hey, you guys should buy it."

"Oh, please," Vine said. "We don't know nothing about the restaurant business, and the only thing I know Italian is bucatini and meat sauce, your bucatini and meat sauce."

"Well, if you know of anyone, I'll probably start finalizing plans after the first of the year," she said. "Put your feelers out, but keep it hush-hush. What y'all want, the usual?"

"Yes, please," Bo said.

"Beauregard, you wanna come in the kitchen and give me a hand?" she cooed.

"No," he replied with a smile that filled his face.

"Well, you wanna come in the kitchen, and I can give you a hand," she said.

"I'm good, Gina," Bo said. "Nasty old Italian woman." She laughed and walked to the kitchen.

"Hey, I can't believe Leg and Thigh is going away," Chiv said. "I wish I had the time, energy, and money. I'd buy this place in a minute. Bo, you should buy it and turn it into that buffet you want to open."

"Naw, that ain't nowhere on the bucket list," Bo said. "In fact, next summer after I retire, I'm going back to school."

"School? What kind of school?" Vine asked.

"I want a college degree," he said. "I'm going back to school to get my bachelor's degree."

"In what?" Chiv asked.

"I don't know. Maybe anthropology or sociology," Bo said. "I've always wanted a degree but never had the time or energy or confidence. After I retire, I'll have nothing but time on my hands, so I'm going back to school."

"Good for you," Sam said. "You'll be the oldest ninja in the class, but hey, it is what it is. And if you stop being so uptight with Gina, she may even pay for it."

"You are stupid, plain and simple," Bo said.

"You know, I've always wanted to ask you something," Sam said.

"Oh, shit, here we go," Vine said. "Please don't say nothing stupid today, Sam. You know you got a habit of saying stupid shit sometimes."

"Have you ever been tempted to cheat on your wife?" Sam said.

"What? What are you talking about?" Bo said nervously. Vine and Chiv looked at each other, picking up on Bo's visible uneasiness.

"I mean Helen or Jackie," Sam said. "Have you ever wondered how it would feel to be with another woman?"

"I love my wife, Sam," Bo said.

"And you are intentionally not answering the question," Sam said.

"And look like you about to come out of your skin," Chiv said.

"You are acting strange all of a sudden," Vine said. "Wait, could it be that Bo parked his car in a strange garage?"

"Nah," Chiv said. "Bo tore up his player card, if he ever had one." The fellas thought Chiv's comment was funny, but Bo didn't laugh—didn't even crack a smile.

"You sure could have when you were with Helen," Vine said. "I don't think even the good Lord would have minded you stepping out on her. She was a trip."

"It was actually while I was with Helen," Bo said. Just then, the waiter brought out their meal. It was the Gina family-style special: a platter of bucatini and sausage with red sauce, chicken alfredo, turkey tetrazzini, and baked ziti. As the waiter placed the four platters on the table, the fellas were silent. Surely, Bo was joking. Their distinguished and respected leader could never be so common and typical. After the waiter left, no one moved. They all sat and stared in horror and disbelief. Bo began filling his plate and telling the story. "Her name was Violet, Vi for short. It was right after my grandson died, and it was a rough time for the entire family. It's also around the time Helen and I started having problems. She told me straight and directly that it was my fault Bo II died. I was a mess and started eating any and everything I could get my hands on. And of course, Helen being Helen reminded me of how big a mess I was. See, she was from the school that taught belittling and insulting people would force them to action. We were from two different schools, which is the primary reason we're not together today."

"Tell the story, Bo," Sam said. "I need to hear this with my own two ears from your two lips."

"It was so hot that day," Bo continued. "Even early in the morning, it was hot and humid. And not to spoil your appetites, but heat and humidity raises the rancid stench of garbage to a level of nearly unbearable. I had seniority, so I got to drive instead of walk and dump. I thought I was fortunate, but I think it may have been worse inside a hot truck. When we pulled into Vi's alley, there she was, smack dab in the middle of the alley with this big long orange Lincoln Town Car with a flat tire. I had to make a decision: help this south-side damsel in distress or risk knocking down fences and crashing in garages trying to back a nine-ton garbage truck out the alley. I went for the damsel. Now from a distance, Vi was as regular and dark and plain as they come. She had that sanctified look: no makeup, showing very little skin, and a general look of fright and misery. And when you got closer to her, well, let's say it didn't get much better. But you wanna know what attracted me to Vi? It was her genuine friendliness and love for people. While we were fixing her tire, she went into the house and came out with a big pitcher of iced tea and a plate of sandwiches. And when we were done, she tried to slip us ten dollars each, but we refused. Instead, we went inside and cooled off in her central air-conditioned kitchen."

"You gotta be careful with that," Vine said. "She could have been a freak or worse yet, some type of serial killer."

"Oh, trust me," Bo said. "The thought crossed my mind, but I felt safe with my crew. And these two Negroes looked like they were just released from jail. She was probably more afraid than I was. I remember being really self-conscious. I know we smelled horrible and was funking up that woman's house."

"You stalling, Bo," Sam said. "Get to the booty part."

"Anyway, we were there for about an hour," Bo continued. "She was down to earth and very funny. I could tell she was genuinely a good person. And the more she laughed and entertained us, her hips got smaller, her hair got longer, her breasts got bigger, and her look of misery faded away. I found myself attracted to Vi. Long story short, we exchanged numbers. She made me dinner a couple of times, and we had an affair. For a couple of months, I spent as much spare time with her as I could. And when I ran out of spare time, I made some up."

"You were with this woman for a couple of months?" Vine said. "I feel like someone just told me that Mr. Rogers was running a sex trafficking ring from the land of make-believe. And the sex was better with her than Helen?"

"Oh my God, yes," Bo said. "I know there is a big college word for this, but she was like a towel that wouldn't get dry." Chiv choked on his alfredo. He was looking at Bo and hearing his voice, but he couldn't believe what he was hearing from the mouth of the head Jolly Boy.

"Where is she now?" Sam asked. "Do y'all ever hook up for old times' sake?"

"No, we shut that down. Actually, she shut it down," Bo said. "I was over there late one Saturday night and overslept. It was like three in the morning, and I needed to hurry up home. She was so irritated. I told her that I had to go home to my wife. That was the first time I disclosed that I was married."

"And she never asked?" Chiv asked. "Two months and she never inquired about your marital status?"

"Nope, not even once," Bo said. "When I uttered those words, she told me to put her key on the table, get out, and never come back."

"Bo, you were strong, bruh," Sam said. "She gave you a key to her crib. I haven't even had a key to somebody's crib."

"I haven't seen or heard from her since," Bo said.

"She didn't ask you because she didn't want to know," Sam said. "I tell chicks up front that I'm married and I ain't leaving my wife. They usually say, 'Damn, why did you tell me that? I just didn't want to know.' Now I feel like a hoe."

"That's playing mind games, and worst of all, mind games with yourself," Chiv said.

"Damn, if someone had told me that the model loving and devoted husband cheated on his wife, I would have slapped them for lying," Sam joked.

"Yeah, but it doesn't' really count," Vine said. "Your actions with Vi were justified. You were married to Helen. Now I couldn't talk about her then because she was your wife, but I can talk about her ass now. I don't see how you could have stayed with that woman all those years. It had to be the Lord."

"No, wrong is wrong," Bo said. "Helen was not the greatest wife nor the nicest person, but she was still my wife. Lying with another woman can't be justified as the right thing to do when its very essence is wrong."

"I guess you're right," Chiv said.

"I know I'm right," Bo said.

"But if you ever cheated on Jackie, all three of us would kick your ass," Vine said. "She's funny, sassy, intelligent, and beautiful. You'd be a fool to mess that up. And because I am a man of God and good-natured, I will take your place as her husband when you go home to be with the Lord."

"Why do I want to punch this fool in his face right now?" Bo joked. "It's funny you mentioned death. I know it's sick, but often, I wonder who's going to die first: me or her? I'm so happy with Jackie, and I love her to the bone. I sometimes think what's worse, dying or living without her? I think living without her would be harder. I hope I go first."

"You don't know how many times I've asked God why he took them and left me here," Chiv said. Bo finally realized how insensitive he was making that comment in Chiv's presence.

"Aw, Chiv man," Bo said, "what was I thinking? I shouldn't have said that. I didn't mean to…"

"Aw, man, we boys," Chiv said. "I know you mean well. I just want you to know I know why and how you're thinking. They were my everything. And I know she would have loved y'all."

"See, I don't feel that way about Marsaleen," Sam said. "And you won't like this, and you'll think I'm crazy. But I do feel that way about Nevaeh."

"Dear Lord Jesus," Vine said. "It's over, Sam. You had your fun with her, and now it's done. You are going to drive yourself and us crazy. Let go."

"I can't," Sam said. "I'm really in love. If she gave me even an inkling that she was stepping away, I'd divorce Marsaleen in a heartbeat. Nevaeh is who I want to be with."

"Damn, what did that girl do to you in the bedroom?" Vine asked. "She covered you with chocolate and licked it off? The girl moved and didn't tell you. How you in love with someone you've got to get a private investigator to find? Don't make me slap you like Cher did that woman in that movie."

"Damn, Chiv man, nothing from the private investigator?" Sam said, ignoring Vine. "I need to find her."

"I'll give him a call," Chiv said. "I guess it's too early to give up."

"Way too early," Sam said. "Y'all don't understand. I'm in love with this woman. She's on my mind all day, every day. And if she has had a child of mine, I need to know him or her, and I need to take care of them. I need them both in my life."

"Damn, you are serious, aren't you?" Vine said.

"Yes, I'm very serious," Sam said. "I've been telling and showing y'all how serious I am. Now don't get me wrong. I've had my fun chasing tail, but that's because she's absent from me. All that stops the day Nevaeh comes back for real. A man can only be miserable so long, and then he's not a man."

"Well, we're gonna find her," Chiv said. "If she's who you want and who you need, we're gonna find her." The fellas shook their heads in blind agreement but only for show. In their brains and in their hearts, they knew Nevaeh was trouble, and trouble was the last thing Sam needed.

"Listen, what would y'all say if I told you I was in love with Hadassah?" Vine posed. Sam was relieved and happy to pivot the attention to someone else.

"I would ask if you were sure," Sam said. "I know we're living in different and more understanding times and all that, but I can't imagine that it would be easy to marry a White woman."

"Aw, see, why we let him answer first?" Chiv said. "Ain't nothing wrong with Vine marrying Hadassah."

"I didn't say there was," Sam said. "Once again, you didn't let me finish my thinking. I just said it wouldn't be easy. Things you take for granted couldn't be taken for granted anymore. People would stare at you when you were together. There would be some places you'd no longer feel comfortable in because you were in those places together. And Black women will treat you like a felon for committing the highest slap-in-the-face crime to Black women: marrying a White woman. And don't forget, you are a pastor and not of some storefront on Halsted. You are the pastor of one of the oldest and respected Baptist churches in the city. How is a White woman gonna be the first lady of GOB? The woman does not believe Jesus was the Messiah. How you gonna parade her up and through GOB? And how will her community treat her? White is one thing, but Jewish is a whole 'nother world. You may know a few Jewish words, but you are still Black. And I like Hadassah once I got to know her. I have nothing against her, but I think you better think about this a little bit more, my friend."

"Wait, you said *love*," Bo clarified. "You didn't say nothing about marriage."

"You're right," Vine said. "But what else is there to do when you love someone than get married? And Sam, I hear you. It won't be a cakewalk, but I want a wife. Bo has Jackie. Chiv has Louise. You got, well, whoever you got. I think you get my point. I want that happiness that you all have. If things keep progressing like they are, I'm going to ask her."

"Well, whatever you do, we'll support you," Chiv said. "If we can support Don Juan over here, we can support the rabbi. In fact, I'll officiate the ceremony."

"How in the hell are you gonna do that?" Sam said. "You've been to church a few Sundays in a row, and now you a preacher?"

"It's easy," Chiv said. "Go online to the Universal Truth Ministries website and click the Instant Ordain button. I've done it already. You are looking at the Right Reverend Arie Eubanks."

"You must have been good and drunk that night," Bo said. "You better check your certificate. Hell, it might say the 'Right Reverend Chivas Regal.' They say that Charles Manson was so diabolical and evil that when he walked into the courtroom, everyone's watch stopped. That's what would happen when your toe hit the pulpit. Look, man, whatever you do, we got you. Just don't break that woman's heart." Those words pierced Vine in the stomach. Bo's words of wisdom matched Vine's prediction. But maybe he was wrong this time. Maybe his spirit man had it all wrong, just this once.

CHAPTER 18

January 27, 2008

When Sam woke up, he realized it was the last Sunday of the month and it was his sixty-fourth birthday. He had been partying since Thursday night with the Jolly Boys and a few of his select lady friends. It was odd but a comforting delight to wake up in his own bed. The weekend was an exciting blur in his mind. He struggled to recall the series of celebrations as he collected himself upright on the side of the bed. When he stood to slip on his robe and slippers, he glanced over at the other side of his bed. That's when all the recollection started flooding his mind. Marsaleen slept with her husband last night. He dropped his head and rubbed his face. He was not dreaming, nor was he reliving some warped and practical joke. His new life with his wife had begun.

As he continued to stir, he could smell the aroma of bacon traveling through the house. He closed his eyes and shook his head. The confirmed player was not a stranger to the logical sequence of ass followed by breakfast, but it had been several years since both were served to him by his wife. "How did this happen?" he asked himself. His memory was coming into focus to help answer that question.

On Saturday night, he had gotten all dressed up, ready to celebrate with the Jolly Boys, after which, he'd celebrate with this week's special someone. While getting dressed, Marsaleen appeared in his bedroom with a box wrapped in silver paper.

"What is that?" he asked.

"I know our marriage has seen better days, but you are still my husband and father of my children," she said. "I have always given you a birthday present. I was going to give it to you tomorrow, but I thought you might want to wear them tonight. It's from me and the girls. Here, open it."

"Marsaleen, you didn't have to do that considering our current situation," Sam said. "It wasn't necessary and makes me feel bad because I forget your birthday every year."

"Yes, I know," she said. "And you say that same ole line every year. Just open the damn present, Sam." He ripped the paper from the box like a little boy on Christmas day. His mouth fell open when he saw his gift. It was a pair of olive-green crocodile Italian loafers.

"These are beautiful," he said. "But you shouldn't have. These shoes are over a thousand dollars."

"Actually, 1,895 dollars, to be exact," she said. "I know you've been wanting these for years. I hope you still like them. Happy birthday, Samaritan."

"Thank you," Sam said and slid the exotic shoes onto his feet. Standing in front of the full-length mirror in the hall, he smiled with adolescent excitement. "I think I'm going to change my clothes. Olive green doesn't go very well with burgundy pants. I can't believe you did this. If you're waiting for me in bed when I get home, I'd love to properly thank you."

"Are you coming in from all that insidious night rambling you've been doing all these years?" she asked. He dropped his head and did not answer. "Precisely what I thought. I will be in my bed when and if you come home. And it's your birthday. You don't have to. Oh, please make sure you say thank you to the girls whenever they call. I'm sure Samaritana will call her precious father. Samita, well, I wouldn't pace the floor waiting if I were you."

"Again, thank you," Sam said. "And when I talk to the girls, I'll thank them and fall all over myself with excitement."

Sam finished dressing and headed out to dinner with the fellas. Vine was watching Levi while Hadassah was out of town on business, so the fellas held Sam's birthday get-together at her house on the gold coast. Worn out from prior days of celebration, he was too tired for his planned after-party, so he went home. When he walked into his bedroom, Marsaleen was in his bed with only a high thread count sheet covering most of her naked body. Sam realized in that moment that he was still in love with her curves. It appeared as if she had changed her mind and was open to the sexual thank you from her husband, to which he gladly obliged. Sam shook his head like an Etch a Sketch toy, washed his face, brushed his teeth, and headed downstairs to the kitchen.

"Good morning, birthday boy," she sang. "You spoiled it. I was going to serve you breakfast in bed."

"You know I don't like eating in bed," Sam said coldly. "That's not what the bed is for."

"Well, sit down," she said. "I'm making scratch biscuits. They'll be ready in five minutes."

"Leen, I hope I didn't give you some false hope by making love to you last night," Sam said. "I was just saying thank you."

"And I appreciate both thank-you sessions this morning," she cooed. Sam did not soften his hardened disposition. "I seduced you, Sam, because I want to satisfy a need I've had for a long time. It doesn't change anything, and I know that. I'm not enough for you anymore. I used to be. But something happened, and I'm no longer your Bathsheba. And I'm sure some other woman received her thank-yous as well. I'm not some little thirtysomething fighting to get you back. I'm a mature adult, and so are you. Let's just leave it at that. Eat your breakfast before it gets cold. I'm going upstairs to get dressed. I'm going to your friend Reverend Oliver's church today."

"That's where I go," Sam said.

"Yes, I know, but I assumed you wouldn't be going today," she said. "Everyone is talking about him and how he's stirring things up over there. I thought I'd go and witness it for myself. Lola is going with me."

"Tell her I said hello, if she doesn't hate me by now," Sam said.

"Oh, she can't stand you," Marsaleen said. "But I'll tell her anyway. Enjoy your breakfast and enjoy your birthday, Sam." She kissed him on the cheek and headed upstairs to get dressed. Sam sat and looked at his cold breakfast. It was his birthday, but he was not happy. He was not pleased with what his life had become.

The sound of the house phone startled Sam, ending his contemplative stare into his breakfast plate. It had been years since he heard that sound, the sound that usually signaled a telemarketer or an emergency. He couldn't imagine an emergency call on Sunday morning. It had to be a telemarketer. He was not in the mood for either.

"Hello," he barked loudly into the phone. "Whatever you selling, I already have it."

"Sam man, it's me, Chiv," Chiv said in a calming voice. "What are you hollering for?"

"I'm sorry, man," Sam said. "The house phone only rings for emergencies and telemarketers. And my mind was somewhere else."

"I tried calling your cell, but it just went to voice mail," Chiv explained. "But check this out. I need you to come by the crib today around four. I need to talk to you about something."

"Oh, damn, an emergency," Sam said. "What's wrong? You haven't been drinking again, have you?"

"No, I haven't been drinking," Chiv lied. "Vine and Bo are coming over after church. I just want to talk to y'all about something important. It's not an emergency, and nothing is wrong."

"Are you sick or something?" Sam said. "It's my birthday, and it hasn't started out all that good. I'm not in the mood for nothing mentally heavy. If you're sick, can we talk about it tomorrow? It will be someone else's birthday tomorrow, so I wouldn't care."

"No, I'm not sick, fool," Chiv said. "And I'm glad I'm not because I wouldn't be able to tell my best friend until tomorrow."

"That was foul, man," Sam said. "I'm sorry. I'll be there. I should be in a better frame of mind by then."

"Come go to church with me," Chiv said. "That would make you feel better. I wasn't planning on going, but I'd go with you."

"Naw, I'm not feeling it today," Sam said. "And besides, Marsaleen and Lola will be there. My brain couldn't process those two together."

"Man, I don't want to be in the same city as you when Marsaleen finds out you've been sleeping with her best friend," Chiv said. "All hell will open and break lose."

"I don't want to talk about that," Sam said. "I'll see you at four."

"A'ight, bet," Chiv said. "And happy birthday, MF."

"Oooooh, you almost said half of a bad word," Sam said, mocking Chiv before hanging up.

After moping around the house for a while, Sam showered, got dressed, and headed to Michigan Avenue. It was his birthday, and he always bought himself a gift on his birthday. And besides, he didn't want to face Marsaleen again until he had to. The way she performed in bed this morning, he wouldn't be surprised if she was waiting for him again in the same spot. He laughed to himself after that thought. "I may be sixty-four, but they're lined up at the door." He couldn't help but to laugh out loud at his self-appraisal.

He strolled through Water Tower Place, hitting only his favorite stores: Lord and Taylor for jackets and pants, Macy's for shirts and jeans, and Saks for shoes. He left the high-end vertical mall bagged up with a smile on his face and just a little later than he had planned. He'd be a good twenty-minutes late for the meeting at Chiv's house. On the drive, he braced himself mentally for bad news. The only good news he'd heard all day was "Mr. Ladeaux, we have that in your size."

When Sam approached Chiv's place, he noticed an unfamiliar car in the driveway. This made his stomach ache. His immediate thought was that Chiv had invited his doctor to explain the details of his fatal disease and how much longer he would live. He parked and sat for a moment, trying to ignore and suppress his fight-or-flight responses, but his loyalty and conscience wouldn't let him. The brotherhood comes before simply not wanting to be bothered. He exited the car and made his way up the walkway. Before his index finger could make contact with the doorbell, Chiv opened the door.

"You had about another two minutes before I came out to get you," Chiv said. "Forty minutes late and then sitting in the car? Makes me think you were contemplating taking off."

"Sorry I'm late," Sam said. "You know how I get when I go shopping. I lose all track of time. I hear Bo and Vine's loud asses." This was a good sign. Everyone was up-spirited. It couldn't be bad news. Sam walked the long and familiar hallway to Chiv's den.

"Good afternoon, my brothers," Sam said. "What y'all in here lying about?"

"Nothing, but we're about to change subjects and talk about those Puerto Rican green shoes you wearing," Vine said. "Those are conversation pieces, that's for sure."

"These are genuine crocodile leather custom-made for my feet," Sam said. "My wife has good taste."

"I would agree," Vine said. "She was almost my girlfriend."

"Vine, I don't want to have to whoop your ass today," Sam said. "Why did you even bring that up?"

"I'm joking, I'm joking. Relax," Vine said.

"I have been eying these shoes for years," Sam said, pivoting from a still sore subject in his mind. "There is this designer up north who does custom-made shoes. You pick the material, and they make the shoe perfectly for your feet. I think in a previous life, I was a designer."

"Could have fooled me," Vine said. "I thought you were a circus clown."

"Chiv, get your boy," Sam said jokingly. "I'd hate to tear up all this pretty shit you got in here, whooping his ass." Once everyone was settled, it was time for business.

"So I know you're wondering what this meeting is about," Bo said.

"Yes, and whose car is that in the driveway?" Sam said.

"Oh, you noticed that?" Bo asked. Sam nodded. "Did you see the license plates?"

"Naw, I didn't pay attention," Sam said with a genuine baffled look on his face.

"Well, we ordered you a present," Chiv said.

"Y'all got me a stripper for my birthday," Sam said. "I didn't think strippers worked on Sunday."

"Speaking of strippers, we have some information to share about Nevaeh," Chiv said.

"Oh no," Sam said, massaging his chest above his heart. "Please don't tell me the girl is dead or something. Is that what the investigator found out? Is she in some sort of legal trouble? Oh my God, is she in jail?"

"Negro, calm down and be cool," Vine said.

"You can come on out now," Chiv yelled in the direction of the kitchen. The expression on Sam's face was that of a man staring at an apparition.

"Is that really you?" Sam asked. "Am I dreaming?"

"No, it's me," she said. "I've put on a few pounds, but it's me."

Sam raced toward her and pulled her in with intensity. He didn't kiss her in front of the fellas, but his confining embrace was more passionate and intense than any kiss either have ever had. Bo, Vine, and Chiv didn't utter a word but were all thinking the same thing. Sam was not lying. It was obvious that he was madly in love with this woman. Sam stroked her face and arms just to make sure he wasn't dreaming or falling prey to some practical joke. Abruptly, his brain caught up with his emotions, and anger seeped in. He stepped back, far back.

"You mind telling me where the hell you've been all these months?" Sam asked. "Why did you move, and why haven't you returned my calls? You certainly cashed my checks. Don't see how you couldn't return my calls. I'm glad you're okay, but you've got a lot of explaining to do."

"I deserve that, and you are entitled to be upset with me," Nevaeh said. "The only thing I can tell you truthfully is that I needed to take a break from us to get my head together. I didn't want to talk to you because I didn't want to hurt you. And because of my circumstances, I moved to Indianapolis to live with my sister. Your friends tracked me down and paid for me to come to Chicago. The unfamiliar car in the driveway with Indiana plates belongs to me."

"Hurt me?" Sam said. "Nevaeh, I was falling in love with you. I was going to leave my wife for you."

"I know, and that's why I didn't connect with you," Nevaeh said. "Things were getting serious and complicated. It was hard, but I knew that the best thing was to end things with you. That would be the best way for me to move on and for you to reconcile with your wife and prevent me from being labeled a home-wrecker."

"My home has been a wreck for a minute now, and it has nothing to do with you," Sam said. "Why are you here, Nevaeh? You getting serious with somebody else? You want my permission to move on with your life without me?"

"I wanted to apologize in person, wish you a happy birthday, and introduce you to your son. He's asleep right now. It's been a long day already for the both of us."

"My son?" Sam repeated. "I have a son?"

"If you say some ignorant shit like they say on those paternity shows like 'I can't make boys,'" Vine said, "we gonna fight you."

"His name is Jeremiah," Nevaeh said. "I named him after my father. We made a boy, a healthy and happy boy. So like I said, things just got really complicated really fast. But you don't have to be in his life. Your wife doesn't have to know. If you help me financially, I won't even file for child support. But I do need some help."

"I'm speechless," Sam said. "But don't you love me? You say you need financial help, but don't you really mean you need me?" The deafening silence was a signal for privacy.

"You know what, we're gonna run to Leon's and get some barbecue," Bo said. "And give you two some time to talk alone. Nevaeh, you like ribs, or would you prefer chicken?"

"She'll take the ribs, large end, hot and mild sauce mixed, extra bread and coleslaw," Sam said.

"Y'all bring me some tips back," Vine said. Everyone, including Nevaeh, turned and looked at him, wondering why he was still seated and still. "Oh, I'm not going nowhere. Somebody got to live to tell the story."

"Divine," Bo barked. "Y'all talk, and we'll be back directly."

Before walking toward the hallway, Vine leaned into Sam's ear. "Don't agree to nothing until all cards are on the table," Vine whispered. "My spirit man is concerned about this. You've been good to this young lady. She needs to make a very strong case for you to do better than that."

"I'm hip," Sam said. "Don't worry. I got this." Sam barely paid attention to Vine's counsel. He wanted them to hurry and leave so he could be alone with the object of his affection and source of his incessant opining of late. When he heard the front door close, he focused his full attention on Nevaeh. He needed to connect with her eyes. Her eyes would tell the real story, regardless of the one flowing from her lips.

"Are you okay?" she asked, rubbing his arm, which was now right in front of her. "I'm not used to you being this quiet."

"I'm quiet because for the first time I think in my life, I don't know what to do or say," Sam said. "I'm so angry. I just want to shake you until your body parts become lose. But I'm also excited and want to have you right here, right now. You got me all messed up, Nevaeh."

"Like I said, I really don't want to create a problem for you and your wife," Nevaeh said.

"All these years and all this time, now you're concerned about my wife?" Sam said. "I don't believe that for a minute. You want me. You want me all to yourself. You're just afraid. See, to be someone's wife, you may have to compromise, you may have to change, you may even have to be vulnerable sometimes and let someone else take charge. You don't want that not because you think we'd fail but because you're afraid that we won't." Nevaeh looked into Sam's eyes before dropping her head and looking away. "I love you. Don't you get that? Don't I get any credit for that? I love you, and I want us to be a family."

"You would just walk away from your marriage for me?" she asked.

"Yes, and that's exactly what you want me to do," Sam said. "I don't know how they found you or what they said to get you to come here, but that's what you came for. You wanted me to tell you that I was leaving my wife for you. Even if you said no, you wanted to hear those words come out of my mouth. So now that you've gotten your wish, what's your answer? You want to be a family and have our son raised by his father, or you just want a money order or a white envelope with cash every month?"

"No, I cannot live with the guilt of destroying another woman's life," she said. She stood and walked to the window. "And I can't help but think that if you do it to her, you'd end up doing it to me too. Look, we had a good time, maybe too much of a good time. We went too far and had a child. I can't. I cannot be your wife, Sam. That job belongs to someone else."

"So you're just going to be a statistic," Sam said, walking toward her. "You're going to settle for being yet another single Black woman raising a child on your own. Another Black woman beating the hell out of a Black boy child trying to make him a man and in turn, making his a straight-up punk."

"Oh, so you can't get me with logic and compassion," she said. "So now we're going for the insults? My mother was a single parent raising me. And as far as statistics go, I'd prefer that one over being demonized as yet another Black woman taking a Black man away from his family and responsibilities."

Sam grabbed her waist and pulled her into himself. "Look at me square on and tell me that you don't love me. Tell me you don't want me in our life."

The words traveled up her throat and tarried on her tongue. They were right there to say and be heard. But when she looked into his sad and glossy eyes, she couldn't. She couldn't lie. He leaned down and kissed her. She kissed him back. Both coolness and heat created a thunderbolt in his body. He wanted her, and she wanted him. Their lips remained locked as they traveled down to the carpeted floor. As if they had the privacy and opportunity of the last two people on the planet, Sam and Nevaeh removed anything that restricted their skin from connecting. It was hurried. It was clumsy. It was intense. It was evitable.

They redressed in silence and exhaustion, returning to the place they started, sitting on the couch, amazed at the presence of each other. Nevaeh took his hand.

"I do love you, Sam," she finally admitted. "The reason I came to Chicago was to hear you say all the things you've said to me. I know I shouldn't, but I want you as mine and mine alone. I know that makes me a home-wrecker and maybe a hoe, but I can't and won't deny it."

A full smile covered Sam's face. "I want you and Jeremiah to go back to Indianapolis and wait for me," he said. "I was going to retire this year, but I think I'm gonna work a few years more." She shook her head while searching for the right words to dissuade him. "No, listen. I'll transfer to Indy, pull out some money from my 401(k), and send to you. Use it to find us an apartment and take care of Jeremiah until I get there. I promise I won't make you wait too long and will see you every chance I get. You're driving distance now. I can see you whenever I want. I just need some time to exit."

"Sam, I understand, and take your time," she said. "It can be next year if you have to. As long as I know you're coming, I can wait. I quit my job at the club. I'm a receptionist at an architecture firm downtown. It's an honest living, and I make pretty good money. But with Jeremiah and paying full rent, it's gonna be a struggle to get an apartment. I'll just stay with my sister…"

"No, you don't have to worry about rent or bills, none of that," Sam said. "My house is almost paid for. I can and will take care of us. I'm going to send you 25,000 dollars. I want you to open a checking account with both our names on it. We'll use that account to pay rent, utilities, and all the expenses for Jeremiah. I don't want you spending one dime of your salary on us. I got that and will take care of it."

"I can't believe this is happening," Nevaeh said. "You are taking care of everything I'm worried about."

"You don't have to worry anymore," Sam said.

"Okay, I won't," Nevaeh said.

"And listen, I'm not going to tell the fellas," Sam said. "I'll tell them after you leave that it's over. That way, they'll stay out of it and stop asking me about you. The next thing they'll know, we'll be at our favorite restaurant having my goodbye dinner." Sam heard the front door open. Nevaeh jumped from the couch and scanned the room for any signs of indiscretion. "Just follow my lead."

"Hello, we're back!" Vine yelled down the hall.

"Why are you hollering?" Chiv said. "You're going to wake the baby."

"Just in case they were doing it on the floor," Vine said. "I ain't trying to see Sam ass-in-air."

"The coast is clear, Pastor," Sam said, winking at Nevaeh.

"Did we give you all enough time?" Bo said. "It must be African American barbecue day. The line at Leon's was out the door. We went to Lem's."

"We're good," Sam said. "We agreed we were better as friends and co-parents, and before anyone says it out loud, yes, Nevaeh has agreed to a paternity test. I'll go to Indy in a couple of weeks to have it done. I'm not leaving my wife and home. That's what these thirty-somethings do. I'm sixty-something, and Nevaeh gets that."

"Sweetheart, I know that's hard to hear, but he's doing the right thing," Bo said. "You both are. You understand that, don't you?"

"Yes, I do," she said. "So let's eat so I can wake Jeremiah up. I want to introduce him to his father and uncles. And then I have a three-hour drive back to Indy. Thank you all so much for sending for me. Sam is lucky to have such good friends like you."

"Thank you, and remember, you can never error doing the right thing," Vine said. "Now that's a good sermon topic. I might drop that on the saints next Sunday."

"Reverend Vine, do you think the Lord will forgive me?" Nevaeh asked.

"If I know God and I know God, he already has," Vine said. "He already has."

CHAPTER 19

Friday, April 20, 2008

It was official. Senator Barack Hussein Obama was the Democratic nominee for president of the United States. Back in February, people in all 102 counties of Illinois came out in record number to vote in the Democratic primary election. Sixty-five percent of them, about 1.3 million, voted for Obama; and 32 percent, about 650,000, voted for the Illinois native and top contender, Clinton—Hillary Clinton, that is. The race wasn't even close.

Exit polls showed that approximately nine out of every ten Black voters voted for Obama. A new wind was blowing across the political landscape of Illinois and the entire country. The nation was on the cusp of electing its first African American president. The general sentiment of the Jolly Boys ranged from skeptical to proud. All paled in comparison to Vine's excitement.

It was a warm Friday night, and the fellas wanted to drink and chill outside as close to the lake as possible. They opted for Riva's at Navy Pier. They chose a table outside on the patio. They started with Bo, Chiv, and Sam. Vine would be along as soon as he was done with a meeting with the church choir. Just as the three were sipping their first cocktail—except Chiv, of course—Vine appeared table side. He was wearing a T-shirt that caught their attention and ridicule almost immediately.

"Vine, please tell me I'm reading that shirt wrong," Bo said. Chiv had already collapsed in hysteria, his body hanging on the side of the wrought iron chair. "Does it really say 'Obama, not a period but a comma'?"

"What does that even mean?" Sam asked.

"He won the Illinois primary, comma, twenty-four states, comma, the Democratic nomination, comma," Vine explained. "We're not inserting a period until after his second term as president. Get it? And I have shirts for the three of you as well."

"Use mine to wash your car with," Sam said. "I'm not wearing a shirt with a saying that requires that much explanation. Obama got Black folks acting road-lizard crazy."

"I'm not acting crazy," Vine said. "I am going to do my part to create a historical event. Doing my part includes getting skeptical people excited about making this happen. Some little Black boy somewhere in America will know that one day, he could actually be president. That's huge."

"Yeah, okay," Sam said, reluctantly sliding over so Vine could sit.

"Hey, I just had an idea," Vine said. "We should go to the convention in August in Denver. That would be an experience of a lifetime. To hear a Black man live, accepting the Democratic party's nomination for president."

"Don't you have to be a worker or affiliated with the party to get invited?" Chiv asked. "How would we get in?"

"I'll take a pass," Sam said. "That would be the perfect chance to take him out and a few delegates right along with him. To tell the truth, I don't want to be in the same room with him for my safety. But back to the shirt. Where did you get it? In the middle of 87th and State?"

"From the flower shops," Vine said. "Pearl and Anne can barely keep them on the shelves. We got this one and the other one that says 'Obama beat your mama.'"

"Now I'll wear that one," Bo said. "For some reason, that one makes sense. The brother is so bad he can beat anyone. Obama can even beat your mama."

"If I get us in the convention, we're all going," Vine said. "I want history to show that I supported my brother for president."

"While you were out T-shirt shopping, I hope you remembered to play our Mega numbers," Bo said. "It's up to forty million this week. That's ten million each. I don't know what I'd do with ten million dollars."

"Well, first, you'd pay Uncle Sam," Chiv said. "I think the taxes on lottery winnings is about 40 percent. Six million ain't that much if you think about it."

"I have thought about it, and that's a lot of damn money still," Bo said. "I put twenty-five dollars in the pool each week. I plan on bankrupting the state of Illinois real soon."

"Oh, I checked the numbers from last week, and it seems we won one hundred dollars," Vine said. "I took the liberty of adding it to our normal weekly contribution. At two dollars a bet, that would give us a hundred bets."

"I'm glad you did," Chiv said. "The more we put in, the greater our chances of winning." The fellas talked about work; Obama, sex, of course, and Vine's big announcement.

"So y'all gonna be at church Sunday, I know," Vine said. "You gotta be there to hear my big announcement."

"That's the plan unless you just tell us tonight," Bo said.

"I won't give it all away, but I'm taking the church in a different direction," Vine said. "I've been reading and studying and have a theory."

"Oh, here we go," Chiv said. "Vine man, you've been doing so well. You haven't cussed out nobody from the pulpit, people are joining, and the church is in the best financial shape it's been in on over a decade. And you have never been with a church this long, not even the one you started. Leave well enough alone."

"No, listen, I've been reading up on positive thinking and New Thought," Vine said. "Now I don't agree with everything I read, but there are some principles that make sense and are biblically supported. It's time for us to change our thinking about God."

"Why you got to make a big announcement about that?" Bo asked.

"I have to tell the people we're going in a new direction, don't I?" Vine replied.

"No, you don't," Bo said. "Your job is to preach and teach. Just preach and teach. Let people decide for themselves whether or not they want to go in a different direction. If they agree, fine. If they don't, then they have to make a decision to go."

"Why does that sound so dishonest?" Vine said. "Feels like I'm trying to trick God's people."

"I don't see it that way at all," Bo said. "Unless we win this money tonight, you need these people. Teach them and lead them. Show them the way. Jesus never made an announcement. He just taught. Some people followed Him, and some didn't. I hear you always referring to Him as the way-shower. Let Him show the church the way through you."

"You got a point, Bo," Vine said. "But now I have a big problem. Now I don't have a big announcement to make. The church is no doubt going to be packed with people wanting to hear some big news. I gots nothing."

"Well, you got forty-eight hours to come up with something," Sam said. "I'm glad you said something tonight. Now I don't have to go on Sunday."

"You old heathen," Vine said, imitating Aunt Ester from the television sitcom *Sanford and Son.*

"Hey, you said you were meeting with the choir," Bo said. "Please tell me you're not changing something with the choir. These folks know they can sing. And when they sing the 'Lord's Prayer,' I'm looking up at the ceiling because I'm expecting Him to break through it. They should record a CD."

"You must be a prophet because that's what the meeting was about," Vine said. "We are getting ready to record."

"We?" Chiv asked. "Are you going to be on the record?"

"Of course," Vine said with a proud smile. "The Reverend D. V. Oliver and the voices of the Grand Ole Baptist Church, live in concert."

"Since when do you have a middle name?" Bo asked.

"Since I was a little boy," Vine answered. "My mama didn't give me one because she said my first name was enough. But I always wanted one, so I took the name of my best friend in grammar school, Victor. I sign everything *D. V. Oliver.*"

"Well, I B damned," Bo joked.

"And Victor is short for *victory*, and that's what I got," Vine said.

"You going to hell, Vine," Sam said. "So are you singing on that record?"

"For your edification, I'm singing and speaking," Vine said. "We're going to record the 'Beatitudes,' originally done by Father Hayes and Cosmopolitan, and I'm singing 'He'll Understand and Say "Well Done."'"

"'No, He won't,'" Chiv said. Bo and Sam were struggling not to burst into a full belly laugh.

"What?" Vine asked. "Why are they laughing?"

"Vine, I don't mean to upset you or hurt your feelings, but you don't sing well," Chiv said.

"Well, thank God you didn't mean it," Vine said. "What's wrong with my singing? I've been singing in church all my life."

"You start out okay, but when you start feeling it, you go off-key," Chiv said.

"You mean *keys*," Sam said. "He goes off all the keys, not just one."

"I can't believe y'all are saying this to me right now," Vine said. He was visibly and genuinely hurt by their comments. "Do I sound that bad?"

"No," Chiv said.

"Yes," Sam said. "Hell, yes."

"Go to hell, the three of you," Vine said.

"Okay, start singing, and it will be just like being there," Sam said.

"Like Dorothy clicking her heels in the *Wizard of Oz*," Bo said.

"Take it as feedback and not criticism," Chiv said. "We just don't want you to embarrass yourself."

"Or us," Sam said. "By now, everyone in that church knows we are close. We don't want you to embarrass yourself, but more importantly, we don't want you to embarrass us either."

"Ease up, Sam," Chiv said. "He is really upset."

"Oh, you two dating now or something?" Sam asked. "There's your big announcement for Sunday. Saints, I'm taking a lover, and his name is Chivas Regal."

"Keep it up, Sam," Vine said.

"Hey, I have the perfect solution," Chiv said. "On the side and without anyone knowing, you should hire a voice coach. He or she can help you, and no one would be the wiser."

"I'm not getting no voice coach because I don't need one," Vine said.

"You're right," Sam said. "You need two."

"And I'm done talking about it," Vine said.

"Good, just as long as you don't sing about it," Sam said. Vine playfully reached for his neck, but he moved away.

The evening ended with more laughs and conversation. Although he didn't appreciate the ridicule and teasing about his singing, Vine did pay attention and seriously tucked the voice-coach idea away for later thinking.

It was Sunday morning, and all were in church. Vine had his sermon all ready to go, including a song he would sing at the end and dedicate to his good friend Sam. What he didn't have was a big announcement. If push came to shove, he would break his promise to the choir and announce the record project to the congregation. In the grand scheme of things, he was more worried about how his sermon would be received. Trying to get hard-shell Baptist folks to focus on living in the here and now and not the by and by was like telling a five-year-old that there was no Santa Claus. When it was time for the sermon, Vine (as he always did) bowed his head in prayer before speaking and imparting what God gave him to share. Right before he opened his mouth to speak, Eric placed a note on the lectern. Vine hated when people did that, but he kept his cool. He had much bigger fish to fry. Vine glanced down at the note and smiled. Eric had handed him his big announcement.

"Good morning, GOB," Vine said, receiving a return salutation in unison. "Every time I stand here, I thank God for you. I'm glad you're here. You passed by a many churches to get here, so I'm glad you stopped here. And we are learning and growing together. Now the big announcement. It has just been confirmed that our next president, Senator Barack Obama, will be speaking to us next Sunday via satellite from the campaign trail. His people asked if he could address the congregation, and we said, 'Of course.' We just had to nail down the date. Thank you, brother Eric, for making this happen." Eric smiled and nodded a thank-you as if he fully understood what Vine was up to. Just like a good and loyal follower, he went along. After a thunderous round of applause, Vine gave his focal scripture and then paused.

"I want to talk to you today on this subject. It's time for a change," he said. "Tap someone on the shoulder and tell them it's time for a change. Imagine placing the stopper in your sink and turning on the faucet just enough to let it drip. Imagine letting the faucet drip for hours, days, weeks, or months. Eventually, the sink would overflow, is that not right? Well, there was this woman in the Bible with an issue of blood. Blood wasn't gushing out of her vagina. She was not hemorrhaging. She was dripping blood. You know that faucet we were talking about? That was her. For days, weeks, months, even years, she was dripping and could not stop. She had gone to every doctor she could and spent every dime that she had. Still drip, drip, drip.

"People stayed away from her. I imagine that she didn't smell all that good. There was blood, no doubt, leaking through her garments. Days, weeks, months, years, drip, drip, drip. But somebody told her about Jesus. Someone told her that there was this man from Galilee, healing and feeding and teaching people. Now her first thought was, *I've got to talk to this man. I'll tell him of my infirmity and he'll touch me and I'll be free.* That was her first thought, but when she got downtown, she changed her mind. Just imagine Jesus walking down the middle of State Street from Jackson to Lake. People would be pushing and shoving through the crowd just to see Him, let alone touch Him. There was no way she'd get to talk to Him. She changed her thinking. She said, 'If I could just touch Him, I would be healed.' So she pushed and shoved her way through. It was nearly impossible and hopeless. She changed her plan yet again. 'If I could just touch His robe, maybe that would slow my bleeding. Maybe some days I would drip and others, not at all.' In her mind, that would be better than days, weeks, months, and years of drip, drip, drip.

"She got closer. He passed, surrounded by the disciples trying to protect Him. She got behind Him. She got closer. People turned their noses up at her. A few pinched their noses not to inhale the scent of her disease. Everyone was reaching for His hands and arms. She changed her plan again. She said, 'If I could just touch the hem of His robe, I'll be okay.' As others were reaching high, she ducked down through the legs of others and touched the bottom of His robe. She didn't hang on. It was just a touch. Jesus stopped and asked, 'Who touched me?' The disciples probably said, 'Master, are you serious right now? Look at all these people. Who's not touching you?' Jesus turned and locked eyes with the woman and told her that her faith had made her whole.

"Famous psychologists, sociologists, and anthropologists have published research about how difficult it is for people to change. Change, no matter what kind of change it is, can snatch people out of their respective zones of comfort into new territory. Change can be stressful. It can evoke feelings of anxiety and uncertainty. It can be uncomfortable, confusing, and dangerous for some people. But if you don't change your thinking or your strategy or your beliefs, you will not burgeon. You will not grow!

"There are too may sick people in this church. There are too many poor people in this church. I have never seen so many church folks with issues until now. Too much depression and loneliness and complacency in this church. It's time for a change. We are God's children. We are supposed to be happy, healthy, and prosperous—not sad, sick, and broke. Stop telling me about the good old days when Pastor Henderson was here fifty years ago. Stop telling me about how you had to wear white on first Sundays. I changed that. You can wear whatever color you want to wear any Sunday. Stop telling me that it's an abomination to allow gay people in the church. Where else are they going to go but the church? Stop telling me that women couldn't wear pants to church back in the day. God doesn't care about your clothes. I used to be that way, but I changed when I realized that there are some great women in this church who happen to wear pants and some skirt, dress, and stocking-wearing sisters who are going to bust hell wide open.

"We are not going to sell chicken wings and taffy apples to meet the financial obligations of this church. We are going to do that with tithes and offerings. We're not having forty clubs in this church. We will have twelve birth-month groups. Get in your group and work it out. We are going to change and grow and change some more.

"Most importantly, we are going to rid our minds of those old backwoods beliefs and rituals about God and replace them with some new thoughts. Long suffering is not a prerequisite of salvation. God is good. He's omnipotent, omnipresent, and omniscient. He wants you to live happy, healthy, and with wallets and purses full of hundred-dollar bills. So it's time for change. That's my ministry. That's what I'll be teaching. You looking for a mourner's bench, we don't have one for you. You looking for an anti-gay ministry, I'm not going to be able to help you. You got problems with White and Latino people and Asian people in the so-called Black church, we're going to disappoint you. If women preachers get on your nerves, take care of yourselves and stay far and away from here. It's time to drop our nets on the other side. It's time to touch the hem of His garment. It's time for change."

As he always did, Vine worked the congregation to a spiritual high. People were clapping and shouting, excited about happiness, health, and those hundred-dollar bills. Mildred, who had been delivered from being wheelchair bound, took off on her weekly sprint around the church. Since she received her healing just as Vine predicted, she does a victory lap around the church each Sunday. Whether she's spirit-filled or not, Vine didn't care. She was a living example of God's goodness and not his wrath. It was a great day at GOB. From Vines vantage point, his true big announcement was well received.

CHAPTER 20

Friday, June 19, 2008

"God knows I am thankful for you being a good man and an amazing husband," Jackie said. "I just wish you could, for one day in your life, be common and trifling and call in sick today. It's your last day on that job. You have 106 sick days on the books. Call them folks and tell them you are staying in bed with your wife. Now go make the call and come get back in bed with me. I'll make it worth your while."

It was 6:30 a.m., and Bo was fully dressed in his uniform and ready for his last day as a waste management specialist. Jackie was still in bed, feeling both proud and amorous. In her heart, she knew Bo would never make an unprofessional and predictable move to call in sick on his last day.

"No, Jacqueline," Bo sang, "you know I'm not going to do that. That's what they expect. It's one of the reasons I'm sure that all the parties and luncheons happened last week and earlier this week. People just assume I would not show up today. Even the deputy director found me on Wednesday to wish me luck and say goodbye before my last day, thinking I wouldn't show up. That's common and ghetto. They won't talk about me like that when I'm gone. I know that there are bets on whether or not I would show today. But I promise you, I'll be home in enough time to change clothes and take my lovely wife out for dinner at Red Lobster."

"I ain't your side chick," Jackie said, playfully throwing her pillow in his direction. "Red Lobster ain't gonna get you no tail. Now you want to fall asleep tonight with a great big smile on your face, I better be going to my favorite restaurant."

"In that case, Houston's, here we come," Bo said. He tied his shoes while sitting on Jackie's side of the bed. "I love you, Mrs. Jackson," he said and kissed her on the cheek. "Can you believe I'm about to retire? I've been with the city for forty years. I've survived rain, snow, heat, and cold. Now this is the final page of my career notebook. I feel proud."

"You should feel proud," Jackie said. "Hell, the sick days you're leaving behind should make you proud in and of itself. Just promise me you'll be extra safe and careful. Don't turn me into a widow before the pension and 401(k) checks start rolling in."

"I'll be fine," Bo said. "See you tonight. I refuse to be late."

As Bo pulled out of the garage, his cell phone rang. It was Vine. It was very early in the morning for Vine. Bo just knew something was wrong. "I don't think in all the years I've known you, you've ever called me this early," Bo said. "Something must be wrong. Just give it to me straight."

"Good morning, retiree," Vine said. "Just calling to wish you a good last day. They ought to be glad it's you instead of me. I wouldn't show up today for nothing in the world."

"I have a conscience and a strong work ethic," Bo said. "What can I say? Hey, have you heard from Chiv?"

"Not yet today," Vine said. "He'll probably call me from the road tomorrow. And rest assured, he'll be back from basketball camp with the ninjas in time to shower, change, and be on time for the party tomorrow night."

"I hope so," Bo said. "It wouldn't feel right if all three of you were not there."

"We'll be there," Vine said. "You don't have to worry about that."

"I don't have to worry about nothing, which is causing me some anxiety," Bo said. "Jackie and the ladies are running the show. She even got Gina to keep Leg and Thigh in business an extra week just to accommodate me."

"Gina would do anything for you," Vine said. "She's on that monkey."

"You a nasty preacher," Bo said. "Get off my phone. I refuse to be late for work today."

"Well, be careful, and I'll see you tomorrow night," Vine said.

After ending his call with Bo, he regretted not sharing his concerns about Chiv. The reason he called Bo was to calm down about this eerie feeling he's had for the last week. It reminded him of how he felt in the days leading up to 9/11. After Bo divulged his anxiety about the party, Vine chose not to pour water on a drowning man, so to speak. And there was really nothing to worry about. Chiv and the team were traveling by deluxe motor coach. There were four other parent chaperones, making it virtually impossible for the ninjas to get into mischief, and Chiv was sober, so there was no worry of him getting drunk and acting an ass. "Lord, I know you are trying to tell me something, but I'm not going to worry. Wrap my friends up in safety, grace, and mercy. Pull them out, up, and through in Jesus's name. Amen."

On Saturday, the fellas and their significant others devoted just about their entire day preparing for the social event of the season: Bo's retirement dinner party. Jackie, the avid planner, gave everyone an assignment and threatened them with bodily harm if their deliverable was anything less than perfect.

At seven on the dot, a long black stretch limousine arrived at the Jackson residence to escort Bo, Jackie, and Ms. Francis to the venue. Bo looked so handsome and distinguished in his black suit and white polo. He would easily stand out as tonight's honoree. When they pulled up to the restaurant, Bo's mouth fell open from shock and excitement. Vine and Hadassah were in charge of the honoree arrival. They rented two jumbo dancing skylights and red carpeting from the curb to the front door of the venue. All the guests were lined up behind the velvet ropes, replicating a star's arrival to the Academy Awards. Bo shook every hand and kissed every cheek on the walk into the venue. He was living out an experience he'd never forget. Entering the restaurant, he could hear Sam's contribution playing in the background. Sam was in charge of the music for the evening. He hired a jazz ensemble for before and during dinner and a DJ for dancing after the big meal. Pearl and Anne made sure the restaurant was adorned with tall vases full of colorful gladiolas, Bo's favorite flower. Over in the corner next to one of the open bars was a tall and deliciously beautiful caramel cake provided by Chiv and Louise. In addition to providing all the liquor for the evening, Chiv and Louise wanted a decadent cake for dessert to go with the champagne toast after Bo's remarks. The dinner was, of course, Italian family style prepared by the cooks of Leg and Thigh. Bo and Jackie took their seats at the head table, which signaled the beginning of the evening's festivities.

Bo was too nervous to eat really. With a highball glass in his hand, he mingled from table to table, spending time with his guests. Alas, it was time for his remarks, champagne and cake. Chiv's absence was alarming and noticeable. It was hard for Bo to fully have a good time wondering where his friend was and if he was okay. Louise got close to the honoree to give him an update.

"Bo, you can relax," she said. "I just got off the phone with Arie. He is headed down Madison to avoid the traffic on the Eisenhower Expressway. The team's bus broke down in Indiana, so they had to wait for hours to be rescued. He's on his way even as we speak."

"Thank you," Bo said. "I know I sound like Vine, but I was beginning to worry. But I'm glad I didn't. He's on the way."

About an hour went by, and Bo couldn't wait any longer for Chiv. He stood, clinked his glass with a dinner fork, and sequestered everyone's attention. "Thank you all for coming," Bo said. "And you all clean up really good. Vine, Anne, Pearl, Sam, and Louise, thank you for what you've done to make this the perfect night. I was trying to wait for Chiv, but that cake looks so good he'll just have to watch the video to hear my speech." The crowd chuckled.

"Congratulations, Bo," one of his female coworkers yelled out.

"Thank you, Ingrid," Bo said. "And thanks to all of you for helping me celebrate forty years working for one employer. And like the old song of the church says, 'I really don't feel no ways tired. I've come too far from where I started from.' Nobody told me that the road would be easy. I don't believe he brought me this far to leave me now. I'm retiring, but I'm not dying. Believe it or not, I will miss work, but I'm looking so forward to starting the next chapter of my life. Do you know what I did on Tuesday? I registered for school. I'm going to earn my bachelor's degree from Loyola. And who knows, maybe I'll keep going and earn a doctorate. So when I call you for help with math, English, and science, don't dodge my call, or you won't be invited to the next gathering in my honor. A special thanks to the owner of this great establishment, Ms. Gina, for letting us take over your restaurant for the evening. I and this entire community will miss you as you close and head off to retirement. And to my lovely wife, Jackie, for producing this event and supporting everything I do. I love you to pieces. And to them Jolly Boys—my brothers. I thank God for you. May God bless you, and that's all I really have to say."

Thunderous applause generated a lot of energy, but where was Chiv? Now Bo was officially worried. Everyone had worked extremely hard to create the perfect event for him. He masked his worry as to not disappoint his family and friends or dilute their energy and efforts.

Jackie assisted Bo in cutting the first slices of cake. He plated a slice for her and then one for himself. As he enjoyed the rich and decadent cake and frosting, his eyes panned the room. People were having a good time. There were huddles of people from all hues, laughing, drinking, eating, and dancing. Even Vine brought all his stiffness to the dance floor, taking a go at the electric slide, the only dance (besides the holy dance) he knew. He often referred to it as the official African American celebratory dance. This made Bo chuckle. "Your boyfriend looks like he could use a couple of squirts of W-D40," Bo said to Jackie. When Jackie panned the floor with her eyes, she laughed out loud when she spotted Vine trying his very best to keep up and remain standing.

As he enjoyed his dessert and scanned the crowd, he noticed Eric on the phone, moving away from the music to be able to hear the caller. When his call had ended, he stood still and began searching the crowd with his eyes. When his eyes met Bo's, he quickly diverted them and continued his search. Bo watched him walk over to Vine and pull him off the dance floor. Something was wrong. After he yelled into Vine's ear, Bo read his friend's face. Something was wrong. Vine's face went flush. Eric helped him sit. After a minute of Vine resting while Eric rubbed his back in comforting circles, they both began walking toward Bo. Sam, Louise, and Hadassah must have been watching as well. Soon, the inner circle was huddled around Jackie and Bo.

"It's Chiv, isn't it?" Bo asked. Bo sat his plate down and walked into the vestibule of the restaurant. The loudness of the party was now muted. "It's Chiv. What's wrong with Chiv, Eric?"

"I just received a call from Northwestern Memorial Hospital," Eric said. "I guess my number was stored as an emergency contact in his phone. He was in a car accident, evidently a really bad one."

"Oh no, where?" Hadassah asked.

"At the corner of Madison and Austin," Eric said. "An eighteen-wheeler grocery truck driver ran a light and collided into the passenger's side of Chiv's car. He's in stable but critical condition."

"Okay, who's driving?" Bo said. "I don't have my car. Sam, how much have you had to drink?"

"Not enough," Sam said. "I'll drive. Let's go. Come on, Louise."

"Uh, you all go ahead," Louise said. "I'll stay here and help Jackie shut down the party."

"Louise, forget about the party," Hadassah said. "Anne, Pearl, and I are here to help Jackie. You go on with them, and we'll connect when we get back to Jackie's. Do you want me to drive and come with you?"

"No, I really want to stay here," Louise said. "I'm not ready for all this, not just yet."

Bo had the look of a disappointed father on his face, but Louise's mental state or her trepidation was not important to Bo right now. He had to get to the hospital.

"We're leaving now," Bo said. "Come on, Eric and Vine. Let's go."

"Okay, baby, I need you to calm down," Jackie said. "We're not going to think the worst. Be the leader, the calm leader."

"Louise, I'm Chiv's power of attorney, but I won't make any decisions without talking to you," Vine said. "I wish you would come and go with us, but I know you need a little time. I'll get as much detail as I can for you."

"Thanks, Vine," Louise said. Her tone was laced with irritation.

Sam, Vine, Eric, and Bo loaded up into Sam's car and headed downtown to the hospital. The ride was somber and quiet. All were having a hard time even imagining losing Chiv.

"It's weird," Vine said. "When he asked me to be his beneficiary for his insurance and his power of attorney, I reluctantly agreed, thinking I would never have to perform those duties. What am I going to do? What if he's brain dead or something and I have to make the decision to turn off the machines? I can't do that. That's not my job. That's Louise's job. And what was all that about from her? She's not ready to deal with it. That's some bullshit."

"Look, he's going to pull through this," Bo affirmed. "He has to. I made you all a promise that I would go first. I plan on keeping my promise. He's going to make it. He has to."

The fellas walked into the emergency department at Northwestern focused and serious as the members of the president's secret service detail. There would be no waiting or wondering. They were going to get answers, and they were going to get them now. The emergency room was full, but it was as if it was abandoned and empty. Knowing that it would be an out-and-out scene if there were any delay in getting to Chiv, Eric stepped to the receptionist to mitigate Vine, Bo, and Sam from imploding.

"Ma'am, I received a call that my father, Arie Eubanks, was in an automobile accident and brought here about an hour or so ago," Eric said. "These are my uncles. Can we see him and speak to his doctor?" The young lady recognized Eric and Vine immediately.

"Pastor Oliver and Brother Eric," she said. "I'm Yolanda. I'm on the usher board at GOB. You all are related to Mr. Eubanks? Pastor, I know you have two sisters. I didn't know you had three brothers." All dropped their heads like little boys who had been caught stealing cookies from the cookie jar.

"Yolanda, can you help us please?" Vine asked.

She smiled, acknowledging that she knew they were not being truthful. She stood from her desk and came around to the four men. "Follow me please," she said and led them through the double-automatic doors into the treatment area. They looked through the opening of each treatment bay they passed, forgetting that Yolanda was leading them to Chiv. Yolanda led them into a small but private waiting room. "You all have a seat and try to relax while I find the doctor. It won't be too long." Yolanda closed the door and left the fellas alone.

"This isn't good," Sam said. "This can't be good. Why would she put us in here? This is where they bring you before they tell you the bad news. This isn't good."

Vine began to pace with his eyes closed. It was as if he were trying to connect to God Himself. Eric joined him. Soon, all four of them were moving and praying.

"In the Bible, there is the story of Hezekiah," Vine began. "Hezekiah had gotten sick with a bad infection and was going to die. Isaiah told him to prepare to die and get his house in order. Hezekiah turned to the wall and prayed. God spoke to Isaiah and told him that Hezekiah would live and that God would add another fifteen years to his life. It was a miracle, and that's what I see, a miracle. No matter the prognosis, just like Sister Mildred ran around the church, healed from being unable to walk and wheelchair bound, Chiv will live. He shall live and not die. In a few minutes, an African American doctor is going to come through those doors to speak to us. No matter what he says, I want you to affirm: he shall live and not die. Chiv is coming out of here." The men ended their pacing and sat, staring at the wall. After about fifteen minutes, the doors opened. When the men saw a tall and very dark African American man wearing a white coat walk into the room, they were relieved.

"Good evening, gentlemen," he said. "I'm Dr. Bradford Mitchell. I'm to understand that you all are the family of Mr. Eubanks." They all nodded. He turned to Eric, who was obviously the youngest in the group. "Are you his son?" Eric nodded. "Then you three must be his brothers."

"That's correct," Bo said. "But you are stalling. We've been here a whole half hour, and we don't know what's going on."

"Mr. Eubanks was struck by a speeding freight truck earlier this evening," Dr. Mitchell explained. "The truck was traveling at an accelerated speed going south on Austin Avenue. Mr. Eubanks was traveling west on Madison. The truck collided with his car on the passenger side. The impact caused the car to spin and eventually flip upside down. He was unconscious when the firefighters cut open the car to get him out. This is all according to the police officers and bystanders on the scene. He was badly injured. His right hip, leg, and arm were broken. He stopped breathing in the ambulance, but the paramedics were successful in resuscitating him. We are running tests to see if there is internal bleeding. Miraculously, he did not suffer any head injuries, from what we can tell. It is a mystery though why he is unconscious. It could be traumatic shock, but I'm not sure."

"Is he on a ventilator?" Sam asked.

"No," Dr. Mitchell said. "He's breathing on his own. We are treating his pain through IV pain medication, so he's not in pain. Again, we will do our due diligence and get him out of this ordeal."

"Is he gonna make it?" Bo asked.

"To be honest, I cannot answer that question now, not until I know the extent of his internal issues," the doctor said. "We are sending him for an MRI to rule that out. If there's no internal bleeding, he'll have to have extensive rehab, but he should be okay. Whether he will ever walk again or have full use of his limbs, I'm not sure. Again, his injuries are very serious."

"Dr. Mitchell, I'm Vine, his power of attorney," Vine said. "I'm telling you now so there is no need to ask: I want you to do everything within and outside of your power to save him."

"I will certainly do my best," the doctor replied.

"No," Bo said, "we need more than that. We need everything you got. We cannot lose our eldest brother."

"You have my word," Dr. Mitchell said.

"Can we see him?" Eric asked.

"Yes," he said. "He should be in a room after this last test. It will be about an hour, and you'll only be able to stay for about fifteen minutes. I'll have Yolanda page you when he can have visitors."

To the fellas, that was the longest sixty minutes or 3,600 seconds that they had ever experienced in their lives. Finally, a nurse came and escorted them to the ICU. When they walked in, each of them gasped and began to shed tears. It was worse than they thought.

Chiv was surrounded by beeping machines, hanging bags, and tubes going into to him and coming out of his body. His skin was pale and ashy gray.

"Look at him," Sam said with tears falling from his chin. Bo sat. He was in a near state of shock. "How in the world will he come back from this?"

"He shall live and not die, Sam," Vine said. "Jesus is a healer."

"Aw, man," Sam said. "Don't nobody want to hear that. I don't know how you define it, but life is not being wheelchair bound, unable to work, drive, or walk. Life isn't having nurses around the clock feeding you, bathing you, and wiping your ass. What if he can't feed himself? What if he's on disability for the rest of his life? Is that living? When you have no quality of life, is that really living?"

Sam left the room before Vine could impart encouraging words. Eric followed him. Vine finally sat. He and Bo just looked at Chiv in silence. After the allowed fifteen minutes, Eric returned to the room.

"Hey, you all, the nurse said we have to go," Eric said.

"Sam outside?" Bo asked.

"Yes. He said he couldn't come back in, not today," Eric said.

"I can't leave him here by himself," Vine said. "What if he wakes up and no one is here?"

"I'm sure Louise will come and stay with him until we get back tomorrow," Vine said. "We'll take shifts so she can have a break."

"I don't know if that will happen," Bo said. "I saw this look in her eyes. I don't know if she's going to be able to handle this."

"She sure as hell better," Vine said. "This is her fiancé. There is no other place she should be than right here."

"Why isn't she here now?" Bo asked. "Let's go. I need to have a talk with her ass."

The entire ride from the hospital to Bo's house was filled with Bo cussing out Louise as if she was sitting in the car next to him. Sam and Vine were mostly quiet but just as irritated. Vine initially resigned to let it be however it was going to be. But Bo's incessant going-on about Louise put him on a low simmer. He was going to let Bo take the lead, but he would not be opposed or shy about tapping in when needed. As they pulled into the driveway, they saw Louise's car. She was no doubt waiting for a report about Chiv's condition and prognosis.

"Okay, Bo, calm way down," Sam said. "You are on rapid boil. At least hear what she has to say. We don't know where she is coming from. Her father or brother or former lover could have been killed in a fatal car crash. We don't know. Hell, for all we know, she could be in shock. I know I'm not 100 percent."

Neither Bo or Vine said a word in response to Sam. They were like two walking sticks of dynamite. One small spark and there would be an explosion.

"Hey, honey, how is he?" Jackie asked, embracing her husband. Hadassah was sitting at the kitchen table next to Louise, nursing a bottle of champagne left over from the party. She smiled in Vine's direction, but he did not return the gesture. In reading his face, she knew he was a bundle of emotions. She had learned this side of Vine. She held back just a little.

"He's not good, baby," Bo said. "The car was hit so hard it flipped over. It's a wonder no one walking near that intersection was hurt. Trying to get to my retirement party and avoiding traffic, two admirable and honest things landed him in the hospital with broken bones and God only knows what else."

"Please tell me you are not blaming yourself for this," Jackie said. "This was in no way your fault. I will not allow you to think that way, you hear me? This is not your fault. Forty years on the job, you deserved a celebration. I don't want to hear another word about that."

"It's so surreal," Vine said. "This is how Catherine and his boys died. He is going to be a mess when that hits him. Louise, this is going to be hard, my friend. He's got to deal with the physical and the mental, but not to worry. You have a village behind you to help."

"Louise, we don't really want him to wake up and hear about what happened from a nurse or doctor," Bo said. "We thought it would be a good idea if someone spent the night with him, just in case he wakes up wanting to know what happened. I'm assuming that's what you want to do. We'll make sure you get there. You don't have to worry about your car."

"I'll go with you to your house to get whatever you need, and then we'll get you to the hospital," Jackie said. "I'll follow you in my car so you can put yours in the garage. And I'm sure visiting hours are over, but you are his fiancée. I'm sure you won't have problems getting in nor spending the night."

"No, Jackie, you've had the longest day of us all," Hadassah said. "I'll go with Louise to her house and then take her to the hospital. And I'm walking distance from Northwestern if you need anything."

"Thanks, everyone," Louise said. "I'm glad to see a lot of love for him, but I'll be okay. I'm going to go on home now."

"We are not letting you drive home and then downtown by yourself," Bo said. "Don't do that to yourself. Let us help you, Louise."

"I'm probably just going home and going to bed," she said. "I am mentally and physically drained. I'll call him first thing in the morning."

"Call him?" Bo said.

"First thing in the morning?" Vine said. "Louise, tell us please what's going on with you right now. You didn't want to go to the hospital, you didn't call one time to check on him while we were there, and you're going to call him in the morning. Did something happen in your relationship that we don't know about because you are not acting like the concerned future spouse of a man in ICU fighting for his life. He is not a mere acquaintance. He's the man who put that ring on your finger."

"Vine, back off," Hadassah said. "Obviously, the woman is in shock and exhausted."

"Stop saying I'm in shock," Louise snapped. "I'm not in shock. I'm angry."

"About what?" Bo asked.

"About the entire situation," she replied. "This is not what we planned. We were saving our money to buy a house. We were picking venues and wedding cakes and tropical destinations for our honeymoon. There was no accident or hospital or rehabilitation in the plan. This is not what I envisioned. This is not what I signed up for. I am so damn angry right now."

"You've got to be strong, Louise," Vine said. "We all do. He's going to need us."

"You mean he's going to need you," Louise said.

"What?" Vine asked.

"I mean you all keep throwing around this *fiancée* word like I'm running the show," Louise said. "He made you his power of attorney, not me. He needs you not me."

"Chiv did that a long time ago," Vine said. "And you know good and damn well he was going to change that after y'all got married."

"I'm not so sure, Vine," Louise said. "He probably chose you because he knew I would not be much of a caregiver."

"Are you really saying that because Chiv made me his power of attorney instead of you, you're not going to that hospital?" Vine asked. "Tell me I've got this all wrong."

"I mean, really, Louise," Sam said. "Would you be acting like this if you two were married?'

"Acting like what, Sam?" Louise asked.

"Like a selfish, narrow-minded, heartless, and unconcerned bitch," Vine said.

"Bitch?" Louise snapped. "You're the bitch. You know, Vine, I would have thought my behavior would make you happy. With me out of the picture, you could finally have him all to yourself."

"Y'all better talk to this broad because I don't like what she is saying to me right now," Vine said. "She's implying the wrong shit. I'm about to go snap, crackle, and pop on her ass."

"Louise, have you gone mad?" Sam asked. "Chiv is our brother. We are supposed to be there for him. I was trying to defend you, but you have crossed the line."

"Okay, everyone, calm down," Hadassah said. "Louise, you owe Vine an apology. You pretty much inferred that Vine and Chiv have some sort of questionable relationship going on, and that's just foul. Now we're chalking your unconcerned behavior and reckless statements to your shock and fear, but you don't get to insult my man like that not while I'm sitting here. If Vine and Chiv were in some sort of relationship, what are you really saying about me? What, I'm just the dumb Jewish White girl?"

"I just need every one of you to mind your own damn business and leave me the hell alone," Louise said. "I'll go to the hospital when I'm good and damn ready."

"Louise, I think it's time for you to leave," Bo said. "I'm about to say some things to you that you won't like and I will never be able to apologize for. Go to the hospital tonight or not. The reality is, we don't need your help in giving our friend, our brother, the help and support he needs. And mark my words, you will look back on this day and name it the day you made one of the worst decisions of your life."

Louise was incensed. She grabbed her purse and stormed out.

It was now July 3 and nearly three weeks of Chiv being in the hospital. A week ago, his condition worsened, and Chiv slipped into a coma. Bo, now officially retired, was at the hospital every morning at ten when visiting hours began and left around six when Sam, Vine, Jackie, Anne, Pearl, or Hadassah came to relieve him until 10:00 p.m. when visiting hours were over. They read to him, prayed for him, talked to him, just as if he were conscious, lucid, and able to speak. According to the doctors, the silver lining in this jet-black cloud was that Chiv being still for so long gave his broken and fractured bones time to heal.

Louise never showed up. During the first week, she called the nurses station in the evenings, avoiding the wrath of Sam, Bo, and Vine, but soon those calls stopped. Louise's behavior was a true head-scratcher and subject of a many conversations among the fellas and ladies. Bo was so exhausted he could hardly get out of bed. The worry and sitting at Chiv's bedside was taking a toll on him. He needed a rest break. He needed Vine to take his place today.

"Good morning, Vine," Bo said. "How you doing this morning?"

"Probably about the same as you," Vine said. "Is it my imagination, or has this whole nightmare made you tired? I get up in the morning, and I feel like a truck has not only hit me but ran me over. Oh, damn, I guess considering the situation, that was a bad example." Bo couldn't help but laugh.

"You all right, man," Bo said. "Stop being so self-conscious. I know what you mean, and I completely understand being tired.

That's one of the reasons I was calling. But you sound just like me, so I'll just push myself."

"What you talking about 'push yourself'?" Vine asked.

"I was calling to see if you could take my shift at the hospital this morning," Bo said. "I know I'm retired and all, but I am so tired. I just can't do it today. Sounds like you can't either, so I'll call Sam."

"Sam is in Indianapolis visiting Jeremiah," Vine said. "He left last night, remember?"

"Yes, now I remember," Bo said. "This situation has got to change, man. I'm losing sleep, energy, and now my damn mind."

"Well, stay at home in the bed," Vine said. "I'll take your place."

"But you have night duty," Bo said. "You can't do both shifts."

"Sure, I can," Vine said. "He's my best friend. I can give him a twelve-hour day."

"Thank you, man," Bo said. "Can you believe tomorrow, it will be fifteen days since the accident? Seems like a lifetime ago. And here I was thinking that by the Fourth of July, we'd be done with this. Guess I was wrong."

"It's interesting you say that," Vine said. "God gave Hezekiah fifteen more years. Tomorrow it will be fifteen days. Wouldn't it be just like God to bring Chiv back on the fifteenth day?"

"That would be a welcomed miracle," Bo said. "But I guess all miracles are welcomed."

"A'ight, let me get to getting," Vine said. "I want to be there at ten on the dot."

"This wouldn't have anything to do with that pretty CNA you be flirting with, does it?" Bo asked. "What's her name—Lorinda?"

"Yes, that's her," Vine said. "Her father wanted to name her Lauren, and her mother wanted to name her Linda. So they came up with Lorinda. Tell me that ain't ignorant and ghetto."

"I wish I could," Bo said.

"And dumb as hell," Vine said.

"Aw, man, don't do that woman like that," Bo said. It had been a few weeks since Bo had a genuine belly laugh.

"Look, we were watching one of those paternity shows," Vine said. "You know, one of those you-are-not-the-father shows. This woman slept with two men in two consecutive days and nine months later had twins. Lorinda was willing to bet me her entire paycheck that it was possible that one man could be the father of one child and the other man could be the father of the other baby. I just looked at her. I couldn't say anything that wasn't mean or cruel."

Bo was laughing so loud he missed the last few words of Vine's statements. "I needed that, although I hate you told me," Bo said. "I won't be able to look at her without laughing. I'm hanging up now. Call me later while you're at the hospital."

"Okay, Bo," Vine said. "Get some rest. Love you, man."

When Vine walked into Chiv's room, he could tell that nothing about his condition had changed. He was lying in the same position, hooked up to the same machines, and received the same medicine. The sounds were the same, the furniture was the same, even the smell was the same. He walked over and placed his hands on Chiv's chest and prayed. That was his routine. When arriving and then every hour on the hour, he prayed. The only way Chiv was going to make it out of this was with the power of prayer. He read to Chiv and filled him in on all the goings-on from Gina finally closing Leg and Thigh to Hadassah's attempt at Kosher soul food. In a move of desperation, Vine poured a cap full of Chivas Regal and placed it under Chiv's nose. Anyone who loved the brown elixir the way he did would surely sit up and ask him to pour. But nothing. Nothing changed.

Teary and defeated, Vine removed his shoes, reclined in the chair next to the bed, and watched television. Around noon, he dozed off and fell into a deep sleep, but something woke him up. He had a vivid dream that he was asleep in the recliner next to the bed and Chiv called his name to wake up. His voice was hoarse and scratchy so he couldn't yell. Just whisper after whisper after whisper until Vine woke up. When Vine woke up, he shook his head to get the whispering to stop, but it wouldn't stop. He turned to look at Chiv. Chiv was calling his name. It was not a dream. Chiv was calling his name. Chiv was conscious and calling his name. Vine couldn't move at first. He didn't want to get excited over a dream or something tentative. He allowed his senses to catch up with his brain before speaking.

"Vine, what happened?" Chiv asked. "Why am I in the hospital? Why am I in so much pain?"

"Oh my God, Chiv, you're awake," Vine said. "You are actually awake. Say something else. Say something else. I can't believe this."

"What are you talking about, Vine?" Chiv said. "Of course, I'm awake. Who could sleep through all that snoring? But you didn't answer my question. Oh my God, my entire body is in so much pain."

"Thank God you are awake," Vine said. "Listen, I'm going to get the doctor so they can give you something for the pain. You were in a bad accident on your way to Bo's retirement party. You have been unconscious for fourteen days."

"What?" Chiv asked. "I was in a car accident? I don't remember no car accident. I remember driving to the party, but I don't remember no accident. I wasn't at the party? For some reason, I feel like I was at the party."

"I assure you that you were not there," Vine said. "Maybe you were thinking about it on the drive if that's your last memory."

"I remember being at the party and dancing with Louise," Chiv said. "Where is Louise? Is she here? I want to see her. She must be worried sick."

"Okay, hold on," Vine said. "First things first. Let me get the doctor, but don't go back to sleep. I want you to recite the alphabet out loud until I get back. This will keep you awake, and I'll be able to hear you. Come on. Real loud. Don't go back to sleep. I need to be able to hear you from the nurse's station."

Chiv didn't ask any questions. Although he didn't fully understand what was going on, he wanted to stay awake just as badly as Vine did. As loud as he could, which wasn't very loud, he began reciting the alphabet. Vine slipped on his shoes and ran out of the room to the nurse's station. Fortunately, Dr. Mitchell was on the floor doing rounds.

Within fifteen minutes, Chiv's room was full of medical personnel. Doctors and nurses examined him and engaged in a discussion about his condition.

"Mr. Eubanks, I'm Dr. Mitchell," he said loudly. "I'm your doctor. It's been a few days, but I am glad to finally meet you."

"I'm glad to meet you too, but why are you hollering?" Chiv asked. "My throat hurts, but my ears are just fine. Bring that down a decibel or two." Dr. Mitchell looked at me as if to ask if this was Chiv's normal behavior. I could only smile, indicating an affirmative answer to his question.

"You were in a serious automobile accident a couple of weeks ago, and you have been unconscious ever since," Dr. Mitchell said, now more softly. "We have run every test on you from here to the sun. The good news is you did not sustain any head trauma, nor are you bleeding internally. The bad news is that you have several broken bones and fractures and will need serious rehabilitation to get mobile again."

"What's broken and fractured?" Chiv asked.

"Your legs, hip, arm, and shoulder," Dr. Mitchell replied. "The nurse just gave you a strong pain medication. Your pain should be subsiding."

"That's why I asked," Chiv said. "I don't feel anything. I must be high as a Georgia pine tree." Dr. Mitchell shook his head and laughed. "Shit, Chivas Regal ain't got nothing on this stuff. As my daddy would say, 'Good Gordon Gin.'"

"Well, that answers my next question," the doctor said. "It's very important that you remain as still as possible. Your healing has had a jump start with you not being able to move. Let's not take any steps backward by you trying to move and interrupt the healing of your bones. I'm going to run some blood tests and another MRI to make sure nothing has changed, and you will be on your way to a long but full recovery."

"When can I go home?" Chiv asked.

"You'll be here another two weeks at least," Dr. Mitchell said. "And then a couple weeks in rehab. We've got to get you up and moving. You may have to retrain your body to do some of the things it used to. If rehab goes well and you can walk and function on your own, you'll be released. It will be awhile before you will be 100 percent. So four more weeks here and then probably another four to six weeks of home rehab."

"Oh, wow," Chiv said. "I messed myself up pretty good. My wife and children were killed several years ago in a car accident. I guess I have a purpose. Although it would have been good to see them again, I'm glad I'm here. Vine, can you call Louise for me?"

Vine didn't answer. After a few more questions and thorough examinations, the doctors and nurse left. Chiv and Vine were now alone. Vine was wondering how he was going to explain Louise's absence.

"Hey, I gotta call Bo," Vine said. Vine dialed Bo's number on the hospital phone. "Hey, Bo, it's me."

"Man, I looked at the caller ID, and it felt like someone kicked me in my stomach," Bo said. "What's the matter? How is he?"

"Wait, I'll let him answer for himself," Vine said and then placed the receiver to Chiv's ear and mouth.

"Hey, Bo," Chiv said. "I'm awake and alive."

"Oh my God, Chiv," Bo screamed into the phone. "Is that really you? Are you awake and conscious after all these days? Say something."

"Why is everyone hollering when they talk to me?" Chiv whispered. "My body is broken up, but my ears are just fine."

"I'm sorry, bruh," Bo said. "I'm just excited to hear your voice. I'm going to get dressed, and I'll be there within the next hour. I gotta call Jackie. You need me to bring you anything?"

"No, but can you call Louise?" Chiv asked.

Bo was silent on the phone. He was sure Vine sidestepped that question, and it was a question that Bo was not ready to answer. He had to say something.

"Listen, I'm going to call everybody, and I'll see you within the hour," Bo said. "And please stay awake."

Chiv nodded for Vine to take the receiver from his ear. "I don't think I've ever heard Bo that excited before," Chiv said. "Wait, I take that back. He was almost giddy at the Bellagio buffet. I'm sure he'll be here soon. Hey, can you call Louise? I know she's probably tired of spending all her free time sitting in a hospital room. I really need to see her and let her know I'm going to be okay."

Vine's body language suggested that something was wrong. "Why don't you just chill for a minute?" Vine said. "Don't push yourself. In a little while, you're going to have a room full of visitors. Just chill for a while."

"Vine, what's wrong?" Chiv asked.

"Nothing is wrong," Vine responded quickly. "You're alive. You're awake. Nothing, absolutely nothing is wrong."

"Is Louise okay?" Chiv asked. "She wasn't in the car with me, was she? I'm starting to remember bits and pieces about the accident, but I'm pretty sure she wasn't in the car with me. I remember calling her from the car."

"You were alone," Vine said. "Louise arrived at the restaurant early to help Jackie with the details."

"Okay, now I remember clearly," Chiv said. "It's interesting how your mind can shut the blinds on certain memories but swing wide open on others." The landline in Chiv's room rang loudly. "That's probably her calling to check on me now."

Vine picked up the phone, glad for another diversion from the message he had to give Chiv about Louise. It was Sam.

"Hey, I just got off the phone with Bo," Sam said. "Let me talk to Lazarus."

"What do you know about Lazarus?" Vine laughed.

"I know he rose from the grave," Sam said. "I may not have memorized the Bible from cover to cover, but I did go to vacation Bible school. Now put him on the phone." Vine laughed and held the phone receiver to Chiv's ear. "Wassup, baby boy?"

"Hey, Sam," Chiv said. "I hear that I am a miracle."

"You are," Sam said. "You certainly are. How you feeling? Don't you hate it when people ask sick people that question?"

"I'm good, man. Well, you know what I mean," Chiv said. "I'm back among the living but got a hell of a physical-therapy road ahead. Thank God for Louise. She might have to take a leave of absence for a couple of months. Hopefully by the fall, I can walk down the aisle as planned."

Sam was silent on the phone before pivoting to another topic. "Well, I'm in Indianapolis, but I'm coming back tomorrow," Sam said. "I'll come straight there from the airport. I gotta put eyes on you for myself."

"Okay, be careful," Chiv said.

"Okay, cool," Sam said and waited for Vine to speak. "So when are we going to tell him about Louise's disappearing act?"

"Oh, I don't know," Vine said. "Bo is on his way. We might call you back then."

"Good idea," Sam said. "Wait and then you and Bo can tell him together. I just don't understand why she is alienating him right when he needs her. I mean, if they were having problems, put that shit on the back burner and tend to him. You know what I mean?"

"Of course, I do," Vine said, masking his sincerity as not to tip Chiv off. "But we gonna call you when Bo gets here."

"All right, bet," Sam said.

"Where you sleeping tonight?" Vine asked.

"At the Hilton Garden Inn," Sam lied proudly. "You want my room number? I told you, that's done!"

"Just checking," Vine said. "That girl is going to get you into a world of trouble. Leave it alone, Sam."

"Done, my friend," Sam said. "I'm done."

"Well, good," Vine said. "A'ight, I'm going to hang up now. Talk back in a bit."

Before he knew it, Chiv had a room full of visitors. The nurses were so overwhelmed they just turned their backs to the rule-breakers. It was good to see a group of people rallying around a loved one who had a second chance at life. Jackie, Bo, Eric, Hadassah, Vine, Anne, Pearl, and Ms. Francis were present to bring Chiv cheer and encouragement and witness the miracle with their own eyes. Chiv was elated, but Louise's absence was glaring. Something was wrong. And whenever he asked about Louise, he never got a straight answer. His inquiries were met with diverted eyes, deep sighs, and erratic changing of the subject. Something was wrong, and it was time to call the question.

"Hey, everyone, I want to say thank you just one more time before this narcotic dripping into my system kicks in," Chiv announced. "I know I've put you through mental hell these past couple of weeks, but you didn't stop praying and hoping for me to regain consciousness. I've got a long recovery ahead, but I know I'm going to be back to normal in no time with your help, hope, and prayers. I love you all. Now that I got that out of the way, where in the hell is Louise?" The room turned silent. Smiles were replaced with blank looks and distant stares. "See, that's what I get. Every time I ask about Louise, I get blank looks and eyes running up and down the wall. Now no one is leaving or wiggling out of this until I get a straight answer to my question. What have you all done or said to Louise to keep her away from me? Give it to me straight."

"Chiv, why don't we discuss this when it's just us?" Bo said.

"Yeah, Chiv, chill," Vine said. "That's Jolly-Boy business."

"The only person you need to be worried about is yourself," Hadassah said. "In fact, we should leave and let you get some rest. Like you said, that narcotic is going to kick in any minute now."

"Enough with the bullshit," Chiv tried to raise his voice, but even the strain on his throat sent shock waves of pain through his body. "If you care about me like you say you do, answer my damn question."

"She hasn't been here, and she's not coming," Jackie said.

"Jackie, no," Vine said, holding up both palms like he was blocking her words from reaching Chiv's ears.

"No, he's right," she continued. "He deserves the truth. Louise cannot handle this, Chiv. Maybe someone close to her in the past was in a similar situation, or maybe she isn't as strong as we think she is. But she cannot handle this. She didn't come to the hospital after the accident. She hasn't been here. In fact, we tried to call her today, and she's not answering her phone or returning our calls."

"That makes no sense," Chiv said. "We were making wedding plans for October around my birthday. We were talking about Jamaica as our honeymoon spot. We made love the night before my trip. This makes no sense. You all must have said something to upset her. Vine, your name is written all over this. What did you do?"

"Vine didn't do or say anything, Chiv," Hadassah said. "I was the last person to speak to her on this subject. I found a psychologist who specialized in traumatic stress and was going to pay for her to go. She was offended. She said that she was not a crazy, nor was she a caregiver. She didn't sign up for this, and she couldn't bear seeing you unable to take care of yourself. She said her man had to be strong and able to take care of himself, not sickly and dependent. She said by the time you're released to come home, she'll be gone."

"Wow, she broke up with me because I was badly injured in a car accident," Chiv said. "What kind of person does that? It's like you all are describing a completely different person." He couldn't help but let a few tears fall from his eyes. He felt betrayed and embarrassed. "Now what am I supposed to do? After the rehab, I'm going to be released to go home. Without her there, I don't feel like I have a home to go to. How could she walk away from me when I needed her? How can you do that to someone you love?"

"Listen, Louise should be the furthest thing from your mind right now," Bo said. "You've got to learn how to walk and dress yourself and get the activity of your limbs and bones back. She don't want to be a caregiver. So what? We'll hire you one."

"But I can't go home," Chiv said. "Not by myself."

"You can hire a nurse," Eric said. "Someone who can help you when you go home."

"I don't want no nurse living with me, robbing me out of house and home," Chiv said. "I don't know what to do. Now I wish I had never woken up."

"Now stop the crazy-ass talk," Vine said. "I know we're not supposed to use this word anymore, but you sound retarded. If Louise is too weak to step up, damn her. We'll change the locks on her ass. You don't need her. You've got me. You've got us. And when you're done with rehab, you are coming to live with me. We're going to hire you a nurse for the days, and I'll be there to take care of you in the evening. God has done what we asked him to do. We're not going to spit in his face by being ungrateful and ignorant, wishing our prayers had not been answered, especially because of some weak, selfish woman like

Louise. Don't say a word. I'm the power of attorney. You're moving in with me, and that's it. Now go to sleep. We're leaving."

Two weeks and one day after Chiv regained consciousness, he was discharged and admitted to a rehabilitation center around the corner from the hospital. He worked extremely hard and made significant progress. Soon after being admitted to rehab, he began walking on his own, which was a major milestone of his healing. When Bo went to Chiv's house to have the locks changed, it was evident that Louise had moved out all her things. It was official. Louise had abandoned the man she said she loved.

CHAPTER 21

Fall 2008

By fall, all were adjusting to playing the cards of life as they were dealt. Bo was enjoying retirement and his new life as a college student. Sam made good on his promise and sent Nevaeh enough money for a spacious three-bedroom apartment and a better day-care solution for Jeremiah. His exit strategy remained a big secret to everyone except Lola, who continued to serve as his secret lover, psychologist, and wife's best friend. But for a minor prostate-cancer concern, Chiv's recovery and return to normal was without incident.

It was the beginning of a new school year, and he was able to return to his administrative role in the Imagination Charter School system. Unfortunately, he had to relinquish his coaching duties to another teacher, but he attended practice and games as often as he could. Vine and Hadassah's relationship hit a rough patch a few weeks ago when Chiv moved in with Vine. He spent his days at the church and his evenings taking care of Chiv. When Hadassah gave him a choice, her or Chiv, Vine chose Chiv. Their relationship had been strained since he made that choice. Also, there were rumblings at the church about Vine's leadership and disposition toward the congregants. The old Vine was coming back. People were starting to dislike his sermons of happiness, health, and prosperity. Slowly but surely, he was turning this bastion of traditional Baptist belief and practice into self-improvement and empowerment. The overall message changed from 'God is gonna get you' to 'God is waiting to bless you.' Words and tone from the pulpit were starting to be a bit much for people to handle.

Marsaleen was starting to see the handwriting on the wall more and more each day regarding her marriage. Sam's withdrawal was more deliberate and unapologetic. Some weeks, he would be home on time every night with takeout for himself and whatever was left over for her. Other weeks, he'd be gone for three or four days at a time without notice, check-in, or consideration. As the time passed, Marsaleen began to question her ability to wait for her husband to end his antics of infidelity. Waiting was getting to be more than she could handle.

Another Friday was in motion, and Marsaleen was finishing up her day at work. She loved Friday up until about three thirty. That was when she was thrown into thought about her weekend. After the whole fiasco with Vine, Marsaleen decided to innocently go on a few dates, not for intimacy but for her own self-esteem. It was important to a gorgeous woman like Marsaleen to feel desired and attractive by men, even men other than her husband. She was a wife, specifically Sam's wife to the core of her sole. A dinner here and there was permissible, but love and making love was for her husband. She longed for the day that Sam would abandon the streets and his "hoeish" ways and return to his duties, accountabilities, and responsibilities as her husband and head of the household. On the way home, she called her best friend and confidant.

"Hey, girl, what are you doing?" Marsaleen asked. "That mystery man you been fornicating with coming over tonight?"

Lola hated when Marsaleen referenced her mystery man. Those comments woke up her sleeping guilt. No man had ever satisfied her like Sam. In her mind, their marriage was none of her business. "Stay out of grown folks' business," Lola joked. "Truth be told, I don't want to see no man for a while, not until I shake this flu. I woke up this morning and felt like a garbage truck ran me over. I stayed at home in the bed. I've made it to the kitchen, looking for a hot toddy recipe."

"Those are easy," Marsaleen said. "I'll come over and make you one. I'll even have one with you. And not to worry, I've had my flu shot. When I'm done with you, you'll forget you even had a cold."

"I can't say no to that," Lola said. "And the weed man has been through, so it's a toddy and weed night."

"Okay, I'm on my way," Marsaleen said. "I'll stop and get the liquor and some Boston Market for dinner. That chicken soup is good and good for a cold."

Marsaleen made it to Lola's within an hour with liquor and soup as promised. After eating, Marsaleen whipped up the toddies and relaxed with her bestie on the couch. "Wait, where the reefer at?"

"'Where the reefer at,'" Lola repeated, mocking Marsaleen's dated slang. "It's upstairs. I'll go get it."

"Naw, you stay your germy ass right there," Marsaleen said. "I'll get it. Where is it, panty drawer?"

"Look in my closet on the floor in my black Bardolino pumps," Lola said.

"You hide your reefer in your pumps?" Marsaleen said, making her way up the stairs. "That's kinda nasty. Hope the fire burns off the smell."

"First of all, heifer, my feet are clean, beautiful, and edible at all times," Lola said. "You won't find loose weed in my shoes. It's in a little brown offering envelope."

"I'm not even gonna ask," Marsaleen said.

When she got to the top of the stairs, the adjusted altitude made her head swim and her eyes blurry. She eased onto her knees in search for the magic shoes. They were in the very last row of shoes. She tilted her head and reached inside the shoe. Her eyes spanned the floor of the closet and fixed on something out of place. She squinted her eyes to focus, just in case they were trying to trick her. Once fully clear, she reached for the misplaced article and examined it inside and out. She was instantly sober. She reached for the other one and held then both in her hands. She was stunned. The contents of her stomach started moving up her throat. She was nauseous. She ran to the bathroom to empty her stomach. All the alcohol left her body and mind. She was now clear to discern and decide how to question her best friend. She was praying that her suspicions were all wrong and there was a believable explanation, but she was not optimistic. She had the evidence of adultery in her hands. She began a slow and trance-like walk down the stairs. The closer she got to Lola, the more the stew of anger, betrayal, disappointment, and rage began to boil.

Only one thing could make her feel better right now. She rushed to her best friend and applied an open-hand slap across her face with her right hand and another with her left.

"Bitch, what is wrong with you?" Lola said, backing as far into the couch as she could, holding her stinging face. "Have you lost your fucking mind?"

Marsaleen then picked up the size 13 weapons and flung them into Lola's body.

"You are sleeping with my husband," Marsaleen said.

"Wait, Leen," Lola said, more surprised than shocked. "Let me explain."

"Who do these belong to?" Marsaleen asked, struggling to keep her distance from Lola. For Lola, everything was moving way too fast. Although she had rehearsed this scene in her mind a thousand times, she couldn't think. She dropped her head and began to sob. "No. Crying won't get you out of this one. I want the words to come out of your mouth." Marsaleen grabbed Lola's neck with one hand, compromising her ability to take in air. "Say it. Say it, bitch, before I choke your ass right out of here."

"Yes, yes!" Lola screamed. Marsaleen released her throat and stepped back.

"I bought these custom-made green crocodile loafers for my husband for his birthday," Marsaleen said. "I even had his initials embossed inside of each shoe. It took nearly an entire paycheck to buy these shoes. I was thinking maybe, just maybe, he would appreciate them. Maybe he would see my value to him as his wife. Maybe he would understand and give me some credit for staying with him and ignoring his indiscretions all these years if I bought him an expensive gift. But what does he do? Puts them in his whore's closet. His whore who is my best friend. How could you do this to me, Lola? I'm so stupid. I've come over here time after time to opine and complain about my marriage to you, and you just lied to me over and over again. You were sleeping with my husband. You are a low-down hoe. You are sleeping with Sam, my husband. I keep saying it out loud to convince myself that this is real."

"Leen, let me explain," Lola said.

"Explain?" Marsaleen said. "This ain't no soap opera. What could you possibly say to me to make me feel better about this situation? What?" She went for Lola again, but stopped herself. She clenched her teeth and pointed her finger. "Don't you ever, ever dial my number or say another word to me as long as you live. You are dead to me. And if you come near me or my husband again, bitch, I'll kill you. And that's not a threat. It's a promise." Marsaleen collected her things and began heading toward the door.

"I am so sorry. I'm going to make this right. Leen, wait," Lola said.

"I don't want to hear a word you have to say," Marsaleen said. "Not one." She stormed out, got into her car, and drove away.

On Sunday, Vine made it to church early with Chiv by his side. He had a special announcement and event prepared for the day. He had to make sure things were in place to support his plan. Just before bringing the message, he stood Chiv up to show the church the latest GOB miracle. The church went quickly into praise. Chiv's recovery was indeed a miracle. Vine let everyone settle down before speaking.

"Brother Eric, are we set to go in the back?" he asked.

"Yes, Pastor, we're ready and waiting on your instructions," Eric said.

"Before I preach, I want to do something," Vine said. "I want all the men in the congregation to stand, please. Don't look around. If you are a man or even think you are a man, rest on your feet, please." Through a few chuckles, the men on the congregation including a few boys stood at Vine's instruction. "If you are age thirty-nine or younger, you may sit. If you are not African American, Black, Negro, colored, or whatever you call yourselves these days, you may sit. If you have had a PSA test and exam between October 2007and now, you may be seated. If you have a PSA scheduled between now and the end of the year, you may be seated." One man who was standing closer to the front raised his hand.

"Brother Pastor, I don't know what PSA means," he said.

"Trust me, you will in a few minutes," Vine said. "Okay, here we go. September is National Prostate Health Awareness month. A PSA (prostate-specific antigen) is a blood test that measures these antigens in your blood. The lower the number, the better. Gentlemen standing, please turn around and look at the congregation." There were about forty to fifty men standing and looking around. Some of them were smiling as if they were being honored or recognized for some great achievement. They were wrong.

"Ladies and gentlemen, Christians and friends, you are looking at the dumbest, most ignorant human beings on the face of the planet," Vine said. "Oh, most of you are thinking that I shouldn't have said that, I'm sure. But I did, and I meant every word. If your house was on fire, you'd call the fire department. If you were in an accident, you'd call the police. I don't understand why African American men, who are twice as likely to get prostate cancer than White men, don't take their health more seriously. One in six of you will develop prostate cancer in your lifetime. The overall five-year survival rate for African American men is 97 percent and 100 percent if caught early. There is a physical exam and a blood test. The physical exam is uncomfortable. The doctor sticks his gloved finger in the rectum and feels for lumps. The PSA is a blood test. I have arranged for all of you to receive the PSA blood test today. If you want to live and stop being ignorant about your health, follow Brother Eric to the annex. Otherwise, you can sit your fool-self down or leave. Continue walking around, refusing to be tested because you don't want to be touched. The funeral director is going to touch you." Most of the men dropped their heads in embarrassment and filed out of the church to the testing area. A few men walked out, and only a handful sat down. The entire church was rumbling with whispers. Vine slapped his hand on the lectern like a judge in the courtroom. "Those were words from the pastor. Now it's time for a word from the Lord."

Vine tried as best he could to get the church past their reaction to his actions, but the looks on the faces of the congregation told it all. They were upset. Aside from a handful of people who would support him whatever he did, there was a spirit of indifference in the temple that morning. He moved past it, tried to ignore it, and let it go. But his spirit man was speaking to him. Although his intentions were good and he, no doubt, helped to save someone's life, it would be difficult to impossible to come back from this one.

After church was over and Vine tended to his pastoral duties, he was hungry and ready for post-church lunch. Although Jackie didn't make it to church, she and Ms. Francis were excited to host Sunday dinner at the Jackson residence in honor of Chiv's recovery. Vine collected his things, and he and Chiv headed to his White Lincoln Towne Car, aka the preacher's car. Once outside, Chiv walked to the driver's side.

"What are you doing?" Vine asked. "You're on the wrong side. Are you getting left and right mixed up again?"

"You know, you're not as funny as you think you are," Chiv said. "I want to drive."

"I don't know, man," Vine said. "Have your reflexes been completely restored? And you're still walking with a little limp in the leg and hip. I think it might be too soon to get behind the wheel, especially with me on the passenger side."

"I am perfectly fine," Chiv said. "It's only a twenty-minute drive to Bo's house from here," Chiv said. "I can handle it. I'm scared that if I don't get behind a wheel real soon, I might be too afraid to drive again."

"Oh, damn," Vine said. "I forgot about the PTSD piece. What if you start driving and have a flashback or something? Something is telling me no."

"How about this: let me drive halfway," Chiv said. "If I take you to the edge of a nervous breakdown, you can have the wheel."

"Why do I feel like I'm talking to a thirteen-year-old who's asking to borrow the car?" Vine said. "Okay, but I plead the blood right now in Jesus's name. And if you put one scratch on my baby, that's exactly what you're going to need."

Reluctantly, Vine climbed into the passenger seat and Chiv behind the wheel. He started the car, took a deep breath, and pulled out of Vine's reserved parking spot with ease and expertise. After a few blocks, Vine relaxed, and so did Chiv. Vine looked over at his friend. Chiv had a big smile on his face. This was the moment he'd been waiting for: some assurance that he was going to be okay. It tickled Vine but made him rejoice on the inside.

"This is about halfway," Chiv said. "You want it?"

"Nah, we're good," Vine said. "Keep going. And besides, you would try your best to whoop my ass if I made you relinquish that steering wheel." After a few minutes of silence, Vine asked the question he had been wanting to ask all afternoon. "So what did you think about today's service?"

"It was good," Chiv said. "The music is always on point, and your sermon was good as usual."

"I hear a *but* coming," Vine said.

"Don't you think you went a bit overboard with that prostate thing?" Chiv asked rhetorically. "I mean, I know my situation scared you, but you stood grown men up in the church and called them dumb. Grown men, some older than you, at church with their wives and sons and daughters, and you called them dumb in open forum. That was not cool, and if I were one of those men, I'd be pissed."

"Oh, I'm sure they are, but they won't be so pissed when they get their results back," Vine said. "My words aside, I helped save somebody's life today, I just know it. And who's kidding who? Some of them jokers would have loved it if a doctor gave them the finger test." Chiv's stoic demeanor fell to the side. He laughed so hard he nearly rear-ended the car in front of him. "Don't make me laugh when I'm trying to give you feedback. You owe those men an apology. You and I both know that you do."

"I don't know about all that," Vine said. "Maybe I shouldn't have called them dumb, although that's what they are."

"Yeah. But you could have said just about anything else, and it would have been okay," Chiv responded. "You could have said, 'This is not a smart position you're in, fellas,' or 'Don't you want to be around for your kids and wives and grandchildren?' Anything would have been better than calling African American men dumb in front of the congregation. You need to get ready. My spirit man is telling me you're in a world of trouble."

"Since when do you have a spirit man?" Vine asked, glaring and the side of Chiv's head.

"Since I moved in with a preacher," Chiv said. "And I know you're tired of me saying this but…"

"Please, Chiv, don't," Vine pleaded.

"I will never be able to thank you enough or repay you for making me move in with you," Chiv said. Vine shook his head and rolled his eyes. Since he moved in with Vine, not a seventy-two-hour period can go by without him thanking Vine. "I mean, you put your engagement on the back burner to take care of me. God is going to blow your mind with a blessing for this. You're not the only one who can see into the future."

"So you have a spirit man, and you're a prophet, huh?" Vine said.

"'Faith cometh by hearing and hearing by the word of God,'" Chiv said. "That's Paul."

"Emm. Hmmm," Vine grunted. "And driving without paying attention makes you run stop signs. That's Divine Oliver."

"I didn't run no stop sign," Chiv said. "See, why you got to spoil all my spiritual moments?"

"You ran the stop sign, man," Vine said. "Go back and see." The two argued and fussed at each other like an old married couple until they arrived at Bo's. Chiv turned off the engine and just sat for a minute. "You all right? You not in pain, are you? Maybe you shouldn't have tried to drive. You feeling some pain in your hip, aren't you?"

"I'm not in physical pain," Chiv said. "I'm in mental pain. Vine, you've got to help me figure this one out. Why did Louise leave me? What did I do to her? She had been wanting to get married for years. I buy her a ring, propose, and help her plan the wedding. And then she up and leaves. This just doesn't make sense. And she even left the school she was at. She transferred to a school in the city on the west side, sources tell me. Vine, promise me you'll get the truth out of her."

"How am I going to do that, Chivas?" Vine asked.

"You just stood up fifty men in the church and called them dumb," Chiv said. "Getting the truth out of Louise will be a cakewalk. Promise me. Between you, Jackie, and Bo, she'll talk to you all. I bet you can get me some answers. Please, man. I need your help."

"Okay, I'll try, but in my own way and time," Vine said. "And on one condition. I don't want to talk about church today at brunch. No one was there, so they don't know what went down. Just don't bring it up."

"That's a deal," Chiv said.

"Chiv, do you want her back?" Vine asked.

"I don't know," Chiv replied. "Some days, I do, and other days, I don't want to ever see her again. What about Hadassah? You want her back?"

"I don't know," Vine said. "Like you, I've thought about it, but that was foul, giving me an ultimatum. I do miss her though. We'll see. We will see."

PART FOUR

Both Sides Now

Tears and fears and feeling proud,
To say, I love you right out loud,
Dreams and schemes and circus crowds,
I've looked at life that way.

But now old friends they're acting strange
And they shake their heads, they say I've changed
Well something's lost, but something's gained,
In living every day.

I've looked at life from both sides now,
From win and lose and still somehow
It's life's illusion I recall
I really don't know life at all.

—Joni Mitchell

CHAPTER 22

Halloween 2008

Not too many people would believe, let alone understand, Chiv's love of Halloween. People would probably peg him as the Independence-Day, Thanksgiving, or Christmas kind of guy. What's known today as Halloween can be traced back to the ancient Celtic end-of-harvest festival of Samhain. During Samhain, people would light bonfires and wear costumes to ward off evil spirits. Christianity embraced Halloween or All Hallow's Eve in the eight century as a precursor to All Saint's Day set for November 1 by Pope Gregory III.

Maybe it was the costumes or the candy or the creativity that lured Chiv in. No matter the reason, Chiv got into it. He was always home, dressed as Dracula, and excited to dispense three handfuls of top-shelf candy to the goblins of all sizes who rang the doorbell. And those with a bag and no costume received one piece of candy and a good talking to about being inappropriately dressed. This year in living with a Baptist minister who referred to the holiday as pagan, Halloween would have to be different. There'd be candy, jack-o'-lanterns, and trick-or-treaters, but no other decorations and certainly no Dracula.

As he sat in Vine's living room waiting to pass out candy, he thought about the last twelve months of his life. Although Vine prophesied health, wealth, and good times, Chiv's experience was full of illness, injury, and heartache. He experienced a life-threating car accident, the abandonment of his fiancée, and dependence on his best friend for care and shelter. A while back, Bo commanded the good times to roll. Chiv felt as if he were waiting in vain. The good times never came, and certainly, there was no rolling. It was also funny to him how much more difficult sobriety had become. When he was more problem and worry-free, he wanted to drink. Now in a constant state of loneliness and depression, he needed to drink. In his mind, the glass of wine here and there didn't really count. Coming from a man who went through a bottle of Chivas Regal a week, a bottle of wine in seven days was still considered sobriety. He could only chuckle when he thought of passing out candy to trick-or-treaters and a neck bone and black-eyed peas dinner with his boys as the highlights of his week. There were three treatments that always helped his depression: booze, friends, and black-eyed peas. Tonight, he was happy with two out of three and a neck bone bonus.

"Trick-or-treat, ninja," Sam said, entering Vine's modest bungalow in Pill Hill. Bo was right behind him. Chiv let them in and led the way to the kitchen. "Man, it smells like straight-up low-country vittles up in here. I smell pork, garlic, and onions."

"Your English isn't that great up in here, but you've got a good nose," Chiv said. "Neck bones with onions and garlic and black-eyed peas with the same is what you smell, my brother. We're eating like poor people tonight."

"We are poor people tonight," Bo said. "Speaking of poor people, where is Vine with our lottery tickets? The jackpot is 44 million dollars."

"He had a ministers' meeting at the church," Chiv said. "He should have been home by now. The meeting was only supposed to last an hour. I guess it takes longer than an hour for Black Baptist church folks to change. He should be on his way. But I bought the tickets this week. I'll pass out the copies at nine. It's funny. In all the years we've been at this lottery-pool approach to retirement, this is the first time we've actually watched the drawing together."

"That damn Vine," Sam said. "He probably achieved millionaire status months ago and cheated us out of our winnings."

"Oh, please," Bo said. "We all know Divine Oliver. If he had won, we'd all know it. And him pulling up his robe and pulling down his pants in the pulpit of GOB, inviting those who wished to kiss his ass, would also be a dead giveaway." All took advantage of a hearty laugh from that one. "They are giving our boy the blues."

"I hear about it all week every week," Chiv said. "I used to think that him insisting on me living here was for my well-being. I'm starting to think it was for his. They question and deride everything he does. And when they found out that his alcoholic friend was living with him, they lost their shit. You would have thought a spaceship landed in the middle of the sanctuary and little one-eyed purple people came out."

"Why is that their business?" Sam asked. "If Vine wasn't my friend and just my pastor, I really don't think I'd care about what went on in his private life as long as it didn't embarrass me."

"And that's the issue," Chiv said. "They are embarrassed by him. The chair of the board said it didn't look right for two men to be living together, especially if they weren't related. It wasn't befitting, whatever the hell that means."

"Oh, Lord, how many MFs did he call them?" Bo asked.

"I asked him the same question," Chiv said. "He said after the first half-dozen, he lost count. They have a problem with him because he's not afraid of them and not afraid to speak his mind."

"You know he's gonna get fired again," Sam said. "Word in the pews is that they are waiting for the annual business meeting in December. It has to be put to a vote since he's been there so long."

"Yeah, I think you're right," Chiv said.

"Enough about him. How are you feeling these days, bruh?" Sam asked. "You back to normal?"

"Physically, I'm fine," Chiv said. "Mentally, I'm messed up. When I'm at work, I'm on it. When work is over and it's just me and my issues, I'm a mess. That's one of the reasons Vine put me on the trustee board. It gives me something to do especially since I'm not coaching no more."

"You seeing somebody?" Bo asked full well knowing the answer.

"Please, I'm like Mister on *The Color Purple* after Celie left," Chiv said. "The last thing I want right now is a woman in my life."

"Naw, man," Bo said. "Are you seeing a counselor or psychologist?"

"Oh, yes," Chiv said. "Twice a week and attending AA meetings. Eric makes sure I get to my meetings. He's a good guy. We should make him a Jolly Boy."

"Oh, no," Sam said. "We've got you and Vine. We don't need no more homosexuals."

"Mrs. Ladeaux's husband is a homosexual," Chiv said, air-punching Sam in the stomach. Come on, y'all, let's eat. I don't know when Vine is getting here, and I'm hungry."

The fellas sat down and began their low country meal and weekly gossip session. Bo asked for help with school as college was proving to be harder than he imagined. Sam played it cool regarding Nevaeh. It was still a big secret to him. He had something more interesting to talk about.

"So y'all know me and Lola was messing around, right?" Sam asked.

"You mean Lola, your wife's best friend?" Bo asked. Chiv laughed, and Sam rolled his eyes.

"Anyway," Sam said. "She called me over a few weeks ago. I thought she wanted to do a little something, but she said she can't continue betraying her friend anymore so we had to stop. I said cool. I just really wanted my gators I'd left over there anyway. Then check this out, right when I was leaving, I leaned down to kiss her. She kissed me like she would never see me again." The kitchen was silent. Chiv and Bo's eyes were wide as saucers.

"You didn't," Bo said.

"Hell, yeah," Sam said.

"And..." Chiv prompted Sam to continue.

"She froze all up and said I was nasty," Sam said. "Only White girls did stuff like that."

"But she did it, didn't she?" Chiv asked.

"Sho did," Sam said. "Like she was being judged in a contest. But sadly enough, that was all I could do, if you know what I mean."

"Yeah, I know what you mean," Bo said. Their eyes widened imagining Jackie and Bo. "No, no, no, that's not what I mean. I'm having issues in the bedroom."

"Oh no, that's a tragedy," Sam said. "You need us to take you to the emergency room? This is truly an emergency."

"Your adulterous ass would label erectile dysfunction as a medical emergency," Chiv said. "What I think Sam was asking is if you've gone to the doctor."

"And say what?" Bo reacted. "'Hey, doc, my dough won't rise.' Oh no, I'm not gonna be the one he laughs about with his other doctor friends. I'm going for the home remedies. Pineapple juice, mint, and turmeric are said to work wonders."

"Yeah, if all you want is a smoothie," Sam said. "If I were you, I'd just kill myself." As if on cue, Vine came in through the attached garage. "Vine, glad you made it. Your timing is perfect. What do you do when your shit don't get hard?"

Vine came in, fixed his plate, and joined the fellas at the table. It was as if he'd been there from the start of the conversation, but that's how them Jolly Boys flowed. "That's God trying to tell you that He has let that nonsense go on long enough," Vine said.

"I just wish somebody would tell me why Louise just walked away from me," Chiv said.

"See, don't nobody care about me," Vine said. "Because if y'all did, you would have discussed Louise's disappearing act before I got here."

"Chiv, you may never know," Bo said. "Just because you keep asking the question doesn't mean the answer is going to change. You act like we know what happened but refuse to tell you. Louise wasn't the one for you. I know it's a big pill to swallow, but you have allowed this situation to put you in emotional agony. You've got to get control of yourself. You're going to have a nervous breakdown." Sam clapped his hands, applauding Bo's eloquent words.

"That was beautiful, Bo," Sam said. "Spoken like a gentleman and a scholar in the making. Now let me break it down. Brace yourself, grasshopper. This might hurt. Louise was a fair-weather girl. She wanted all the good stuff that came from two people in love like a wedding and holding hands in the mall. She wanted flowers sent to her classroom and a big ole diamond on her finger so all her friends could ooooh and aaaah while gazing at the stone. She wanted to be the pretty girl with the short dress, holding the trophy y'all won at the stepping contest. She was about coordination. If she wore a pink dress, she wanted you to have on a pink sock, shirt, handkerchief, something so people could comment on how cute you two were. So when she imagined herself sleeping in a hard recliner next to your hospital bed or holding a straw up to your chapped lips so you could take a drink, she freaked the hell out. She closed her eyes and imagined herself feeding you, bathing you, and wiping your ass, and she was done. She was fair weather, bruh. The accident shook her."

"And when you wouldn't wake up," Vine continued the explanation, "she couldn't see a happy ending. If something happened to Bo right now, we'd have to pry Jackie away from him. That wasn't Louise. She was not ride-or-die, and I don't know how many times or how else to say it."

"It's hard to accept," Chiv said. "I think your theory makes sense, but it's hard to accept. After I lost Catherine and the boys, I asked, 'Why me?' Becoming an alcoholic, I asked, 'Why me?' Then the accident, I asked again, 'Why me?' Now Louise just walks away without warning or the courtesy of a 'Dear John' letter. You're right. I've got to get past this. But mark my words, she's gonna regret this. I'm sure of it."

"Of course, she is," Vine said. "But you wait until she sees you walking hand in hand all color coordinated with another woman. The dead in Christ shall rise. It might be time for some fresh fruit. No more fruit out of the can." This time, it was Chiv glaring at Vine. "It's time for Mona."

"It was official," Chiv said. "You can't hold onions on your breath, let alone a secret on your tongue."

"So this ninja is punking us?" Sam said. "You been to the fruit market, Chiv?"

"No, it ain't even like that," Chiv said. "I made the mistake of telling my landlord here about one of the new counselors at the high school. She's thick and light and smart and reserved, which I find very attractive. I kinda like her. She's flirted, and I've flirted back. I can tell from her clothes, shoes, and purses that she likes the finer things in life. She must have a man. You can't buy Louis Vuitton on a teacher's salary. But I don't want to start nothing new until I've settled this thing with Louise."

"For God's sake, man," Bo yelled, which very seldom happened. "Damn, damn, damn, the thing with Louise has been settled. Let it go."

"You know what," Vine said. "Leave him alone. It might just be time for a Jolly-Boy love intervention."

"What's that?" Chiv asked.

"You'll see," Vine said. "But when she calls you and thanks you for the two-dozen teacup roses, just play along."

"Vine, don't do that," Chiv said. "I mean it. Stay out of this. I know how to step to a woman. I'm just not ready."

"Yeah, okay," Vine said.

"Uh-oh, it's ten thirty," Bo said. "We missed the lottery drawing."

"Oh, I never watch the drawing," Vine said. "We have fifty numbers. I just usually go to the White Hen and scan the tickets. If one is a winner, the machine will let you know."

"Well, can you or your house guest do that tomorrow, please?" Bo said. "Sitting here eating low-country cuisine, I could be a millionaire."

It wasn't actually until the following Thursday when Vine stopped to purchase Friday's tickets when he thought about last Friday's tickets. Why no one called to remind him, he'd never know. They must have assumed they didn't win. He scanned each one, holding the last ticket in hope of a winner. He placed the ticket in the palms of his hands and said a little prayer. He would have been happy with two hundred dollars for three winning numbers and the lucky ball. That would at least keep the pool going for the next couple of weeks. He scanned the final ticket. He heard a chime, and the LCD screen was blinking "winner." He slyly handed the ticket to the cashier who also scanned it. The young Latino dude handed the ticket back to Vine and instructed him to follow him to the manager's office. When he walked into the freezer-size office, an older but beautiful Latina looked at Vine and smiled.

"You got three numbers and the lucky ball plus the multiplier," she said. "That's fifty grand. Unfortunately, you will need to claim your prize at the state lottery office downtown. Keep that ticket in a very safe place and get downtown tomorrow morning early."

"I will," Vine said. "Thank you." Vine made a mad dash to the door. He couldn't wait to tell the fellas. He called them all individually. Everyone was happy and thankful for the 12,550-dollar windfall, but everyone said the same thing: why couldn't it be the jackpot? The fellas agreed to continue playing until they hit the jackpot. They could now certainly afford it.

CHAPTER 23

Sunday, November 2, 2008

It was the Sunday before the presidential election. The church was still excited about the possibility of electing the first African American president of the United States of America, especially after his virtual appearance and plea to the congregation a few weeks ago. According to Vine, God told him it was a done deal. He declared Sunday, November 2, Barack Obama Day and asked everyone to wear their favorite Obama shirt with jeans and comfortable shoes. It was also the day of the special board meeting in preparation for the annual business meeting next month. Vine was excited to share his ideas for the format of the meeting, not knowing that his job was officially on the line.

After service, there was a two-hour break before the meeting. Vine didn't feel like going out, so he snacked on pork rinds and the Pepsi Eric picked up for him at the corner store. Admittedly, he was nervous but felt comfortable that he could defend himself with the facts if confronted by the board.

For effect, Vine was intentionally five minutes late for the meeting. When he entered the room, everyone stood. When Vine made his way to the head of the table, everyone joined hands and prayed along with Vine as usual. Everyone sat, and Vine jumped right in. He was quickly halted by the board chair.

"Reverend Oliver, before we get to the first agenda item, there are some sensitive issues we need to discuss," Deacon George Porter, the board chair, explained.

"What is it, George?" Vine asked, using the deacon's first name and tilting his head, indicating that he was already annoyed. "Now who did I piss off?"

"Pastor, your language," Mildred Hutchins, another board member, said.

"The congregation has been complaining about you," Porter said. "They don't like all the changes you're making around here. And they are really disturbed with how you speak to people from the pulpit."

"Like what, George?" Vine asked. "I'm intrigued."

"Well, for starters, they don't like this new doctrine," Porter said. "All this self-empowerment and happy, healthy, and wealthy talk is offensive to people, especially those who have been here for a long time. I mean, telling people that there is only one power in the universe implies that there is no devil. That's just ludicrous. And all this metaphysical scripture interpretation is confusing to people."

"George and all of you, let me ask you question," Vine said, leaning back in his chair and clasping his fingers behind his head. "If we preach and believe that God is omnipotent or all power, can there really be a devil?" The room was quiet. All fourteen pairs of eyes were on him. "Why is the devil so important and necessary in the Christian church? All I'm trying to do is to get people to focus on God and only God. That's where the victory is. Otherwise, we are nothing but a bunch of down-low hypocritical devil worshipers." He finished and looked around the table anticipating a response, but nothing.

"And what about communion on the fourth Sunday night?" Porter continued without answering Vine's question. "We are Baptist. We take communion on the first Sunday wearing white. And this casual dress code is bad. Women are wearing blue jeans and flip-flops to church, parading down the center aisle. Pastor Henderson consecrated that aisle as holy. It's not holy having women inappropriately dressed standing in the aisle."

"Another question," Vine said. "Hopefully, I'll get an answer to this one. There is nothing in the gospel that says you have to be dressed a certain way to attend worship. Dress codes of stockings, hats, and ties reflect minister preferences, not religious doctrine and teaching. But if we're going to roll with minister preference, I am the minister here, and as such, my preference is casual. Churches all over the country, the world even, are doing the same thing. What makes all of them right and me wrong?"

"It just doesn't look right," another board member chimed in. "Coming in here with no girdle and no stockings and cheap bras. All that stuff jiggling and wiggling. It makes me sick."

"Tell that to the 175 new members we took in over the last two years," Vine said. "I bet you'd get a different reaction. These new changes is what attracted them here."

"And when you stood those men up and called them dumb, that was despicable," Mattie Rainy, the former board chair, said. "You better be glad it wasn't me. I would have given you some not-so-kind words from the pew."

"Mattie, you know I apologized for that," Vine said. "I stood those men up the next Sunday and apologized to them all in front of the congregation. And if you weren't so busy keeping up confusion, you would know that fourteen of those men I offended had high PSA results. And three of those offended men are now undergoing chemotherapy for prostate cancer. If I didn't have on-site testing, they never would have known until it was too late. Believe it or not, I am led and directed by Spirit. Spirit told me to do that. So you can be mad at what I said, but you can't be mad at the leadings of the Lord."

"Pastor, with this diversity thing and making your best friend a trustee and marrying gay couples," Deacon Porter continued, "I don't think you're going to win the reelection vote next month. Why don't you just resign? We'll pay you a year's severance, and you can be on your way with no hard feelings."

"Absolutely not," Vine said. "This church is growing. We have younger people in here now. You have a half million dollars in the bank, and the choir will be recording its first album as soon as I can learn to stay on key. Why on earth would I resign? I'm the best thing next to Jesus that ever happened to this church."

"No, you are not," Mildred said. "Pastor John Henderson, the founder, was the best thing that ever happened since I've been here."

"Oh, really?" Vine said. "Mildred, this time last year, you were in a wheelchair. Now every Sunday, you run around this church like you've got ants crawling up your legs. Did Reverend Henderson ever touch someone and they were healed? Your silence is deafening. So if you don't like me, it's okay because I don't like some of you. This board is old, country, and weak. How about this? I've got a great idea. Why don't you all resign? Be on your way and leave me and the rest of the church alone."

"I ain't going no damn where," George said.

"George, two wrongs don't make a right," another board member, Deacon Jordan, spoke up. "He's a man of God. Watch your language."

"I ain't got to watch a damn thing," Deacon Porter said. "And *damn* is in the Bible. You wanna know what's not in the bible? The word *homosexual, sissy, gal boy*."

"Deacon Porter, is there something you want to tell me?" Vine said. "I'm not a priest, but I can take a confession privately if there is something you need to get off your chest." Vine had had enough of this nonsense. It was time to fight fire with fire.

"Cute, Pastor," Deacon Porter said, "and very cleaver. Let's be clear. I have nothing to confess, but perhaps this is a good time for you to do so. I mean, why would two grown men who are not related be living together? The girlfriend of one disappeared for no reason, and the White Jewish girlfriend of the other was pushed to the side for the best friend. And don't ask how I know things, just know I know things. How are you gonna lead God's people living a sinful life?"

"Let me get you and the rest of this so-called board of directors crystal clear," Vine said. He was leaning forward with both fists on the table with a controlled cadence through clenched teeth. "I am the elected pastor of this church. You are going to respect me whether you want to or not. You are not going to sit here and bring my sexuality into question. Not that it's any of your business, but I invited my best friend to come and live with me after his accident. That's what Christians do. They look after one another. They take care of one another. When others walk out, Christians walk in. I am not gay nor bisexual, but as you very well know, I don't have a problem with same-sex loving Christians. In fact, if I'm hearing my spirit man correctly, there are a few sitting in this room. Don't come for me because you're not equipped to handle my gift. God speaks to me and reveals to me. And if you keep talking reckless to me, I'll start revealing what has been revealed to me." Vine closed his eyes. "I see a lot of sin around this table. So unless you have the courage and nerve to fire me, you will leave me alone to run this church the way I see fit. That is really your only option. Don't play with me. I'm not afraid of you at all. How dare you come at me with this bullshit? All y'all can kiss my—oh, never mind."

The meeting was officially over. Vine stood, and out of respect, so did the others. They started grabbing hands for the closing prayer, but Vine was halfway to the door. The meeting was over. Vine made a beeline to his office, gathered his things, grabbed his black diamond mink coat, and headed for the parking lot through his private exit. He was praying not to run into anyone as the look on his face told a story he didn't want to tell.

It was now Tuesday, and that meant Election Day. Vine got up early, got dressed, and hit the pavement. He canvased the neighborhood encouraging, sometimes aggressively, people to vote and vote for Barack Obama. In the afternoon, he shuttled people from the nearby bus stop to the church, which was a polling place. At the church, he supervised the poll supervisors, making sure that every ballot was completed and read appropriately. There would be no "hanging chads" at the GOB church, not on his watch. When the line got long enough to extend out the door, Vine changed the traffic pattern to keep people out of the cold. By 3:00 p.m., he was exhausted, but he didn't stop working. In his mind, he was helping to create history. In his office, he was watching the tallies. Eric brought in dinner for his shepherd and friend.

"Eric, thanks for the food, man," Vine said. "I think this is the first real meal I've eaten today. I've been so heads down working I forgot to eat. And quiet as it's kept, there is no better Tuesday night meal than Lem's rib tips."

"I wish I could forget to eat," Eric said. "While I'm eating one meal, I'm thinking about or planning my next meal. Michael, my partner, is the same way. We plan our week's menu on Sunday night. We're a little OCD that way."

"You know, that is the first time you've talked about your lover," Vine said. "Wait, should I be using lover or partner?"

"Although he is my lover, more than that, he is my partner," Eric said. "I guess soon, I'll be able to say *husband.* One day, it will happen. I just know it."

"Tell me about you and Michael," Vine said, sincerely interested in Eric's personal affairs. "What does he look like? What does he do for a living? Is he saved? Please tell me the boy is saved."

"Yes, Pastor." Eric laughed in responding. "Michael is saved and a member of Old Time Way Church."

"Oh no," Vine said. "Not OTW? I find those people a little strange, and their pastor is from another planet. I just don't see how people can be comfortable thinking that you are right and everyone else is wrong when it comes to salvation. And you talking about happy? Those are some happy people. Those folks shout on the Lord's Prayer. I'm kind of surprised you would be attached to someone who subscribed to that fire-and-brimstone doctrine."

"Michael hates that church," Eric said. "But he grew up there. His parents are still there. He wants to leave so badly, but he thinks his parents would kill him. They are already secretly dealing with his sexuality. If he left the church, that secret might get out, and the family would be shamed. He loves our church and the diversity work I'm doing here. He would be such a good cocaptain, but he won't leave."

"Oh, he will," Vine said. "I'm hearing in spirit that he will. I just hope that I'm here to welcome him in."

"Why wouldn't you be here?" Eric asked with sincere concern.

"Oh, Brother Eric," Vine said. "I should be counseling you, not you counseling me. I think I'm taking the church in a direction it may not want to go. I'm taking them from get-right church and let's-go-home-to-get-right church and let's-enjoy-this-gift-of-life. The board is not happy with me. I may not get enough votes to stay."

"So what?" Eric said. Vine's expression was shock and surprise. "Yes, I said it. This could be happening for a reason. When my friends bemoan about their pastors and churches not accepting of their lifestyle, I tell them how blessed and fortunate we are. There used to be a time when there was nowhere for us to go. Now we have options. It's up to us to move. So who cares if the Baptist can't handle some new thinking? Maybe you should start your own."

"I love young people," Vine said. "Anything is possible. Do you know what it takes to start a ministry?"

"Nope, but a great preacher I heard said that nothing to my highest good is impossible with God," Eric said. "I'm just saying."

"Man, look at the tallies," Vine said, pointing at the mounted television in office. "Barack is taking the map by storm."

"If God can put a Black man in the White House," Eric said, "he can help another one create and build a ministry. Think about it, Pastor." Eric went back into the polling area.

It was six thirty, and polls would be closing at eight. Vine finished his rib tips and continued watching television while cleaning out his bag. He came across the lottery tickets and remembered he had to play before Friday for Friday's drawing. And like a brick to the back of the head, it hit him: the drawings were on Tuesday's and Fridays. He'd never played on Tuesday before. He began having a conversation with himself. "Naw, I can't do that. They would kill me if I played tonight and not on Friday. I'd have to pay for Friday's drawing out of my pocket, but if I did that and we won, I wouldn't be obligated to share. That doesn't feel right. Maybe I'll take my own money and play the numbers tonight. But if I won, did we win, or did I win? And today, all this talk with Eric about change and the election—is God trying to tell me something? Maybe I should do like the disciples and drop my net on the other side. Maybe I should do this differently. I could have some kind of church with 26 million dollars. I'm doing this."

Vine slipped on his jacket and walked out through his private exit as not to be seen. He walked two blocks to the convenient store hoping that not too many people would recognize him. As luck would have it, the store was basically empty, no doubt from people engaged in election-night activities. He placed his bet and made it back to the church quickly before being spotted. Once back inside, no one was of the wiser. It was as if he had never left. He made his rounds and continued in his volunteer duties until the polls closed at 8:00 p.m. It was a record-breaking night. The election officials on site had to send people away. It was then that Vine realized that he had done all he could do. It was in the Lord's hands. He chatted with Eric and then made his exit.

As he drove home, he could feel something different in all that he saw. The lights were brighter, the view was clearer, and the streets were calmer. It was as if everyone was on their best behavior. People drove by, honking their horns and yelling "Obama" out of their windows. The communities—Black and White, Hispanic and Asian, democrats and some republicans on the low—were bracing themselves for a shift. A prophet of change was coming. God was getting ready to move. When Vine got home, Chiv was sitting in front of the television fully dressed, shoes and all.

"Hey, man," Vine said, removing his coat and throwing it on the empty chair in the den. "Are you going or coming? You are fully dressed."

"I am ready to roll," he said.

"You going out?" Vine said. "You up to going out by yourself? I don't think that's a good idea."

"I'm not going out by myself," Chiv said. "We're going out. Sam and Bo are on their way over."

"Oh, I'm not moving off this couch until McCain concedes," Vine said.

"Sure, you are, after I tell you what I found out today," Chiv said. Vine looked at him in silence. "When Obama wins, he's moving his acceptance speech from the Hyatt Regency to Grant Park. We're going down in anticipation of the crowd, so don't relax. They'll be here in a minute."

"You won't have to twist my arm," Vine said. "I am feeling so emotional. It's like I want to burst out into tears. I should be happy, not sad."

"Maybe they are happy emotions and happy tears," Chiv said. "I say embrace it. I don't know about you, but I'm tired of sad-ass tears."

At 11:30 p.m., Vine, Chiv, Sam, and Bo were standing in Grant Park amid thousands of men and women, girls and boys from every neighborhood, age group, and hue. And no one was afraid. There was too much joy in the air to entertain fear on any level. Barack Hussein Obama had just accepted a concession call from John McCain and was on his way to Grant Park. When he and his family walked out onto the stage, this dream-like feeling was a reality. The Jolly Boys had lived long enough to see a Black man elected to the highest office in the nation. They danced, they cheered, and they listened to the prophet of change.

"This election had many firsts and many stories that will be told for generations," the president elect said. "But one that's on my mind tonight is about a woman who cast her ballot in Atlanta. She's a lot like the millions of others who stood in line to make their voice heard in this election except for one thing: Ann Nixon Cooper is 106 years old. She was born just a generation past slavery, a time when there were no cars on the road or planes in the sky, when someone like her couldn't vote for two reasons—because she was a woman and because of her skin color. And tonight, I think about all that she's seen throughout her century in America—the heartache and the hope, the struggle and the progress, the times we were told that we can't, and the people who pressed on with that American creed: Yes, we can. At a time when women's voices were silenced and their hopes dismissed, she lived to see them stand up and speak out and reach for the ballot. Yes, we can. When there was despair in the dust bowl and depression across the land, she saw a nation conquer fear itself with a New Deal, new jobs, a new sense of common purpose. Yes, we can. When the bombs fell on our harbor and tyranny threatened the world, she was there to witness a generation rise to greatness and a democracy was saved. Yes, we can. She was there for the buses in Montgomery, the hoses in Birmingham, a bridge in Selma, and a preacher from Atlanta who told a people that we shall overcome. Yes, we can. A man touched down on the moon, a wall came down in

Berlin, a world was connected by our own science and imagination. And this year, in this election, she touched her finger to a screen and cast her voice, because after 106 years in American, through the best of times and the darkest of hours, she knows how America can change. This is our time to put our people back to work and open doors of opportunity for our kids; to restore prosperity and promote the cause of peace; to reclaim the American dream and reaffirm that fundamental truth that, out of many, we are one; that while we breath, we hope. And where we are met with cynicism and doubts and those who tell us that we can't, we will respond with that timeless creed that sums up the spirit of a people: Yes, we can. Thank you. God bless you. And may God bless the United States of America."

CHAPTER 24

Friday, November 11, 2008

After election night, the rest of the week was a wash. Managers all over the United States shared a common sentiment of frustration in trying to get people to focus on work. Absenteeism was sky-high, and liquor outlets reported a very low inventory of champagne. Deliveries were late, crime was down, and spirits were up. There was something almost paranormal blowing in the wind. Hope, probability, and chance were the go-to words felt and expressed by many. The Jolly Boys were on a high, but none like Vine. Have him tell it, his efforts changed the course of history. Who better than to host a Friday night get-together than the great history maker himself?

"I just hope this ninja don't get into office and forget what color he really is," Sam said.

"See, there you go," Vine said. "We've been following this man ever since he announced that he was running. What has he said or done to give you the impression that he would forget the many bridges that brought him over?"

"It happens," Sam continued. "And he's part White too? If that joker wakes up one morning confused, we gonna be in a heap of trouble."

"Okay, I'm not lauding myself as a history maker like the gentleman from Pill Hill, but let's give the man some credit," Bo said. "If ever we had a chance, we have one now. What did he say? 'Yes, we can.'"

"Oh, damn," Vine said as if he had forgotten something. "What is wrong with me? We should have 'Yes, We Can' T-shirts made, with a checkbox. We could make a fortune."

"I'm sure someone has already thought of that," Chiv said. "Michelle got Sasha and Melia selling shirts on the corner of 87th and State."

"You going straight to hell for that one," Vine said. "I just need a couple hundred to get started. I'm working on this idea first thing tomorrow morning."

"Okay, wait, it's nine," Bo said. "Turn to channel 9 so we can see the lottery drawing. Vine, give us our copies so we can check the numbers. It might bring us luck sitting in front the television. Maybe our positive vibes will make the right balls come on through." Vine looked as if he had seen a ghost do cartwheels down his hallway. "Vine, what's the matter with you?"

"I forgot to play the numbers today," Vine said.

"What?" Sam said. "You forgot to play the numbers?"

"Yes, with all the excitement of the week, I forgot to play the numbers," Vine said.

"Divine Oliver, if these numbers fall tonight and we don't have tickets for them, we gonna break up all this pretty shit in here beating yo ass."

"I did something different," Vine said. "I played them Tuesday instead."

"And I take it we didn't win," Sam said.

"I don't know," Vine said. "With the—"

"Excitement of the week, you forgot to check the numbers," Sam said, completing Vine's sentence. "Go on the internet to see if we can pull up the winning numbers for Tuesday. We have been consistent for all these months, and all of a sudden, we change our routine? This won't be good."

Chiv sat at the computer and began searching the lottery website for the numbers. It took several clicks, but he was able to find them. He printed out the numbers and handed them to Vine, who, in the meantime, retrieved the tickets from his briefcase.

"Here, somebody else check," Vine said. "I just got nervous all of a sudden."

Chiv took the tickets, laid them side by side on the cocktail table and held the printout in his hand. The fellas went on in conversation as they were not hopeful that Vine's deviation from the plan would yield any results.

"Bo, Bo," Chiv called out. "Come over here. Compare the numbers on this ticket to the printout."

"Everybody done gone plantation crazy," Bo said, standing and walking over to the table. His eyes bounced back and forth, comparing the printout to the ticket in question. "I don't believe this shit. Wait, Sam, take this ticket. I'm going to read some numbers. You tell me all the numbers that match."

"Okay," Sam said, wondering why Chiv and Bo had begun pacing.

"Okay, 8, 24, 28, 42, 62, and extra ball 21," Bo read, slowing his pace. "Did any of those numbers match?"

"Yes, they all did," Sam said and then paused. His brain was catching up with his eyes. "All the numbers match, including the extra ball. What does this mean?"

"This means that we just won 165 million dollars," Bo said. "We just won 165 million dollars. We just won 165 million dollars."

Sam ran to Bo and snatched the printout from him to compare the numbers with his own eyes. "They match," Sam said. "They really match." This time, screaming. "Vine, we won, man. Your plan worked. We won the jackpot. We're rich."

Vine's eyes rolled back, and he spiraled to the floor. Sam and Bo ran to him and started slapping his face. Still stiff, Chiv just stood over the three of them on the floor, trying to revive Vine.

"Vine, bruh, snap out of it," Sam said, slapping him in the face. Bo took his highball glass, which held his now watered-down drink and threw it in his face, ice cubes and all. Vine snapped back, sitting straight up.

"What the hell you do that for?" Vine asked.

"I'm sorry, bruh," Bo said. "I panicked. I saw that in a movie once. Are you okay?"

"Yeah, I think so," Vine said, groggy as if he'd been asleep all afternoon. "Someone said we won. That's the last thing I heard."

"We did," Chiv said. "We are millionaires. After taxes, we have one hundred million dollars. That's 25 million apiece."

"Okay, okay," Sam said. "Everybody, calm down. We could have this wrong."

"Let's go to the convenience store around the corner," Bo said. "We'll run the ticket through the machine. If it's a winner, we run the hell out of the store."

Sam and Bo ran out of the house and to Sam's car. Chiv walked over and helped Vine off the floor. Before long, Sam and Bo returned with the confirmed news. They won. The(m) Jolly Boys were rich.

"Okay, this isn't funny anymore," Vine said. "I only faint when I preach too hard or receive shocking, startling news. Please don't shock me with this being a practical joke or something."

"Preacher man, you might as well get back down on the floor," Sam said, popping the cork on what looked like an expensive bottle of champagne. "The(m) Jolly Boys, us Jolly Boys, we Jolly Boys is rich."

As sore as his body was, Chiv tried to jump up and down. But the tightness of muscles just wouldn't let him, and everyone in the room felt it.

"Chiv, please sit your ass down," Sam said. "You making me hurt just by looking at you."

"So how much did we win exactly?" Vine said, looking through his cabinets for champagne glasses.

"I have it written here on this here piece of paper," Bo said. He was so happy he could hardly contain himself. "We won 165,000,000 dollars. After taxes, we are left with 25,000,000 dollars each. We get all if we go public and half if we want to remain anonymous. Also we get half if we want all cash right now. If we elect the annuity, we get five million dollars in cash now and one million January 1st of each year for twenty years plus interest for the year."

"We should get the cash," Sam said. "And stay anonymous. That's six million right now."

"You stupid as hell," Chiv said. "If we take an annuity, we get five million now, another one million on January 1, which is only a little over a month away, and then one million every year for the next twenty years."

"But what if I die in the next twenty years?" Sam said.

"The money goes to your beneficiary," Bo said.

"Aw, hell, naw," Sam said. "We getting our cash now."

"I'm not going to die within the next twenty years," Bo said. "We're taking the annuity. I ain't leaving no money on the table. Now we have to call the lottery commission on Monday and make an appointment. We'll go down on Tuesday to smile at the cameras and get our checks. But we have to decide annuity or lump sum."

"Sam is the only one for lump sum," Vine said. "We're getting the annuity." Sam was so hoping for the cash. Marsaleen wouldn't have to know, and he and Nevaeh could live comfortably together for the next twenty years. The annuity made sense to the normal man but created all kinds of problems for the adulterous brother with a clandestine plan to leave his wife for his pole-dancing lover. "In fact, where is the ticket?"

"It's in my wallet, which I will not let out of my sight until Monday morning," Bo said. "If I have to put it in my mouth when I go the bathroom, I will not let that wallet out of my sight."

"That's just nasty," Chiv said. "First thing in the morning, go to the bank and put it in your safety deposit box. We'll pick it up before we go to the appointment on Tuesday. That way, you piss in peace."

"I'm scared to go to sleep," Vine said. "I'm scared of waking up and finding out that this was all a dream. I am a millionaire." Vine found the crystal flutes, and Sam filled them full of champagne. "Thank you, God, for keeping your promise." Everyone took a sip. Chiv emptied the contents of his glass down his throat in a matter of seconds. "Chiv, you know you ain't supposed to be drinking."

"Leave him alone," Sam said. "He don't have to do nothing he don't want to do. He's rich. We're rich."

"We should do something wild and crazy like fly to Vegas tonight," Sam said.

"Hold on. Now everybody get a leveled head," Bo said. "We're going to get some financial advice about this before we lose our minds. It would be a shame to live from lottery check to lottery check." The fellas sat down and slowly but surely came down from their high. The champagne was gone, so now everyone was nursing their Chivas and ginger ale.

"I just don't want to end up like those people who get excited, quit their jobs, and go on wild spending sprees and end up having to work again," Vine said.

"Ain't that the truth," Sam said. "Folks go in and tell their bosses to kiss their ass, and less than a year later, they are right back in that boss's office begging for their old job back. That will not be our testimony."

"The trajectory of our lives is about to change in a matter of days," Vine said.

"You know what I'm going to do?" Bo said. "I'm going to pay off my house, fix it up a bit, and then sell it. "Then I'm going to build my dream home from the ground up. I'm staying in Beverly, but I'm going to find some land and build a new modern home that will put those old, drafty, historical money pits to shame. Then me and Jackie are going to travel. I've always wanted to go to Paris and take the train to London. Of course, we'll go to Africa, the motherland, and Jerusalem, the Holy Land. I want to see the Taj Mahal in India, get some suits custom-made in Hong Kong, some shoes in Millan, and attend a Papal mass in Rome."

"Now that sounds like a lot of fun," Chiv said. "But there are places here we haven't seen."

"That's true," Bo said, "so I'll add a visit to the Sequoia National Forest in California to see the big trees, the Grand Canyon, Mount Rushmore, and the Golden Gate Bridge. Imagine eating fresh pineapple and homemade coconut cream pie in Hawaii. And the icing on the cake will be to fly first class everywhere all the time. The days of being stuffed into a coach seat are gone."

"All that traveling," Chiv said, "you'll never finish your degree."

"Oh, I'm done with that," Bo said.

"Done," Sam said. "How can you be done? You're not even done with the first semester, are you?"

"They don't know I'm done, but I'm done," Bo said. "I'm not a defeatist, but that's not for me. I don't have to because now I don't have to do nothing I don't want to do."

"I was all ready to call you Dr. Beauregard Jeramiah Jackson," Chiv said.

"I don't give a damn about no degree," Bo said. They were cracking up. Bo was always amusing when he had been slightly over-served. "Vine, what you gonna do? And please don't tell those people on Sunday to kiss your natural Black ass from the pulpit."

"I ain't gonna lie," Vine said and began laughing. "In the last few hours, I was imagining doing just that and being completely naked under my robe. I'd give them a little peep show on my way out the door. I don't usually watch the recordings of the services, but I'd get a few copies of that one."

"Just to see your own ass on camera?" Sam said. "Now that's somebody's nasty."

"Naw, to see the looks," Vine responded. "Now that would be hilarious. But in answer to your question, I'd go downtown and buy a two- or three-bedroom condo just like Hadassah's. I've always wanted to live downtown and have a doorman and look out at the lake every morning. That's first, and then I would find the New Thought people, go to the New Thought school, get ordained as a New Thought minister, and open my own New Thought church. I won't have to slip new ideas in or ease people into a new way of thinking. They'll walk in the door expecting not to be yelled at and spit on and horrified about their lives. I won't be popular, but I think that is my calling."

"Well, I support you and wish you well, but I gotta stick to what I know," Bo said. "And that's the Baptist way. My beliefs have served me well in these sixty-five years. I'm too old and set in my ways to do God differently. I'll write you a check, but I'm staying at GOB."

"Bo, that is okay," Vine said. "Actually, it illustrates my point very well. Salvation is a personal thing. There is no right or wrong when it comes down to how you choose to work out your soul salvation, as the old folks used to say. You support me, and I support you."

"Vine, don't you want to do something wild and exotic?" Sam said. "You gonna buy a crib and start your own church. How boring is that? Don't you want to get you a fine sister and shower her with gifts and flaunt her around Chicago?"

"I think you've got your dream mixed up with mine," Vine said. "I wonder what Hadassah is going to say when she hears that I'm rich."

"She'll probably want you back," Bo said. "I still don't understand what happened between you two. At one dinner party, you were hinting at marriage, and at the next, y'all had gone your separate ways."

"Hadassah is a good person," Vine said. "But she had a hard time with me being a Jolly Boy. And when she said it's Arie or me, well, you see what happened."

"Wait, did that really happen?" Chiv asked. "Did she really give an ultimatum and you chose me? Please tell me that didn't happen."

"Well, it did, but don't blame yourself," Vine said. "It wasn't that deep. She could have said it's either a gorilla or me, and I would have chosen the gorilla."

"Looks like you did," Bo said, nearly falling off the couch laughing at his own wit.

"No, but if I let her get away with 'it's either this or me,' it would always be her trump card," Vine said. "Now I meant what I said about not leaving you alone and taking care of you, but no one gives Vine Oliver an ultimatum."

"Well, I didn't like her at first, but she grew on me," Sam said. "She wasn't able to change her skin color, but she was all right, as White women would go. I'll loan you Lola sometime, you know, just to take the edge off."

"I thought you were done with that?" Bo asked. "Sleeping with your wife's best friend. Now that is a guaranteed first-class ticket to the south side of hell."

"Please, all I gotta do is say I'm a millionaire, and she'll open her door and anything else for me," Sam said. "In fact, I might stop over there on my way home."

"Are you going to tell Marsaleen?" Chiv asked.

"Yeah, you never said what you were going to do with your money," Vine said. "Now this ought to be good."

"Oh, mine is simple," Sam said. "I'm going to give Marsaleen two million, and then I'm moving to Indianapolis. I'm going to leave her and marry Nevaeh."

"You can't be serious," Vine asked.

"I'm very serious," Sam said. "I wasn't going to say anything, but I've been sending her money. She's setting up house for us. I told her that I needed some time, but I was leaving my wife. Now I have no reason to stay. I'm retiring and moving to Indianapolis."

"Sam, I don't think—" Bo began before Sam interrupted him.

"It's a good idea. I know, Bo," Sam said. "You are a man of valor and standards and all that, and you couldn't imagine doing this to Jackie. I get it. But you and I are not the same person. I love Marsaleen, but she knew I was a player when she married me. Nevaeh is the only woman I've been with that I deem worth ending my marriage for. And I have a son that needs a father, even an old father like me. I'm sixty-four years old and may have ten or fifteen good years left. I want to spend those days fully happy, not happy enough. And Indianapolis is a three-hour drive from here. I won't miss a Jolly-Boys meeting, I promise." The mood turned solemn. Bo, Vine, and Chiv were trying to wrap their heads around Sam leaving. It wasn't right to leave his wife and the brotherhood, but they had to support him. That was the Jolly-Boy way. "Jeremiah is going to live a good life not wanting for a thing, living in a home with a mother and father. You all have to give me some credit for that."

"I think you're making a mistake, but it's your mistake to make," Vine said. "It's gonna be weird not having you in the city. But we'll support you, whatever that means, I guess."

"Well, Chiv, your turn," Sam said. "I know I am a hard act to follow, but what's your plan? You are the only one who has experience with big money. How does this feel?"

"You know, after I got the settlement money from Catherine and the boys, I just put it away and forgot about it," Chiv said. "It couldn't tout myself as well-off with my wife and boys dead. There was no glory or joy in that. And the little money they gave me was piddling at best compared to what I lost. For me, I'm going to adjust to living well alone. I might follow Vine downtown and get a crib in the Hancock. I've always wanted to live there. And then by a couple of cases of CR and adjust to living well alone."

"You're going to retire at least, aren't you?" Bo asked.

"Probably not," Chiv said. "The only normal and stable thing in my life right now is those kids. And I don't have nothing else to do."

"Man, that sounds sad as hell," Sam said. "There has got to be a dream you've got buried inside of you somewhere. I know you got more than working, drinking, and living alone."

"All my dreams got deferred," Chiv said. "It's like I feel guilty for being happy."

"Aw, you got to come out of that shit," Vine said. "Happiness, health, and wealth are a given. I heard a New Thought preacher say it was your birthright. Come on. Think really hard. What is your dream, Chiv?" Chiv stared off for a minute and then smiled and chuckled. "Oh, here it comes. He's got something, y'all."

"When I was in college, I had a business class," Chiv said. "One of our assignments was to create a business. For the entire semester, we had to apply what we learned to our business idea. I had this idea for a business I called BMS: Black Man's Saturday."

"The hell?" Sam said.

"What do Black men do on Saturday?" Chiv asked. "They get their car washed, go to the dry cleaners, sit for hours in the barbershop, and make a trip to the liquor store. Imagine all that under one roof." As Chiv explained his idea, he lit up with excitement. "You'd pull up to the front and hand your keys to the valet. They'd take your dry-cleaning bag out of your car (everybody would get a purple bag for their dry cleaning) and take it to the dry-cleaning department before taking your car around back to the car wash. You'd go to the barbershop for your appointment. While you waited, you could play pool, enjoy the buffet, hang out in the theater and watch a movie, get a manicure and pedicure, or work out in the gym. You'd also be able to place your liquor order. When you were done with your haircut, your car would be waiting for you in a reserved parking spot with your dry cleaning and your liquor order in the trunk."

"Wow, that sounds good, but you know these cheap ninjas ain't gonna pay for all that," Bo said.

"Correct," Chiv said. "There would be a special clientele who would pay for a monthly membership, maybe 250 dollars. It would be exclusive. It would start slow, but soon everyone would want in. Black men love the idea of having access to something exclusive."

"See, that's a great idea," Bo said. "Instead of sitting home looking out the window and sipping on CR, you should work that idea. But I don't like the name. You should call it the Millionaire Boys Club."

"How about this?" Vine said. "How about the Jolly Boys Club? We'll invest. And, Bo, you could open Beauregard's Buffet in there. Ms. Francis could run the buffet. Think about it."

"But I want to do something with kids," Chiv said.

"Jackie will want to open a boys-and-girls club," Bo said. "Somewhere in the South Loop, we could have a boys-and-girls club with all kinds of activities and homework help. And you could name it after your boys."

"The Nero and Arie Jr. Eubanks Young Citizen's Club," Chiv said. "That would be amazing. I've been looking for a way to spend that settlement money that would make me feel good. That's the seed money I'd need."

"Now you're talking," Sam said. "But by all means, get you a woman. You need some loving in your life. And not Louise's ass. I can't wait to walk up on her one day. I ain't never hit a woman, but as Eddie Murphy said, 'I'd shake the shit out one.'"

"If you walk up on her, leave her alone," Chiv said. "Louise has shown me exactly what type of woman she is. If I yoke up with that one, don't shake me. Knock me all the way out."

CHAPTER 25

MEETING OF THE MINDS

On Monday, Vine sat on the side of his bed waiting for the clock to strike 9:00 a.m. That's when he would carry out the delegated task of calling the lottery office and reporting the names of the jackpot winners. He was given an appointment for 9:30 a.m. the next day. The next morning, Vine stood in front of his closet, perplexed with what to wear to collect his portion of the jackpot. He settled for a thin sweater, dress slacks, and expensive shoes. The fellas provided their own transportation as they would head straight to the bank after their meeting at the lottery office. At 9:30 a.m. as planned, Bo, Vine, Chiv, and Sam appeared in the state lottery office and presented their winning ticket. Their minds were on one accord as they all had on thin sweaters, dress slacks, and expensive shoes. The rest of the day was spent completing paperwork, taking pictures, eating a lavish lunch, and staring at the five-million-dollar checks each held in their hands. Vine was wrong. It was not a dream. At approximately 2:19 p.m., he and his close friends were officially millionaires. And because of a misunderstanding, the fellas could remain anonymous. There would be a news story that evening, but it would not include their photographs and names. Their pictures, however, would line the hollowed halls of the lottery office, next to winners who came before them. At the end of the day, the fellas gathered in the massive and open lobby of the State of Illinois Building, with smiles of the rich and famous.

"Well, life from here on out sure gonna be different," Bo said. "Jackie has been trying to play it cool, but I know she's at home pacing and itching to spend my money."

"It's like I don't know what to do now," Chiv said. "The day is kinda anticlimactic. I didn't expect a parade or nothing, but I thought there would be more fanfare than this."

"I'm on my way to Indianapolis," Sam said. "I'm going to make my own fanfare, if you know what I mean."

"You better wear a condom or two," Vine said. "Just in case there is some residual fanfare crawling in and through that…"

"Vine, come on, man," Sam said. "We are talking about the next Mrs. Ladeaux. I'm going to the bank and hitting the road. I'll be back on Saturday. Let's play golf and have brunch on Saturday. Rich men play golf and have brunch on Saturdays."

"It's November in Chicago," Chiv said. "Ain't nobody playing golf."

"They have indoor golf courses," Sam said. "I'll hook it up. Keep your Saturday free. All right, I'm out. Love y'all."

On Thursday, Chiv, Bo, and Vine received a text message from Sam. He had obviously come back from Indianapolis and wanted them to meet him at an old catalog-printing company near the convention center. He had a great business idea that he needed to discuss. Vine and Chiv scooped up Bo, and they headed that way. When they arrived, the description was accurate. The building was old and very abandoned. The side door was propped open. The fellas took that as their way inside. The building had been gutted to the studs and was as massive high as it was wide. Just at the point where they felt afraid, they heard footsteps. They thought it was Sam's big feet, but it sounded more like heels on concrete. In an instant, they understood why.

"Well, good afternoon, gentlemen," Marsaleen said, hugging and kissing each one. "I know you are shocked to see me."

"Yes, we are," Bo said. "Where is Sam?"

"Hold on a minute," Marsaleen said. "Let me get these folding chairs for the millionaires." When the fellas looked in the direction of her gait, they saw four folding chairs against the wall. Vine and Bo followed her to assist. “Here we go. Now that’s better. I should know better than to make a millionaire stand.”

“I’m sorry. Where is Sam?” Bo asked again.

“I would have thought he told you all everything,” Marsaleen said. “Sam is in Indianapolis visiting his hoe and bastard child. My God, the looks on your faces are priceless right now. It’s like I’m staring into the eyes of horror and her distant cousin, dismay.”

“Marsaleen, if you have an issue with Sam’s indiscretions, I think you should talk to him, not us,” Bo said.

“Spoken like a true Jolly Boy, Bo,” she said. “Let’s get into it, shall we? As you know, my former best friend, Lola, was sleeping with my husband,” Marsaleen said. “After I caused her inability to taste and smell by slapping the shit out of her, I walked out of her house for what I thought would be forever. I guess the guilt and shame was too much for her. She had to somehow do right by me. So she came to my house and told me that my husband had won a significant amount of money from the state lottery. She also told me that my husband plans on giving me a portion of his winnings and then moving to Indianapolis to be with his whore, Nevaeh Miller, and his bastard child, Jeremiah. In fact, I was told that he has been setting up house with her for some time now, planning the perfect time to make his exit. He’s no doubt there now house hunting, getting ready for the big move.”

“I’m sorry, Marsaleen,” Chiv said. “No disrespect, but our loyalty is to Sam. It wasn’t our place to tell you any of this.”

“Oh, I understand the boy code very well, Arie,” she said. “I’m not mad at you for standing in solidarity with your friend. But I want you to know that Sam’s plans will never happen. And we are going to make sure that they don’t.”

“We?” Vine said. “We aren’t going to do a thing. We are going to mind our own business. We are not married or obligated to you. Sam is.”

“Oh, that’s where you’re wrong, Brother Pastor,” Marsaleen said. “See, the thing that you three have that Sam doesn’t is a moral compass. You don’t like the idea of him setting up house with this woman no more than I do. And you sure don't want him living in another city. We are going to fix this little problem together."

"You think so, huh?" Chiv said.

"Oh, I know so, baby," she said. "Just so we're on the same page, Ms. Miller is a scam artist. She's been arrested for everything from prostitution to extortion. Her real name Linda Tavelon. Nevaeh Miller is her stage name. See, that's how she does it. She strips at the club, targets older men with money, and milks them for all she can. And that's what she has been doing to Sam. She still lives in Vegas but flies to Indianapolis to perpetrate a fraud with Sam. On one of his future trips, he'll discover that she has taken his money, his identity, and disappear."

"Well, I'll be damned," Vine said. "What about the baby? Sam says that she got a paternity test and the baby is his."

"I had some of my nurse friends contact some of their nurse friends in Vegas and Indianapolis to check her medical records," Marsaleen said. "She has never had a baby. She has had a few abortions, but she has never had a baby."

"But she has been here," Chiv said. "We got her to come here, and she brought Jeremiah with her. What did she do, rent a baby?"

"That's exactly what she did," Marsaleen said. "She is a conniving, low-down, trick whore. Conniving, low-down, trick whores don't hang out with doctors and lawyers. They hang out with other conniving, low-down, trick whores. I'm sure she paid one of her friends to rent a baby. I don't know. All I know is the baby isn't his. And I got to give it to her. She's a pro. She has a tracking device on his phone and his car. She knows his every move. So when he made that surprise trip, she knew he was coming and was waiting."

"Wow, this is messed up," Vine said. "But I'm confused. What is it you think we can do?"

"That's the easy part," Marsaleen said. "You're going to Indianapolis to put a stop to her little scheme."

"And how are we supposed to do that?" Bo said.

"Well, it seems she has two choices," Marsaleen said. "She can continue with this masquerade and go to jail, or she can disappear from his life forever."

"No offense, but aren't you capable of doing that yourself?" Vine said. "Why do we have to get involved? Sam has convinced himself that he is in love with this girl. His heart will be broken. We'll have to be there to help him through that. It's like we're cooking and doing the dishes."

"I don't know nothing about no dishes, but if I go to Indianapolis, I will shoot her in the head," Marsaleen said. "I've planned it out. I have the gun already. There will be no communication, no conversation, no sharing of evidence. I will walk up to her, make sure it's her, and shoot her in the head. Then I'll get in my car and come back to Chicago. They'll eventually find me, and I'll go to jail. But I'll be damned if I'm going to let some hoe scam my husband out of millions of dollars. Not on my watch. And if you three care about him and want to see him protected, you will do this for me. The choice is yours. And when Sam gives me the two million he's supposed to give me, I'll turn it over to you, and eventually, everyone will be happy." Marsaleen handed Bo an envelope with pictures and documents she assembled to validate what she had said. "He's coming home Saturday morning. The first afternoon flight from Indianapolis to Vegas leaves at two thirty. No doubt, she'll be on that flight. You have from the time his flight leaves at ten until she leaves at two thirty to get this trick in check. Oh, my flight for Vegas leaves Saturday night. By my estimation, she'll be dead Sunday morning."

"Okay, calm down," Bo said. "We'll go."

"We will?" Vine asked.

"Yes, we will," Bo said. "But how do you know Lola won't call him and tell him she told you?"

"Because she knows I'll kill her too," Marsaleen said. "I have a gun. She knows I'm not messing around. In fact, she knows that if she comes anywhere near my husband again, that trick-whore bullet that was for Nevaeh will be for her." Marsaleen stood, buttoned her coat, and looked at the three men still seated. "Does anyone have any questions?"

"No, we'll take care of this," Bo said. "We owe it to you."

"And just so you know, we've tried very hard to get him to come out of the streets and home to you," Vine said. "We've never counseled him to leave you. You've got to believe that."

"I believe you tried, but you obviously didn't try hard enough," Marsaleen said. "And let's be clear, if Sam comes back to Chicago, he doesn't have to come back to me. One day, I'll wake up and realize that my marriage is over. I just don't want him made a fool of. I love that man. Otherwise, I wouldn't care. If you care, help me save his life. Thank you for your time and attention. I have to go now and polish my borrowed gun." Marsaleen walked away and never looked back.

"I knew it. I knew it," Bo said. "When that nasty wench licked his face on stage, I knew she was dirty. I should shoot her my damn self."

"We've got to figure out how we're gonna play this," Vine said. "I guess the first question is, are we driving to Indianapolis on Saturday?"

"No," Chiv said. "We're going Friday night, and I know exactly how we should do this."

"Chiv, you up to a long drive?" Vine asked.

"For my friend, I'm up to just about anything," Chiv said.

Bo hated lying to his wife, but he had to in order to save his friend. He told her that the four of them were going to Indianapolis for a preaching engagement Vine had on Saturday morning. At least if Linda or Nevaeh or whatever her name was met him in the alley with a gun of her own and he didn't return, Jackie would know where to start looking. They arrived Friday night, stopped at Best Buy, and then headed to their hotel. Chiv explained the plan, and then they turned in. The next morning, they sat outside of her apartment complex just to make sure Sam was there and to know exactly when she'd be in her apartment. At 7:45, she pulled out of the complex with Sam in tow, no doubt on their way to the airport. The fellas sat in the car and awaited her return. An hour later, Nevaeh entered the complex, parked her car, and headed toward her apartment. The fellas got out and followed her, keeping their distance. They let her go in and waited about ten minutes to make sure no one else was there. They listened at the door and could only hear her talking on the phone. It was time. Vine knocked on the door like he was the police about to do a drug raid.

"Man, take it easy," Bo said. "I know she's a prostitute, but you can't bang on her door like that. She's gonna think you're the police. We've got to play this cool. We don't want to spook her." About a minute later, she came to the door, opened it widely, and acted as if she was pleasantly surprised to see them.

"Hi, guys," she said and hugged them one by one. "You all drove all the way up here to surprise him, didn't you?" She was oblivious to the reason they were there.

"We sure did," Chiv said. "He must be out getting coffee or something."

"No, he had to get back to Chicago for work tomorrow," she said. "I just took him to the airport. He is going to be so bombed when I call him."

"Where's Jeremiah?" Chiv asked.

"Uh, he, uh, he's at my sister's place," Nevaeh said, stumbling on her words. It was obvious that she was not prepared for the question. "It was Sam's last night, and I wanted some alone time with him. He loves his son, but I wanted him all to myself."

"I could vomit right now," Vine whispered to Bo.

"Let me try to call him before he takes off," she said. "Hopefully, his plane was delayed."

"No need to call him," Chiv said. "We really didn't come for him. We came for you, Linda. Linda Tavelon. That is your real name, isn't it?"

A look of horror and panic filled her face. She knew she had been busted. The fellas were hoping she'd be cool. They studied her every move.

"What's this all about?" she said nervously. "Why are you all coming in here all gangster and using my government name?"

"Come. Let's sit at this beautiful kitchen table," Chiv said. "Was it a gift from Sam? Looks like his taste."

"I'm good," she said. "I don't need to sit because I'm going to walk you all out." The three of them sat at her table as if she hadn't said a word.

"Not a problem, Linda, but when we leave, we're going straight to the police department to report yet another victim of your extortion scheme."

"Sit your ass down," Vine snapped. "I'm starting to lose patience with you."

She sat at the table and folded her arms across her full bosom. "I'm sitting. Now what do you want?" she asked.

"Oh, we have a list," Chiv said, "but I'll cover them slowly one by one." Chiv pulled out the handheld tape recorder that he purchased from Best Buy. "We are going to interview you on tape—that's first. Confession is good for the soul. When I give you the signal, you are going to start this recording with your name, and you're going to grant us permission to tape you. Then I'm just going to ask you a series of questions and want you to respond accurately."

"And for your cooperation in granting us this interview, there is a check for five hundred thousand dollars in this envelope made out to you," Vine said. Her eyes lit up, but then she deflated as she thought about the strings that were surely attached to this gift.

"Oh, I get it," she said. "You all are trying to pay me off. You don't want Sam and I to be together. Well, good luck with that. My man and the father of my son is a millionaire. That measly five hundred thousand dollars is a drop in the bucket compared to the five million that will be leaving Chicago and moving to Indianapolis. So, gentlemen, I think your offer is quite an insult. I've told Sam everything about my past, and he does not care. I'm who he wants. You'll never be able to keep him away from me, and you will probably lose a friend in the process. So are we done yet?"

"Oh, sweetheart, we haven't even started," Vine said. "Had you exercised some manners and let me finish my statement, there is also some other stuff in that envelope. For one, your arrest record and all your aliases are in there. You've done every lose and despicable thing from prostitution to pushing counterfeit money all up and through Las Vegas. And I almost fell out of my chair thinking of how my friend was going to leave his wife for a woman who sold and used drugs. And how you got your last victim to drop the charges for extortion and blackmail, I'll never know."

"Tell me, what did Sam say exactly when you told him that the little boy he's been bonding with is not his?" Bo asked. "You said you told him everything about your past. Did you mention anything about your present? Did you mention to him that not only is this child not yours, you have had more abortions than the law should allow? The truth is, you've never had a child. You don't seem to like them very much. You kill them before they even get here."

"Y'all are starting to piss me off," Nevaeh said, raising her voice. "Get you old dusty asses out of my house."

"The truth is, you are a low-down trifling hoe who would rather cook up schemes and scams and take advantage of people than to live a halfway decent life," Chiv said. "So let me make this as clear as I can. There is no way we are going to let you add Sam to your victim list. It's just not going to happen. So if I were you, I'd take this measly five hundred thousand dollars and disappear. It's either that or go back to jail. Either way, you and our friend are through."

Nevaeh sat in silence for a moment, and then the tears came. "I love him," she said. "I care for him. I want to be with him. I was eventually gonna tell him the whole story and tell him about Jeremiah, I swear."

"You make me sick to my stomach," Vine said. "And if you think we are going to believe and fall for one of your tricks, you got another thing coming. I could just vomit right now looking at you. Come on, Chiv. Let's get this shit over with. The longer I sit here, the more I want to choke the tongue out of this hoe's mouth."

"So this is what's going to happen," Chiv said. "You are going to answer my questions, and then we're going to leave. Before the sun goes down, you are going to disappear. You will never answer his calls, you will never call him, you will never set foot in the state of Illinois. You will tear up every check he sends you. You are going to forget he even existed. If you don't, we will play the tape for him and then for the police."

"Where am I supposed to go?" she asked, slowing becoming hysterical.

"You'll have half a million dollars, sweetheart," Bo said. "I really don't see a problem."

"When we're done, you are going to leave him a voice mail saying that you cannot see him anymore, and if we are not successful in keeping him from driving here to find you, when he gets here, you'll be gone," Chiv said. "You see, we are more than friends of Sam. He's our brother. We love him."

"And because we love him, we'll do just about anything to protect him from everything," Bo said.

"Even if that means protecting him from gutter trash like you," Vine said. "So take a chance if you want to. Do all the stupid shit you big enough to do. You will regret it for the rest of your short life."

CHAPTER 26

Thanksgiving 2013

"You know what would be good right now?" Vine said to the fellas in an exaggerated whisper. "Some reefer."

"Uh, excuse me, Reverend," Chiv said.

"You heard me," Vine repeated. "I'm full and sleepy, and it would be the end of a perfect Thanksgiving here in Los Angeles with some good reefer."

"First of all, you ignorant, hell-bound sinner," Sam said, "it's not called reefer anymore. It's called weed."

"Hell, it's been weed for a long time, ain't it?" Bo said, laughing at his own quip. "I think it changed when we became African Americans. If you want to be hip, you've got to keep up. Like Little Richard said, 'Get out of the mustard and catch up.'"

"We need us an LA connection," Vine said, ignoring all who were not taking him seriously.

"No, we don't," Chiv said. "Just go down to Venice Beach and stand there for a minute. The weed man might come to you."

"Y'all are stupid, old and stupid," Chiv said. "I'm tripping on it being Thanksgiving, and I'm sitting on the deck of this Malibu house in shorts and a polo. I'm from Chicago. It's cold on Thanksgiving. Feels like I'm in an alternate universe."

"Money does have the power to make you experience things you've never experienced before," Bo said. "I think about our lives over the last five years and can't imagine that it could get much better than this."

As an early Christmas gift, Bo, Sam, Chiv, and Vine sent Jackie, Marsaleen, Pearl, Anne, and Ms. Francis to Italy for Thanksgiving.

They started in Milan, then traveled to Tuscany, and ended their tour in Rome. They've been gone for ten days and will be returning home on Saturday. As the date of the trip drew near, the fellas thought it would be a good idea to visit a warmer place to thaw out and take a break from their new lives as millionaire businessmen. One of Vine's members owned a home in Malibu and offered it to the Jolly Boys for their excursion west. They catered their Thanksgiving meal, with plans to eat and then take a nap on the netted deck facing the ocean. Their lives were stressful, hectic, and challenging, but it was all good. They were finally happy—well, mostly happy.

Sam moped around for weeks after Nevaeh aka Linda Tavelon broke up with him. He couldn't understand how his well-developed plan for happiness turned into a nightmare overnight. After Nevaeh left him a voicemail message while he was flying back to Chicago from spending nearly a week with her in Indianapolis, he dismissed it as some sort of joke or, at best, her second-guessing her home-wrecking actions. But when she didn't return his calls and when he received the check he'd written to her back in the mail, he knew it was over. He and Chiv even drove to Indianapolis looking for her, but she was gone. The apartment they leased was empty. The love of his life and well-spring of his happiness left him and took his son with her. He would never know what his fellow Jolly Boys did to protect him. And they would never tell.

Needless to say, his plans changed. Tired of seeing him so miserable, Marsaleen created a business opportunity that caught his attention. She had an idea to start a school-bus company. They started with four yellow school buses catering to parents and guardians of school-age children to forty school buses and thirteen state-of-the-art deluxe motor coaches. They were successful in outbidding their competitors for contracts with Chicago Public Schools and a few neighboring school districts in the suburbs. Churches, schools, and sports teams kept their coach business in the green. Working together as business partners brought Sam and Marsaleen closer, and she got her wish. She waited for him to come home, and he was glad she did.

After a few months, Bo grew bored of traveling. It was exciting, and he took a lot of pictures. But it was wearing him down. He felt old and not as spry as he used to be. He had planned on becoming a road warrior. Instead, he became road weary. He needed another diversion. He turned his focus on designing and building his dream home. That diversion didn't last long as he found his dream home already built in Oak Brook, an affluent suburb just west of Chicago. He finally found his mojo, teaming up with Jackie and Ms. Francis to open Beauregard's Buffet or BB's, for short. He actually purchased the building that housed Leg and Thigh from Gina, who was still smitten with him. It was an instant success. Soon thereafter, they opened a second location in Hyde Park. The lines were out the door and down the street. And as Vine predicted, divine collard greens was their signature dish. With the onset of Bo's digestive issues, he pretty much turned the business over to Jackie and Ms. Francis, but he showed up when he had to and often when he wanted to.

Chiv went to work right away on the Jolly Boys Club. He found an old strip mall and bought it for cash. He rented out some stores on the end but started with the barbershop and dry cleaners. It was a failure. To him, it was the beginning of his dream. To everyone else, it was just another barbershop and dry cleaner. Slowly but surely, he was ready to open the doors. Unfortunately, no one came when he did. He noticed that there was always a line and a lot of activity at the Laundromat across the street. It was run-down and dirty but cheap and had a lot of machines. The idea hit him like a bolt of lightning. He would invest in a modern, clean, and well-kept chain of laundromats. The overhead was low, and people seem to enjoy doing their laundry while working in the office area or watching their favorite television shows and movies. It was a huge success. In January, he will open his tenth location out in Hammond, Indiana, near the casino. After a year living with Vine, he, too, found a spacious high-rise home downtown in the Hancock Building and moved out on his own. In fact, with Vine on East Delaware, he and Vine were within walking distance from each other. Although the Jolly Boys Club idea didn't pan out, Chiv never waned from his desire to help young kids and honor his deceased wife and sons. It would take a little more time than he originally envisioned, but it was going to happen. The money from ten machines in each laundromat was held in trust.

Soon, he would be able to open the Nero, and Arie Jr. Eubanks, Boys and Girls Club.

Vine left Grand Old Baptist and attended the Metaphysical Seminary, where he learned the New Thought body of Christian knowledge. He was ordained a metaphysical practitioner and minister and opened the Pinnacle Temple of Truth and Awareness. He began by holding services in the banquet room in his building. He started with Eric and his partner Michael and a few defectors from GOB. A year later, they were moving into their million-dollar temple in the south loop warehouse district, financed primarily by Vine. After a year, they'd outgrown that space. On their third-year anniversary, the congregation moved into their new location near the McCormick Place Convention Center. Ironically, it was the same abandoned property where the Jolly Boys met with Marsaleen years ago. Personally, Vine bought and invested in several businesses including Bo, Chiv, and Sam's. He was even a silent partner in an upscale nightclub on the Northside. That was a big secret. Anne and Pearl opened two new flower shops, which were very profitable. After meeting a prominent funeral director, Pearl married and moved with her new husband to Jackson, Mississippi. With Vine's help, she opened two shops in Jackson. Anne remained a serious businesswoman and single.

"You know, I've been meaning to ask you, Bo," Vine said, horizontal on the outdoor chaise lounge. "How are things at GOB?"

"Oh, here we go," Bo said. "You want me to tell you how awful things are without you being there, don't you?"

"That's exactly what I want you to say," Vine said. "But we all know I wouldn't have to ask you if you were a member of PTTA and not GOB, but it's whatever."

"Vine, now stop acting like we haven't talked about this," Bo said. "I don't knock or judge your doctrine, but it's not for everyone. I've been Baptist all my life. I don't know nothing else. And out of guilt, I made a sizeable donation to the seminary you attended."

"Yes, I know," Vine said. "I'm on the Chicago board. They want to give you an honorary doctorate degree. We give at least one per year. They were impressed that you gave and was not a member of a New Thought church."

"Well, I do believe that all God's children should be rich and happy and in good health, but I don't have to change denominations to believe that, do I?"

"No, you don't, Dr. Jackson," Vine said. "You are exactly right. Speaking of good health, how are we feeling these days? Feels strange sitting out here, sipping on whiskey and wanting some reefer, and you drinking milk."

"Man, believe me when I tell you when you get older, your body changes," Bo said. "I used to be able to eat those collard greens with hot sauce, pickle juice, red onions, and skin from the hock. Now if a drop of acid hits my stomach, I could do flips down Stony Island."

"Man, you need to check that out," Sam said. "You slimming down, and that's good. But you could have an ulcer or something."

"I've been to a couple of doctors," Bo said. "They give me Pantoprazole and Prilosec and send me home. I've just got to watch what and how much I eat. Here I am, owner of two successful restaurants, and can't eat half the shit on the menu. I wish I could get into Mayo Clinic. They say if anything is wrong with you, Mother Mayo will find it. But I think it's by referrals, and I don't know nobody."

"Oh, I can get you into Mayo," Chiv said.

"How you gonna get me into Mayo?" Bo asked. "You are the laundromat king."

"I'm also well-connected," Chiv said. "You want in, I can get you in. But you gotta be ready to travel to Rochester, Minnesota, whenever they call. They don't call you to work out a convenient time. They call you and tell you when to show up. You gotta be ready."

"You get me in, and I'll be ready," Bo said.

"I'll even roll with you," Chiv said. "I've never been to Minneapolis before. While you're getting poked and prodded, I'll hit the Mall of America. I'll call my contact when we get home."

"Chiv, don't you want to tell Vine and Bo the news?" Sam said with a huge and devilish smile on his face.

"Oh no," Vine said. "You gonna try sobriety again."

"For your information, ass hat, I don't have a drinking problem," Chiv said. "I drink when I feel like it and when I want to.

Some weeks, I want to more than others, but I'm controlling it. It's not controlling me."

"So what's the news?" Bo asked.

"I had a surprise visitor last week," Chiv said. "It was Louise."

"Louise. I damn near forgot she even existed," Vine said. "We haven't heard that name in years."

"She called and wanted to meet," Chiv said.

"I hope you laid her out," Vine said.

"No, we met and even had dinner," Chiv said.

"So what happened?" Bo asked.

"She told me that I scared her," Chiv said. "She said she actually came to the hospital, and when she saw me lying there unconscious with all the machines beeping and half my body bandaged up, she got really spooked and ran away."

"Money does keep the ghetto away," Sam said. "What did you say?"

"'Spend the night with me,'" Chiv said.

"You didn't," Vine said. "You are seeing Louise again? Don't you know she wants some of that money?"

"Damn, Vine," Chiv said. "Of course, I know that. I ain't stupid. But it has been a minute since I had me some good-good, and she had the good-good. So I invited her to spend the night. In fact, she spent a couple of nights. It was around my birthday."

"So where do y'all stand now?" Bo asked.

"We don't," Chiv said. "She seems to think I owe her my forgiveness because I made her wait so long to get engaged. I don't think I owe her a damn thing because when I needed her, she ran away."

"See, I didn't know all that," Sam said. "The news I was talking about was Geraldine."

"Who the hell is Geraldine?" Vine asked.

"Oh, she's a lady I met at one of the laundromats," Chiv said. "We struck up a conversation, and we've been out a few times. But that's about it. I've never even been in her house, let alone her bedroom. I was trying to impress her with my wealth, and she wasn't impressed. As owner of a couple popular hamburger franchises, she doesn't have to suppress her morals to be with a man. Those were her words. And as funny as it sounds, that turned me on. I done found myself a lady."

"So you cheating on your new girlfriend with your old girlfriend," Vine said. "I want to be just like you when I grow up."

"Vine, as usual, you all in everybody's business," Sam said. "Whose bed have your boots been under?"

"Please," Vine said. "I think that part of my life is officially over. The church is more than enough for me right now and for a long time. Hadassah and I hook up from time to time, but that's about it. I've chosen to make love to the Lord."

"You might be making love to a Jew, but it sho ain't the Lord," Sam said. The deck was full of laughter. It felt like old times.

"I'm serious," Vine said. "I don't have time for nothing. It's funny. Y'all retired and went right back to work. Just because you work for yourselves don't mean you ain't working hard. In essence, we will never really retire. Well, y'all won't. I'm seventy years old. I'm going to go hard for about two or three more years, and then I'm retiring. Eric will be preaching by then, and if he ain't, they'll find somebody. I'm going to be done."

"I don't get this new trend in the Black church, preachers retiring from preaching," Sam said. "I thought preaching was a lifelong calling?"

"Oh, I can't give up preaching," Vine said. "But I can certainly give up pastoring Black folks. I'm retiring and moving to a warmer climate. Wouldn't it be amazing to wake up to this view every morning? Hey, we should do that. We should retire and move here."

"You know, I've never thought about ever living anywhere but Chicago," Bo said. "I wonder if Jackie would move."

"Well, Marsaleen would leave Chicago in a heartbeat," Sam said. "As long as the city we move to has an international airport, she's good."

"Chiv, would you move?" Sam asked.

"I don't know," Chiv said. "Ain't we too old to pack up and move to another city?"

"Yes, if we were broke," Vine said. "But we're millionaires, and our money is making money. And if I can find a pastor to take over,

I know y'all can find some business managers to run your businesses. We could at least live here in the winter and Chicago in the summer."

"We should really think about that," Bo said. "I think we should have a five-year plan to relocate to LA."

"Count me in," Vine said. "Thanksgiving 2018, we'll be having dinner on the deck of my Malibu home."

"I'll drink to that," Chiv said.

CHAPTER 27

April 5, 2014

"Divine Oliver," Bo said, greeting Vine at the door. "What are you doing here? You taking us to the airport?"

"Well, something like that," Vine said. "Chiv is having issues with some of his new machines, so he asked if I would take his place. So I'm going with you to Rochester."

"Aw, Vine," Bo said. "You don't have to do that. You got too much going on. I'm the one retired. I can go by myself."

"You are not going by yourself, Beauregard," Jackie said. She always called him by his full first name when she was irritated with him or was putting her foot down. "You're going to be there through Friday. You won't let me go, and now you don't want Vine to go. Do you know something we don't?"

"Not at all," Bo said. "Nothing like that. I just don't want everybody to put their lives on hold to go with me to Mayo Clinic. It's really a waste of everybody's time. They are going to run some heavy-duty tests on my stomach and will probably prescribe some magic pill to make all these issues go away. It's Mayo Clinic, not the county hospital. Gone back to your church, man. I got this."

"So what I say don't matter?" Jackie said, with her hand on her hip. "What if you get up there and something happens? No matter how routine you think this is, you can't do this by yourself, sweetheart. Now you have a choice, me or Vine. And if I were you, I'd be very careful with your choice."

"Okay, fine," Bo said. "You're right. Although I know nothing is going to happen, it will be good to have a preacher with me. Okay, preacher man, let's go."

"See, Jackie, if I were your husband, you wouldn't have all these problems," Vine said. "You know, David had Bathsheba's husband put on the front line so he could get killed. That was the only way he could have her. I might leave this ninja in Rochester."

"Divine Oliver, if you come back to Chicago without my husband, it better be horizontal with a tag on your toe," Jackie said. Vine and Bo thought that was pretty hysterical. "Now I completed all the forms, his medical records have been sent electronically, and all the medications he's taken for his stomach are on the spreadsheet named Drugs. Also, the X-rays he took before his gallbladder removal are in there. Call me if they need something else." Jackie hugged Bo and kissed him on the jaw. "Oooh, I don't like being able to wrap my arms all around you. You hurry home with some good drugs so I can fatten you back up."

"Okay, baby," Bo said. "I love you."

"Of course, you do because I love you," Jackie said and kissed him on the cheek. Vine stood behind Bo as if he were waiting in line at a kissing booth. When Bo moved, Vine opened his arms, closed his eyes, and stuck out his tongue.

"Come on, Jackie Jackson," he said. "I'm waiting on it."

"I wish I had some ammonia and bleach," Jackie said, wrapping her arms around Vine. "I'd sprinkle it all on your tongue. Ain't no telling where that tongue has been. I'd have to get it cleaned first." Vine squeezed her tightly and picked her up off the floor. "Put me down, fool. Bo, tell Vine to put me down."

"Don't fight it, baby," Vine joked.

"Vine, put my wife down and come on here before I miss my flight," Bo said. "You can flirt with her when we get back."

"Please keep him in good spirits," Jackie whispered in Vine's ear. "I'm glad you're going instead of Chiv. I think you can handle his mood swings. Just be methodical and patient. And don't baby him."

"Okay, you know I got him," Vine said. "I'll sneak off and call you when I can to let you know what's going on."

"Okay, thank you, Vine," Jackie said. "I'm counting on you."

"Divine!" Bo yelled from the front door. "Come on, Negro."

"Okay, I'm coming," Vine said. "I had to get me some more of that good sugar."

"You make me miss my flight, you gonna get some of this good foot in your ass," Bo said.

"Might as well start now, keeping him in good spirits," Vine said and trotted to the front door.

Their flight to Rochester was smooth and without incident. Once they arrived at the airport, a short White gentleman holding a sign, which displayed Bo's name, walked up to us. "You must be Dr. Jackson," he said.

"I am Bo Jackson, yes," Bo said. "I would love to see the description they gave you for me. You picked me out very quickly."

"Yes, a James Earl Jones-look-alike is not too hard to miss," he said. "I'm Quentin. I'll be driving you to the clinic."

"Hello, Quentin," Bo said. "This is my best friend, Rev. Oliver. Thank you for driving us."

"No problem," he said. "Let's get your bags, and we'll be on our way."

The limo ride to the hotel was not short but not too long. Bo was asleep for most of the ride. Vine stared at his friend sleeping so peacefully and smiled. Although his body and his spirit man were giving him signs of danger, he continued to smile. Subconsciously, he was thinking that if he smiled long enough and hard enough, his actions would take the fear and dismay away. Not since Chiv's accident had he had this feeling.

They checked into the hotel and into their joining rooms. Without asking permission, Bo opened the walk-through door. He said it would feel like one big room instead of two smaller rooms. Vine unpacked his clothes and set up the iron to press their clothes for the next day. He repacked Bo's bag as he'd be staying at the clinic. By the time he was done unpacking, packing, and ironing, Bo was sound asleep. He shook him and pleaded with him to eat, but he was not hungry, just tired. Vine ordered room service and ate alone in his room. After two bites of his overcooked hotel hamburger, he couldn't eat anymore. That feeling was all over him. He stopped and prayed and turned in. The next morning, it was Bo shaking him to wake up. It was six, and Quentin would be back to pick them up in an hour. They dressed and checked out of Bo's room in record time. Like clockwork, Quentin was there at seven and had Bo all checked in, sitting in his hospital gown in time for his first appointment. A gorgeous female nurse and a portly physician entered the room.

"Good morning, Mr. Jackson," the doctor said. "I'm Doctor Matthew Tephanopolis." Bo frowned as if the doctor was speaking a different language. "Not to worry. Everyone calls me Dr. T."

"Oh, good," he said. "I'm from Mississippi. We can't flip the tongue that fast. This is my friend, Rev. Oliver."

"Rev. Oliver, welcome to Mayo Clinic," he said. "This is Nurse Casio. She will be coordinating your care while you're here. So, Mr. Jackson, tell me, what's going on? I've scheduled an aggressive battery of diagnostic tests for you, but I want to make sure I hear what's going on with you just in case I need to test you for something else. So what's going on?"

Bo looked over at Vine. He had to quickly assess if he was comfortable discussing his infirmities with Vine in the room. There had been so much that he withheld from the Jolly Boys, he didn't want Vine to go into shock or anger. He decided to proceed and hoped that Vine would understand.

"Well, I had my gallbladder removed a few years ago, and to be honest, I haven't felt 100 percent since," Bo explained. "I was initially thinking malpractice but really didn't have the energy to revisit and fight. I used to be an overeater, so I know some of my issues are from that and my weight. I can't even look at anything with tomato sauce or barbecue or anything spicy. I get a heartburn that takes days to shake off. I have these stabbing-like pains in my upper stomach that pound inside my guts for about fifteen minutes and then go away. Sometimes I feel so nauseous I feel like I'm going to pass out. I break into a sweat and feel like crap. Those are more like spasms, and I feel those in my lower belly. After one of those, I'm wiped out. I take a shower and sleep ten hours. I don't have much of an appetite anymore. I eat bland foods and drink tons of milk. Our housekeeper makes a big pot of oatmeal at the beginning of the week. And when I get tired of yogurt, pudding, and bananas, I heat up some oatmeal.

It is really delicious. I think she puts honey in it. Anyway, I'll have a shot of Chivas Regal every now and then, but it feels like it's peeling and stripping the walls of my esophagus as it goes down. And I'm tired. I have no get-up. I think that's because I've stopped drinking coffee because it bothers my stomach."

"What does your doctor back home say?" Dr. T. asked.

"He thinks I might have an ulcer," Bo said. "But the tests don't show it. He keeps changing my medication, but nothing really takes the edge off. I've been to the emergency room a few times, but they give me something and send me home. That's why I know this isn't bad. The hospital would have surely caught it on one of those trips, don't you think?"

"How are your bowel movements?" Dr. T. asked, not answering Bo's question. "Any blood or blackness in your stool?"

"I have two or three bowel movements a day, and they are very brown," Bo said. "I don't think they are black, but no blood. You know, today is the best my stomach has felt in months."

"We gave you some abdominal-pain medication through your IV," Dr. T. said.

"Does it come in pill form?" Bo said, excited. "If it does, this is all I need. I feel no pain."

"Well, we'll see," Dr. T said. "We're gonna rule out all the big stuff like diabetes and cancer. Once we do that, we'll figure out what's really happening and will treat it at that time. But we'll figure it out. You know what our motto is around here?" Bo shook his head. "'We'll figure it out.'" Dr. T.'s attempt at levity was ineffective at best. "Okay, Nurse Casio, he's in your hands. I'll see you on Friday, Mr. Jackson. And don't worry. We're gonna take good care of you. I will be monitoring your results electronically as they come in, but chances are, I won't see you until Friday. If you need me, however, just tell Nurse Casio, and she'll put us in touch. Do you have any questions?"

"No, Doc," Bo said. "I just really feel good right now. You've got to send me home with some of this stuff."

"Rev. Oliver, do you have any questions?" Dr. T. asked.

"No," Vine said. "I'm just glad he's feeling better. He looks like his old self."

"Well, we have a lot of weapons in our arsenal to control pain around here," Dr. T. said.

"Rev. Oliver, are you staying here or at a hotel?" Nurse Casio asked. "Since for all intents and purposes, you are his next of kin on site, you are free to stay here with him."

"No," Bo and Vine said in unison and broke out into laughter.

"No further explanation needed," Nurse Casio said. "You'll let me know if that changes."

"I do have one question," Vine said. "What test will he have today? Should I hang out or go to my room until this evening?"

"He'll be very busy today," she said. "He'll have most of his scoping work, ultrasound, and MRI today. You probably won't see him until around two, and he'll be groggy from the anesthesia. If you're back by three, you'll be good."

"Well, I'm going to go to the cafeteria for a while and then hang out in your room," Vine said. "I'll be here when you get back."

"Thanks, Vine," Bo said. "Okay, fix me."

A team of nurses and transporters came in to prepare Bo for his day. They took blood, hooked him up to a portable blood-pressure machine, and a lot of other stuff that Vine nor Bo understood or could explain. Eventually, they wheeled him out. Vine closed the room door and dropped to his face. He prayed seriously and hard, but the more he prayed, the more that feeling he got in distressful situations would not leave. He sat in the chair and cried himself to sleep. When Bo returned, he was indeed groggy and not very talkative. He was resting, which was good and needed. Vine kissed him on the forehead and headed back to the hotel. When he spoke to Jackie, he pulled his spirits up and was as positive as he could be without being unintelligently optimistic or fake.

On Thursday, Vine got an opportunity to travel with Bo to his various appointments within the clinic. He had another endoscopic ultrasound, MRI, CT scan, an ERC, and a CPT. They both were drained at the end of Thursday but were able to eat a meal together and watch some television and have a conversation.

"Vine, have you ever thought about dying?" Bo asked.

"Thoughts are things, Bo," Vine said. "We're not going to think or talk about that now. They are going to give you some good drugs, and you're going to be okay."

"Oh, I'm not declaring doom or defeat," Bo said. "But all these tests, even the most positive person would question the number of days he had left on the planet. But do you ever think about how you're going to die?"

"It's funny," Vine said. "I always imagined that I would just die from old age, but old age is not a disease. And then when Chiv was in that wreck, I thought about death coming swiftly and without warning. I don't want that either. I don't know. I guess that's God's business."

"I guess," Bo said. "I mean, we are entrusted with these temples. It's up to us to take care of them. I just don't want years and years of agonizing and suffering. I had an aunt who had colon cancer. She was just in excruciating pain for months on end. It was a relief for her to finally leave here. You know, this might be the end. And before you start hitting me with positive this and positive that, this could be the end. I'm not ready, Vine. I got to get my affairs in order. You know what I told the Lord today? I told him that I just wanted one more chance. I just wanted one more trip, one more dinner party with the Jolly Boys, one more night of passion with my wife, one more hug and kiss from my girls, just one more chance, and then I'm ready to go. And do me a favor, take care of Jackie. Help her make good decisions, and by all means, if it looks like my breathing is the only thing keeping me here, nothing else is working, don't let her keep me here. Let me go. We make the mistake of praying to keep people alive, and they're in agony. Just let me go."

"I will take care of Jackie and your girls, Bo," Vine said. "You know that, but don't give up so soon. You know God can block this."

"He certainly can," Bo said. "I just wonder if he will. I just wonder if he will."

On Friday morning, the nurse came in and woke Bo. She needed one more vial of blood before his meeting with Dr. T., which was scheduled for 9:00 a.m. Vine fell asleep at his friend's side and woke when he heard Bo stirring. While Bo showered and got dressed, Vine went to the cafeteria to have his morning coffee, toast, and prayer. Once back upstairs, he brushed his teeth and freshened up before Dr. T.'s scheduled arrival. They had a 2:00 p.m. flight, so everything would have to stay on schedule. After meeting with Dr. T., they would have to go back to the hotel so Vine could shower, change, and get Quentin to take them to the airport. At 8:55, Dr. T. was knocking on the door.

"Good morning, Mr. Jackson, Rev. Oliver," Dr. T. said, adjusting the other chair to face Bo and Vine. "Did they make you comfortable last night?"

"Yes, I was very comfortable and had a great night sleep," Bo said. "I'm telling you, I've haven't felt this good in months. I hope you have a folder full of prescriptions for all the drugs you gave me."

"I'm glad you slept well, and I'm glad you're feeling better," Dr. T. said. "There are some things that I love about this job and some things I hate. Meeting and treating good people like yourself is one of the things I love. Delivering bad news is one of the things I hate."

"So you have bad news?" Bo asked.

"Bo, do you want me to leave?" Vine asked.

"Vine, sit down," Bo snapped. "What do you have to tell me, Doc?"

"There is a tumor on your pancreas, and it's blocking the flow of bile from your liver as well as the flow of enzymes from your pancreas," Dr. T. said. "The tumor has wrapped itself around a blood vessel."

"Well, go in and get it," Bo said. "Go get the tumor. If you take the tumor out, then I'll be okay."

"Trust me," Dr. T. said. "I wish that was a viable option, but I'm afraid it's not. The procedure is known as the Whipple Operation, where we would remove a large part of the pancreas, the duodenum, and a portion of the bile duct. But there are very few surgeons in the country who would be able to successfully perform the surgery, and your chances of survival would be less than 10 percent."

"So what exactly are you saying to me, Doctor?" Bo asked, confused by all the medical terms.

"I'm telling you, Mr. Jackson, that you have stage 3 pancreatic cancer," Dr. T. said.

"That's impossible," Vine said. His voice was cracking, and he did everything in his power to hold back the tears. "This is not your typical male. He does not have to see blood and guts before he goes to the doctor. You heard him on Wednesday. He has been to several doctors and has been admitted more than once into the hospital. They tested him for everything and couldn't find anything. How all of a sudden does he have cancer? I don't understand."

"Rev. Oliver, this is Mayo Clinic," Dr. T. said. "Someone who presents with his symptoms or abdominal pain, lethargy, and weight loss can't be given a pill and sent home. I knew you had some type of abdominal cancer when you told me you were feeling better. The medication I gave you is a low dosage of morphine. It is the common medication to treat severe pain from cancer-related illnesses."

"I have cancer," Bo said. "I didn't think you had good news for me today, but I never imagined that it would be cancer. What does stage 3 even mean?"

"Well, there are four stages of pancreatic cancer before a person expires," Dr. T. said. "Your cancer is far along and already attacking your blood vessels. Also, this form of cancer is very aggressive. It's hard to diagnose, and it's hard to treat. Following a good care plan, you probably have six to eight months at the most. I am so very sorry."

"I have cancer," Bo said again. "This time last year, I was cutting the ribbon at the opening of my second restaurant, and one year later, I have eight months to live."

"Come on, Bo," Vine said. "We're not claiming that."

"Vine, whether I claim it or not, I have cancer, and I'm going to die in eight months," Bo said. "I don't mean to snap at you, but try to suppress that positive thinking stuff until I can come to grips with this."

Vine dropped his head. His friend had just received a death sentence, and there was nothing he could do to help.

"You can certainly get another opinion," Dr. T. said.

"Like you said, Doc, this is the Mayo Clinic," Bo said. "I can't imagine the story getting any better. So what now? What do I do now?"

"There is a great oncologist in Chicago at Northwestern, Dr. Bledsoe," Dr. T. said. "I've already contacted him and sent him your records. You need to see him on Monday. He will develop a care and treatment plan for you. He'll evaluate your candidacy for chemo and will probably talk to you about having a stent put in. A stent inserted into the tubes leading from your liver and pancreas will help them function and give you a better quality of life. I'm sending you home with enough morphine to get you to Monday. Dr. Bledsoe will prescribe medications for your care."

"Dr. T., may I ask a question?" Vine asked. "What causes this cancer?"

"We don't know, Reverend," he said. "It is known to be hereditary and more prevalent in African Americans."

"I was thinking the same thing," Bo said. "This has to be my fault. What did I do wrong? What was the dessert or cut of red meat or shot of alcohol or toilet seat I sat on that made this thing start growing in my body?" Bo said. "What did I do?"

"Nothing, Mr. Jackson," Dr. T. said. "You did nothing. Don't even beat yourself up like that. It's energy wasted."

"Oh, Dr. T.," Vine said. "I think my friend is saying it to himself before someone else does. Believe it or not, some ding-dong will say to him, 'You should have watched your diet,' or 'You should have exercised.' Black folks can't help blaming you for something even if it's not your fault. They never let you forget that you had a role in the situation even if it's your own demise."

"Well, tell those people to call me," Dr. T. said, somewhat irritated. "I will give them a piece of my mind. We Greeks have a hard time with blame." That was the first time Bo had laughed all day. "Mr. Jackson, I know this was a lot and that you weren't expecting this, so please, as you process this, do not hesitate to call me. I also suggest that you engage in psychotherapy in parallel to your treatment. But please call me. I will always make time for you and always return my phone calls. It was a pleasure meeting you. You are such a good patient. I am so very sorry for your plight, but please try to enjoy your time left. Don't spend more than a minute trying to understand why. Our souls occupy bodies that can't hold our spirit forever. It's science, and it happens. Spend your time with your family and friends and think of all the good things you've encountered, like winning all that money. You've been blessed. Don't let cancer erase those blessings from your memory. Take care, Reverend. Take care, Mr. Jackson. I hope you get the miracle you deserve, but if you don't, I wish you peace and strength for your journey."

"Thank you, Doctor," Bo said. "You all have been amazing, but I'm going to make it. You'll see."

"That is certainly my prayer," Dr. T. said.

Vine was a ball of emotion, but he had to hold it together for Bo. Vine decided to follow Bo's lead through this journey instead of trying to lead for it was not his journey. It was Bo's.

"So, do you want to call Jackie now, or you want to wait and tell her in person?" Vine asked.

"I would love to tell her in person, but knowing my wife, she has mapped out my schedule for the day and will be expecting a call right about now," Bo said. "If I try to avoid her, she'll be upset. What should I do, Vine?"

"Let's do this," Vine said. "Let's not call, but if she calls, we talk to her. I think that's a fair compromise."

"Okay, that sounds good," Bo said. "Vine, I have cancer. I have eight months to live. What am I going to do?"

"I think you should take Dr. T.'s advice and live the best possible life you can while you can," Vine said. "And remember, we're going to follow your lead. You feel like walking and crying, we'll walk and cry with you. You feel like smoking some reefer looking out the window, we'll roll and smoke right along with you and make sure your windows are clean. But I don't want you to worry about a thing. Anything you want or need, you'll have it. You've been such a good friend to me, Bo. I'm really going to miss you, but not yet because you're still here."

"That's what people always say in the beginning," Bo said. "In the beginning, everyone has time and energy for you, but at the end, you end up alone."

"Do you think we would fizzle out on you like that?" Vine asked with a tone of tempered irritation. "I can't believe you would think that about us."

"Look at Louise and how she abandoned Chiv," Bo said. "That's what happens. When my moods start swinging and I start looking weak and forgetting what I was saying in the middle of a sentence, y'all ain't gonna want to see that. You'll stop coming and start telling that old standard lie: 'I just want to remember him the way he was. I can't stand to see him suffer.'"

"You know, it's probably poor taste to cuss someone out after they've received a cancer diagnosis, but I'll take the chance," Vine said. "Now these other folks you speak of, I wouldn't expect much from them. But me, Chiv, Sam, and Jackie, we would never do that to you, and I ought to kick you in your ass for even thinking that shit. Wait until I tell the rest of the gang you opened your mouth and spewed out such bullshit."

"Vine, Vine, man, calm down," Bo said. Vine was on a roll getting him told. "I'm sorry. You're absolutely right. I don't know what I was thinking."

"I don't know what you were thinking either," Vine said, slowly returning to a normal temperament.

"I just don't want to end up suffering and alone," Bo said. "I think of my aunt lying in the nursing home just calling on the name of Jesus because she was in so much pain. I can't do that, Vine. I'll jump out of the window before I do that."

"Yes, but with your luck, yo ass would break a leg or hip and wind up alive and in more agony," Vine said. Bo's whole body shook from laughing. "Now me, I could get a paper cut and check out of here. It's like the old folks used to say, 'God don't want me, and the devil can't use me.'"

"Oh, I don't know about that," Bo said, standing and grabbing his bag. "You've run a few errands for the devil."

"You got that right," Vine said, "and quiet as it's kept, I still got a full tank of gas to run a few more."

"You ain't got good sense, Vine," Bo said. "If someone accused you of being sane, you should sue them for slander." Bo and Vine walked down the hall toward the exit. When they got on the elevator, Bo turned to Vine. "I love you, man. Now I ain't no punk or nothing, but I want you to know I love you."

"I love you too, Dr. Jackson," Vine said and hugged his friend.

"Listen, when we get in the limo, I'm going to cry as hard as I can," Bo said. "I'm going to scream and holler and grunt and moan like never before, but when I get to the airport, all crying will stop. I've got to be strong for my wife, kids, and friends."

"No, you don't," Vine said. "You don't have to do nothing you don't want to do. You can't carry everyone else's burdens right now. You've got your own. Cry when and however you want to. Damn being strong."

"Nah, you know that ain't even me," Bo said. "It might be my turn to go, but I'm not leaving before I show people how to live."

"You are a remarkable man, Dr. Beauregard Jeremiah Jackson," Vine said.

"That's what I want on my tombstone: 'a remarkable man,'" Bo said.

"Consider it done," Vine said.

By the time Bo and Vine made it back to Chicago, he had spoken to Jackie, had his gut-wrenching cry, and made his plea to God that His will be done and he not suffer long. When he and Vine pulled up to the Jackson estate, the driveway was jam-packed with cars. When he walked in, he was greeted with a foyer full of friends: Jackie, Pearl, Ms. Francis, Chiv, Sam, Marsaleen, his girls Jarrah and Maya, and Eric and his partner Michael. He studied their faces. Some conveyed sadness and concern, some intimated fear and worry, and a couple radiated with hope and optimism. There were tears, but there were also smiles. A few people were quiet, but a few vocal. He hugged and kissed them all, the men and women. He saved Jackie for last.

"Hey, baby," he said, squeezing his wife. "You ready?"

"Yes," she replied. "We are gonna kick cancer's ass."

"Or die trying," he said. She laughed and led him into the family room.

"Well, I've been thinking about this, and I'm going to give everyone an assignment," Vine said.

"Oh, here we go," Sam said out loud. Bo just smiled. He wanted to say the same thing.

"Marsaleen is a nurse, so she can help with all things medical," Vine said before being interrupted.

"Vine, Vine," Bo said. "Please sit down. I've been with this ninja for the last three days. I just want to hear someone else's voice." Everyone laughed. "Listen, the news isn't good, but the doctor said something to me that I will never forget. This body can only hold the real us for so long before it starts to expire. Just because it expires doesn't me we, the real us, dies. I know that once I give up this body, I'll be in perfect peace, but while I still have this body, I'm going to enjoy my life. I want to laugh and reminisce. I want to look at old pictures and tell stories. I want to pack my mind with all the good memories of my life. So the only assignment you have is to help me celebrate my life. That's all I want you to do. Okay?" Everyone nodded in agreement, including Vine.

Over the course of the weeks that followed, Bo experienced more and more pain, which required more and more morphine and less and less optimism. After discussing treatment options with Dr. Bledsoe, Bo reluctantly opted to try one round of chemo and radiation, but if it didn't work, he would not do another. He did not do another. He had developed an addiction to morphine, but it was the only thing that gave him the slightest bit of relief. Bo was swimming in an ocean of drugs. There were digestive enzymes that had to be taken prior to eating, beta blockers, heart medication, anxiety medication, insulin for the diabetes caused by the shutdown of the pancreas, vitamins, blood thinners for blood clots, and so many other medications that his daughter Maya had to create an Excel spreadsheet just to keep track of them all. And then there were the side effects of either the cancer or the medication or both at the same time. Around the third month, Bo would often forget what he was saying in the middle of a sentence. Jackie and the Jolly Boys told him many things over and over again. He started to experience extreme swelling in his stomach and feet to the point that only house shoes could be worn. In month four, the infections and trips to the emergency room began. One evening, he passed out from weakness due to internal bleeding. Blood was in his bowels, and blood transfusions had to be issued in order to get his blood count back up to normal.

Bo began to really pass away in September. His disposition changed. The morphine started messing with his mind, changed his personality, and caused aggression and paranoia. This was the hardest for everyone. It was like Bo hated the people he loved. It was hard to watch and hard to be around him. In October, he refused to take the medication. He was ready to go. His communication drastically changed. He stopped talking and didn't want visitors, not even Jackie. And then came the night of October 7.

"Why don't you just let me die?" he asked Jackie. He had not said two or three words all day.

"Oh, you're talking to me again, huh?" she said lightly. "I'm not going to let you die because I'm not ready for you to go."

"You are so selfish," he said. "I've made you a millionaire, put you in a beautiful house that's paid for, left you with a grip in the bank, and a life-insurance policy. Aren't you ready for me to go so you and your boyfriend can spend my money?"

"Stop talking ridiculousness," Jackie said. "You're just trying to make me angry. You really should stop. It's starting to work."

"I know you're mad at me either for getting sick or taking so long to die," Bo said. He was angry today, more than normal. "Boy, won't you be surprised at the reading of the will when you find out I left all my money to the church. Is that me stinking or you?" Bo was in the fetal position. As if he hadn't uttered word, Jackie laid in bed with him and began massaging his back. For some reason, whenever he was ornery, her firm touch on his back calmed him down.

"Relax, baby," she said, applying pressure to his lumbar and upper back.

"Jack, I'm ready to go," Bo said. He had not cried since the limo ride in Rochester. His back was to her, but she could hear him crying. "All day, every day, just pains in my stomach, back, legs, feet. It's unbearable."

"Bo, please let me give you some medicine," Jackie said.

"It's only going to prolong it," Bo said. "Jackie, let me go please. I can't take another pill or another shot or another sad face staring across from me. Just let me go."

"Bo, what are you saying?" Jackie asked. She jumped out of bed and ran to the other side. She dropped to her knees on the side of the bed to look him in his eyes.

"If you make a mistake and give me an extra dosage of the medication, I can go," Bo said. "I can't suffer another day. At the beginning, it was tolerable, but now, I want to go on."

"Bo, I'm not going to kill you," Jackie said. "Just take the medicine, the right way, so you won't feel so bad."

"Do you think the medicine makes me feel good?" Bo said, raising his voice. "Nothing makes me feel good. Let me go, please. I can't leave until you let me go."

"You know what, you're going to hate me for this, but I'm giving you a shot," Jackie said.

"No, please don't," Bo pleaded, grabbing her hand. His body was shaking so that it made her hand shake. She looked into his eyes and saw that her husband was leaving her.

"Oh, Bo, I'm not ready," she pleaded. "I'm not ready."

"Yes, you are," he said. "You're a strong woman. You made a man out of me. Only a strong woman can turn a man into a man. I love you more than you'll ever know. Do you love me?"

"Of course," she said.

"Then let me go. Please, Jackie, let me go," he pleaded. She stood and went to the medication container in their bedroom refrigerator. She pulled his pajamas down part way and administered the shot. "Now another one." She hesitated. She knew if she gave him another shot, he'd be gone in an hour, free from pain, agony, and misery. Her hand started shaking from fear, guilt, and defeat.

"Bo, I can't," she said. "I can't." She dropped the full syringe and ran out of the bedroom. She was hysterical. She went on the deck and cried like he had gone mad. When she finally calmed herself, she went back into the room. Bo was asleep with the empty syringe in his hand. She checked his pulse. He was free.

CHAPTER 28

THE EULOGY CONTINUED

October 16, 2014

When Vine realized that he had said all that with his eyes closed, he quickly opened them. Nearly every face was wet with tears, and every head continued to nod in agreement. The church was on one accord. He didn't want to, but this was the perfect time to get the house in order. He was hesitant for a moment, but it was time for, as he often called it, the morning read.

"Now I'm Vine Oliver, and as such, I have to tell it like it is," he said. "There is a spirit of confusion and disruption in here that needs to be rebuked. Just call me Vine the rebuker." A few people in the congregation cheered him on with an amen. "In preparing to write the obituary, Jackie realized that she had no record of Bo being baptized." A collective moan and sigh rose from the crowd. "Wait, hold on. We contacted his church back home, went through all his things—nothing. All we knew was when he joined this church, he came on his Christian experience, which he had plenty of. A distant relative confirmed that he had never been baptized, not to her recollection. So we went with the standard: Bo accepted Christ at an early age. Now you know negative news can run five miles and back before the truth can get its Nikes on. I was not surprised when just this morning, I had a woman tell me that Bo going to hell makes this truly a sad occasion. I want to say to you, my dear, sitting over there in your beautiful white dress and expensive funeral wig, and to all of you in here who have condemned my friend to hell: Dr. Beauregard Jeremiah Jackson will never spend a minute in hell. He loved God, his church, his wife [even that first one], his children, his friends, and anyone in his presence. I have never met someone who was so positive, so caring, so loving as my brother Beauregard Jeremiah Jackson. And he was a giver. He gave generously to this church, his family, and his friends. The wealth I now enjoy did not come from church folks. The successful restaurants, Laundromats, bus companies, and other businesses we own and operate did not come from tithes and offerings. It came from God through the channel known as Dr. Beauregard Jeremiah Jackson. If you were doing the right thing and sometimes when you weren't, if Bo could help you, he would. And ain't no skeletons in this man's closet. Some of you have been baptized, purged, slain in the spirit a number of times and have so many secrets, cover-ups, and lies that you can't even open your closet for fear of being injured by skeleton bones. This man was as clean and honest as they come. Besides Barack Obama and Bo, I can't think of too many men who wouldn't mind their life story being published on the front page of the *Chicago Tribune*." The church was stirring. People were yelling "Amen," "Tell it, Preacher," and "Read, Vine, read, read."

"Let me tell you the greatest salvation story I know," Vine continued. "It happened at Calvary. To mock Jesus, they hung Him between two thieves. The one on the left mocked Him and said, 'Aren't you Jesus? Aren't you the Messiah? Save yourself and save us too.' But the one on the right was paying attention to what was happening. It was in the afternoon, but the sky was black. There was thunder and lightning. People were weeping and wailing. This man in the middle, named Jesus, was talking to His Father. He had been beaten, made to carry His own cross to Calvary, stabbed in the side, hands and feet nailed, had a crown of thorns pressed into His head, and given vinegar instead of water to drink. He was in bad shape. By all accounts, He should have been dead before they nailed Him to the cross. He should have died hours ago, but He was talking to His heavenly Father and His earthly mother. He'd heard of this man claiming to be the Messiah but didn't think much of it. There had been a few before Him who claimed to be the same thing. But He was talking to His Father, and things were happening. When He asked His father to pardon His abusers, saying, 'Father, forgive them,' the thief on the right realized that it was indeed Him. He must be the Messiah. This must be the son of God. The thief on the right told the thief on the left to shut up. He acknowledged that they were being hanged because of their crimes and transgressions, but Jesus had done nothing wrong. This was the savior of the world. He then looked over in Jesus's direction and said, 'Please, Savior, remember me when you get to your kingdom.' Jesus stopped dying and opened the doors of the church. He didn't sing a special song, nor did He place a special chair in the aisle. He told the thief, 'Today, you will be with me in paradise.' There was no orientation class. There was no special uniform. There were no forms to complete. He didn't receive the right hand of fellowship. No one asked him what club he wanted to join. And no, he was not baptized. But Jesus forgave his transgressions, saved him, and took him to paradise. If Jesus saved a self-confessed thief hanging on a cross without the sacrament of baptism, I know for certain that Bo is in paradise right now with his Father. So to you, ma'am and all you other church folks, you can stop asking if you're going to see Bo again. Your question should be, is he going to see you again?"

The church erupted in applause and praise. Vine had set the church on fire. He took a seat in the chair that used to be his. He felt a stirring. He wasn't done. He stood up and walked back to the microphone. The funeral directors were on their way down the aisle to facilitate the final viewing, but Vine stopped them.

"Brothers, funeral directors, hold on just one more second," he said. "I can see the look on Bo's face as he smelled the perfume from the heavenly flowers, flowers with a beauty he'd never seen. I can see Bo's expression as he drank the cool, crisp, and the clean fountain's healing water. I can see the look on Bo's face as he touched and acknowledged the softness and quality of the robe he had been given to wear. I can see Bo looking for and finding his mother, father, sister, and grandson, hugging them and greeting them. But, oh, I can hear.

I said I can hear. You might not be able to hear it. But I can hear Jesus saying, 'Beauregard Jeremiah Jackson, well done.' I can hear Jesus saying, 'Bo, I know you tried and sometimes failed in your trying. Your hands were sore and worn from the work you had begun. I saw you taking up your cross and running quickly to meet me. I understand, my child, and I say well done. Well done, Beauregard Jeremiah Jackson—well done."

Every parishioner stood to their feet to applaud Vine. Tears flowed from his eyes. He knew that Bo was right—this was his assignment. He sat down again. The nurse gave him the old gold chalice he favored and drank from for many years while there. The water was icy cold and felt good going down his hoarse and dry throat. He looked toward the ceiling as if no one was there but him and said, "Thank you, God, for my friend."

The final viewing, entombment, and repass went off without a hitch. No one showed out, overperformed, or got out of line. Who would? Who could with Vine, Chiv, and Sam in charge? No matter where she was, Jackie had Vine, Chiv, Sam or some combination of the three by her side. After a few bites of food and a few last hugs, Jackie gave the signal, and it was time to go. A few people offered to come by the house to keep Jackie company, but she just wanted her family and friends. She gave the excuse of being tired, and within a few minutes, all were in the limos on their way to Oak Brook. Once inside, everyone made themselves comfortable, ending up with Jackie on the extended deck attached to their palatial mansion. The air was cool but not cold. The sun was easing itself down. It was tranquil and quiet. The perfect way to end a day of putting a giant to rest. Chiv, Sam, Vine, Eric, Michael, Marsaleen, Hadassah, Anne, and Pearl sat in silence, no doubt reflecting on their individual relationships with Bo. Because it was hard for silence and Vine to occupy the same space, no one was surprised when he broke the silence by laughing out loud.

"Oh, here we go," Sam said. "What is it, Vine?"

"I'm just thinking about Bo watching the faces of everyone as they slid his casket into the wall," Vine said. "I'm sure it was the first time that many of them witnessed an entombment. I know he is cracking up."

"I'm sure Bo found a lot of humor in people's reactions today," Jackie said. "From the operetta, to the roped-off mahogany couch casket, to the entombment, and the passed hors d'oeuvres at the repass, I put my husband away like royalty. Funeral by Jacqueline Jackson. I'm the widow to beat, baby."

"And, Jackie, you were amazing today," Chiv said. "How many Black women would get up and speak at their husband's funeral? Certainly none I know."

"That's for sure," Vine said. "You held a queenly spirit about you from beginning to end, which was nothing short of magnificent."

"And although I hate to admit it, Vine, you did a great job, man," Sam said. "Even tried to hoop a little at the end. You got them ninjas straight. People are going to be talking about this funeral for years."

"Hey, did you all see Louise?" Chiv asked.

"Yeah, I saw her weak ass," Jackie said. "She tried to hug me, but when I stiffened, she got the message and soon moved on. I can't stand no weak-ass woman. A weak man I can handle if only for a short period of time. But a weak woman, especially a Black woman, gets on my nerves. Did you see our girls up there today? Did you see how they fought their tears and spoke about their father? I'm raising strong women. And if those girls could speak like professional keynoters at their father's funeral, surely a grown-ass woman could tend to her injured fiancé."

"I got to give some props to Anne and Pearl," Eric said. "Those flowers were the most beautiful flowers I've ever seen. Those roses were as big as coffee mugs and perfect."

"Bo said he wanted nothing but yellow roses," Marsaleen said. "That was my assignment: to make sure there were a hundred yellow roses around him and on the Jolly Boys."

"And they weren't easy to come by, but we got 'em in," Pearl said.

"Where is your husband, Ms. Pearl?" Michael asked. "I was looking forward to meeting him."

"Oh, baby, I had to leave him at home," Pearl said, evoking more laughter on the deck. "I love him, and he's God's gift to me. But I needed a break. I spent so many years alone it's hard for me to be around someone all the time."

"And I spent so many years with someone," Jackie said. "I wonder just how hard it will be to be alone?"

"Oh, you won't be alone," Vine said. "You're gonna get tired of us at your door. We promised Bo we'd look after you, and that's what we're going to do."

"Yeah, I know you'll try," Jackie said. "But one day, the visits will stop, the calls will stop, and the cards will stop flowing in. And I'm going to be alone. That's when it will get hard. It's easy right now because I have you all around me, but what am I going to do when I'm alone and lonely? God, I hope I can take this."

"When you get alone and lonely, you're going to call one of us," Sam said. "And that's all there is to that."

"Thanks, guys," Jackie said. "He loved me, but he loved them Jolly Boys. I don't know what I would have done if I didn't have y'all. You're my brothers."

"We got you, sister," Chiv joked.

"Chiv, go in there and get that bottle of champagne in the back of the refrigerator and bring out some glasses," Jackie said. "How can we celebrate the life of a remarkable man without champagne?"

"I'll go," Sam said. "That's like sending a witch into a broom factory. We may never see him again. What are we doing this week, Chiv? On the wagon or dragging behind it?"

"I don't know," Chiv said. "Why don't we ask your mama?" More laughter erupted.

"Jackie, do you mind if I smoke out here?" Pearl asked.

"Pearl, when you start smoking?" Vine asked.

"When my vision started getting blurry, my knees started predicting rain, and when I said I do," Pearl responded.

"Gone girl with your bad self," Jackie said. After a few minutes, the stench of marijuana started attacking everyone's nose. "Pearl, are you smoking reefer?"

"Yes," she responded flatly.

"Oh, I can't believe this," Vine said. "My oldest sister who I love and adore. I can't believe this. All these months I've been looking for some reefer, and my oldest sister who I love and adore wouldn't give me none."

"Pastor," Eric said. "You just preached a whole sermon today and read a woman from the pulpit. You can't smoke that. But I can."

"Uh-oh, y'all," Sam said. "We got us a Jolly Boy in the making." Sam and Chiv passed out the glasses and poured the champagne.

"I was saving this for after the reading of the will, but I'm learning to live in the moment," Jackie said. "Y'all got to be here Monday morning at ten. The attorney said we can do it from here."

"I can't believe that Bo put us in his will," Vine said.

"And I can't believe you can't believe it," Jackie said. "With the way he loved y'all, I just hope he left me enough to get by on, in the lifestyle to which I've become accustomed. But that's for tomorrow. Let's all raise a glass tonight to the greatest man I know, Dr. Beauregard Jeremiah Jackson. Thank you for changing our lives for the better."

"To Bo," Vine said, raising his glass, "truly a remarkable man."

EPILOGUE

Monday, August 18, 2014

After introductions and some legal mumbo jumbo, the attorney stood before Jackie, Sam, Vine, Chiv, and Ms. Francis in the theater of their home. Bo opted to record a video to direct his final wishes instead of a boiler plate paper document. Jackie held her stomach, bracing herself to see her husband again. When the attorney hit the play button, music began. As Joni Mitchell began to sing "Both Sides Now" in the background, Bo's upper torso filled the screen. It was not the swollen, thin, and hairless Bo they saw last. He looked good, pleasingly plump, and well-dressed sitting in a high-back chair and holding a highball glass of cola, ice, and Chivas Regal.

"Well, hello, everyone," he began. "I know the last few days have been difficult. Black funerals can be so exhausting, entertaining, but exhausting. I know my plans were followed down to the yellow roses. Thank you, Jackie, for being strong, and thank you, fellas, my brothers, for holding my family up in my absence. The four of you came into my life at the right time for the right reasons. Jackie, you were sent to me so I could experience real love, partnership, and confidence. And although I was an old man when you met me, you made a man out of me. I can never repay you for that. Chiv, you came to show me intelligence and stature. And although I didn't finish, it's because of you that I wanted to go back to school. Like you, I wanted to be an example for young Black boys of what could be achieved with perseverance and preparation. Sam, you came to teach me courage and fortitude. No matter how many times you got knocked down, you always bounced back. You taught me how to fight for what I wanted and to never be afraid. And Vine, I know

God because of you. I know my gifts because of you. You are a testament that God truly can use ordinary flawed people for a higher purpose. The three of you came in the beginning so you would be here for my family in the end. Whoever finds you as a friend has indeed found a treasure.

"So here we go. Get ready! Francis, my love, you are precious and kind and sweet, and I love you for taking care of my family all these years. You are the invisible super glue that kept us together. You are now the proud owner of Beauregard's Buffet. And for your willingness to take over the reins, a check for three million dollars will be deposited into your account before the sun goes down. To my wife, Jackie, I cannot begin to compensate you for what you mean to me. Even a billion dollars wouldn't be enough. Every worldly good I have including the six buildings I own (yes, I know I kept that from you) are now yours. With the proceeds from my three insurance policies and the lottery annuity, I leave you an estate worth forty million dollars. Like I said, it ain't nearly enough. The attorney should have a brown envelope to hand you. Please take it, but don't open it until I tell you." The attorney handed Jackie the envelope, which felt like it included pictures, papers, and a set of keys. She was smiling and crying at the same time.

"Vine, Chiv, and Sam," Bo's recording continued, "you are my brothers, and I love you. I can't begin to express what you mean to me, even from this distance. My prayer is and has always been for you to be happy, safe, and comfortable. I think I can help you accomplish those things. Counselor, pass them their envelopes now." The attorney handed envelopes to the fellas, similar to the one he passed to Jackie. "Last year, we talked about really retiring and moving to California. I can't be there to participate, but I want you to have that opportunity. You can open your envelopes now. Each one of you are holding the keys, photos, and deeds to a home in Malibu on the water. I purchased them for you and made sure they were furnished and paid for. Don't let my death stop you from enjoying your life. You've worked too long and hard. It's time to relax because, believe me when I tell you, you don't have as much time as you think you have. I want you to enjoy your homes in the winter and come back to Chicago in the summer if you want. Just enjoy your lives. You'll also find a check for two million dollars, just to (as my mother would say) keep the ghetto away.

"Now I know what you're asking yourselves: where did he get all this money from? That's none of your business. Let's just say, I won the lottery again. Now don't sulk around worried about me. I'm having dinner with Ella and Satchmo tonight. Oh, just one last thing: Vine, don't sing. You sound terrible. Love and peace, Bo."

"I'm in a state of shock," Jackie said.

"That ninja kept playing after we won and hit the number again," Sam said. "He must have taken the anonymous lump sum. That's why we didn't know about it."

"So let's talk," Vine said. "Are we really retiring and moving to California?

"Of course, we are," Chiv said. "We've always done what Bo told us to do."

"And it has served us well," Sam said.

"Well, California, here we come," Vine said. "Here we come."

One year later—Circa 2015

Jackie missed her husband more than she thought she would. Although she was glad to know that he was free from pain and agony, she longed for their long talks in the middle of the night, traveling, and just being in each other's presence. She made the move to LA and fell in love with her new home in the affluent town of Malibu. Considering the weather, there was no reason to be a snowbird. In one year's time, she became a Californian. The girls visited often and vowed to eventually become Californians as well. Retirement didn't suit her, nor did the nine to five grind, so she opened the third Beauregard's Buffet in downtown LA. She hired a chef to replicate Ms. Francis's delicious soul food and manage the day-to-day operations. It was a small place with only a few regular customers who did not mind the rich and highly caloric ingredients of a soul-food diet. She met with the fellas just about every Friday for supper and to watch the lottery drawing. A few of her friends encouraged her to date, but she refused. She could never cheat on her husband.

Sam and Marsaleen also made the move west. Although they both vowed to retire for real, within two months, they had purchased a small fleet of buses and expanded their transportation company to LA. Sam was excited to add limousine service as well, often driving himself in hopes of meeting as many famous people as he could. He remained faithful to Marsaleen, who was excited that her husband "finally came home."

Chivas sold his Laundromat business and moved to LA. He discovered Muscle Beach and turned himself into a fitness fanatic. When teased about it, he said he was sculpting a masterpiece—himself. He no longer considered himself an alcoholic and strayed away from the hard stuff. He rebranded himself as a wine connoisseur. Geraldine didn't make the move with him but was encouraged to visit often.

Vine was the last to finally move full-time to LA. He tried the bicostal approach, but it didn't work. Just a few months ago, he installed Eric and Michael as the new pastors of his church and joined his friends in retirement. He and Chiv decided to live together and chose Vine's house as their main domicile. Chiv's house was reserved as the bachelor pad. That's where they entertained Hadassah and Geraldine when they came to visit. Vine attended several New Thought churches in the LA area and occasionally preached a sermon whenever asked. He started his first book, *The Greatest Salvation Story Ever Told*, which was scheduled to be released on February 10 of next year, on Bo's birthday.

Ms. Francis purchased Bo and Jackie's home in Oak Brook. She continued to oversee the restaurants. She's planning on retiring soon to travel and just enjoy being a millionaire. She and her new love interest, Ms. Eva, visited Malibu regularly just like members of the family.

Louise, Lola, and Linda aka Nevaeh were never spoken to or heard from again.

The End

ABOUT THE AUTHOR

Larry LaDell Robertson is a prolific and up-and-coming storyteller and writer always on the lookout for a unique story to share that will make you laugh, make you cry, but more importantly, make you think. In his first book released in 2019, *Five Smooth Stones: What I Know about God for Sure*, Larry tells the story of his spiritual journey from religious complacency to spiritual empowerment. In this, his first fiction novel, he examines the beauty and nuances of a meaningful relationship of men—a story that is rarely told. Whether fiction or nonfictional, Larry's goal is to inspire men and women to be extraordinary. Larry currently works as an accomplished Human Resources, Diversity and Inclusion, and Information Technology leader for an association in Washington, DC, and resides in Upper Marlboro, Maryland, with his wife of thirty years, Ramona (Mony), his two adult daughters, Jesseca (Scooter Bug) Jazzmin (CoCo), and their Yorkie Bashan, Dougie.

CPSIA information can be obtained
at www.ICGtesting.com
Printed in the USA
LVHW030935280621
691317LV00004B/26